AUTHOR	CLASS
QUEEN . E .	AF.

TITLE *Best of Ellery Queen*

D1583044

6

The Best of
ELLERY
QUEEN
2

The Best of
ELLERY QUEEN
2

ROBERT HALE · LONDON

© *This omnibus edition Robert Hale Limited 1984*
First published in Great Britain 1984

ISBN 0 7090 1793 6

Robert Hale Limited
Clerkenwell House
Clerkenwell Green
London EC1R 0HT

Printed in Great Britain by
St Edmundsbury Press, Bury St Edmunds, Suffolk
and bound by Hunter & Foulis Ltd

Contents

Acknowledgements

Grateful acknowledgement of permission to reprint the stories in this volume is hereby made to:

Scott Meredith Inc. for *The Nine Mile Walk* by Harry Kemelman, copyright 1947 by The American Mercury, Inc., renewed 1974 by Davis Publications, Inc.; *Death at the Excelsior* by P. G. Wodehouse, copyright 1976 by the estate of P. G. Wodehouse, from The Uncollected Wodehouse; *Death between Dances* by Cornell Woolrich, copyright 1947 by Cornell Woolrich, renewed; *The Purple Shroud* by Joyce Harrington, © 1972 by Joyce Harrington; *The Adventure of the Three R's* by Ellery Queen, copyright 1946, 1952 by Ellery Queen, renewed;

Harold Matson Co. Inc. for *The Widow's Walk* by Jack Finney, copyright 1947 by Jack Finney, renewed; *Mrs. Craggs' Sixth Sense* by H. R. F. Keating; © 1978 by H. R. F. Keating;

Harold Ober Associates Inc. for *Gone Girl* by Ross Macdonald, © 1953 by Kenneth Millar, renewed; *The Rose Murders* by E. X. Ferrars, © 1977 by E. X. Ferrars;

Curtis Brown Ltd. for *The Speciality of the House* by Stanley Ellin, copyright 1948 by Stanley Ellin, renewed; *Credit to Shakespeare* by Julian Symons, © Julian Symons 1961; *Chain of Terror* by Patricia McGerr, © 1979 by Patricia McGerr; *A More-or-Less Crime* by Edgar Wallace, copyright 1975 by Penelope Wallace;

Georges Borchardt, Inc. for *The Strong and the Weak* by Ruth Rendell, © 1976 by Ruth Rendell;

John Cushman Associates, Inc. for *The Sark Lane Mission* by Michael Gilbert, © 1958 by Michael Gilbert; *Dover Does Some Spadework* by Joyce Porter, © 1976 by Joyce Porter;

Estate of Ernest Bramah for *The Tragedy at Brookbend Cottage* by Ernest Bramah;

James Brown Associates, Inc. for *Blind Man's Buff* by Roy Vickers, copyright 1947 by The American Mercury, Inc., renewed;

the Author for *The Dead Past* by Thomas Walsh; *Gentleman's Agreement* by Lawrence Block, © 1977 by Lawrence Block; *The Glory Hunter* by Brian Garfield, © 1977 by Brian Garfield; *The Man Who Never Told a Lie* by Isaac Asimov, © 1972 by Isaac Asimov;

McIntosh & Otis, Inc. for *The Gracious, Pleasant Life of Mrs. Afton* by Patricia Highsmith, © 1962 by Patricia Highsmith;

Brandt & Brandt Literary Agents, Inc. for *Blood Brothers* by Christianna Brand, © 1965 by Christianna Brand;

A. Searle Pinney, executor of the Author's estate for *The Sweet Corn Murder* by Rex Stout, © 1962 by Rex Stout and first published in the Saturday Evening Post.

Introduction

So enthusiastically was *The Best of Ellery Queen* received that the publisher has now compiled a new selection of outstanding stories from Ellery Queen's Mystery Magazine. *The Best of Ellery Queen # 2* includes work from a remarkably wide range of writers and, indeed, to the *aficionado* of the mystery story there can hardly be a name that is not known and widely respected.

Rex Stout

The Sweet Corn Murder

When the doorbell rang that Tuesday evening in September and I stepped to the hall for a look and through the one-way glass saw Inspector Cramer on the stoop, bearing a fair-sized carton, I proceeded to the door, intending to open it a couple of inches and say through the crack, "Deliveries in the rear."

Inspector Cramer was uninvited and unexpected, we had no case and no client, and we owed him nothing, so why pretend he was welcome?

But by the time I reached the door I had changed my mind. Not because of him. He looked perfectly normal—big and burly, round red face with bushy gray eyebrows, broad heavy shoulders straining the sleeve seams of his coat. It was the carton. It was a used one, the right size, the cord around it was the kind McLeod used, and the NERO WOLFE on it in blue crayon was McLeod's style of printing.

Having switched the stoop light on, I could observe those details as I approached, so I swung the door open and asked politely, "Where did you get the corn?"

I suppose I should explain a little. Usually Wolfe comes closest to being human after dinner, when we leave the dining room to cross the hall to the office, and he gets his bulk deposited in his favorite chair behind his desk, and Fritz brings coffee; and either Wolfe opens his current book or, if I have no date and am staying in, he starts a conversation.

The topic may be anything from women's shoes to the importance of the new moon in Babylonian astrology. But that evening he had taken his cup and crossed to the big globe over by the bookshelves and stood twirling the globe, scowling at it, probably picking a place he would rather be.

For the corn hadn't come. By an arrangement with a farmer named Duncan McLeod up in Putnam County, every Tuesday from July 20 to October 5, sixteen ears of just-picked corn were delivered. They were roasted in the husk, and we did our own shucking as we ate—four ears for me, eight for Wolfe, and four in the kitchen for Fritz. The corn had to arrive no earlier than 5:30 and no later than 6:30. That day it hadn't arrived at all and Fritz had had to do some stuffed eggplant, so Wolfe was standing scowling at the globe when the doorbell rang.

And now here was Inspector Cramer with the carton. Could it possibly be it? It was. Handing me his hat to put on the shelf, he tramped down the hall to the office, and when I entered he had put the carton on Wolfe's desk and had his knife out to cut the cord, and Wolfe, cup in hand, was crossing to him.

Cramer opened the flaps, took out an ear of corn, and said, "If you were going to have this for dinner, I guess it's too late."

Wolfe moved to his elbow, turned the flap to see the inscription, his name, grunted, circled around the desk to his chair, and sat. "You have your effect," he said. "I am impressed. Where did you get it?"

"If you don't know, maybe Goodwin does." Cramer shot a glance at me, went to the red-leather chair facing the end of Wolfe's desk, and sat. "I've got some questions for you and for him, but of course you want grounds. You would. At a quarter past five, four hours ago, the dead body of a man was found in the alley back of Rusterman's restaurant. He had been hit in the back of the head with a piece of iron pipe which was there on the ground by the body. The station wagon he had come in was alongside the receiving platform of the restaurant, and in the station wagon were nine cartons containing ears of corn."

Cramer pointed. "That's one of them, your name on it. You get one like it every Tuesday. Right?"

Wolfe nodded. "I do. In season. Has the body been identified?"

"Yes. Driver's license and other items in his pockets, including cash, eighty-some dollars. Kenneth Faber, twenty-eight years old. Also men at the restaurant identified him. He had been delivering the corn there the past five weeks, and then he had been coming on here with yours. Right?"

"I don't know."

"The hell you don't. If you're going to start that kind—"

I cut in. "Hold it. Stay in the buggy. As you know, Mr. Wolfe is up in the plant rooms from four to six every day except Sunday. The corn usually comes before six, and either Fritz or I receive it. So Mr. Wolfe doesn't know, but I do. Kenneth Faber has been bringing it the past five weeks. If you want—"

I stopped because Wolfe was moving. Cramer had dropped the ear of corn onto Wolfe's desk, and Wolfe had picked it up and felt it, gripping it in the middle, and now he was shucking it. From where

I sat, at my desk, the rows of kernels looked too big, too yellow, and too crowded.

Wolfe frowned at it, muttered, "I thought so," put it down, stood up, reached for the carton, said, "You will help, Archie," took an ear, and started shucking it. As I got up Cramer said something but was ignored.

When we finished we had three piles, as assorted by Wolfe. Two ears were too young, six were too old, and eight were just right. He returned to his chair, looked at Cramer, and declared, "This is preposterous."

"So you're stalling," Cramer growled.

"No. Shall I expound it?"

"Yeah. Go ahead."

"Since you have questioned men at the restaurant, you know that the corn comes from a man named Duncan McLeod, who grows it on a farm some sixty miles north of here. He has been supplying it for four years, and he knows precisely what I require. It must be nearly mature, but not quite, and it must be picked not more than three hours before it reaches me. Do you eat sweet corn?"

"Yes. You're stalling."

"No. Who cooks it?"

"My wife. I haven't got a Fritz."

"Does she cook it in water?"

"Sure. Is yours cooked in beer?"

"No. Millions of American women, and some men, commit that outrage every summer day. They are turning a superb treat into mere provender. Shucked and boiled in water, sweet corn is edible and nutritious; roasted in the husk in the hottest possible oven for forty minutes, shucked at the table, buttered and salted, nothing else, it is ambrosia. No chef's ingenuity and imagination have ever created a finer dish. American women should themselves be boiled in water. Ideally the corn—"

"How much longer are you going to stall?"

"I'm not stalling. Ideally the corn should go straight from the stalk to the oven, but of course that's impractical for city dwellers. If it's picked at the right stage of development it is still a treat for the palate after twenty-four hours, or even forty-eight; I have tried it. But look at this." Wolfe pointed to the assorted piles. "This is preposterous. Mr. McLeod knows better. The first year I had him send two dozen ears, and I returned those that were not acceptable. He knows what I require, and he knows how to choose it without opening the husk. He is supposed to be equally meticulous with the supply for the restaurant, but I doubt if he is—they take fifteen to twenty dozen. Are they serving what they got today?"

"Yes. They've admitted that they took it from the station wagon even before they reported the body." Cramer's chin was down and his eyes were narrowed under the eyebrow hedge. "You're the boss at that restaurant."

Wolfe shook his head. "Not the boss. My trusteeship, under the will of my friend Marko Vukcic when he died, will end next year. You know the arrangement; you investigated the murder; you may remember that I brought the murderer back from Yugoslavia."

"Yeah. Maybe I never thanked you." Cramer's eyes came to me. "You go there fairly often—not to Yugoslavia, to Rusterman's. How often?"

I raised one brow. That annoys him because he can't do it. "Oh, once a week, sometimes twice. I have privileges, and it's the best restaurant in New York."

"Sure. Were you there today?"

"No."

"Where were you at five-fifteen this afternoon?"

"In the Heron sedan which Mr. Wolfe owns and I drive. Five fifteen? Grand Concourse, headed for the East River Drive."

"Who was with you?"

"Saul Panzer."

He grunted. "You and Wolfe are the only two men alive Panzer would lie for. Where had you been?"

"Ball game. Yankee Stadium."

"What happened in the ninth inning?" He flipped a hand. "To hell with it. You'd know all right, you'd see to that. How well do you know Max Maslow?"

I raised the brow again. "Connect it, please."

"I'm investigating a murder."

"So I gathered. And apparently I'm a suspect. Connect it."

"One item in Kenneth Faber's pockets was a little notebook. One page had the names of four men written in pencil. Three of the names had checkmarks in front of them. The last one, no checkmark, was Archie Goodwin. The first one was Max Maslow. Will that do?"

"I'd rather see the notebook."

"It's at the laboratory." His voice went up a notch. "Look, Goodwin. You're a licensed private detective."

I nodded. "But that crack about who Saul Panzer would lie for.

Okay, I'll file it. I don't know any Max Maslow and have never heard the name before. The other two names with checkmarks?"

"Peter Jay. J-A-Y."

"Don't know him and never heard of him."

"Carl Heydt." He spelled it.

"That's better. Couturier?"

"He makes clothes for women."

"Including a friend of mine, Miss Lily Rowan. I have gone with her a few times to his place to help her decide. His suits and dresses come high, but I suppose he'd turn out a little apron for three Cs."

"How well do you know him?"

"Not well at all. I call him Carl, but you know how that is. We have been fellow weekend guests at Miss Rowan's place in the country a couple of times. I have seen him only when I have been with Miss Rowan."

"Do you know why his name would be in Faber's notebook with a checkmark?"

"I don't know and I couldn't guess."

"Do you want me to connect Susan McLeod before I ask you about her?"

I had supposed that would be coming as soon as I heard the name Carl Heydt, since the cops had had the notebook for four hours and had certainly lost no time making contacts. Saving me for the last, and Cramer himself coming, was of course a compliment, but more for Wolfe than for me.

"No, thanks," I told him. "I'll do the connecting. The first time Kenneth Faber came with the corn, six weeks ago today, the first time I ever saw him, he told me Sue McLeod had got her father to give him a job on the farm. He was very chatty. He said he was a free-lance cartoonist, and the cartoon business was in a slump, and he wanted some sun and air and his muscles needed exercise, and Sue often spent weekends at the farm and that would be nice. You can't beat that for a connection. Go ahead and ask me about Susan McLeod."

Cramer was eying me. "You're never slow, are you, Goodwin?"

I gave him a grin. "Slow as cold honey. But I try hard to keep up."

"Don't overdo. How long have you been intimate with her?"

"Well. There are several definitions for 'intimate.' Which one?"

"You know damn well which one."

My shoulders went up. "If you won't say, I'll have to guess." The shoulders went down. "If you mean the very worst, or the very best, depending on how you look at it, nothing doing. I have known her three years, having met her when she brought the corn one day. Have you seen her?"

"Yes."

"Then you know how she looks, and much obliged for the compliment. She has points. I think she means well, and she can't help it if she can't keep the come-on from showing because she was born with it. She didn't pick her eyes and voice, they came in the package. Her talk is something special. Not only do you never know what she will say next; she doesn't know herself. One evening I kissed her, a good healthy kiss, and when we broke she said, 'I saw a horse kiss a cow once.' But she's a lousy dancer, and after a show or prizefight or ball game I want an hour or two with a band and a partner.

"So I haven't seen much of her for a year. The last time I saw her was at a party somewhere a couple of weeks ago. I don't know who her escort was, but it wasn't me. As for my being intimate with her, meaning what you mean, what do you expect? I haven't, but even if I had I'm certainly not intimate enough with you to blab it. Anything else?"

"Plenty. You got her a job with that Carl Heydt. You found her a place to live, an apartment that happens to be only six blocks from here."

I cocked my head at him. "Where did you get that? From Carl Heydt?"

"No. From her."

"She didn't mention Miss Rowan?"

"No."

"Then I give her a mark. You were at her about a murder, and she didn't want to drag in Miss Rowan. One day, the second summer she was bringing the corn, two years ago, she said she wanted a job in New York and asked if I could get her one. I doubted if she could hold a job any friend of mine might have open or might make room for, so I consulted Miss Rowan, and she took it on. She got two girls she knew to share their apartment with Sue—it's only five blocks from here, not six—she paid for a course at the Midtown Studio—Sue has paid her back—and she got Carl Heydt to give Sue a tryout at modeling.

"I understand that Sue is now one of the ten most popular models in New York and her price is a hundred dollars an hour, but that's hearsay. I haven't seen her on a magazine cover. I didn't get her a job or a place to live. I know Miss Rowan better than Sue does; she won't mind my dragging her in. Anything else?"

"Plenty. When and how did you find out that Kenneth Faber had shoved you out and taken Sue over?"

"Nuts." I turned to Wolfe. "Your Honor, I object to the question on the ground that it is insulting, impertinent, and disgusticulous. It assumes not only that I am shovable but also that I can be shoved out of a place I have never been."

"Objection sustained." A corner of Wolfe's mouth was up a little. "You will rephrase the question, Mr. Cramer."

"The hell I will." Cramer's eyes kept at me. "You might as well open up, Goodwin. We have a signed statement from her. What passed between you and Faber when he was here a week ago today?"

"The corn. It passed from him to me."

"So you're a clown. I already know that. A real wit. What else?"

"Well, let's see." I screwed my lips, concentrating. "The bell rang and I went and opened the door and said, quote, 'Greetings. How's things on the farm?' As he handed me the carton he said, 'Lousy, thank you, hot as hell and I've got blisters.' As I took it I said, 'What's a few blisters if you're the backbone of the country?' He said, 'Go soak your head,' and went, and I shut the door and took the carton to the kitchen."

"That's it?"

"That's it."

"Okay." He got up. "You don't wear a hat. You can have one minute to get a toothbrush."

"Now listen." I turned a palm up. "I can throw sliders in a pinch, and do, but this is no pinch. It's close to bedtime. If I don't check with something in Sue McLeod's statement, of course you want to work on me before I can get in touch with her, so go ahead, here I am."

"The minute's up. Come on."

I stayed put. "No. I now have a right to be sore, so I am. You'll have to make it good."

"You think I won't?" At least I had him glaring. "You're under arrest as a material witness. Move!"

I took my time getting up. "You have no warrant, but I don't want to be fussy." I turned to Wolfe. "If you want me around tomorrow, you might give Parker a ring."

"I shall." He swiveled. "Mr. Cramer. Knowing your considerable talents as I do, I am sometimes dumfounded by your fatuity. You were so bent on baiting Mr. Goodwin that you completely ignored the point I was at pains to make." He pointed at the piles on his desk. "Who picked that corn? Pfui!"

"That's *your* point, " Cramer rasped. "Mine is who killed Kenneth Faber. Move, Goodwin."

At twenty minutes past eleven Wednesday morning, standing at the curb on Leonard Street with Nathaniel Parker, I said, "Of course in a way it's a compliment. Last time the bail was a measly five hundred. Now twenty grand. That's progress."

Parker nodded. "That's one way of looking at it. He argued for fifty thousand, but I got it down to twenty. You know what that means. They actually—here's one."

A taxi headed in to us and stopped. When we were in and I had told the driver Eighth Avenue and Thirty-fifth Street, and we were rolling, Parker resumed, leaning to me and keeping his voice down. The legal mind. Hackies are even better listeners than they are talkers, and that one could be a spy sicked on us by the District Attorney.

"They actually," Parker said, "think you may have killed that man. This is serious, Archie. I told the judge that bail in the amount that was asked would be justified only if they had enough evidence to charge you with murder, and he agreed. As your counsel, I must advise you to be prepared for such a charge at any moment. I didn't like Mandel's attitude. By the way, Wolfe told me to send my bill to you, not him. He said this is your affair and he isn't concerned. I'll make it moderate."

I thanked him. I already knew that Assistant District Attorney Mandel, and maybe Cramer too, regarded me as a real candidate for the big one. Cramer had taken me to his place, Homicide South, and after spending half an hour on me had turned me over to Lieutenant Rowcliff and gone home. Rowcliff had stood me for nearly an hour—I had him stuttering in fourteen minutes, not a record—and had then sent me under convoy to the D.A.'s office, where Mandel had taken me on, obviously expecting to make a night of it.

Which he did, with the help of a pair of dicks from the D.A.'s Homicide Bureau. He had of course been phoned by both Cramer and Rowcliff, and it was evident from the start that he didn't merely think I was holding out on details that might be useful, to prevent either bother for myself or trouble for someone else; he had me tagged as a real prospect. Naturally I wanted to know why, so I played along. I hadn't with Cramer because he had got me sore in front of Wolfe, and I hadn't with Rowcliff because playing along is impossible with a double-breasted baboon, but with Mandel I could.

Of course he was asking the questions, him and the dicks, but the trick is to answer them in such a way that the next question, or maybe one later on, tells you something you want to know, or at least gives you a hint. That takes practise, but I had had plenty, and it makes it simpler when one guy pecks away at you for an hour or so and then backs off, and another guy starts in and goes all over it again.

For instance, the scene of the crime—the alley and receiving platform at the rear of Rusterman's. Since Wolfe was the trustee, there was nothing about that restaurant I wasn't familiar with. From the side street it was only about fifteen yards along the narrow alley to the platform, and the alley ended a few feet farther on at the wall of another building.

A car or small truck entering to deliver something had to back out. Knowing, as I had, that Kenneth Faber would come with the corn sometime after five o'clock, I could have walked in and hid under the platform behind a concrete post with the weapon in my hand, and when Faber drove in, got out, and came around to open the tailgate he would never know what hit him.

If I could have done that, who couldn't? I would have had to know one other thing, that I couldn't be seen from the windows of the restaurant kitchen because the glass had been painted on the inside so boys and girls couldn't climb onto the platform to watch Leo boning a duck or Felix stirring goose blood into a Sauce Rouennaise.

In helping them get it on the record that I knew all that, I learned only that they had found no one who had seen the murderer in the alley or entering or leaving it, that Faber had probably been dead five to ten minutes when someone came from the kitchen to the platform and found the body, and that the weapon was a piece of two-inch galvanized iron pipe sixteen and five-eighths inches long, threaded male at one end and female at the other, old and battered. Easy to hide under a coat. Where it came from might be discovered by one man in ten hours, or by a thousand men in ten years.

Getting those details was nothing, since they would be in the morning papers, but regarding their slant on me I got some hints that the papers wouldn't have. Hints were the best I could get, no facts to check, so I'll just report how it looked when Parker came to spring me in the morning.

They hadn't let me see Sue's statement, but there must have been something in it, or something she had said, or something someone else, maybe Carl Heydt or Peter Jay or Max Maslow, had said, either to her or to the cops. Or possibly something Duncan McLeod, Sue's father, had said. That didn't seem likely, but I included him because I saw him.

When Parker and I entered the anteroom on our way out he was there on a chair in the row against the wall, dressed for town, with a necktie, his square deep-tanned face shiny with sweat. I crossed over and told him good morning, and he said it wasn't, it was a bad morning, a day lost and no one to leave to see to things. It was noplace for a talk, with people there on the chairs, but I might at least have asked him who had picked the corn if someone hadn't come to take him inside.

So when I climbed out of the taxi at the corner and thanked Parker for the lift and told him I'd call him if and when, and walked the block and a half on Thirty-fifth Street to the old brownstone, I was worse off than when I had left, since I hadn't learned anything really useful, and no matter how Parker defined "moderate," the cost of a twenty-grand bond is not peanuts. I couldn't expect to pass the buck to Wolfe, since he had never seen either Kenneth Faber or Sue McLeod, and as I mounted the seven steps to the stoop and put my key in the lock I decided not to try to.

The key wasn't enough. The door opened two inches and stopped. The chain bolt was on. I pushed the button, and Fritz came and slipped the bolt; and his face told me something was stirring before he spoke. If you're not onto the faces you see most of, how can you expect to tell anything from strange ones?

As I crossed the sill I said, "Good morning. What's up?"

He turned from closing the door and stared. "But Archie. You look terrible."

"I feel worse. Now what?"

"A woman to see you. Miss Susan McLeod. She used to bring—"

"Yeah. Where is she?"

"In the office."

"Where is he?"

"In the kitchen."

"Has he talked with her?"

"No."

"How long has she been here?"

"Half an hour."

"Excuse my manners. I've had a night."

I headed for the end of the hall, the swinging door to the kitchen, pushed it open, and entered. Wolfe was at the center table with a glass of beer in his hand. He grunted. "So. Have you slept?"

"No."

"Have you eaten?"

I got a glass from the cupboard, went to the refrigerator and got milk, filled the glass, and took a sip. "If you could see the bacon and eggs they had brought in for me and I paid two bucks for, let alone taste it, you'd never be the same. You'd be so afraid you might be hauled in as a material witness you'd lose your nerve. They think maybe I killed Faber. For your information, I didn't."

I sipped the milk. "This will hold me till lunch. I understand I have a caller. As you told Parker, this is my affair and you are not concerned. May I take her to the front room? I'm not intimate enough with her to take her up to my room."

"Confound it," he growled. "How much of what you told Mr. Cramer was flummery?"

"None. All straight. But he's on me and so is the D.A. and I've got to find out why." I sipped milk.

He was eying me. "You will see Miss McLeod in the office."

"The front room will do. It may be an hour. Two hours."

"You may need the telephone. The office."

If I had been myself I would have given that offer a little attention, but I was somewhat pooped. So I went, taking my half a glass of milk. The door to the office was closed and, entering, I closed it again.

She wasn't in the red-leather chair. Since she was there for me, not for Wolfe, Fritz had moved up one of the yellow chairs for her, but hearing the door open and seeing me she had sprung up, and by the time I had shut the door and turned she was to me, gripping my arms, her head tilted back to get my eyes.

If it hadn't been for the milk I would have used my arms for one of their basic functions, since that's a sensible way to start a good frank talk with a girl. That being impractical, I tilted my head forward and kissed her. Not just a peck. She not only took it, she helped, and her grip on my arms tightened, and I had to keep the glass plumb by feel since I couldn't see it. It wouldn't have been polite for me to quit, so I left it to her.

She let go, backed up a step, and said, "You haven't shaved."

I crossed to my desk, sipped milk, put the glass down, and said,

"I spent the night at the District Attorney's office, and I'm tired, dirty, and sour. I could shower and shave and change in half an hour."

"You're all right." She plumped onto the chair. "Look at me."

"I am looking at you." I sat. "You'd do fine for a before-and-after vitamin ad. The before. Did you get to bed?"

"I guess so, I don't know." Her mouth opened to pull air in. Not a yawn, just helping her nose. "It couldn't have been a jail because the windows didn't have bars. They kept me until after midnight asking questions, and one of them took me home. Oh, yes, I went to bed, but I didn't sleep, but I must have, because I woke up. Archie, I don't know what you're going to do to me."

"Neither do I." I drank milk, emptying the glass. "Why, have you done something to me?"

"I didn't mean to."

"Of course not."

"It came out. You remember you explained it for me one night."

I nodded. "I said you have a bypass in your wiring. With ordinary people like me, when words start on their way out they have to go through a checking station for an okay, except when we're too mad or scared or something. You may have a perfectly good checking station, but for some reason, maybe a loose connection, it often gets bypassed."

She was frowning. "But the trouble is, if I haven't got a checking station I'm just plain dumb. If I do have one, it certainly got bypassed when the words came out about my going to meet you there yesterday."

"Meet me where?"

"On Forty-eighth Street. There at the entrance to the alley where I used to turn to deliver the corn to Rusterman's. I said I was to meet you there at five o'clock and we were going to wait there until Ken came because we wanted to have a talk with him. But I was late, I didn't get there until a quarter past five, and you weren't there, so I left."

I kept my shirt on. "You said that to whom?"

"To several people. I said it to a man who came to the apartment, and in that building he took me to downtown I said it to another man, and then to two more, and it was in a statement they had me sign."

"When did we make the date to meet there? Of course they asked that."

"They asked everything. I said I phoned you yesterday morning and we made it then."

"It's just possible that you *are* dumb. Didn't you realize they would come to me?"

"Why, of course. And you would deny it. But I thought they would think you just didn't want to be involved, and I said you weren't there, and you could probably prove you were somewhere else, so that wouldn't matter, and I had to give them some reason why I went there and then came away without even going in the restaurant to ask if Ken had been there."

She leaned forward. "Don't you see, Archie? I couldn't say I had gone there to see Ken, could I?"

"No. Okay, you're not dumb." I crossed my legs and leaned back. "You *had* gone there to see Ken?"

"Yes. There was something—about something."

"You got there at a quarter past five?"

"Yes."

"And came away without even going in the restaurant to ask if Ken had been there?"

"I didn't— Yes, I came away."

I shook my head. "Look, Sue. Maybe you didn't want to get me involved, but you have, and I want to know. If you went there to see Ken and got there at a quarter past five, you *did* see him. Didn't you?"

"I didn't see him alive." Her hands on her lap, very nice hands, were curled into fists. "I saw him dead. I went up the alley and he was there on the ground. I thought he was dead, but, if he wasn't, someone would soon come out and find him, and I was scared. I was scared because I had told him just two days ago that I would like to kill him. I didn't think it out, I didn't stop to think, I was just scared. I didn't realize until I was several blocks away how dumb *that* was."

"Why was it dumb?"

"Because Felix and the doorman had seen me. When I came I passed the front of the restaurant, and they were there on the sidewalk, and we spoke. So I couldn't say I hadn't been there and it was dumb to go away, but I was scared. When I got to the apartment I thought it over and decided what to say, about going there to meet you, and when a man came and started asking questions I told him about it before he asked." She opened a fist to gesture. "I did think about it, Archie. I did think it couldn't matter to you, not much."

That didn't gibe with the bypassing-the-checking-station theory, but there was no point in making an issue of it. "You thought wrong," I said, not complaining, just stating a fact. "Of course they asked you why we were going to meet there to have a talk with Ken, since he would be coming here. Why not here instead of there?"

"Because you didn't want to. You didn't want to talk with him here."

"I see. You really thought it over. Also they asked what we wanted to talk with him about. Had you thought about that?"

"Oh, I didn't have to. About what he had told you, that I thought I was pregnant and he was responsible."

That was a little too much. I goggled at her, and my eyes were in no shape for goggling. "He had told *me* that?" I demanded. "When?"

"You know when. Last week. Last Tuesday when he brought the corn. He told me about it Saturday—no, Sunday. At the farm."

I uncrossed my legs and straightened up. "I may have heard it wrong. I may be lower than I realized. Ken Faber told you on Sunday that he had told me on Tuesday that you thought you were pregnant and he was responsible? Was that it?"

"Yes. He told Carl too—you know, Carl Heydt. He didn't tell me he had told Carl, but Carl did. I think he told two other men too—Peter Jay and Max Maslow. I don't think you know them. That was when I told him I would like to kill him, when he told me he had told you."

"And that's what you told the cops we wanted to talk with him about?"

"Yes. I don't see why you say I thought wrong, thinking it wouldn't matter much to you, because you weren't there. Can't you prove you were somewhere else?"

I shut my eyes to look it over. The more I sorted it out, the messier it got. Mandel hadn't been fooling when he asked the judge to put a fifty-grand tag on me; the wonder was that he hadn't hit me with the big one.

I opened my itching eyes and had to blink to get her in focus. "For a frame," I said, "it's close to perfect, but I'm willing to doubt if you meant it. I doubt if you know the ropes well enough, and why pick on me? I am not a patsy. But whether you meant it or not, what are you here for? Why bother to come and tell me about it?"

"Because—I thought— don't you understand, Archie?"

"I understand plenty, but not why you're here."

"But don't you see, it's my word against yours. They told me last night that you denied that we had arranged to meet there. I wanted to ask you—I thought you might change that, you might tell them that you denied it just because you didn't want tᴏ be involved, that you had agreed to meet me there but you decided not to go, and they'll have to believe you because of course you were somewhere else. Then they won't have any reason not to believe me."

She put out a hand. "Archie—will you? Then it will be all right."

"Holy saints. You think so?"

"Of course it will. The way it is now they think either I'm lying or you're lying, but if you tell them—"

"Shut up!"

She gawked at me; then all of a sudden she broke. Her head went down and her hands up to cover her face. Her shoulders started to tremble and then she was shaking all over. If she had sobbed or groaned or something I would have merely waited it out, but there was no sound effect at all, and that was dangerous. She might crack.

I went to Wolfe's desk and got the vase of orchids, *Dendrobium nobile* that day, removed the flowers and put them on my desk pad, went to her, got fingers under her chin, forced her head up, and sloshed her good. The vase holds two quarts. Her hands came down and I sloshed her again, and she squealed and grabbed for my arm. I dodged, put the vase on my desk, went to the bathroom, which is over in the corner, and came back with a towel. She was on her feet, dabbing at her front.

"Here," I said, "use this."

She took it and wiped her face. "You didn't have to do that," she said.

"The hell I didn't." I got another chair and put it at a dry spot, went to my desk, and sat. "It might help if someone did it to me. Now listen. Whether you meant it or not, I am out on an extremely rickety limb. Ken did not tell me last Tuesday that you thought you were pregnant and he was responsible, he told me nothing whatever, but whether he lied to you or you're lying to the cops and me, they *think* he did.

"They also think or suspect that you and I have been what they call intimate. They also expect you to say under oath that I agreed to meet you at the entrance of that alley yesterday at five o'clock, and I can't prove I wasn't there. There's a man who will say he was with me somewhere else, but he's a friend of mine and he often works with me when Mr. Wolfe needs more help, and the cops don't have to believe him and neither would a jury. I don't know what else the cops have or haven't got, but any time now—"

"I didn't lie to you, Archie." She was on the dry chair, gripping the towel. A strand of wet hair dropped over her eye and she pushed it back. "Everything I told—"

"Skip it. Any time now, any minute, I may be hauled in on a charge of murder, and then where am I? Or suppose I somehow made it stick that I did not agree to meet you there, that you're lying to them, and I wasn't there. Then where will *you* be? The way it stands, the way you've staged it, today or tomorrow either you or I will be in the jug with no out. So either I—"

"But Archie, you—"

"Don't interrupt. Either I wriggle off by selling them on you—and by the way, I haven't asked you." I got up and went to her. "Stand up. Look at me." I extended my hands at waist level, open, palms up. "Put your hands on mine, palms down. No, don't press, relax, just let them rest there. Damn it, relax! Right. Look at me. Did you kill Ken?"

"No."

"Again. Did you kill him?"

"No, Archie!"

I turned and went back to my chair. She came a step forward, backed up, and sat. "That's my private lie detector," I told her. "Not patented. Either I wriggle off by selling them on you, and it would take some wriggling, which is not my style, or I do a job that *is* my style—I hope.

"As you know, I work for Nero Wolfe. First I see him and tell him I'm taking a leave of absence—I hope a short one. Then you and I go someplace where we're sure we won't be interrupted, and you tell me things, a lot of things, and no fudging. Where I go from there depends on what you tell me. I'll tell *you* one thing now, if you—"

The door opened and Wolfe was there. He crossed to the corner of his desk, faced her, and spoke. "I'm Nero Wolfe. Will you please move to this chair?" He indicated the red-leather chair by a nod, circled around his desk, and sat. He looked at me. "A job that is your style?"

Well. As I remarked when he insisted that I see her in the office, if I hadn't been pooped I would have given that offer a little attention. If I had been myself I would have known, or at least suspected, what he intended. I suppose he and I came as close to trusting each other as any two men can, on matters of joint concern, but as he had told

Parker, this was my affair, and I was discussing it with someone in his office, keeping him away from his favorite chair, and I had just told him that nothing of what I had told Cramer was flummery. So he had gone to the hole in the alcove.

I looked back at him. "I said I hope. What if I heard the panel open and steered clear?"

"Pfui. Clear of what?"

"Okay. Your trick. But I think she has a right to know."

"I agree." Sue had moved to the red-leather chair, and he swiveled. "Miss McLeod. I eavesdropped, without Mr. Goodwin's knowledge. I heard all that was said, and I saw. Do you wish to complain?"

She had fingered her hair back, but it was still a sight. "Why?" she asked.

"Why did I listen? To learn how much of a pickle Mr. Goodwin was in. And I learned. I have intruded because the situation is intolerable. You are either a cockatrice or a witling. Whether by design or stupidity, you have brought Mr. Goodwin to a desperate pass. That is—"

I broke in. "It's my affair. You said so."

He stayed at her. "That is his affair, but now it threatens me. I depend on him. I can't function properly, let alone comfortably, without him. He just told you he would take a leave of absence. That would be inconvenient for me but bearable, even if it were rather prolonged, but it's quite possible that I would lose him for good, and that would be a calamity. I won't have it. Thanks to you, he is in grave jeopardy." He turned. "Archie. This is now our joint affair. By your leave."

I raised both eyebrows. "Retroactive? Parker and my bail?"

He made a face. "Very well. Intimate or not, you have known Miss McLeod three years. Did she kill that man?"

"No and yes."

"That doesn't help."

"I know it doesn't. The 'no' because of a lot of assorted items, including the lie-detector test I just gave her, which of course you would hoot at if you hooted. The 'yes,' chiefly because she's here. Why did she come? She says to ask me to change my story and back hers up, that we had a date to meet there. That's a good deal to expect, and I wonder.

"If she killed him, of course she's scared stiff and she might ask anybody anything, but if she didn't, why come and tell me she went in the alley and saw him dead and scooted? I wonder. On balance, one will get you two that she didn't. One item for 'no,' when a man gets a girl pregnant her normal procedure is to make him marry her, and quick. What she wants most and has got to have is a father for the baby, and not a dead father. She certainly isn't going to kill him unless—"

"That's silly," Sue blurted, "I'm not pregnant."

I stared. "You said Ken told you he told me."

She nodded. "Ken would tell anybody anything."

"But you thought you were?"

"Of course not. How could I? There's only one way a girl can get pregnant, and it couldn't have been that with me because it's never happened."

Like everybody else, I like to kid myself that I know why I think this or do that, but sometimes it just won't work, and that was once. I don't mean why I believed her about not being pregnant and how she knew she couldn't be; I do know that; it was the way she said it and the way she looked. I *had* known her three years. But since, if I believed her on that, I had to scrap the item I had just given Wolfe for "no" on her killing Faber, why didn't I change the odds to even money?

I pass. I could cook up a case—for instance if she was straight on one thing, about not being pregnant and why not, she was probably straight on other things too—but who would buy it? It's even possible that every man alive, of whom I am one, has a feeling down below that an unmarried girl who knows she *can't* be pregnant is less apt to commit murder than one who can't be sure. I admit that a good private detective shouldn't have feelings down below, but have you any suggestions?

Since Wolfe pretends to think I could qualify on the witness stand as an expert on attractive young women, of course he turned to me and said, "Archie?" and I nodded yes. An expert shouldn't back and fill, and as I just said, I believed her on the pregnancy issue. Wolfe grunted, told me to take my notebook, gave her a hard eye for five seconds, and started in.

An hour and ten minutes later, when Fritz came to announce lunch, I had filled most of a new notebook and Wolfe was leaning back with his eyes shut and his lips tight. It was evident that he was going to have to work. She had answered all his questions with no apparent fumbling, and it still looked very much as if either I was going to ride the bumps or she was. Or possibly both.

As she told it, she had met Ken Faber eight months ago at a party at the apartment of Peter Jay. Ken had been fast on the follow-up, and four months later, in May, she had told him she would marry him someday—say in two or three years, when she was ready to give up modeling—if he had shown that he could support a family. From the notebook: "I was making over eight hundred dollars a week, ten times as much as he was, and of course if I got married I couldn't expect to keep that up. I don't think a married woman should model anyway because if you're married you ought to have babies, and there's no telling what that will do to you, and who looks after the babies?"

In June, at his request, she had got her father to give him a job on the farm, but she had soon regretted it. From the notebook: "Of course he knew I went to the farm weekends in the summer, and the very first weekend it was easy to see what his idea was. He thought it would be different on the farm than in town, it would be easy to get me to do what he wanted, as easy as falling off a log.

"The second week it was worse, and the third week it was still worse, and I was seeing what he was really like and I wished I hadn't said I would marry him. He accused me of letting other men do what I wouldn't let him do, and he tried to make me promise I wouldn't date any other man, even for dinner or a show.

"Then the last week in July he seemed to get some sense and I thought maybe he had just gone through some kind of phase or something, but last week, Friday evening, he was worse than ever all of a sudden, and Sunday he told me he had told Archie Goodwin that I thought I was pregnant and he was responsible, and of course Archie would pass it on, and if I denied it no one would believe me, and the only thing to do was to get married right away.

"That was when I told him I'd kill him. Then the next day, Monday, Carl—Carl Heydt—told me that Ken had told him the same thing, and I suspected he had told two other men, on account of things they had said, and I decided to go there Tuesday and see him. I was going to tell him he had to tell Archie and Carl it was a lie, and anybody else he had told, and if I had to I'd get a lawyer."

If that was straight, and the part about Carl Heydt and Peter Jay and Max Maslow could be checked, that made it more like ten to one that she hadn't killed him. She couldn't have ad-libbed it; she would have had to go there intending to kill him, or at least bruise him, since she couldn't have just happened to have with her a piece of two-inch pipe sixteen inches long. Say twenty to one.

But if she hadn't who had? Better than twenty to one, not some thug. There had been eighty bucks in Ken's pockets, and why would a thug go up that alley with the piece of pipe, much less hide under the platform with it? No. It had to be someone out for Ken specifically who knew that spot, or at least knew about it, and knew he would come there, and when.

Of course it was possible the murderer was someone Sue had never heard of and the motive had no connection with her, but that would make it really tough, and there she was, and Wolfe got all she had—or at least everything she would turn loose of. She didn't know how many different men she had had dates with in the twenty months she had been modeling—maybe thirty. More in the first year than recently; she had thought it would help to get jobs if she knew a lot of men, and it had, but now she turned down as many jobs as she accepted.

When she said she didn't know why so many men wanted to date her Wolfe made a face, but I knew she really meant it. It was hard to believe that a girl with so much born come-on actually wasn't aware of it, but I knew her, and so did my friend Lily Rowan, who *is* an expert on women.

She didn't know how many of them had asked her to marry them; maybe ten; she hadn't kept count. Of course you don't like her; to like a girl who says things like that, you'd have to see her and hear her, and if you're a man you wouldn't stop to ask whether you liked her or not. I frankly admit that the fact that she couldn't dance had saved me a lot of wear and tear.

From the time she had met Ken Faber she had let up on dates, and in recent months she had let only three other men take her places. Those three had all asked her to marry them, and they had stuck to it in spite of Ken Faber. Carl Heydt, who had given her her first modeling job, was nearly twice her age, but that wouldn't matter if she wanted to marry him when the time came. Peter Jay, who was something important in a big advertising agency, was younger, and Max Maslow, who was a fashion photographer, was still younger.

She had told Carl Heydt that what Ken had told him wasn't true, but she wasn't sure that he had believed her. She couldn't remember exactly what Peter Jay and Max Maslow had said that made her think that Ken had told them too; she hadn't had the suspicion until Monday, when Carl had told her what Ken had told him. She had told no one that she was going to Rusterman's Tuesday to see Ken.

it. I ask you to have those three here this evening. Not you with them."

She was frowning. "But you can't—you said identify him. How can you?"

"I don't know. Perhaps I can't, but I must try. Nine o'clock?"

She didn't want to, even after the concessions he had made, but she had to admit that we had to get some kind of information from somebody, and who else was there to start with? So she finally agreed, definitely, and Wolfe leaned back with his eyes shut and his lips tight, and Fritz came to announce lunch.

Sue got up to go, and when I returned after seeing her to the door and out, Wolfe had crossed to the dining room and was at the table. Instead of joining him, I stood and said, "Ordinarily I would think I was well worth it, but right now I'm no bargain at any price. Have we a program for the afternoon?"

"No. Except to telephone Mr. McLeod."

"I saw him at the D.A.'s office. Then I'm going up and rinse off. I think I smell. Tell Fritz to save me a bite in the kitchen."

I went to the hall and mounted the two flights to my room. During the forty minutes it took to do the job I kept telling my brain to lay off until it caught up, but it wouldn't. It insisted on trying to analyze the situation, with the emphasis on Sue McLeod. If I had her figured wrong, if she was it, it would almost certainly be a waste of time to try to get anything from three guys who were absolutely hooked, and if there was no program for the afternoon I had damn well better think one up. If it would be a calamity for Wolfe to lose me for good, what would it be for me?

By the time I stepped into the shower the brain had it doped that the main point was the piece of pipe. She had not gone into that alley toting that pipe; that was out. But I hadn't got that point settled conclusively by Cramer or Mandel, and I hadn't seen a morning paper. I would consult *The Times* when I went downstairs. But the brain wanted to know now, and when I left the shower I dried in a hurry, went to the phone on the bedtable, dialed the *Gazette*, got Lon Cohen, and asked him.

Of course he knew I had spent the night downtown and he wanted a page or two of facts, but I told him I was naked and would catch cold, and how final was it that whoever had conked Faber had brought the pipe with him? Sewed up, Lon said. Positively. The pipe was at the laboratory, revealing—maybe—its past to the scientists, and three or four dicks with color photos of it were trying to pick

All three of them knew about the corn delivery to Rusterman and Nero Wolfe; they knew she had made the deliveries for two summers and had kidded her about it; Peter Jay had tried to get her to pose in a cornfield, in an evening gown, for a client of his. They knew Ken was working at the farm and was making the deliveries.

From the notebook, Wolfe speaking: "You know those men quite well. You know their temperaments and bents. If one of them, enraged beyond endurance by Mr. Faber's conduct, went there and killed him, which one? Remember it was not a sudden fit of passion, it was planned. From your knowledge of them, which one?"

She was staring. "They didn't."

"Not 'they.' One of them. Which?"

She shook her head. "None of them."

Wolfe wiggled a finger at her. "That's twaddle, Miss McLeod. You may be shocked at the notion that someone close to you is a murderer; anyone would be; but you may not reject it as inconceivable. By your foolish subterfuge you have made it impossible to satisfy the police that neither you nor Mr. Goodwin killed that man except by one procedure: demonstrate that someone else killed him, and identify him. I must see those three men, and, since I never leave my house on business, they must come to me. Will you get them here? At nine o'clock this evening?"

"No," she said. "I won't."

He glared at her. If she had been merely a client, with nothing but a fee at stake, he would have told her to either do as she was told or clear out; but the stake was an errand boy it would be a calamity to lose—me—as he had admitted in my hearing. So he turned the glare off and turned a palm up.

"Miss McLeod. I concede that your refusal to think ill of a friend is commendable. I concede that Mr. Faber may have been killed by someone you have never heard of with a motive you can't even conjecture—and by the way, I haven't asked you: do you know of anyone who might have had a ponderable reason for killing him?"

"No."

"But it's possible that Mr. Heydt does, or Mr. Jay or Mr. Maslow. Even accepting your conclusion that none of them killed him, I must see them. I must also see your father, but separately—I'll attend to that. My only possible path to the murderer is the motive, and one or more of those four men, who knew Mr. Faber, may start me on up its trail. I thanked him and promised him something for a headline if and when. So that was settled.

As I went to a drawer for clean shorts the brain started in on Carl Heydt, but it was darned little to work on, and by the time I tied my tie it was buzzing around trying to find ₒ place to land.

Downstairs Wolfe was still in the dining room, but I went on by to the kitchen, got at my breakfast table with *The Times,* and was served by Fritz with what do you think? Corn fritters. There had been eight perfectly good ears, and Fritz hates to throw good food away. With bacon and homemade blackberry jam they were ambrosia, and in *The Times* report on the Faber murder Wolfe's name was mentioned twice and mine four times, so it was a fine meal.

I had finished the eighth fritter and was deciding whether to take on another one and a third cup of coffee when the doorbell rang, and I got up and went to the hall for a look. Wolfe was back in the office, and I stuck my head in and said, "McLeod."

He let out a growl. True, he had told Sue he must see her father and was even going to phone to ask him to come in from the country, but he always resents an unexpected visitor, no matter who. Ignoring the growl, I went to the front and opened the door, and when McLeod said he wanted to see Mr. Wolfe, with his burr on the *r,* I invited him in, took his Sunday hat, a dark-gray antique fedora in good condition, put it on the shelf, and took him to the office. Wolfe, who is no hand-shaker, told him good afternoon and motioned to the red-leather chair.

McLeod stood. "No need to sit," he said. "I've been told about the corn and I came to apologize. I'm to blame, and I'd like to explain how it happened. I didn't pick it; that young man did. Kenneth Faber."

Wolfe grunted. "Wasn't that heedless? I telephoned the restaurant this morning and was told that theirs was as bad as mine. You know what we require."

He nodded. "I ought to by now. You pay a good price, and I want to say it'll never happen again. I'd like to explain it. A man was coming Thursday with a bulldozer to work on a lot I'm clearing, but Monday night he told me he'd have to come Wednesday instead, and I had to dynamite a lot of stumps and rock before he came.

"I got at it by daylight yesterday and I thought I could finish in time to pick the corn, but I had some trouble and I had to leave the corn to that young man. I had showed him and I thought he knew.

So I've got to apologize and I'll see it don't happen again. Of course I'm not expecting you to pay for it."

Wolfe grunted. "I'll pay for the eight ears we used. It was vexatious, Mr. McLeod."

"I know it was." He turned and aimed his gray-blue eyes, with their farmer's squint, at me. "Since I'm here I'm going to ask you. What did that young man tell you about my daughter?"

I met his eyes. It was a matter not only of murder, but also of my personal jam that might land me in the jug any minute, and all I really knew of him was that he was Sue's father and he knew how to pick corn.

"Not a lot," I said. "Where did you get the idea he told me anything about her?"

"From her. This morning. What he told her he told you. So I'm asking you, to get it straight."

"Mr. McLeod," Wolfe cut in. He nodded at the red-leather chair. "Please sit down."

"No need to sit. I just want to know what that young man said about my daughter."

"She has told you what he said he said. She has also told Mr. Goodwin and me. We have spoken with her at length. She came shortly after eleven o'clock this morning to see Mr. Goodwin and stayed two hours."

"My daughter Susan? Came here?"

"Yes."

McLeod moved. In no hurry he went to the red-leather chair, sat, focused on Wolfe, and demanded, "What did she come for?"

Wolfe shook his head. "You have it wrong side up. That tone is for us, not you. We may or may not oblige you later; that will depend. The young man you permitted to pick my corn has been murdered, and because of false statements made by your daughter to the police, Mr. Goodwin may be charged with murder. The danger is great and imminent. You say you spent yesterday dynamiting stumps and rocks. Until what hour?"

McLeod's set jaw made his deep-tanned seamed face even squarer.

"My daughter doesn't make false statements," he said. "What were they?"

"They were about Mr. Goodwin. Anyone will lie when the alternative is intolerable. She may have been impelled by a desperate need to save herself, but Mr. Goodwin and I do not believe she killed that man. Archie?"

I nodded. "Right. Any odds you want to name."

"And we're going to learn who did kill him. Did you?"

"No. But I would have, if—" He let it hang.

"If what?"

"If I had known what he was saying about my daughter. I told them that, the police. I heard about it from them, and from my daughter, last night and this morning. He was a bad man, an evil man. You say you're going to learn who killed him, but I hope you don't. I told them that too. They asked me what you did, about yesterday, and I told them I was there in the lot working with the stumps until nearly dark and it made me late with the milking. I can tell you this, I don't resent you thinking I might have killed him, because I might."

"Who was helping you with the stumps?"

"Nobody, not in the afternoon. He was with me all morning after he did the chores, but then he had to pick the corn and then he had to go with it."

"You have no other help?"

"No."

"Other children? A wife?"

"My wife died ten years ago. We only had Susan. I told you, I don't resent this, not a bit. I said I would have killed him if I'd known. I didn't want her to come to New York, I knew something like this might happen—the kind of people she got to know and all the pictures of her. I'm an old-fashioned man and I'm a righteous man, only that word righteous may not mean for you what it means for me. You said you might oblige me later. What did my daughter come here for?"

"I don't know." Wolfe's eyes were narrowed at him. "Ask her. Her avowed purpose is open to question. This is futile, Mr. McLeod, since you think a righteous man may wink at murder. I wanted—"

"I didn't say that. I don't wink at murder. But I don't have to want whoever killed Kenneth Faber to get caught and suffer for it. Do I?"

"No. I wanted to see you. I wanted to ask you, for instance, if you know a man named Carl Heydt, but since—"

"I don't know him. I've never seen him. I've heard his name from my daughter; he was the first one she worked for. What about him?"

"Nothing, since you don't know him. Do you know Max Maslow?"

"No."

"Peter Jay?"

"No. I've heard their names from my daughter. She tells me about people; she tries to tell me they're not as bad as I think they are, only their ideas are different from mine. Now this has happened, and I knew it would, something like this. I don't wink at murder and I don't wink at anything sinful."

"But if you knew who killed that man or had reason to suspect anyone, you wouldn't tell me—or the police."

"I would not."

"Then I won't keep you. Good afternoon, sir."

McLeod stayed put. "If you won't tell me what my daughter came here for I can't make you. But you can't tell me she made false statements and not say what they were."

Wolfe grunted. "I can and do. I will tell you nothing." He slapped the desk. "Confound it, after sending me inedible corn you presume to come and make demands on me? Go!"

McLeod's mouth opened and closed again. In no hurry he got up. "I don't think it's fair," he said. "I don't think it's right." He turned to go and turned back. "Of course you won't be wanting any more corn."

Wolfe was scowling at him. "Why not? It's only the middle of September."

"I mean not from me."

"Then from whom? Mr. Goodwin can't go scouring the countryside with this imbroglio on our hands. I want corn this week. Tomorrow?"

"I don't see— There's nobody to bring it."

"Friday, then?"

"I might. I've got a neighbor— Yes, I guess so. The restaurant too?"

Wolfe said yes, he would tell them to expect it, and McLeod turned and went. I stepped to the hall, got to the front ahead of him to hand him his hat, and saw him out. When I returned to the office Wolfe was leaning back, frowning at the ceiling. As I crossed to my desk and sat I felt a yawn coming, and I stopped it.

A man expecting to be tagged for murder is in no position to yawn, even if he has had no sleep for thirty hours. I had my nose fill the order for more oxygen, swiveled, and said brightly, "That was a big help. Now we know about the corn."

Wolfe straightened up. "Pfui. Call Felix and tell him to expect a delivery on Friday."

"Yes, sir. Good. Then everything's jake."

"That's bad slang. There is good slang and bad slang. How long will it take you to type a full report of our conversation with Miss McLeod, yours and mine, from the beginning?"

"Verbatim?"

"Yes."

"The last half, more than half, is in the notebook. For the first part I'll have to dig, and though my memory is as good as you think it is, that will be a little slower. Altogether, say four hours. But what's the idea? Do you want it to remember me by?"

"No. Two carbons."

I cocked my head. "Your memory is as good as mine—nearly. Are you actually telling me to type all that stuff just to keep me off your neck until nine o'clock?"

"No. It may be useful."

"Useful how? As your employee I'm supposed to do what I'm told, and I often do, but this is different. This is our joint affair now—trying to save you from the calamity of losing me. Useful how?"

"I don't know!" he bellowed. "I say it *may* be useful, if I decide to use it. Can you suggest something that may be more useful?"

"Offhand, no."

"Then *if* you type it, two carbons."

I got up and went to the kitchen for a glass of milk. I might or might not start on it before four o'clock, when he would go up to the plant rooms for his afternoon session with the orchids.

At five minutes past nine that evening the three men whose names had had checkmarks in front of them in Kenneth Faber's little notebook were in the office, waiting for Wolfe to show. They hadn't come together; Carl Heydt had arrived first, ten minutes early, then Peter Jay, on the dot at nine, and then Max Maslow. I had put Heydt in the red-leather chair, and Jay and Maslow on two of the yellow ones facing Wolfe's desk. Nearest me was Maslow.

I had seen Heydt before, of course, but you take a new look at a man when he becomes a homicide candidate. He looked the same as ever—medium height with a slight bulge in the middle, round face with a wide mouth, quick dark eyes that kept on the move.

Peter Jay, the something important in a big advertising agency, tall as me but not as broad, with more than his share of chin and thick dark mane that needed a comb, looked as if he had the regulation ulcer, but it could have been just the current difficulty.

Max Maslow, the fashion photographer, was a surprise. With the twisted smile he must have practised in front of a mirror, the trick haircut, the string tie dangling, and the jacket with four buttons buttoned, he was a screwball if I ever saw one, and I wouldn't have supposed that Sue McLeod would let such a specimen hang on. I admit it could have been just that his ideas were different from mine, but I like mine.

Wolfe came. When there is to be a gathering he stays in the kitchen until I buzz on the house phone, and then he doesn't enter, he makes an entrance. Nothing showy, but it's an entrance. A line from the door to the corner of his desk just misses the red-leather chair, so with Heydt in the chair he would have had to circle around his feet and also pass between Heydt and the other two; and he detoured to his right, between the chair and the wall, to his side of the desk, stood, and shot me a glance.

I pronounced their names, indicating who was which, and he gave them a nod, sat, moved his eyes from left to right and back again, and spoke.

"This can be fairly brief," he said, "or it can go on for hours. I think, gentlemen, you would prefer brevity, and so would I. I assume you have all been questioned by the police and by the District Attorney or one of his assistants?"

Heydt and Maslow nodded, and Jay said yes. Maslow had his twisted smile on.

"Then you're on record, but I'm not privy to that record. Since you came here to oblige Miss McLeod, you should know our position, Mr. Goodwin's and mine, regarding her. She is not our client; we are under no commitment to her; we are acting solely in our own interest. But as it now stands we are satisfied that she didn't kill Kenneth Faber."

"That's damn nice of you," Maslow said. "So am I."

"Your own interest?" Jay asked. "What's your interest?"

"We're reserving that. We don't know how candid Miss McLeod has been with you, any or all of you, or how devious. I will say only that, because of statements made to the police by Miss McLeod, Mr. Goodwin is under heavy suspicion, and that because she knew the suspicion was unfounded she agreed to ask you gentlemen to come to see me. To lift the suspicion from Mr. Goodwin we must find out where it belongs, and for that we need your help."

"My God," Heydt blurted, "*I* don't know where it belongs."

The other two looked at him, and he looked back. There had been a feel in the atmosphere, and the looks made it more than a feel.

Evidently each of them had ideas about the other two, but of course it wasn't as simple as that if one of them had killed Faber, since he would be faking it. Anyhow, they all had ideas and they were itching.

"Quite possibly," Wolfe conceded, "none of you knows. But it is not mere conjecture that one of you has good reason to know. All of you knew he would be there that day at that hour, and you could have gone there at some previous time to reconnoiter. All of you had an adequate motive—adequate, at least, for the one it moved: Mr. Faber had either debased or grossly slandered the woman you wanted to marry.

"All of you had some special significance in his private thoughts or plans; your names were in his notebook, with checkmarks. You are not targets chosen at random for want of better ones; you are plainly marked by circumstances. Do you dispute that?"

Maslow said, "All right, that's our bad luck."

Heydt, biting his lip, said nothing.

Jay said, "It's no news that we're targets. Go on from there."

Wolfe nodded. "That's the rub. The police have questioned you, but I doubt if they have been importunate; they have been set at Mr. Goodwin by Miss McLeod. I don't know—"

"That's your interest," Jay said. "To get Goodwin from under."

"Certainly. I said so. I—"

"He has known Miss McLeod longer than we have," Maslow said. "He's the hero type. He rescued her from the sticks and started her on the path of glory. He's her hero. I asked her once why she didn't marry him if he was such a prize, and she said he hadn't asked her, Now you say she has set the police on him. Permit me to say I don't believe it. If they're on him they have a damn good reason. Also permit me to say I hope he *does* get from under, but not by making me the goat. I'm no hero."

Wolfe shook his head. "As I said, I'm reserving what Miss McLeod has told the police. She may tell you if you ask her. As for you gentlemen, I don't know how curious the police have been about you. Have they tried seriously to find someone who saw one of you in that neighborhood Tuesday afternoon?

"Of course they have asked you where you were that afternoon, that's mere routine, but have they properly checked your accounts? Are you under surveillance? I doubt it; and I haven't the resources for those procedures. I invite you to eliminate yourselves from consideration if you can. The man who killed Kenneth Faber was in that alley, concealed under that platform, shortly after five o'clock yesterday afternoon. Mr. Heydt. Can you furnish incontestable evidence that you weren't there?"

Heydt cleared his throat. "If I could, I don't have to furnish it to you. It seems to me—oh, what the hell. No, I can't."

"Mr. Jay?"

"Incontestable, no." Jay leaned forward, his chin out. "I came here because Miss McLeod asked me to, but if I understand what you're after I might as well go. You intend to find out who killed Faber and pin it on him. To prove it wasn't Archie Goodwin. Is that it?"

"Yes."

"Then count me out. I don't want Goodwin to get it, but neither do I want anyone else to. Not even Max Maslow."

"That's damn nice of you, Pete," Maslow said. "A real pal."

Wolfe turned to him. "You, sir. Can you eliminate yourself?"

"Not by proving I wasn't there."Maslow flipped a hand. "I must say, Wolfe, I'm surprised at you. I thought you were very tough and cagey, but you've swallowed something. You said we all wanted to marry Miss McLeod. Who fed you that? I admit I do, and as far as I know Carl Heydt does, but not my pal Pete. He's the pay-as-you-go type. I wouldn't exactly call him a Casanova, because Casanova never tried to score by talking up marriage, and that's Pete's favorite gambit. I could name—"

"Stand up." It was his pal Pete, on his feet, with fists, glaring down at him.

Maslow tilted his head back. "I wouldn't, Pete. I was merely—"

"Stand up or I'll slap you out of the chair."

Of course I had plenty of time to get there and in between them, but I was curious. It was likely that Jay, not caring about his knuckles, would go for the jaw, and I wanted to see what effect it would have on the twisted smile.

My curiosity didn't get satisfied. As Maslow came up out of the chair he sidestepped, and Jay had to turn, hauling his right back. He started it for Maslow's jaw by the longest route, and Maslow ducked, came on in, and landed with his right at the very best spot for a bare fist. A beautiful kidney punch.

As Jay started to bend, Maslow delivered another one to the same spot, harder, and Jay went down. He didn't tumble, he just wilted. By then I was there. Maslow went to his chair, sat, breathed, and fingered his string tie. The smile was intact, maybe twisted a little more.

He spoke to Wolfe. "I hope you didn't misunderstand me. I wasn't suggesting that I think he killed Faber. Even if he did I wouldn't want him to get it. On that point we're pals. I was only saying I don't see how you got your reputation if you— You all right, Pete?"

I was helping Jay up. A kidney punch doesn't daze you, it just makes you sick. I asked him if he wanted a bathroom, and he shook his head, and I steered him to his chair. He turned his face to Maslow, muttered a couple of vulgar words, and belched.

Wolfe spoke. "Will you have brandy, Mr. Jay? Whiskey? Coffee?" Jay shook his head and belched again.

Wolfe turned. "Mr. Heydt. The others have made it clear that if they have information that would help to expose the murderer they won't divulge it. How about you?"

Heydt cleared his throat. "I'm glad I don't have to answer that," he said. "I don't have to answer it because I have no information that would help. I know Archie Goodwin and I might say we're friends. If he's really in a jam I would want to help if I could. You say Miss McLeod has said something to the police that set them on him, but you won't tell us what she said."

"Ask her. You can give me no information whatever?"

"No."

Wolfe's eyes moved right, to the other two, and back again. "I doubt if it's worth the trouble," he said. "Assuming that one of you killed that man, I doubt if I can get at him from the front; I must go around. But I may have given you a false impression, and if so I wish to correct it. I said that to lift the suspicion from Mr. Goodwin we must find out where it belongs, but that isn't vital, for we have an alternative.

"We can merely shift the suspicion to Miss McLeod. That will be simple; and it will relieve Mr. Goodwin of further annoyance. We'll discuss it after you leave, and decide. You gentlemen may view the matter differently when Miss McLeod is in custody, charged with murder, without bail, but that is your—"

"You're a damn liar." Peter Jay.

"Amazing." Max Maslow. "Where *did* you get your reputation? What do you expect us to do, kick and scream or go down on our knees?"

"Of course you don't mean it." Carl Heydt. "You said you're satisfied that she didn't kill him."

Wolfe nodded. "I doubt if she would be convicted. She might not even go to trial; the police are not blockheads. It will be an ordeal for her, but it will also be a lesson; her implication of Mr. Goodwin may not have been willful, but it was inexcusable." His eyes went to Maslow. "You have mentioned my reputation. I made it and I don't risk it rashly. If tomorrow you learn that Miss McLeod has been arrested and is inaccessible, you may—"

" 'If.' " That crooked smile.

"Yes. It is contingent not on our power but on our preference. I am inviting you gentlemen to have a voice in our decision. You have told me nothing whatever, and I do not believe that you have nothing whatever to tell. Do you want to talk now, to me, or later, to the police, when that woman is in a pickle?"

"You're bluffing," Maslow said. "I call." He got up and headed for the hall. I got up and followed him out, got his hat from the shelf, and opened the front door; and as I closed it behind him and started back down the hall here came the other two. I opened the door again, and Jay, who had no hat, went by and on out, but Heydt stood there. I got his hat and he took it and put it on.

"Look, Archie," he said. "You've got to do something."

"Check," I said. "What, for instance?"

"I don't know. But about Sue—my God, he doesn't mean it, does he?"

"It isn't just a question of what he means, it's also what I mean. Damn it, I'm short on sleep, and I may soon be short on life, liberty, and the pursuit of happiness. Get the news every hour on the hour. Pleasant dreams."

"What did Sue tell the police about you?"

"No comment. My resistance is low and with the door open I might catch cold. If you don't mind?"

He went. I shut the door, put the chain bolt on, returned to the office, sat at my desk, and said, "So you thought it might be useful."

He grunted. "Have you finished it?"

"Yes. Twelve pages."

"May I see it?"

Not an order, a request. At least he was remembering that it was now a joint affair. I opened a drawer, got the original, and took it to him. He inspected the heading and the first page, flipped through the sheets, took a look at the end, dropped it on his desk, and said, "Your notebook, please." I sat and got my notebook and pen.

"There will be two," he said, "one for you and one for me. First mine. Heading in caps, affidavit by Nero Wolfe. The usual State of New York, County of New York. The text: I hereby depose that the twelve foregoing typewritten pages attached hereto, comma, each page initialed by me, comma, are a full and accurate record of a conversation that took place in my office on September thirteenth, nineteen sixty-one, by Susan McLeod, comma, Archie Goodwin, comma, and myself, semicolon; that nothing of consequence has been omitted or added in this typewritten record, semicolon; and that the conversation was wholly impromptu, comma, with no prior preparation or arrangement. A space for my signature, and, below, the conventional formula for notarizing. The one for you, on the same sheet if there is room, will be the same with the appropriate changes."

I looked up. "All right, it wasn't just to keep me off your neck. Okay on the power. But there's still the if on the preference. She didn't kill him. She came to me and opened the bag. I'm her hero. She as good as told Maslow that she'd marry me if I asked her. Maybe she could learn how to dance if she tried hard, though I admit that's doubtful. She makes a lot more than you pay me, and we could postpone the babies. You said you doubt if she would be convicted, but that's not good enough. Before I sign that affidavit I would need to know that you won't chuck the joint affair as soon as the heat is off of me."

"Rrrhhh," he said.

"I agree," I said, "it's a damn nuisance. It's entirely her fault, she dragged me in without even telling me, and if a girl pushes a man in a hole he has a right to wiggle out, but you must remember that I am now a hero. Heroes don't wiggle. Will you say that it will be our joint affair to make sure she doesn't go to trial?"

"I wouldn't say that I will make sure of anything whatever."

"Correction: that you will be concerned?"

He took air in, all the way, through his nose, and let it out through his mouth. "Very well. I'll be concerned." He glanced at the twelve pages on his desk. "Will you bring Miss Pinelli to my room at five minutes to nine in the morning?"

"No. She doesn't get to her office until nine-thirty."

"Then bring her to the plant rooms at nine-forty with the affidavit." He looked at the wall clock. "You can type it in the morning. You've had no sleep for forty hours. Go to bed."

That was quite a compliment, and I was appreciating it as I mounted the stairs to my room. Except for a real emergency he will permit no interruptions from nine to eleven in the morning, when he is in the plant rooms, but he wasn't going to wait until he came down to the office to get the affidavit notarized.

As I got into bed and turned the light off I was considering whether to ask for a raise now or wait till the end of the year, but before I made up my mind I didn't have a mind. It was gone.

I never did actually make up my mind about passing the buck to Sue. I was still on the fence after breakfast Thursday morning when I dialed the number of Lila Pinelli, who adds maybe two bucks a week to the take of her secretarial service in a building on Eighth Avenue by doubling as a notary public. Doing the affidavits didn't commit me to anything; the question was, what then?

So I asked her to come, and she came, and I took her up to the plant rooms. She was in a hurry to get back, but she had never seen the orchids, and no one alive could just breeze on by those benches, with everything from the neat little *Oncidiums* to the big show-offs like the *Laeliocattleyas*. So it was after ten o'clock when we came back down and I paid her and let her out, and I went to the office and put the document in the safe.

As I say, I never did actually make up my mind; it just happened. At ten minutes past eleven Wolfe, having come down at eleven as usual, was at his desk looking over the morning crop of mail, and I was at mine sorting the germination slips he had brought, when the doorbell rang. I stepped to the hall for a look, turned, and said, "Cramer. I'll go hide in the cellar."

"Confound it," he growled. "I wanted— Very well."

"There's no law about answering doorbells."

"No. We'll see."

I went to the front, opened up, said good morning, and gave him room. He crossed the sill, took a folded paper from a pocket, and handed it to me. I unfolded it, and a glance was enough, but I read it through. "At least my name's spelled right," I said. I extended my hands, the wrists together. "Okay, do it right."

"You'd clown in the chair," he said. "I want to see Wolfe."

He marched down the hall and into the office. Very careless. I could have scooted on out and away, and for half a second I considered it, but I wouldn't have been there to see the look on his face when he found I was gone. When I entered the office he was lowering his fanny onto the red-leather chair and putting his hat on the stand beside it. Also he was speaking.

"I have just handed Goodwin a warrant for his arrest," he was saying, "and this time he'll stay."

I stood. "It's an honor. Anyone can be banged by a bull or a dick. It takes me to be pinched by an Inspector twice in one week."

His eyes stayed at Wolfe. "I came myself," he said, "because I want to tell you how it stands. A police officer with a warrant to serve is not only allowed to use his discretion, he's supposed to. I know damn well what Goodwin will do—he'll clam up, and a crowbar wouldn't pry him open. Give me that warrant, Goodwin."

"It's mine. You've served it."

"I have not. I just showed it to you." He stretched an arm and took it. "When I was here Tuesday night," he told Wolfe, "you were dumfounded by my fatuity. So you said in your fancy way. All you cared about was who picked that corn. I came myself to see how you feel now. Goodwin will talk if you tell him to. Do you want me to wait in the front room while you discuss it? Not all day, say ten minutes. I'm giving you a—"

He stopped to glare. Wolfe had pushed his chair back and was rising, and of course Cramer thought he was walking out. It wouldn't have been the first time. But Wolfe headed for the safe, not the hall. As he turned the handle and pulled the door open, there I was. If he had told me to bring it instead of going for it himself, I could have stalled while I made up my mind, even with Cramer there; but as I have said twice before I never did actually make up my mind.

I merely went to my desk and sat. I owed Sue McLeod nothing. If either she or I was going to be cooped, there were two good reasons why it should be her: she had made the soup herself, and I wouldn't be much help in the joint affair if I was salted down. So I sat, and Wolfe got it from the safe, went and handed it to Cramer, and spoke. "I suggest that you look at the affidavits first. The last two sheets."

Over the years I have made a large assortment of cracks about Inspector Cramer, but I admit he has his points. Having inspected the affidavits, he went through the twelve pages fast, and then he went back and started over and took his time. Altogether, more than half an hour; and not once did he ask a question or even look up. And when he finished, even then no questions.

Lieutenant Rowcliff or Sergeant Purley Stebbins would have kept at us for an hour. Cramer merely gave each of us a five-second-straight hard look, folded the document, put it in his inside breast pocket, rose and came to my desk, picked up the phone, and dialed. In a moment he spoke.

"Donovan? Inspector Cramer. Give me Sergeant Stebbins." In another moment: "Purley? Get Susan McLeod. Don't call her, get her.

Go yourself. I'll be there in ten minutes and I want her there fast. Take a man along. If she balks, wrap her up and carry her."

He cradled the phone, went and got his hat, and marched out.

Of all the thousand or more times I have felt like putting vinegar in Wolfe's beer, I believe the closest I ever came to doing it was that Thursday evening when the doorbell rang at a quarter past nine, and after a look at the front I told him that Carl Heydt, Max Maslow, and Peter Jay were on the stoop, and he said they were not to be admitted.

In the nine and a half hours that had passed since Cramer had used my phone to call Purley Stebbins I had let it lie. I couldn't expect Wolfe to start any fur flying until there was a reaction, or there wasn't, say by tomorrow noon, to what had happened to Sue. However, I had made a move on my own.

When Wolfe had left the office at four o'clock to go up to the plant rooms, I had told him I would be out on an errand for an hour or so, and I had taken a walk, to Rusterman's, thinking I might pick up some little hint.

I didn't. First I went out back for a look at the platform and the alley, which might seem screwy, since two days and nights had passed and the city scientists had combed it, but you never know. I once got an idea just running my eye around a hotel room where a woman had spent a night six months earlier. But I got nothing from the platform or alley except a scraped ear from squeezing under the platform and out again, and after talking with Felix and Joe and some of the kitchen staff I crossed it off.

No one had seen or heard anyone or anything until Zoltan had stepped out for a cigarette (no smoking is allowed in the kitchen) and had seen the station wagon and the body on the ground.

I would have let it ride that evening, no needling until tomorrow noon. When Lily Rowan phoned around seven o'clock and said Sue had phoned her from the D.A.'s office that she was under arrest and had to have a lawyer and would Lily send her one, and Lily wanted me to come and tell her what was what, I would have gone if I hadn't wanted to be on hand if there was a development. But when the development came Wolfe told me not to let it in.

I straight-eyed him. "You said you'd be concerned."

"I am concerned."

"Then here they are. You tossed her to the wolves to open them up, and here—"

"No. I did that to keep you out of jail. I am considering how to deal with the problem, and until I decide there is no point in seeing them. Tell them they'll hear from us."

The doorbell rang again. "Then I'll see them. In the front room."

"No. Not in my house." He went back to his book.

Either put vinegar in his beer or get the Marley .32 from my desk drawer and shoot him dead, but that would have to wait; they were on the stoop. I went and opened the door enough for me to slip through, did so, bumping into Carl Heydt, and pulled the door shut. "Good evening," I said. "Mr. Wolfe is busy on an important matter and can't be disturbed. Do you want to disturb me instead?"

They all spoke at once. The general idea seemed to be that I would open the door and they would handle the disturbing.

"You don't seem to realize," I told them, "that you're up against a genius. So am I, only I'm used to it. You were damn fools to think he was bluffing. You might have known he would do exactly what he said."

"Then he did?" Peter Jay. "He did it?"

"We did. I share the glory. We did."

"Glory, hell." Max Maslow. "You know Sue didn't kill Ken Faber. He said so."

"He said we were satisfied that she didn't. We still are. He also said that we doubt if she'll be convicted. He also said that our interest was to get me from under, and we had alternatives. We could either find out who killed Faber, for which we needed your help; or, if you refused to help, we could switch it to Sue.

"You refused, and we switched it, and I am in the clear, and here you are. Why? Why should he waste time on you now? He is busy on an important matter; he's reading a book entitled *My Life in Court,* by Louis Nizer. Why should he put it down for you?"

"I can't believe it, Archie." Carl Heydt had hold of my arm. "I can't believe you'd do a thing like this—to Sue—when you say she didn't—"

"You never can tell, Carl. There was that woman who went to the park every day to feed the pigeons, but she fed her husband arsenic. I have a suggestion. This is Mr. Wolfe's house and he doesn't want you in it, but if you guys have changed your minds, at least two of you, about helping to find out who killed Faber, I'm a licensed detective too and I could spare a couple of hours. We can sit here on the steps, or we can go somewhere—"

"And you can tell us," Maslow said, "what Sue told the cops that got them on you. I may believe that when I hear it."

"You won't hear it from me. That's not the idea. *You* tell *me* things. I ask questions and you answer them. If I don't ask them, who will? I doubt if the cops or the D.A. will; they've got too good a line on Sue. I'll tell you this much, they know she was there Tuesday at the right time, and they know that she lied to them about about what she was there for and what she saw. I can spare an hour or two."

They exchanged glances, and they were not the glances of buddies with a common interest. They also exchanged words and found they agreed on one point: if one of them took me up they all would. Peter Jay said we could go to his place and they agreed on that too, and we descended to the sidewalk and headed east. At Eighth Avenue we flagged a taxi with room for four. It was ten minutes to ten when it rolled to the curb at a marquee on Park Avenue in the Seventies.

Jay's apartment, on the fifteenth floor, was quite a perch for a bachelor. The living room was high, wide, and handsome, and it would have been an appropriate spot for our talk, since it was there that Sue McLeod and Ken Faber had first met; but Jay took us on through to a room, smaller but also handsome, with chairs and carpet of matching green, a desk, bookshelves, and a TV-player cabinet. He asked us what we would drink but got no orders, and we sat.

"All right, ask your questions," Maslow said. The twisted smile.

He was blocking my view of Heydt, and I shifted my chair. "I've changed my mind," I said. "I looked it over on the way, and I decided to take another tack. Sue told the police, and it was in her signed statement, that she and I had arranged to meet there at the alley at five o'clock, and she was late, she didn't get there until five-fifteen, and I wasn't there, so she left. She had to tell them she was there because she had been seen in front of the restaurant, just around the corner, by two of the staff who know her."

Their eyes were glued on me. "So you weren't there at five-fifteen," Jay said. "The body was found at five-fifteen. So you had been and gone?"

"No. Sue also told the police that Faber had told her on Sunday that he had told me on Tuesday that she was pregnant and he was responsible. He had told you that, all three of you. She said that was why she and I were going to meet there, to make Faber swallow his lies. So it's fair to say she set the cops on me, and it's no wonder they turned on the heat. The trouble—"

"Why not?" Maslow demanded. "Why isn't it still on?"

"Don't interrupt. The trouble was, she lied. Not about what Faber had told her on Sunday he had told me on Tuesday; that was probably *his* lie; he probably had told her that, but it wasn't true; he had told me nothing on Tuesday. That's why your names in his notebook had checkmarks but mine didn't; he was going to feed us that to put the pressure on Sue, and he had fed it to you but not me. So that was his lie, not Sue's. Hers was about our arranging to meet there Tuesday afternoon to have it out with Faber. We hadn't arranged anything. She also—"

"So *you* say." Peter Jay.

"Don't interrupt. She also lied about what she did when she got there at five-fifteen. She said she saw I wasn't there and left. Actually she went down the alley, saw Faber's body there on the ground with his skull smashed, panicked, and blew. The time thing—"

"So *you* say." Peter Jay.

"Shut up. The time thing is only a matter of seconds. Sue says she got there at five-fifteen, and the record says that a man coming from the kitchen discovered the body at five-fifteen. Sue may be off half a minute, or the man may. Evidently she had just been and gone when the man came from the kitchen."

"Look, pal." Maslow had his head cocked and his eyes narrowed. "Shut up? Go soak your head. Who's lying, Sue or you?"

I nodded. "That's a fair question. Until noon today, a little before noon, they thought I was. Then they found out I wasn't. They didn't just guess again, they found out, and that's why they took her down and they're going to keep her. Which—"

"How did they find out?"

"Ask them. You can be sure it was good. They were liking it fine, having me on a hook, and they hated to see me flop off. It had to be good, and it was. Which brings me to the point. I think Sue's lie was part truth. I think she *had* arranged with someone to meet her there at five o'clock.

"She got there fifteen minutes late and he wasn't there, and she went down the alley and saw Faber dead, and what would she think? That's obvious. No wonder she panicked. She went home and looked it over. She couldn't deny she had been there because she had been seen. If she said she had gone there on her own to see Faber, alone, they wouldn't believe she hadn't gone in the alley, and they certainly *would* believe she had killed him.

"So she decided to tell the truth, part of it, that she had arranged to meet someone and she got there late and he wasn't there and she had left—leaving out that she had gone in the alley and seen the body. But since she thought that the man she had arranged to meet had killed Faber she couldn't name him; but they would insist on her naming him. So she decided to name me. It wasn't so dirty really; she thought I could prove I was somewhere else, having decided not to meet her. I couldn't, but she didn't know that." I turned a palm up. "So the point is, who had agreed to meet her there?"

Heydt said, "That took a lot of cutting and fitting, Archie."

"You were going to ask questions," Maslow said. "Ask one we can answer."

"I'll settle for that one," I said. "Say it was one of you, which of course I *am* saying. I don't expect him to answer it. If Sue stands pat and doesn't name him and it gets to where he has to choose between letting her go to trial and unloading, he might come across, but not here and now. But I do expect the other two to consider it.

"Put it another way: if Sue decided to jump on Faber for the lies he was spreading around and to ask one of you to help, which one would she pick? Or still another: which one of you would be most likely to decide to jump Faber and ask Sue to join in? I like the first one better because it was probably her idea." I looked at Heydt. "What about it, Carl? Just a plain answer to a plain question. Which one would she pick? You?"

"No. Maslow."

"Why?"

"He's articulate and he's tough. I'm not tough, and Sue knows it."

"How about Jay?"

"My God, no. I hope not. She must know that nobody can depend on him for anything that takes guts."

Jay left his chair, and his hands were fists as he moved. Guts or not, he certainly believed in making contact. Thinking that Heydt probably wasn't as well educated as Maslow, I got up and blocked Jay off, and darned if he didn't swing at me, or start to. I got his arm and whirled him and shoved, and he stumbled but managed to stay on his feet. As he turned, Maslow spoke.

"Hold it, Pete. I have an idea. There's no love lost among us three, but we all feel the same about this Goodwin. He's a persona non grata if I ever saw one." He got up. "Let's bounce him. Not just a nudge, the bum's rush. Care to help, Carl?"

Heydt shook his head. "No, thanks. I'll watch."

"Okay. It'll be simpler if you just relax, Goodwin."

I couldn't turn and go, leaving my rear open. "I hope you won't tickle," I said, backing up a step.

"Come in behind, Pete," Maslow said, and started, slow, his elbows out a little and his open hands extended and up some. Since he had been so neat with the kidney punch he probably knew a few tricks, maybe the armpit or the apple, and with Jay on my back I would have been a setup, so I doubled up and whirled, came up bumping Jay, and gave him the edge of my hand, as sharp as I could make it, on the side of his neck, the tendon below the ear.

It got exactly the right spot and so much for him, but Maslow had my left wrist and was getting his shoulder in for the lock, and in another tenth of a second I would have been meat. The only way to go was down, and I went, sliding off his shoulder and bending my elbow into his belly, and he made a mistake. Having lost the lock, he reached for my other wrist. That opened him up, and I rolled into him, brought my right arm around, and had his neck with a knee in his back.

"Do you want to hear it crack?" I asked him, which was bad manners, since he couldn't answer. I loosened my arm a little. "I admit I was lucky. If Jay had been sideways you would have had me."

I looked at Jay, who was on a chair, rubbing his neck. "If you want to play games you ought to take lessons. Maslow would be a good teacher." I unwound my arm and got erect. "Don't bother to see me out," I said and headed for the front.

I was still breathing a little fast when I emerged to the sidewalk, having straightened my tie and run my comb through my hair in the elevator. My watch said twenty past ten. Also in the elevator I had decided to make a phone call, so I walked to Madison Avenue, found a booth, and dialed one of the numbers I knew best.

Miss Lily Rowan was in and would be pleased to have me come and tell her things, and I walked the twelve blocks to the number on 63rd Street where her penthouse occupies the roof.

Since it wasn't one of Wolfe's cases with a client involved, but a joint affair, and since it was Lily who had started Sue on her way at my request, I gave her the whole picture. Her chief reactions were (a) that she didn't blame Sue and I had no right to, I should feel flattered; (b) that I had to somehow get Sue out of it without involving whoever had removed such a louse as Kenneth Faber from circulation; and (c) that if I did have to involve him she hoped to heaven it wasn't Carl Heydt because there was no one else around who could make clothes that were fit to wear, especially suits.

She had sent a lawyer to Sue, Bernard Ross, and he had seen her and had phoned an hour before I came to report that she was being held without bail and he would decide in the morning whether to apply for a writ.

It was after one o'clock when I climbed out of a cab in front of the old brownstone on West 35th Street, mounted the stoop, used my key, went down the hall to the office and switched the light on, and got a surprise. Under a paperweight on my desk was a note in Wolfe's handwriting. It said:

AG: Saul will take the car in the morning, probably for most of the day. His car is not presently available.   NW

I went to the safe, manipulated the knob, opened the door, got the petty-cash book from the drawer, flipped to the current page, and saw an entry:

9/14 SP exp AG 100

I put it back, shut the door, twirled the knob, and considered. Wolfe had summoned Saul, and he had come and had been given an errand for which he needed a car. What errand, for God's sake? Not to drive to Putnam County to get the corn that had been ordered for Friday; for that he wouldn't need to start in the morning, he wouldn't need a hundred bucks for possible expenses, and the entry wouldn't say "exp AG." It shouldn't say that anyway since I wasn't a paying client; it should say "exp JA" for joint affair.

And if we were going to split the outlay I should damn well have been consulted beforehand. But up in my room, as I took off and put on, what was biting me was the errand. In the name of the Almighty Lord what and where was the errand?

Wolfe eats breakfast in his room from a tray taken up by Fritz, and ordinarily I don't see him until he comes down from the plant rooms at eleven o'clock. If he has something important or complicated for me he sends word by Fritz for me to go up to his room; for something trivial he gets me on the house phone. That Friday morning there was neither word by Fritz nor the buzzer, and after a late and leisurely breakfast in the kitchen, having learned nothing new from the report of developments in the morning papers on the Sweet

Corn Murder, as the *Gazette* called it, I went to the office and opened the mail.

If Wolfe saw fit to keep Saul's errand strictly private, he could eat wormy old corn boiled in water before I'd ask him. I decided to go out for a walk and was starting for the kitchen to tell Fritz when the phone rang. I got it, and a woman said she was the secretary of Mr. Bernard Ross, counsel for Miss Susan McLeod, and Mr. Ross would like very much to talk with Mr. Wolfe and Mr. Goodwin at their earliest convenience. He would appreciate it if they would call at his office today, this morning if possible.

I would have enjoyed telling Wolfe that Bernard Ross, the celebrated attorney, didn't know that Nero Wolfe, the celebrated detective, never left his house to call on anyone whoever, but since I wasn't on speaking terms with him I had to skip it. I told the secretary that Wolfe couldn't but I could and would, went and told Fritz I would probably be back for lunch, put a carbon copy of the twelve-page conversation with affidavits in my pocket, and departed.

I did get back for lunch, just barely. Including the time he took to study the document I had brought, Ross kept me a solid two hours and a half. When I left he knew nearly everything I did, but not quite; I omitted a few items that were immaterial as far as he was concerned—for instance, that Wolfe had sent Saul Panzer somewhere to do something. Since I couldn't tell him where, to do what, there was no point in mentioning it.

I would have preferred to buy my lunch somewhere, say at Rusterman's, rather than sit through a meal with Wolfe, but he would be the one to gripe, not me, if he didn't know where I was. Entering his house, and hearing him in the dining room speaking to Fritz, I went first to the office, and there on my desk under a paperweight were four sawbucks. Leaving them there, I went to the dining room and said good morning, though it wasn't.

Wolfe nodded and went on dishing shrimps from a steaming casserole. "Good afternoon. That forty dollars on your desk can be returned to the safe. Saul had no expenses and I gave him sixty dollars for his six hours."

"His daily minimum is eighty."

"He wouldn't take eighty. He didn't want to take anything, since this is our personal affair, but I insisted. This shrimp Bordelaise is without onions but has some garlic. I think an improvement, but Fritz and I invite your opinion."

"I'll be glad to give it. It smells good." I sat. That was by no means the first time the question had arisen whether he was more pig-headed than I was strong-minded. I was supposed to explode. I was supposed to demand to know where and how Saul had spent the six hours, and he would then be good enough to explain that he had got an idea last night in my absence, and, not knowing where I was, he had had to call Saul. So I wouldn't explode. I would eat shrimp Bordelaise without onions but with garlic and like it.

Obviously, whatever Saul's errand had been, it had been a wash-out, since he had returned, reported, and been paid off. So it was Wolfe's move, since he had refused to see the three candidates when they came and rang the bell, and I would not explode. Nor would I report on last night or this morning unless and until he asked for it.

Back in the office after lunch, he got settled in his favorite chair with *My Life in Court,* and I brought a file of cards from the cabinet and got busy with the germination records. At one minute to four he put his book down and went to keep his date with the orchids. It would have been a pleasure to take the Marley .32 from the drawer and plug him in the back.

I was at my desk, looking through the evening edition of the *Gazette* that had just been delivered, when I heard a noise I couldn't believe. The elevator. I looked at my watch: half past five. That was unprecedented. He never did that. Once in the plant rooms he stuck there for the two hours, no matter what. If he had a notion that couldn't wait he buzzed me on the house phone, or Fritz if I wasn't there. I dropped the paper and got up and stepped to the hall. The elevator jolted to a stop at the bottom, the door opened, and he emerged.

"The corn," he said. "Has it come?"

For Pete's sake. Being finicky about grub is all right up to a point, but there's a limit. "No," I said. "Unless Saul brought it."

He grunted. "A possibility occurred to me. When it comes—if it comes—no. I'll see for myself. The possibility is remote, but it would be—"

"Here it is," I said. "Good timing." A man with a carton had appeared on the stoop. As I started to the front the doorbell rang, and as I opened the door Wolfe was there beside me. The man, a skinny little guy in pants too big for him and a bright-green shirt, spoke. "Nero Wolfe?"

"I'm Nero Wolfe." He was on the sill. "You have my corn?"

"Right here." He put the carton down and let go of the cord.

"May I have your name, sir?"

"My name's Palmer. Delbert Palmer. Why?"

"I like to know the names of men who render me a service. Did you pick the corn?"

"Hell, no. McLeod picked it."

"Did you pack it in the carton?"

"No, he did. Look here, I know you're a detective. You just ask questions from habit, huh?"

"No, Mr. Palmer. I merely want to be sure about the corn. I'm obliged to you. Good day, sir." He bent over to slip his fingers under the cord, lifted the carton, and headed for the office. Palmer told me distinctly, "It takes all kinds," turned, and started down the steps, and I shut the door.

In the office Wolfe was standing eying the carton, which he had put on the seat of the red-leather chair. As I crossed over he said without looking up, "Get Mr. Cramer."

It's nice to have a man around who obeys orders no matter how batty they are and saves the questions for later. That time the questions got answered before they were asked. I went to my desk, dialed Homicide South, and got Cramer, and Wolfe, who had gone to his chair, took his phone.

"Mr. Cramer? I must ask a favor. I have here in my office a carton which has just been delivered to me. It is supposed to contain corn, and perhaps it does, but it is conceivable that it contains dynamite and a contraption that will detonate it when the cord is cut and the flaps raised. My suspicion may be groundless, but I have it.

"I know this is not your department, but you will know how to proceed. Will you please notify the proper person without delay? . . . That can wait until we know what's in the carton . . . Certainly. Even if it contains only corn I'll give you all relevant information . . . No, there is no ticking sound. If it does contain explosive there is almost certainly no danger until the carton is opened . . . Yes, I'll make sure."

He hung up, swiveled, and glared at the carton. "Confound it," he growled, "again. We'll get some somewhere before the season ends."

The first city employee to arrive, four or five minutes after Wolfe hung up, was one in uniform. Wolfe was telling me what Saul's errand had been when the doorbell rang, and since I resented the interruption I trotted to the front, opened the door, saw a prowl car at the curb, and demanded rudely, "Well?"

"Where's that carton?" he demanded back.

"Where it will stay until someone comes who knows something."
I was shutting the door but his foot was there.

"You're Archie Goodwin," he said. "I know about you. I'm coming
in. Did you yell for help or didn't you?"

He had a point. An officer of the law doesn't have to bring a search
warrant to enter a house whose owner has asked the police to come
and get a carton of maybe dynamite. I gave him room to enter, shut
the door, took him to the office, pointed to the carton, and said, "If
you touch it and it goes off we can sue you for damages."

"You couldn't pay me to touch it," he said. "I'm here to see that
nobody does."

He glanced around, went over by the big globe, and stood, a good
fifteen feet away from the carton. With him there, the rest of the
explanation of Saul's errand had to wait, but I had something to
look at to pass the time—a carbon copy, one sheet, which Wolfe had
taken from his desk drawer and handed me, of something Saul had
typed on my machine during my absence Thursday evening.

The second city employee to arrive, at ten minutes to six, was
Inspector Cramer. When the bell rang and I went to let him in, the
look on his face was one I had seen before. He knew Wolfe had
something fancy by the tail, and he would have given a month's pay
before taxes to know what. He tramped to the office, saw the carton,
turned to the cop, got a salute but didn't acknowledge it, and said,
"You can go, Schwab."

"Yes, sir. Stay out front?"

"No. You won't be needed."

Fully as rude as I had been, but he was a superior officer. Schwab
saluted again and went. Cramer looked at the red-leather chair. He
always sat there, but the carton was on it. I moved up one of the
yellow ones, and he sat, took his hat off, dropped it on the floor, and
asked Wolfe, "What is this, a gag?"

Wolfe shook his head. "It may be a bugaboo, but I'm not crying
wolf. I can tell you nothing until we know what's in the carton."

"The hell you can't. When did it come?"

"One minute before I telephoned you."

"Who brought it?"

"A stranger. A man I had never seen before."

"Why do you think it's dynamite?"

"I think it may be. I reserve further information until—"

I missed the rest because the doorbell rang and I went. It was the bomb squad, two of them. They were in uniform, but one look and you knew they weren't flatties—if nothing else, their eyes. When I opened the door I saw another one down on the sidewalk, and their special bus, with its made-to-order enclosed body, was double-parked in front.

I asked, "Bomb squad?" and the shorter one said, "Right," and I convoyed them to the office. Cramer, on his feet, returned their salute, pointed to the carton, and said, "It may be just corn. I mean the kind of corn you eat. Or it may not. Nero Wolfe thinks not. He also thinks it's safe until the flaps are opened, but you're the experts. As soon as you know, phone me here. How long will it take?"

"That depends, Inspector. It could be an hour, or ten hours—or it could be never."

"I hope not never. Will you call me here as soon as you know?"

"Yes, sir."

The other one, the taller one, had stooped to press his ear against the carton and kept it there. He raised his head, said, "No comment," eased his fingers under the carton's bottom, a hand at each side, and came up with it. I said, "The man who brought it carried it by the cord," and got ignored. They went, the one with the carton in front, and I followed to the stoop, watched them put it in the bus, then I returned to the office. Cramer was in the red-leather chair, and Wolfe was speaking.

"But if you insist, very well. My reason for thinking it may contain an explosive is that it was brought by a stranger. My name printed on it was as usual, but naturally such a detail would not be overlooked. There are a number of people in the metropolitan area who have reason to wish me ill, and it would be imprudent—"

"My God, you can lie."

Wolfe tapped the desk with a fingertip. "Mr. Cramer. If you insist on lies you'll get them. Until I know what's in that carton. Then we'll see." He picked up his book, opened to his place, and swiveled to get the light right.

Cramer was stuck. He looked at me, started to say something, and vetoed it. He couldn't get up and go because he had told the Bomb Squad to call him there, but an Inspector couldn't just sit. He took a cigar from a pocket, looked at it, put it back, arose, came to me, and said, "I've got some calls to make." Meaning he wanted my chair, which was a good dodge since it got *some* action; I had to move.

He stayed at the phone nearly half an hour, making four or five calls, none of which sounded important, then got up and went over to the big globe and started studying geography. Ten minutes was enough for that and he switched to the bookshelves. Back at my desk, leaning back with my legs crossed, my hands clasped behind my head, I noted which books he took out and looked at.

Now that I knew who had killed Ken Faber, little things like that were interesting. The one he looked at longest was *The Coming Fury* by Bruce Catton. He was still at that when the phone rang. I turned to get it, but by the time I had it to my ear he was there. A man asked for Inspector Cramer and I handed it to him and permitted myself a grin as I saw Wolfe put his book down and reach for his phone. He wasn't going to take hearsay, even from an Inspector.

It was a short conversation; Cramer's end of it wasn't more than twenty words. He hung up and went to the red-leather chair. "Okay," he growled. "If you had opened that carton they wouldn't have found all the pieces. You didn't think it was dynamite, you knew it was. Talk."

Wolfe, his lips tight, was breathing deep. "Not me," he said. "It would have been Archie or Fritz, or both of them. And of course my house. The possibility occurred to me, and I came down, barely in time. Three minutes later . . . Pfui. That man is a blackguard."

He shook his head, as if getting rid of a fly. "Well. Shortly after ten o'clock last evening I decided how to proceed, and I sent for Saul Panzer. When he came—"

"Who put that dynamite in that carton?"

"I'm telling you. When he came I had him type something on a sheet of paper and told him to drive to Duncan McLeod's farm this morning and give it to Mr. McLeod. Archie. You have the copy,"

I took it from my pocket and went and handed it to Cramer. He kept it, but this is what it said:

MEMORANDUM FROM NERO WOLFE

TO DUNCAN MCLEOD

I suggest that you should have in readiness acceptable answers to the following questions if and when they are asked:

1. When did Kenneth Faber tell you that your daughter was pregnant and he was responsible?

2. Where did you go when you drove away from your farm Tuesday afternoon around two o'clock—perhaps a little later—and returned around seven o'clock, late for milking?

3. Where did you get the piece of pipe? Was it on your premises?

4. Do you know that your daughter saw you leaving the alley Tuesday afternoon? Did you see her?

5. Is it true that the man with the bulldozer told you Monday night that he would have to come Wednesday instead of Thursday?

There are many other questions you may be asked; these are only samples. If competent investigators are moved to start inquiries of this nature, you will of course be in a difficult position, and it would be well to anticipate it.

Cramer looked up and aimed beady eyes at Wolfe. "You knew last night that McLeod killed Faber."

"Not certain knowledge. A reasoned conclusion."

"You knew he left his farm Tuesday afternoon. You knew his daughter saw him at the alley. You knew—"

"No. Those were conclusions." Wolfe turned a palm up. "Mr. Cramer. You sat there yesterday morning and read a document sworn to by Mr. Goodwin and me. When you finished it you knew everything that I knew, and I have learned nothing since then. From the knowledge we shared I had concluded that McLeod had killed Faber. You haven't. Shall I detail it?"

"Yes."

"First, the corn. I presume McLeod told you, as he did me, that he had Faber pick the corn because he had to dynamite some stumps and rock."

"Yes."

"That seemed to me unlikely. He knows how extremely particular I am, and also the restaurant. We pay him well, more than well; it must be a substantial portion of his income. He knew that young man couldn't possibly do that job. It must have been something more urgent than stumps and rocks that led him to risk losing such desirable customers. Second, the pipe. It was chiefly on account of the pipe that I wanted to see Mr. Heydt, Mr. Maslow, and Mr. Jay. Any man—"

"When did you see them?"

"They came here Wednesday evening, at Miss McLeod's request. Any man, sufficiently provoked, might plan to kill, but very few men would choose a massive iron bludgeon for a weapon to carry through the streets. Seeing those three, I thought it highly improbable that any of them would. But a countryman might, a man who does rough work with rough and heavy tools."

"You came to a conclusion on stuff like that?"

"No. Those details were merely corroborative. The conclusive item came from Miss McLeod. You read that document. I asked her—I'll quote from memory. I said to her, 'You know those men quite well. You know their temperaments. If one of them, enraged beyond endurance by Mr. Faber's conduct, went there and killed him, which one? It wasn't a sudden fit of passion, it was planned. From your knowledge of them, which one?' How did she answer me?"

"She said, 'They didn't.' "

"Yes. Didn't you think that significant? Of course I had the advantage of seeing and hearing her."

"Sure it was significant. It wasn't the reaction you always get to the idea that some close friend has committed murder. It wasn't shock. She just stated a fact. She *knew* they hadn't."

Wolfe nodded. "Precisely. And I saw and heard her. And there was only one way she could know they hadn't, with such certainty in her words and voice and manner: She knew who had. Did you form that conclusion?"

"Yes."

"Then why didn't you go on? If she hadn't killed him herself but knew who had, and it wasn't one of those three men—isn't it obvious?"

"You slipped that in, if she hadn't killed him herself. Why hadn't she?"

A corner of Wolfe's mouth went up. "There it is, your one major flaw: a distorted conception of the impossible. You will reject as inconceivable such a phenomenon as a man being at two different spots simultaneously, though any adroit trickster could easily contrive it; but you consider it credible that that young woman—even after you had studied her conversation with Mr. Goodwin and me—that she concealed that piece of pipe on her person and took it there with the intention of crushing a man's skull with it. Preposterous. That *is* inconceivable."

He waved it away. "Of course that's academic, now that that wretch has betrayed himself by sending me dynamite instead of corn, and the last step to my conclusion was inevitable. Since she knew who had killed Faber but wouldn't name him, and it wasn't one of those three, it was her father; and since she was certain—I

heard and saw her say, 'They didn't'—she had seen him there. I
doubt if he knew it, because— But that's immaterial. So much for—"

He stopped because Cramer was up, coming to my desk. He picked
up the phone, dialed, and in a moment said, "Irwin? Inspector Cramer. I want Sergeant Stebbins." After another moment: "Purley?
Get Carmel, the sheriff's office. Ask him to get Duncan McLeod and
hold him, and no mistake . . . Yes, Susan McLeod's father. Send two
men to Carmel and tell them to call in as soon as they arrive. Tell
Carmel to watch it, McLeod is down for murder and he may be
rough . . . No, that can wait. I'll be there soon—half an hour, maybe
less."

He hung up, about-faced to Wolfe, and growled, "You knew all
this Wednesday afternoon, two days ago."

Wolfe nodded. "And you have known it since yesterday morning.
It's a question of interpretation, not of knowledge. Will you please
sit? As you know, I like eyes at my level. Thank you. Yes, as early
as Wednesday afternoon, when Miss McLeod left, I was all but certain of the identity of the murderer, but I took the precaution of
seeing those three men that evening because it was just possible
that one of them would disclose something cogent.

"When you came yesterday morning with that warrant, I gave
you that document for two reasons: to keep Mr. Goodwin out of jail,
and to share my knowledge with you. I wasn't obliged to share also
my interpretation of it. Any moment since yesterday noon I have
rather expected to hear that Mr. McLeod had been taken into custody, but no."

"So you decided to share your interpretation with him instead of
me."

"I like that," Wolfe said approvingly. "That was neat. I prefer to
put it that I decided not to decide. Having given you all the facts I
had, I had met my obligation as a citizen and a licensed private
detective. I was under no compulsion, legal or moral, to assume the
role of a nemesis. It was only conjecture that Faber had told Mr.
McLeod that he had debauched his daughter, but he had told others,
and McLeod must have had a potent motive, so it was highly probable. If so, the question of moral turpitude was moot, and I would
not rule on it.

"Since I had given you the facts, I thought it only fair to inform
Mr. McLeod that he was menaced by a logical conclusion from those
facts; and I did so. I used Mr. Panzer as my messenger because I
chose not to involve Mr. Goodwin. He was unaware of the conclusion

I had reached, and if I had told him there might have been disagreement regarding the course to take. He can be—uh—difficult."

Cramer grunted. "Yeah. He can. So you deliberately warned a murderer. Telling him to have answers ready. Nuts. You expected him to lam."

"No. I had no specific expectation. It would have been idle to speculate, but if I had, I doubt if I would have expected him to scoot. He couldn't take his farm along, and he would be leaving his daughter in mortal jeopardy. I didn't consciously speculate, but my subconscious must have, for suddenly, when I was busy at the potting bench, it struck me.

"Saul Panzer's description of McLeod's stony face as he read the memorandum; the stubborn ego of a self-righteous man; dynamite for stumps and rocks; corn; a closed carton. Most improbable. I resumed the potting. But conceivable. I dropped the trowel and went to the elevator, and within thirty seconds after I emerged in the hall the carton came."

"Luck," Cramer said. "Your damn incredible luck. If it had made mincemeat of Goodwin you might have been willing to admit for once—okay, it didn't." He got up. "Stick around, Goodwin. They'll want you at the D.A.'s office, probably in the morning." To Wolfe: "What if that phone call had said the carton held corn, just corn? You think you could have talked me off, don't you?"

"I could have tried."

"By God. Talk about stubborn egos." Cramer shook his head. "That break you got on the carton. You know, any normal man, if he got a break like that, coming down just in the nick of time, what any normal man would do, he would go down on his knees and thank God. Do you know what you'll do? You'll thank *you*. I admit it would be a job for you to get down on your knees, but—"

The phone rang. I swiveled and got it, and a voice I recognized asked for Inspector Cramer. I turned and told him, "Purley Stebbins," and he came and took it. The conversation was even shorter than the one about the carton, and Cramer's part was only a dozen words and a couple of growls. He hung up, went and got his hat, and headed for the hall, but a step short of the door he stopped and turned.

"I might as well tell you," he said. "It'll give you a better appetite for dinner, even if it's not corn. About an hour ago Duncan McLeod sat or stood or lay on a pile of dynamite and it went off. They'll want to decide whether it was an accident or he did it. Maybe you can help them interpret the facts." He turned and went.

One day last week there was a party at Lily Rowan's penthouse. She never invites more than six to dinner—eight counting her and me—but that was a dancing party and around coffee time a dozen more came and three musicians got set in the alcove and started up. After rounds with Lily and three or four others, I approached Sue McLeod and offered a hand.

She gave me a look. "You know you don't want to. Let's go outside."

I said it was cold, and she said she knew it and headed for the foyer. We got her wrap—a fur thing which she probably didn't own, since topflight models are offered loans of everything from socks to sable—went back in, on through, and out to the terrace. There were evergreens in tubs, and we crossed to them for shelter.

"You told Lily I hate you," she said. "I don't."

"Not 'hate,'" I said. "She misquoted me or you're misquoting her. She said I should dance with you and I said when I tried it a month ago you froze."

"I know I did." She put a hand on my arm. "Archie. It was hard, you know it was. If I hadn't got my father to let him work on the farm—it was my fault, I know it was—but I couldn't help thinking if you hadn't sent him that—letting him know you knew—"

"I didn't send it, Mr. Wolfe did. But I would have. Okay, he was your father, so it was hard. But no matter whose father he was, I'm not wearing an armband for the guy who packed dynamite in that carton."

"Of course not. I know. Of course not. I tell myself I'll have to forget it . . . but it's not easy." She shivered. "Anyway, I wanted to say I don't hate you. You don't have to dance with me, and you know I'm not going to get married until I can stop working and have babies, and I know you never are, and even if you do, it will be Lily, but you don't have to stand there and let me *really* freeze, do you?"

I didn't. You don't have to be rude, even with a girl who can't dance, and it was cold out there.

Ross Macdonald

Gone Girl

It was a Friday night. I was tooling home from the Mexican border in a light blue convertible and a dark blue mood. I had followed a man from Fresno to San Diego and lost him in the maze of streets in Old Town. When I picked up his trail again, it was cold. He had crossed the border, and my instructions went no farther than the United States.

Halfway home, just above Emerald Bay, I overtook the worst driver in the world. He was driving a black fishtail Cadillac as if he were tacking a sailboat. The heavy car wove back and forth across the freeway, using two of its four lanes, and sometimes three. It was late, and I was in a hurry to get some sleep. I started to pass it on the right, at a time when it was riding the double line. The Cadillac drifted toward me like an unguided missile, and forced me off the road in a screeching skid.

I speeded up to pass on the left. Simultaneously, the driver of the Cadillac accelerated. My acceleration couldn't match his. We raced neck and neck down the middle of the road. I wondered if he was drunk or crazy or afraid of me.

Then the freeway ended. I was doing 80 on the wrong side of a two-lane highway, and a truck came over a rise ahead like a blazing double comet. I floorboarded the gas pedal and cut over sharply to the right, threatening the Cadillac's fenders and its reckless driver's life. In the approaching headlights his face was as blank and white as a piece of paper, with charred black holes for eyes. His shoulders were naked.

At the last possible second he slowed enough to let me get by. The truck went off onto the shoulder, honking angrily. I braked gradually, hoping to force the Cadillac to stop.

It looped past me in an insane arc, tires skittering, and was sucked away into darkness.

When I finally came to a full stop, I had to pry my fingers off the wheel. My knees were remote and watery.

After smoking part of a cigarette, I U-turned and drove very cautiously back to Emerald Bay. I was long past the hot-rod age, and I needed rest.

The first motel I came to, the Siesta, was decorated with a vacancy sign and a neon Mexican sleeping luminously under a sombrero. Envying him, I parked on the gravel apron in front of the motel office. There was a light inside. The glass-paned door was standing open, and I went in.

The little room was pleasantly furnished with rattan and chintz. I jangled the bell on the desk a few times. No one appeared, so I sat down to wait and lit another cigarette. An electric clock on the wall said a quarter to one.

I must have dozed for a few minutes. A dream rushed by the threshold of my consciousness, making a gentle noise. Death was in the dream. He drove a black Cadillac loaded with flowers. When I woke up, the cigarette was starting to burn my fingers. A thin man in a gray flannel shirt was standing over me with a doubtful look on his face.

He was big-nosed and small-chinned, and he wasn't as young as he gave the impression of being. His teeth were bad, the sandy hair was thinning and receding. He was the typical old youth who scrounged and wheedled his living around motor courts and restaurants and hotels, and hung on desperately to the frayed edges of other people's lives.

"What do you want?" he said. "Who are you? What do you want?" His voice was reedy and changeable like an adolescent's.

"A room."

"Is that all you want?"

From where I sat, it sounded like an accusation.

I let it pass. "What else is there? Circassian dancing girls? Free popcorn?"

He tried to smile without showing his bad teeth. The smile was a dismal failure, like my joke.

"I'm sorry, sir," he said. "You woke me up. I never make much sense right after I just wake up."

"Have a nightmare?"

His vague eyes expanded like blue bubblegum bubbles. "Why did you ask me that?"

"Because I just had one. But skip it. Do you have a vacancy or don't you?"

"Yessir. Sorry, sir."

He swallowed whatever bitter taste he had in his mouth, and assumed an impersonal obsequious manner.

"You got any luggage, sir?"

"No luggage."

Moving silently in tennis sneakers like a frail ghost of the boy he once had been, he went behind the counter, and took my name, address, license number, and ten dollars. In return, he gave me a key numbered 14 and told me where to use it. Apparently he despaired of a tip.

Room 14 was like any other middle-class motel room touched with the California-Spanish mania. Artificially roughened plaster painted adobe color, poinsettia-red curtains, imitation parchment lampshade on a twisted black iron stand. A Rivera reproduction of a sleeping Mexican hung on the wall over the bed. I succumbed to its suggestion right away, and dreamed about Circassian dancing girls.

Along toward morning one of them got frightened, through no fault of mine, and began to scream her little Circassian lungs out. I sat up in bed, making soothing noises, and woke up. It was nearly nine by my wristwatch. The screaming ceased and began again, spoiling the morning like a fire siren outside the window. I pulled on my trousers over the underwear I'd been sleeping in, and went outside.

A young woman was standing on the walk outside the next room. She had a key in one hand and a handful of blood in the other. She wore a wide multicolored skirt and a low-cut gypsy sort of blouse. The blouse was distended and her mouth was open, and she was yelling her head off. It was a fine dark head, but I hated her for spoiling my morning sleep.

I took her by the shoulders and said, "Stop it."

The screaming stopped. She looked down sleepily at the blood on her hand. It was as thick as axle grease, and almost as dark in color.

"Where did you get that?"

"I slipped and fell in it. I didn't see it."

Dropping the key on the walk, she pulled her skirt to one side with her clean hand. Her legs were bare and brown. Her skirt was stained at the back with the same thick fluid.

"Where? In this room?"

She faltered. "Yes."

Doors were opening up and down the drive. Half a dozen people began to converge on us. A dark-faced man about four and a half feet high came scampering from the direction of the office, his little pointed shoes dancing on the gravel.

"Come inside and show me," I said to the girl.

"I can't. I won't." Her eyes were very heavy, and surrounded by the bluish pallor of shock.

The little man slid to a stop between us, reached up, and gripped the upper part of her arm. "What is the matter, Ella? Are you crazy, disturbing the guests?"

She said, "Blood," and leaned against me with her eyes closed.

His sharp glance probed the situation. He turned to the other guests, who had formed a murmuring semicircle around us.

"It is perfectly okay. Do not be concerned, ladies and gentlemen. My daughter cut herself a little bit. It is perfectly all right."

Circling her waist with one long arm, he hustled her through the open door and slammed it behind him. I caught it on my foot and followed them in.

The room was a duplicate of mine, including the reproduction over the unmade bed, but everything was reversed as in a mirror image. The girl took a few weak steps by herself and sat on the edge of the bed. Then she noticed the blood spots on the sheets. She stood up quickly. Her mouth opened, rimmed with white teeth.

"Don't do it," I said. "We know you have a very fine pair of lungs."

The little man turned on me. "Who do you think you are?"

"The name is Archer. I have the next room."

"Get out of this one, please."

"I don't think I will."

He lowered his greased black head as if he were going to butt me. Under his sharkskin jacket a hunch protruded from his back like a displaced elbow. He seemed to reconsider the butting gambit and decided in favor of diplomacy.

"You are jumping to conclusions, mister. It is not so serious as it looks. We had a little accident here last night."

"Sure, your daughter cut herself. She heals remarkably fast."

"Nothing like that." He fluttered one long hand. "I said to the people outside the first thing that came to my mind. Actually, it was a little scuffle. One of the guests suffered a nosebleed."

The girl moved like a sleepwalker to the bathroom door and switched on the light. There was a pool of blood coagulating on the black and white checkerboard linoleum, streaked where she had slipped and fallen in it.

"Some nosebleed," I said to the little man. "Do you run this joint?"

"I am the proprietor of the Siesta motor hotel, yes. My name is Salanda. The gentleman is susceptible to nosebleed. He told me so himself."

"Where is he now?"

"He checked out early this morning."

"In good health?"

"Certainly in good health."

I looked around the room. Apart from the unmade bed with the brown spots on the sheets, it contained no signs of occupancy. Someone had spilled a pint of blood and vanished.

The little man opened the door wide and invited me with a sweep of his arm to leave. "If you will excuse me, sir, I wish to have this cleaned up as quickly as possible. Ella, will you tell Lorraine to get to work on it right away pronto? Then maybe you better lie down for a little while, eh?"

"I'm all right now, father. Don't worry about me."

When I checked out a few minutes later, she was sitting behind the desk in the front office, looking pale but composed. I dropped my key on the desk in front of her.

"Feeling better, Ella?"

"Oh. I didn't recognize you with all your clothes on."

"That's a good line. May I use it?"

She lowered her eyes and blushed. "You're making fun of me. I know I acted foolishly this morning."

"I'm not so sure. What do *you* think happened in Room Thirteen last night?"

"My father told you, didn't he?"

"He gave me a version, two of them in fact. I doubt that they're the final shooting script."

Her hand went to the central hollow in her blouse. Her arms and shoulders were slender and brown, the tips of her fingers carmine. "Shooting?"

"A cinema term," I said. "But there might have been a real shooting at that. Don't you think so?"

Her front teeth pinched her lower lip. She looked like somebody's pet rabbit. I restrained an impulse to pat her sleek brown head.

"That's ridiculous. This is a respectable motel. Anyway, father asked me not to discuss it with anybody."

"Why would he do that?"

"He loves this place, that's why. He doesn't want any scandal made out of nothing. If we lost our good reputation here, it would break my father's heart."

"He doesn't strike me as the sentimental type."

She stood up, smoothing her skirt. I saw that she'd changed it.

"You leave him alone. He's a dear little man. I don't know what you think you're doing, trying to stir up trouble where there isn't any."

I backed away from her righteous indignation—female indignation is always righteous—and went out to my car. The early spring sun was dazzling. Beyond the freeway and the drifted sugary dunes, the bay was Prussian blue. The road cut inland across the base of the peninsula and returned to the sea a few miles north of the town. Here a wide blacktop parking space shelved off to the left of the highway, overlooking the white beach and whiter breakers. Signs at each end of the turnout stated that this was a County Park, No Beach Fires.

The beach and the blacktop expanse above it were deserted except for a single car, which looked very lonely. It was a long black Cadillac nosed into the cable fence at the edge of the beach. I braked and turned off the highway and got out. The man in the driver's seat of the Cadillac didn't turn his head as I approached him. His chin was propped on the steering wheel, and he was gazing out across the endless blue sea.

I opened the door and looked into his face. It was paper-white. The dark brown eyes were sightless. The body was unclothed except for the thick hair matted on the chest, and a clumsy bandage tied around the waist. The bandage was composed of several blood-stained towels, held in place by a knotted piece of nylon fabric whose nature I didn't recognize immediately. Examining it more closely, I saw that it was a woman's slip. The left breast of the garment was embroidered in purple with a heart, containing the name *Fern*. I wondered who Fern was.

The man who was wearing her purple heart had dark curly hair, heavy black eyebrows, a heavy chin sprouting black beard. He was rough-looking in spite of his anemia and the lipstick smudged on his mouth.

There was no registration on the steeringpost, and nothing in the glove compartment but a half-empty box of shells for a .38 automatic. The ignition was still turned on. So were the dash and headlights, but they were dim. The gas gauge registered empty. Curlyhead must have pulled off the highway soon after he passed me, and driven all the rest of the night in one place.

I untied the slip, which didn't look as if it would take fingerprints, and went over it for a label. It had one: Gretchen, Palm Springs. It occurred to me that it was Saturday morning and that I'd gone all winter without a weekend in the desert. I retied the slip the way I'd found it, and drove back to the Siesta Motel.

Ella's welcome was a few degrees colder than absolute zero. "Well!" She glared down her pretty rabbit nose at me. "I thought we were rid of you."

"So did I. But I just couldn't tear myself away."

She gave me a peculiar look, neither hard nor soft, but mixed. Her hand went to her hair, then reached for a registration card. "I suppose if you want to rent a room, I can't stop you. Only please don't imagine you're making an impression on me. You're not. You leave me cold, mister."

"Archer," I said. "Lew Archer. Don't bother with the card. I came back to use your phone."

"Aren't there any other phones?" She pushed the telephone across the desk. "I guess it's all right, long as it isn't a toll call."

"I'm calling the Highway Patrol. Do you know their local number?"

"I don't remember." She handed me the telephone directory.

"There's been an accident," I said as I dialed.

"A highway accident? Where did it happen?"

"Right here, sister. Right here in Room Thirteen."

But I didn't tell that to the Highway Patrol. I told them I had found a dead man in a car on the parking lot above the county beach. The girl listened with widening eyes and nostrils. Before I finished she rose in a flurry and left the office by the rear door.

She came back with the proprietor. His eyes were black and bright like nailheads in leather, and the scampering dance of his feet was almost frenzied. "What is this?"

"I came across a dead man up the road a piece."

"So why do you come back here to telephone?" His head was in butting position, his hands outspread and gripping the corners of the desk. "Has it got anything to do with us?"

"He's wearing a couple of your towels."

"What?"

"And he was bleeding heavily before he died. I think somebody shot him in the stomach. Maybe you did."

"You're loco," he said, but not very emphatically. "Crazy accusations like that, they will get you into trouble. What is your business?"

"I'm a private detective."

"You followed him here, is that it? You were going to arrest him, so he shot himself?"

"Wrong on both accounts," I said. "I came here to sleep. And they don't shoot themselves in the stomach. It's too uncertain, and slow. No suicide wants to die of peritonitis."

"So what are you doing now, trying to make scandal for my business?"

"If your business includes trying to cover up a murder."

"He shot himself," the little man insisted.

"How do you know?"

"Donny. I spoke to him just now."

"And how does Donny know?"

"The man told him."

"Is Donny your night keyboy?"

"He was. I think I will fire him, for stupidity. He didn't even tell me about this mess. I had to find it out for myself. The hard way."

"Donny means well," the girl said at his shoulder. "I'm sure he didn't realize what happened."

"Who does?" I said. "I want to talk to Donny. But first let's have a look at the register."

He took a pile of cards from a drawer and riffled through them. His large hands, hairy-backed, were calm and expert, like animals that lived a serene life of their own, independent of their emotional owner. They dealt me one of the cards across the desk. It was inscribed in block capitals: RICHARD ROWE, DETROIT, MICH.

I said, "There was a woman with him."

"Impossible."

"Or he was a transvestite."

He surveyed me blankly, thinking of something else. "The HP, did you tell them to come here? They know it happened here?"

"Not yet. But they'll find your towels. He used them for bandage."

"I see. Yes. Of course." He struck himself with a clenched fist on the temple. It made a noise like someone maltreating a pumpkin. "You are a private detective, you say. Now if you informed the police that you were on the trail of a fugitive, a fugitive from justice . . . He shot himself rather than face arrest . . . For five hundred dollars?"

"I'm not that private," I said. "I have some public responsibility. Besides, the cops would do a little checking and catch me out."

"Not necessarily. He *was* a fugitive from justice, you know."

"I hear you telling me."

"Give me a little time and I can even present you with his record."

The girl was leaning back away from her father, her eyes starred with broken illusions. "Daddy," she said weakly.

He didn't hear her. All his bright black attention was fixed on me. "Seven hundred dollars?"

"No sale. The higher you raise it, the guiltier you look. Were you here last night?"

"You are being absurd," he said. "I spent the entire evening with my wife. We drove up to Los Angeles to attend the ballet." By way of supporting evidence, he hummed a couple of bars from Tchaikovsky. "We didn't arrive back here in Emerald Bay until nearly two o'clock."

"Alibis can be fixed."

"By criminals, yes," he said. "I am not a criminal."

The girl put a hand on his shoulder. He cringed, his face creased by monkey fury, but his face was hidden from her.

"Daddy," she said. "Was he murdered, do you think?"

"How do I know?" His voice was wild and high, as if she had touched the spring of his emotion. "I wasn't here. I only know what Donny told me."

The girl was examining me with narrowed eyes, as if I were a new kind of animal she had discovered and was trying to think of a use for.

"This gentleman is a detective," she said, "or claims to be."

I pulled out my photostat and slapped it down on the desk. The little man picked it up and looked from it to my face. "Will you go to work for me?"

"Doing what, telling little white lies?"

The girl answered for him. "See what you can find out about this—this death. On my word of honor, father had nothing to do with it."

I made a snap decision, the kind you live to regret. "All right. I'll take a fifty-dollar advance. Which is a good deal less than five hundred. My first advice to you is to tell the police everything you know. Provided that you're innocent."

"You insult me," he said.

But he flicked a fifty-dollar bill from the cash drawer and pressed it into my hand fervently, like a love token. I had a queasy feeling that I had been conned into taking his money, not much of it but enough. The feeling deepened when he still refused to talk. I had to use all the arts of persuasion even to get Donny's address out of him.

The keyboy lived in a shack on the edge of a desolate stretch of dunes. I guessed that it had once been somebody's beach house, before sand had drifted like unthawing snow in the angles of the walls and winter storms had broken the tiles and cracked the concrete foundations. Huge chunks of concrete were piled haphazardly on what had been a terrace overlooking the sea.

On one of the tilted slabs Donny was stretched like a long albino lizard in the sun. The onshore wind carried the sound of my motor to his ears. He sat up blinking, recognized me when I stopped the car, and ran into the house.

I descended flagstone steps and knocked on the warped door. "Open up, Donny."

"Go away," he answered huskily. His eye gleamed like a snail through a crack in the wood.

"I'm working for Mr. Salanda. He wants us to have a talk."

"You can go and take a running jump for yourself, you and Mr. Salanda both."

"Open it or I'll break it down."

I waited for a while. He shot back the bolt. The door creaked reluctantly open. He leaned against the doorpost, searching my face with his eyes, his hairless body shivering from an internal chill. I pushed past him, through a kitchenette that was indescribably filthy, littered with the remnants of old meals, and gaseous with their odors. He followed me silently on bare soles into a larger room whose sprung floorboards undulated under my feet. The picture window had been broken and patched with cardboard. The stone fireplace was choked with garbage. The only furniture was an army cot in one corner where Donny apparently slept.

"Nice homey place you have here. It has that lived-in quality."

He seemed to take it as a compliment, and I wondered if I was dealing with a moron. "It suits me. I never was much of a one for fancy quarters. I like it here, where I can hear the ocean at night."

"What else do you hear at night, Donny?"

He missed the point of the question, or pretended to. "All different things. Big trucks going past on the highway. I like to hear those night sounds. Now I guess I can't go on living here. Mr. Salanda owns it, he lets me live here for nothing. Now he'll be kicking me out of here, I guess."

"On account of what happened last night?"

"Uh-huh." He subsided onto the cot, his doleful head supported by his hands.

I stood over him. "Just what did happen last night, Donny?"

"A bad thing," he said. "This fella checked in about ten o'clock—"

"The man with the dark curly hair?"

"That's the one. He checked in about ten, and I gave him Room Thirteen. Around about midnight I thought I heard a gun go off from there. It took me a little while to get my nerve up, then I went back to see what was going on. This fella came out of the room, without no clothes on. Just some kind of a bandage around his waist. He looked like some kind of a crazy Indian or something. He had a gun in his hand, and he was staggering, and I could see that he was bleeding some. He come right up to me and pushed the gun in my gut and told me to keep my trap shut. He said I wasn't to tell anybody I saw him, now or later. He said if I opened my mouth about it to anybody he would come back and kill me. But now he's dead, isn't he?"

"He's dead."

I could smell the fear in Donny: there's an unexplained trace of canine in my chromosomes. The hairs were prickling on the back of my neck, and I wondered if Donny's fear was of the past or for the future. The pimples stood out in bas-relief against his pale lugubrious face.

"I think he was murdered, Donny. You're lying, aren't you?"

"Me lying?" But his reaction was slow and feeble.

"The dead man didn't check in alone. He had a woman with him."

"What woman?" he said in elaborate surprise.

"You tell me. Her name was Fern. I think she did the shooting, and you caught her red-handed. The wounded man got out of the room and into his car and away. The woman stayed behind to talk to you. She probably paid you to dispose of his clothes and fake a new registration card for the room. But you both overlooked the blood on the floor of the bathroom. Am I right?"

"You couldn't be wronger, mister. Are you a cop?"

"A private detective. You're in deep trouble, Donny. You'd better talk yourself out of it before the cops start on you."

"I didn't do anything." His voice broke like a boy's. It went strangely with the glints of gray in his hair.

"Faking the register is a serious rap, even if they don't hang accessory to murder on you."

He began to expostulate in formless sentences that ran together. At the same time his hand was moving across the dirty gray blanket. It burrowed under the pillow and came out holding a crumpled card.

He tried to stuff it into his mouth and chew it. I tore it away from between his discolored teeth.

It was a registration card from the motel, signed in a boyish scrawl: *Mr. and Mrs. Richard Rowe, Detroit, Mich.*

Donny was trembling violently. Below his cheap cotton shorts his bony knees vibrated like tuning forks. "It wasn't my fault," he cried. "She held a gun on me."

"What did you do with the man's clothes?"

"Nothing. She didn't even let me into the room. She bundled them up and took them away herself."

"Where did she go?"

"Down the highway towards town. She walked away on the shoulder of the road and that was the last I saw of her."

"How much did she pay you, Donny?"

"Nothing, not a cent. I already told you, she held a gun on me."

"And you were so scared you kept quiet until this morning?"

"That's right. I was scared. Who wouldn't be scared?"

"She's gone now," I said. "You can give me a description of her."

"Yeah." He made a visible effort to pull his vague thoughts together. One of his eyes was a little off center, lending his face a stunned, amorphous appearance. "She was a big tall dame with blondey hair."

"Dyed?"

"I guess so, I dunno. She wore it in a braid like, on top of her head. She was kind of fat, built like a lady wrestler, great big watermelons on her. Big legs."

"How was she dressed?"

"I didn't hardly notice, I was so scared. I think she had some kind of a purple coat on, with black fur around the neck. Plenty of rings on her fingers and stuff."

"How old?"

"Pretty old, I'd say. Older than me, and I'm going on thirty-nine."

"And she did the shooting?"

"I guess so. She told me to say if anybody asked me, I was to say that Mr. Rowe shot himself."

"You're very suggestible, aren't you, Donny? It's a dangerous way to be, with people pushing each other around the way they do."

"I didn't get that, mister. Come again." He batted his pale blue eyes at me, smiling expectantly.

"Skip it," I said and left him.

A few hundred yards up the highway I passed an HP car with two

uniformed men in the front seat looking grim. Donny was in for it
now. I pushed him out of my mind and drove across country to Palm
Springs.

Palm Springs is still a one-horse town, but the horse is a Palomino
with silver trappings. Most of the girls are Palomino too. The main
street was a cross-section of Hollywood and Vine transported across
the desert by some unnatural force and disguised in western cos-
tumes which fooled nobody. Not even me.

I found Gretchen's lingerie shop in an expensive-looking arcade
built around an imitation flagstone patio. In the patio's center a
little fountain gurgled pleasantly, flinging small lariats of spray
against the heat. It was late in March, and the season was ending.
Most of the shops, including the one I entered, were deserted except
for the hired help.

It was a small shop, faintly perfumed by a legion of vanished dolls.
Stockings and robes and other garments were coiled on the glass
counters or hung like brilliant treesnakes on display stands along
the narrow walls. A henna-headed woman emerged from rustling
recesses at the rear and came tripping toward me on her toes.

"You are looking for a gift, sir?" she cried with a wilted kind of
gaiety. Behind her painted mask she was tired and aging and it was
Saturday afternoon and the lucky ones were dunking themselves in
kidney-shaped swimming pools behind walls she couldn't climb.

"Not exactly. In fact, not at all. A peculiar thing happened to me
last night. I'd like to tell you about it, but it's kind of a complicated
story."

She looked me over quizzically and decided that I worked for a
living too. The phony smile faded away. Another smile took its place,
which I liked better. "You look as if you'd had a fairly rough night.
And you could do with a shave."

"I met a girl," I said. "Actually she was a mature woman, a stat-
uesque blonde to be exact. I picked her up on the beach at Laguna,
if you want me to be brutally frank."

"I couldn't bear it if you weren't. What kind of a pitch is this,
brother?"

"Wait. You're spoiling my story. Something clicked when we met,
in that sunset light, on the edge of the warm summer sea."

"It's always bloody cold when I go in."

"It wasn't last night. We swam in the moonlight and had a gay
time and all. Then she went away. I didn't realize until she was

gone that I didn't know her telephone number, or even her last name."

"Married woman, eh? What do you think I am, a lonely hearts club?" Still, she was interested, though she probably didn't believe me. "She mentioned me, is that it? What was her first name?"

"Fern."

"Unusual name. You say she was a big blonde?"

"Magnificently proportioned," I said. "If I had a classical education I'd call her Junoesque."

"You're kidding me, aren't you?"

"A little."

"I thought so. Personally I don't mind a little kidding. What did she say about me?"

"Nothing but good. As a matter of fact, I was complimenting her on her—er—garments."

"I see." She was long past blushing. "We had a customer last fall some time by the name of Fern. Fern Dee. She had some kind of a job at the Joshua Club, I think. But she doesn't fit the description at all. This one was a brunette, a middle-sized brunette, quite young. I remember the name Fern because she wanted it embroidered on all the things she bought. A corny idea if you ask me, but that was her girlish desire and who am I to argue with girlish desires."

"Is she still in town?"

"I haven't seen her lately, not for months. But it couldn't be the woman you're looking for. Or could it?"

"How long ago was she in here?"

She pondered. "Early last fall, around the start of the season. She only came in that once, and made a big purchase, stockings and nightwear and underthings. The works. I remember thinking at the time, here was a girlie who suddenly hit the chips but heavily."

"She might have put on weight since then, and dyed her hair. Strange things can happen to the female form."

"You're telling me," she said. "How old was—your friend?"

"About forty, I'd say, give or take a little."

"It couldn't be the same one then. The girl I'm talking about was twenty-five at the outside, and I don't make mistakes about women's ages. I've seen too many of them in all stages, from Quentin quail to hags, and I certainly do mean hags."

"I bet you have."

She studied me with eyes shadowed by mascara and experience. "You a policeman?"

"I have been."

"You want to tell mother what it's all about?"

"Another time. Where's the Joshua Club?"

"It won't be open yet."

"I'll try it anyway."

She shrugged her thin shoulders and gave me directions. I thanked her.

It occupied a plain-faced one-story building half a block off the main street. The padded leather door swung inward when I pushed it. I passed through a lobby with a retractable roof, which contained a jungle growth of banana trees. The big main room was decorated with tinted desert photomurals. Behind a rattan bar with a fishnet canopy a white-coated Caribbean type was drying shot glasses with a dirty towel. His face looked uncommunicative.

On the orchestra dais beyond the piled chairs in the dining area a young man in shirt sleeves was playing bop piano. His fingers shadowed the tune, ran circles around it, played leap-frog with it, and managed never to hit it on the nose. I stood beside him for a while and listened to him work. He looked up finally, still strumming with his left hand in the bass. He had soft-centered eyes and frozen-looking nostrils and a whistling mouth.

"Nice piano," I said.

"I think so."

"Fifty-second Street?"

"It's the street with the beat and I'm not effete." His left hand struck the same chord three times and dropped away from the keys. "Looking for somebody, friend?"

"Fern Dee. She asked me to drop by sometime."

"Too bad. Another wasted trip. She left here end of last year, the dear. She wasn't a bad little nightingale but she was no pro, Joe, you know? She had it but she couldn't project it. When she warbled the evening died, no matter how hard she tried, I don't wanna be snide."

"Where did she lam, Sam, or don't you give a damn?"

He smiled like a corpse in a deft mortician's hands. "I heard the boss retired her to private life. Took her home to live with him. That is what I heard. But I don't mix with the big boy socially, so I couldn't say for sure that she's impure. Is it anything to you?"

"Something, but she's over twenty-one."

"Not more than a couple of years over twenty-one." His eyes darkened, and his thin mouth twisted sideways angrily. "I hate to see it happen to a pretty little girl like Fern. Not that I yearn—"

I broke in on his nonsense rhymes: "Who's the big boss you mentioned, the one Fern went to live with?"

"Angel. Who else?"

"What heaven does he inhabit?"

"You must be new in these parts—" His eyes swiveled and focused on something over my shoulder. His mouth opened and closed.

A grating tenor said behind me, "Got a question you want answered, bud?"

The pianist went back to the piano as if the ugly tenor had wiped me out, annulled my very existence. I turned to its source. He was standing in a narrow doorway behind the drums, a man in his thirties with thick black curly hair and a heavy jaw blue-shadowed by closely shaven beard. He was almost the living image of the dead man in the Cadillac. The likeness gave me a jolt. The heavy black gun in his hand gave me another.

He came around the drums and approached me, bull-shouldered in a fuzzy tweed jacket, holding the gun in front of him like a dangerous gift. The pianist was doing wry things in quickened tempo with the dead march from *Saul*. A wit.

The dead man's almost-double waved his cruel chin and the crueler gun in unison. "Come inside, unless you're a government man. If you are, I'll have a look at your credentials."

"I'm a freelance."

"Inside then."

The muzzle of the automatic came into my solar plexus like a pointing iron finger. Obeying its injunction, I made my way between empty music stands and through the narrow door behind the drums. The iron finger, probing my back, directed me down a lightless corridor to a small square office containing a metal desk, a safe, a filing cabinet. It was windowless, lit by fluorescent tubes in the ceiling. Under their pitiless glare, the face above the gun looked more than ever like the dead man's face. I wondered if I had been mistaken about his deadness, or if the desert heat had addled my brain.

"I'm the manager here," he said, standing so close that I could smell the piney stuff he used on his crisp dark hair. "You got anything to ask about the members of the staff, you ask me."

"Will I get an answer?"

"Try me, bud."

"The name is Archer," I said. "I'm a private detective."

"Working for who?"

"You wouldn't be interested."

"I am, though, very much interested." The gun hopped forward like a toad into my stomach again, with the weight of his shoulder behind it. "Working for who did you say?"

I swallowed anger and nausea, estimating my chances of knocking the gun to one side and taking him bare-handed. The chances seemed pretty slim. He was heavier than I was, and he held the automatic as if it had grown out of the end of his arm. You've seen too many movies, I told myself. I told him, "A motel owner on the coast. A man was shot in one of his rooms last night. I happened to check in there a few minutes later. The old boy hired me to look into the shooting."

"Who was it got himself ventilated?"

"He could be your brother," I said. "Do you have a brother?"

He lost his color. The center of his attention shifted from the gun to my face. The gun nodded. I knocked it up and sideways with a hard left uppercut. Its discharge burned the side of my face and drilled a hole in the wall. My right sank into his neck. The gun thumped the cork floor.

He went down but not out, his spread hand scrabbling for the gun, then closing on it. I kicked his wrist. He grunted but wouldn't let go of it. I threw a punch at the short hairs on the back of his neck. He took it and came up under it with the gun, shaking his head from side to side.

"Up with the hands now," he murmured. He was one of those men whose voices go soft and mild when they are in a killing mood. He had the glassy impervious eyes of a killer. "Is Bart dead? My brother?"

"Very dead. He was shot in the belly."

"Who shot him?"

"That's the question."

"Who shot him?" he said in a quiet white-faced rage. The single eye of the gun stared emptily at my midriff. "It could happen to you, bud, here and now."

"A woman was with him. She took a quick powder after it happened."

"I heard you say a name to Alfie, the piano player. Was it Fern?"

"It could have been."

"What do you mean, it could have been?"

"She was there in the room, apparently. If you can give me a description of her?"

His hard brown eyes looked past me. "I can do better than that. There's a picture of her on the wall behind you. Take a look at it. Keep those hands up high."

I shifted my feet and turned uneasily. The wall was blank. I heard him draw a breath and move, and tried to evade his blow. No use. It caught the back of my head. I pitched forward against the blank wall and slid down it into three dimensions of blankness.

The blankness coagulated into colored shapes. The shapes were half human and half beast and they dissolved and reformed. A dead man with a hairy breast climbed out of a hole and doubled and quadrupled. I ran away from them through a twisting tunnel which led to an echo chamber. Under the roaring surge of the nightmare music, a rasping tenor was saying:

"I figure it like this. Vario's tip was good. Bart found her in Acapulco, and he was bringing her back from there. She conned him into stopping off at this motel for the night. Bart always went for her."

"I didn't know that," a dry old voice put in. "This is very interesting news about Bart and Fern. You should have told me before about this. Then I would not have sent him for her and this would not have happened. Would it, Gino?"

My mind was still partly absent, wandering underground in the echoing caves. I couldn't recall the voices, or who they were talking about. I had barely sense enough to keep my eyes closed and go on listening. I was lying on my back on a hard surface. The voices were above me.

The tenor said: "You can't blame Bartolomeo. She's the one, the dirty treacherous lying little bitch."

"Calm yourself, Gino. I blame nobody. But more than ever now, we want her back, isn't that right?"

"I'll kill her," he said softly, almost wistfully.

"Perhaps. It may not be necessary now. I dislike promiscuous killing—"

"Since when, Angel?"

"Don't interrupt, it's not polite. I learned to put first things first. Now what is the most important thing? Why did we want her back in the first place? I will tell you: to shut her mouth. The government heard she left me, they wanted her to testify about my income. We wanted to find her first and shut her mouth, isn't that right?"

"I know how to shut her mouth," the younger man said very quietly.

"First we try a better way, my way. You learn when you're as old as I am there is a use for everything, and not to be wasteful. Not even wasteful with somebody else's blood. She shot your brother, right? So now we have something on her, strong enough to keep her mouth shut for good. She'd get off with second degree, with what she's got, but even that is five to ten in Tehachapi. I think all I need to do is tell her that. First we have to find her, eh?"

"I'll find her. Bart didn't have any trouble finding her."

"With Vario's tip to help him, no. But I think I'll keep you here with me, Gino. You're too hot-blooded, you and your brother both. I want her alive. Then I can talk to her, and then we'll see."

"You're going soft in your old age, Angel."

"Am I?" There was a light slapping sound, of a blow on flesh. "I have killed many men, for good reasons. So I think you will take that back."

"I take it back."

"And call me Mr. Funk. If I am so old, you will treat my gray hairs with respect. Call me Mr. Funk."

"Mr. Funk."

"All right, your friend here, does he know where Fern is?"

"I don't think so."

"Mr. Funk."

"Mr. Funk." Gino's voice was a whining snarl.

"I think he's coming to. His eyelids fluttered."

The toe of a shoe prodded my side. Somebody slapped my face a number of times. I opened my eyes and sat up. The back of my head was throbbing like an engine fueled by pain. Gino rose from a squatting position and stood over me.

"Stand up."

I rose shakily to my feet. I was in a stone-walled room with a high beamed ceiling, sparsely furnished with stiff old black oak chairs and tables. The room and the furniture seemed to have been built for a race of giants.

The man behind Gino was small and old and weary. He might have been an unsuccessful grocer or a superannuated barkeep who had come to California for his health. Clearly his health was poor. Even in the stifling heat he looked pale and chilly, as if he had caught chronic death from one of his victims. He moved closer to me, his legs shuffling feebly in wrinkled blue trousers that bagged

at the knees. His shrunken torso was swathed in a heavy blue tur-
tleneck sweater. He had two days' beard on his chin, like moth-eaten
gray plush.

"Gino informs me that you are investigating a shooting." His
accent was Middle-European and very faint, as if he had forgotten
his origins. "Where did this happen, exactly?"

"I don't think I'll tell you that. You can read it in the papers
tomorrow night if you are interested."

"I am not prepared to wait. I am impatient. Do you know where
Fern is?"

"I wouldn't be here if I did."

"But you know where she was last night."

"I couldn't be sure."

"Tell me anyway to the best of your knowledge."

"I don't think I will."

"He doesn't think he will," the old man said to Gino.

"I think you better let me out of here. Kidnaping is a tough rap.
You don't want to die in the pen."

He smiled at me, with a tolerance more terrible than anger. His
eyes were like thin stab wounds filled with watery blood. Shuffling
unhurriedly to the head of the mahogany table behind him, he
pressed a spot in the rug with the toe of one felt slipper. Two men
in blue serge suits entered the room and stepped toward me briskly.
They belonged to the race of giants the room had been built for.

Gino moved behind me and reached to pin my arms. I pivoted,
landed one short punch, and took a very hard counter below the
belt. Something behind me slammed my kidneys with the heft of a
trailer truck bumper. I turned on weakening legs and caught a chin
with my elbow. Gino's fist, or one of the beams from the ceiling,
landed on my neck. My head rang like a gong. Under its clangor
Angel was saying pleasantly, "Where was Fern last night?"

I didn't say.

The men in blue serge held me upright by the arms while Gino
used my head as a punching bag. I rolled with his lefts and rights
as well as I could, but his timing improved and mine deteriorated.
His face wavered and receded. At intervals Angel inquired politely
if I was willing to assist him now. I asked myself confusedly in the
hail of fists what I was holding out for or who I was protecting.
Probably I was holding out for myself. It seemed important to me
not to give in to violence. But my identity was dissolving and receding like the face in front of me.

I concentrated on hating Gino's face. That kept it clear and steady for a while: a stupid square-jawed face barred by a single black brow, two close-set brown eyes staring glassily. His fists continued to rock me like an air-hammer.

Finally Angel placed a clawed hand on his shoulder, and nodded to my handlers. They deposited me in a chair. It swung on an invisible wire from the ceiling in great circles. It swung out wide over the desert, across a bleak horizon, into darkness.

I came to, cursing. Gino was standing over me again. There was an empty water glass in his hand, and my face was dripping. Angel spoke up beside him, with a trace of irritation in his voice.

"You stand up good under punishment. Why go to all the trouble, though? I want a little information, that is all. My friend, my little girl friend, ran away. I'm impatient to get her back."

"You're going about it the wrong way."

Gino leaned close and laughed harshly. He shattered the glass on the arm of my chair, held the jagged base up to my eyes. Fear ran through me, cold and light in my veins. My eyes were my connection with everything. Blindness would be the end of me. I closed my eyes, shutting out the cruel edges of the broken thing in his hand.

"Nix, Gino," the old man said. "I have a better idea, as usual. There is heat on, remember."

They retreated to the far side of the table and conferred there in low voices. The young man left the room. The old man came back to me. His storm troopers stood one on each side of me, looking down at him in ignorant awe.

"What is your name, young fellow?"

I told him. My mouth was puffed and lisping, tongue tangled in ropes of blood.

"I like a young fellow who can take it, Mr. Archer. You say you're a detective. You find people for a living, is that right?"

"I have a client," I said.

"Now you have another. Whoever he is, I can buy and sell him, believe me. Fifty times over." His thin blue hands scoured each other. They made a sound like two dry sticks rubbing together on a dead tree.

"Narcotics?" I said. "Are you the wheel in the heroin racket? I've heard of you."

His watery eyes veiled themselves like a bird's. "Now don't ask foolish questions or I will lose my respect for you."

"That would break my heart."

"Then comfort yourself with this." He brought an old-fashioned purse out of his hip pocket, abstracted a crumpled bill, and smoothed it out on my knee. It was a five-hundred-dollar bill.

"This girl of mine you are going to find for me, she is young and foolish. I am old and foolish, to have trusted her. No matter. Find her for me and bring her back and I will give you another bill like this one. Take it."

"Take it," one of my guards repeated. "Mr. Funk said for you to take it."

I took it. "You're wasting your money. I don't even know what she looks like. I don't know anything about her."

"Gino is bringing a picture. He came across her last fall at a recording studio in Hollywood where Alfie had a date. He gave her an audition and took her on at the club, more for her looks than for the talent she had. As a singer she flopped. But she is a pretty little thing, about five foot four, nice figure, dark brown hair, big hazel eyes. I found a use for her."

"You find a use for everything."

"That is good economics. I often think if I wasn't what I am, I would make a good economist. Nothing would go to waste." He paused and dragged his dying old mind back to the subject. "She was here for a couple of months, then she ran out on me, silly girl. I heard last week that she was in Acapulco, and the federal Grand Jury was going to subpoena her. I have tax troubles, Mr. Archer, all my life I have tax troubles. Unfortunately I let Fern help with my books a little bit. She could do me great harm. So I sent Bart to Mexico to bring her back. But I meant no harm to her. I still intend her no harm, even now. A little talk, a little realistic discussion with Fern, that is all that will be necessary. So even the shooting of my good friend Bart serves its purpose. Where did it happen, by the way?"

The question flicked out like a hook on the end of a long line.

"In San Diego," I said, "at a place near the airport: the Mission Motel."

He smiled paternally. "Now you are showing good sense."

Gino came back with a silver-framed photograph in his hand. He handed it to Angel, who passed it on to me. It was a studio portrait, of the kind intended for publicity cheesecake. On a black velvet divan, against an artificial night sky, a young woman reclined in a gossamer robe that was split to show one bent leg. Shadows accentuated the lines of her body and the fine bones in her face. Under the heavy makeup which widened the mouth and darkened the half-closed eyes, I recognized Ella Salanda. The picture was signed in white, in the lower righthand corner: *To my Angel, with all my love, Fern.*

A sickness assailed me, worse than the sickness induced by Gino's fists. Angel breathed into my face: "Fern Dee is a stage name. Her real name I never learned. She told me one time that if her family knew where she was they would die of shame." He chuckled. "She will not want them to know that she killed a man."

I drew away from his charnel-house breath. My guards escorted me out. Gino started to follow, but Angel called him back.

"Don't wait to hear from me," the old man said after me. "I expect to hear from you."

The building stood on a rise in the open desert. It was huge and turreted, like somebody's idea of a castle in Spain. The last rays of the sun washed its walls in purple light and cast long shadows across its barren acreage. It was surrounded by a ten-foot hurricane fence topped with three strands of barbed wire.

Palm Springs was a clutter of white stones in the distance, diamonded by an occasional light. The dull red sun was balanced like a glowing cigar butt on the rim of the hills above the town. A man with a bulky shoulder harness under his brown suede windbreaker drove me toward it. The sun fell out of sight, and darkness gathered like an impalpable ash on the desert, like a column of blue-gray smoke towering into the sky.

The sky was blue-black and swarming with stars when I got back to Emerald Bay. A black Cadillac followed me out of Palm Springs. I lost it in the winding streets of Pasadena. So far as I could see, I had lost it for good.

The neon Mexican lay peaceful under the stars. A smaller sign at his feet asserted that there was No Vacancy. The lights in the long low stucco buildings behind him shone brightly. The office door was open behind a screen, throwing a barred rectangle of light on the gravel. I stepped into it, and froze.

Behind the registration desk in the office a woman was avidly reading a magazine. Her shoulders and bosom were massive. Her hair was blonde, piled on her head in coroneted braids. There were rings on her fingers, a triple strand of cultured pearls around her thick white throat. She was the woman Donny had described to me. I opened the screen door and said, "Who are you?"

She glanced up, twisting her mouth in a sour grimace. "Well! I'll thank you to keep a civil tongue in your head."

"Sorry. I thought I'd seen you before somewhere."

"Well, you haven't." She looked me over coldly. "What happened to your face, anyway?"

"I had a little plastic surgery done. By an amateur surgeon."

She clucked disapprovingly. "If you're looking for a room, we're full up for the night. I don't believe I'd rent you a room even if we weren't. Look at your clothes."

"Uh-huh. Where's Mr. Salanda?"

"Is it any business of yours?"

"He wants to see me. I'm doing a job for him."

"What kind of a job?"

I mimicked her. "Is it any business of yours?" I was irritated. Under her mounds of flesh she had a personality as thin and hard and abrasive as a rasp.

"Watch who you're getting flip with, sonny boy." She rose, and her shadow loomed immense across the back door of the room. The magazine fell closed on the desk: it was *Teen-age Confessions.* "I am Mrs. Salanda. Are you a handyman?"

"A sort of one," I said. "I'm a garbage collector in the moral field. You look as if you could use me."

The crack went over her head. "Well, you're wrong. And I don't think my husband hired you, either. This is a respectable motel."

"Uh-huh. Are you Ella's mother?"

"I should say not. That little snip is no daughter of mine."

"Her stepmother?"

"Mind your own business. You better get out of here. The police are keeping a close watch on this place tonight, if you're planning any tricks."

"Where's Ella now?"

"I don't know and I don't care. She's probably gallivanting off around the countryside. It's all she's good for. One day at home in the last six months, that's a fine record for a young unmarried girl." Her face was thick and bloated with anger against her stepdaughter. She went on talking blindly, as if she had forgotten me entirely. "I told her father he was an old fool to take her back. How does he know what she's been up to? I say let the ungrateful filly go and fend for herself."

"Is that what you say, Mabel?" Salanda had softly opened the door behind her. He came forward into the room, doubly dwarfed by her blonde magnitude. "I say if it wasn't for you, my dear, Ella wouldn't have been driven away from home in the first place."

She turned on him in a blubbering rage. He drew himself up tall and reached to snap his fingers under her nose. "Go back into the house. You are a disgrace to women, a disgrace to motherhood."

"I'm not *her* mother, thank God."

"Thank God," he echoed, shaking his fist at her. She retreated like a schooner under full sail, menaced by a gunboat. The door closed on her. Salanda turned to me.

"I'm sorry, Mr. Archer. I have difficulties with my wife, I am ashamed to say it. I was an imbecile to marry again. I gained a senseless hulk of flesh and lost my daughter. Old imbecile!" he denounced himself, wagging his great head sadly. "I married in hot blood. Passion has always been my downfall. It runs in my family, this insane hunger for blondeness and stupidity and size." He spread his arms in a wide and futile embrace on emptiness.

"Forget it."

"If I could." He came closer to examine my face. "You are injured, Mr. Archer. Your mouth is damaged. There is blood on your chin."

"I was in a slight brawl."

"On my account?"

"On my own. But I think it's time you leveled with me."

"Leveled with you?"

"Told me the truth. You knew who was shot last night, and who shot him, and why."

He touched my arm, with a quick tentative grace. "I have only one daughter, Mr. Archer, only the one child. It was my duty to defend her, as best as I could."

"Defend her from what?"

"From shame, from the police, from prison." He flung one arm out, indicating the whole range of human disaster. "I am a man of honor, Mr. Archer. But private honor stands higher with me than public honor. The man was abducting my daughter. She brought him here in the hope of being rescued. Her last hope."

"I think that's true. You should have told me this before."

"I was alarmed, upset. I feared your intentions. Any minute the police were due to arrive."

"But you had a right to shoot him. It wasn't even a crime. The crime was his."

"I didn't know that then. The truth came out to me gradually. I feared that Ella was involved with him." His flat black gaze sought my face and rested on it. "However, I did not shoot him, Mr. Archer. I was not even here at the time. I told you that this morning, and you may take my word for it."

"Was Mrs. Salanda here?"

"No, sir, she was not. Why should you ask me that?"

"Donny described the woman who checked in with the dead man. The description fits your wife."

"Donny was lying. I told him to give a false description of the woman. Apparently he was unequal to the task of inventing one."

"Can you prove that she was with you?"

"Certainly I can. We had reserved seats at the theater. Those who sat around us can testify that the seats were not empty. Mrs. Salanda and I, we are not an inconspicuous couple." He smiled wryly.

"Ella killed him then."

He neither assented nor denied it. "I was hoping that you were on my side, my side and Ella's. Am I wrong?"

"I'll have to talk to her before I know myself. Where is she?"

"I do not know, Mr. Archer, sincerely I do not know. She went away this afternoon, after the policemen questioned her. They were suspicious, but we managed to soothe their suspicions. They did not know she had just come home, from another life, and I did not tell them. Mabel wanted to tell them. I silenced her." His white teeth clicked together.

"What about Donny?"

"They took him down to the station for questioning. He told them nothing damaging. Donny can appear very stupid when he wishes. He has the reputation of an idiot, but he is not so dumb. Donny has been with me for many years. He has a deep devotion for my daughter. I got him released tonight."

"You should have taken my advice," I said, "taken the police into your confidence. Nothing would have happened to you. The dead man was a mobster, and what he was doing amounts to kidnaping. Your daughter was a witness against his boss."

"She told me that. I am glad that it is true. Ella has not always told me the truth. She has been a hard girl to bring up, without a good mother to set her an example. Where has she been these last six months, Mr. Archer?"

"Singing in a night club in Palm Springs. Her boss was a racketeer."

"A racketeer?" His mouth and nose screwed up, as if he sniffed the odor of corruption.

"Where she was isn't important, compared with where she is now. The boss is still after her. He hired me to look for her."

Salanda regarded me with fear and dislike, as if the odor originated in me. "You let him hire you?"

"It was my best chance of getting out of his place alive. I'm not his boy, if that's what you mean."

"You ask me to believe you?"

"I'm telling you. Ella is in danger. As a matter of fact, we all are." I didn't tell him about the second black Cadillac. Gino would be driving it, wandering the night roads with a ready gun in his armpit and revenge corroding his heart.

"My daughter is aware of the danger," he said. "She warned me of it."

"She must have told you where she was going."

"No. But she may be at the beach house. The house where Donny lives. I will come with you."

"You stay here. Keep your doors locked. If any strangers show and start prowling the place, call the police."

He bolted the door behind me as I went out. Yellow traffic lights cast wan reflections on the asphalt. Streams of cars went by to the north, to the south. To the west, where the sea lay, a great black emptiness opened under the stars. The beach house sat on its white margin, a little over a mile from the motel.

For the second time that day I knocked on the warped kitchen door. There was light behind it, shining through the cracks. A shadow obscured the light.

"Who is it?" Donny said. Fear or some other emotion had filled his mouth with pebbles.

"You know me, Donny."

The door groaned on its hinges. He gestured dumbly to me to come in, his face a white blur. When he turned his head, and the light from the living room caught his face, I saw that grief was the emotion that marked it. His eyes were swollen as if he had been crying. More than ever he resembled a dilapidated boy whose growing pains had never paid off in manhood.

"Anybody with you?"

Sounds of movement in the living room answered my question. I brushed him aside and went in. Ella Salanda was bent over an open suitcase on the camp cot. She straightened, her mouth thin, eyes wide and dark. The .38 automatic in her hand gleamed dully under the naked bulb suspended from the ceiling.

"I'm getting out of here," she said, "and you're not going to stop me."

"I'm not sure I want to try. Where are you going, Fern?"

Donny spoke behind me, in his grief-thickened voice. "She's going away from me. She promised to stay here if I did what she told me. She promised to be my girl—"

"Shut up, stupid." Her voice cut like a lash, and Donny gasped as if the lash had been laid across his back.

"What did she tell you to do, Donny? Tell me just what you did."

"When she checked in last night with the fella from Detroit, she made a sign I wasn't to let on I knew her. Later on she left me a note. She wrote it with a lipstick on a piece of paper towel. I still got it hidden, in the kitchen."

"What did she write in the note?"

He lingered behind me, fearful of the gun in the girl's hand, more fearful of her anger.

She said, "Don't be crazy, Donny. He doesn't know a thing, not a thing. He can't do anything to either of us."

"I don't care what happens, to me or anybody else," the anguished voice said behind me. "You're running out on me, breaking your promise to me. I always knew it was too good to be true. Now I just don't care any more."

"I care," she said. "I care what happens to me." Her eyes shifted to me, above the unwavering gun. "I won't stay here. I'll shoot you if I have to."

"It shouldn't be necessary. Put it down, Fern. It's Bartolomeo's gun, isn't it? I found the shells to fit it in his glove compartment."

"How do you know so much?"

"I talked to Angel."

"Is he here?" Panic whined in her voice.

"No. I came alone."

"You better leave the same way then, while you can go under your own power."

"I'm staying. You need protection, whether you know it or not. And I need information. Donny, go in the kitchen and bring me that note."

"Don't do it, Donny. I'm warning you."

His sneakered feet made soft indecisive sounds. I advanced on the girl, talking quietly and steadily, "You conspired to kill a man, but you don't have to be afraid. He had it coming. Tell the whole story to the cops, and my guess is they won't even book you. Hell, you can

even become famous. The government wants you as a witness in a
tax case."

"What kind of a case?"

"A tax case against Angel. It's probably the only kind of rap they
can pin on him. You can send him up for the rest of his life like
Capone. You'll be a heroine, Fern."

"Don't call me Fern. I hate that name." There were sudden tears
in her eyes. "I hate everything connected with that name. I hate
myself."

"You'll hate yourself more if you don't put down that gun. Shoot
me and it all starts over again. The cops will be on your trail, Angel's
troopers will be gunning for you."

Now only the cot was between us, the cot and the unsteady gun
facing me above it.

"This is the turning point," I said. "You've made a lot of bum
decisions and almost ruined yourself, playing footsie with the evilest
men there are. You can go on the way you have been, getting in
deeper until you end up in a refrigerated drawer, or you can come
back out of it now, into a decent life."

"A decent life? Here? With my father married to Mabel?"

"I don't think Mabel will last much longer. Anyway, I'm not Mabel.
I'm on your side."

I waited. She dropped the gun on the blanket. I scooped it up and
turned to Donny. "Let me see that note."

He disappeared through the kitchen door, head and shoulders
drooping on the long stalk of his body.

"What could I do?" the girl said. "I was caught. It was Bart or me.
All the way up from Acapulco I planned how I could get away. He
held a gun in my side when we crossed the border; the same way
when we stopped for gas or to eat at the drive-ins. I realized he had
to be killed. My father's motel looked like my only chance. So I
talked Bart into staying there with me overnight. He had no idea
who the place belonged to. I didn't know what I was going to do. I
only knew it had to be something drastic. Once I was back with
Angel in the desert, that was the end of me. Even if he didn't kill
me, it meant I'd have to go on living with him. Anything was better
than that. So I wrote a note to Donny in the bathroom, and dropped
it out the window. He was always crazy about me."

Her mouth had grown softer. She looked remarkably young and
virginal. The faint blue hollows under her eyes were dewy. "Donny
shot Bart with Bart's own gun. He had more nerve than I had. I lost

my nerve when I went back into the room this morning. I didn't know about the blood in the bathroom. It was the last straw."

She was wrong. Something crashed in the kitchen. A cool draft swept the living room. A gun spoke twice, out of sight. Donny fell backward through the doorway, a piece of brownish paper clutched in his hand. Blood gleamed on his shoulder like a red badge.

I stepped behind the cot and pulled the girl down to the floor with me. Gino came through the door, his two-colored sports shoe stepping on Donny's laboring chest. I shot the gun out of his hand. He floundered back against the wall, clutching at his wrist.

I sighted carefully for my second shot, until the black bar of his eyebrows was steady in the sights of the .38. The hole it made was invisible. Gino fell loosely forward, prone on the floor beside the man he had killed.

Ella Salanda ran across the room. She knelt, and cradled Donny's head in her lap. Incredibly he spoke, in a loud sighing voice, "You won't go away again, Ella? I did what you told me. You promised."

"Sure I promised. I won't leave you, Donny. Crazy man. Crazy fool."

"You like me better than you used to? Now?"

"I like you, Donny. You're the most man there is."

She held the poor insignificant head in her hands. He sighed, and his life came out bright-colored at the mouth. It was Donny who went away.

His hand relaxed, and I read the lipstick note she had written him on a piece of paper towel:

"Donny: This man will kill me unless you kill him first. His gun will be in his clothes on the chair beside the bed. Come in and get it at midnight and shoot to kill. Good luck. I'll stay and be your girl if you do this, just like you always wished. Love. Ella."

I looked at the pair on the floor. She was rocking his lifeless head against her breast. Beside them, Gino looked very small and lonely, a dummy leaking darkness from his brow.

Donny had his wish and I had mine. I wondered what Ella's was.

Brian Garfield

The Glory Hunter

On the evening when the kid came to kill him, the man returned from the day's labor at his usual time.

The man and the woman went out each morning from the ruined fort to the cliff. It was about a half-mile walk. They worked side by side inside the mountain.

In the course of four years of work they had tunneled deep into the quartz. Hardrocking was not easy work, especially for a man and a woman both in their fifties and neither of them very large in size; but they accepted the arduous work because it had a goal and the goal was in sight.

Inside the tunnel they would crush the rock together and shovel it into the wooden dumpcart. They would wheel the cart out of the tunnel and dump it into the sluice that the man had designed in the second year to replace the rocker-box they'd begun with. The sluice carried water at high speed. This was water that came down through a wooden flume from a creek 70 yards above them, above the top of the low cliff. The floor of the sluice was rippled with wooden barriers; these were designed to separate the particles and retain the heaviest ones—the gold flakes—while everything else washed away downstream.

It was a good lode and during the four years they had washed a great deal of gold out of the mountain, flake by flake. Most of it was hidden in various caches. When they made the forty-mile muleback ride to Florence Junction for stocking up, they would take only enough gold dust to pay for their purchases; the town knew they had a claim back in the Superstitions but from the amount they spent it appeared they were barely making ends meet. They had never been invaded by gold-rush crowds.

They'd started working the claim when the man was 51 and the woman 48 and he figured to quit when he was 56, at which time they should have enough money to live handsomely in one of those big new gabled houses over in San José or Palo Alto or San Francisco. They'd be able to afford all the genteel things. In the meantime they worked hard to pay for it, pitting their muscles and pickaxes against the hard skeleton of the mountain.

The mountain was called Longshot Bluff because it was topped by a needle-shaped pinnacle like the spike on a Prussian helmet; from up there you could command everything in sight with an unobstructed circle of fire and because of the altitude you could make a bullet travel an extremely long distance.

The cavalry, back in 1879, had chased a small band of warriors onto the mountain and the Apaches had taken up positions on top of the spire. There were only five Apaches; there were 40 soldiers in the troop but the Indians barricaded themselves and there was no way the army could get at them. A siege had ensued and finally the Apaches were starved out.

After that the army built the little outpost on a hilltop about a mile out from the base of Longshot Bluff. Troops had occupied the post for five years; then the Indian wars came to an end and the camp was abandoned. It was the ruins of this fort that the man and the woman used as their home.

The abandoned camp had no stockade around it; the simple outpost consisted merely of a handful of squat adobes built around a flat parade ground. There had been a post-and-rail corral, but travelers had consumed the rails for firewood over the twelve years since the camp had been decommissioned by the army. The man and the woman had kept their four mules loose-hobbled for the first few weeks of their residence; after that they let the animals graze at will because this had become home and the mules had nowhere else to go.

When you sat on the veranda after supper, as the man and the woman often did, you faced the east. You looked down a long easy hardpan slope dotted with a spindle tracery of desert growth—catclaw and ocotillo, manzanita and cholla and sage. The foot of the slope was nearly a half-mile away.

At that point you saw the low cliff where the man and the woman had drilled their mining tunnel. Beyond it lofted the abrupt mass of Longshot Bluff. The pinnacle was perhaps 800 feet higher than the fort. From this angle the spire appeared as slender as a lance, sharp enough to pierce the clouds. It stood, as the crow flies, perhaps three miles from the veranda.

They came in from work in the late afternoon and the man packed his pipe on the veranda while he waited for supper. Over on the southern slope of Longshot Bluff he saw briefly the movement of an approaching horseman. From the window the woman must have seen it as well; she appeared on the veranda. "He'll be too late for supper unless we wait on him."

"Then we'll wait on him," the man said.

It would take the rider at least an hour to get here and it would be about 45 minutes short of sunset by then. But the man went inside immediately and opened the threadbare carpetbag that he kept under the bed.

The woman said, "I hope he's not another glory hunter." She said it without heat; when the man glanced at her she cracked her brief gentle smile.

He unwrapped his revolver from the oiled rags that protected it. The revolver was a single-action Bisley model with a 7½-inch barrel, caliber .45 Long Colt. It had been designed for match target competition and the Colt people had named it after the shooting range at Bisley in England where marksmen met every year to decide the championship.

The man put the revolver in his waistband and snugged it around until it didn't abrade his hipbone.

On his way to the door he glanced at the woman. She was, he thought, a woman of rare quality. When he'd met her she'd been working in a brothel in Leadville. After they'd known each other a few years the man had said, "We're both getting kind of long in the tooth," and they'd both left their previous occupations and gone out together looking for gold.

At the door he said, "I'll be back directly," and walked down toward the cliff.

He covered the distance briskly; it took some 15 minutes and when he reached the mouth of the tunnel he ran the empty ore cart out past the sluice and pushed it up onto a little hump of rocky ground. In the debris of the tailings dump he found two cracked half-gallon jugs they'd discarded. He set the jugs on two corners of the ore cart; they balanced sturdily and nothing short of a direct blow would knock them off.

Then he walked back up toward the fort, but he moved more slowly now, keeping to cover because it wasn't certain just when the approaching horseman would come into sight down along the far end of the base of the mountain.

The man laid up in a clump of manzanita about 30 feet from the veranda and kept his eye on the little stand of cottonwoods a mile away. That was where the creek flowed off the mountain. The creek went underground there but you could trace the line of its passage out onto the desert plain by the deep green row of mesquite and scrub sycamore. The rider would appear somewhere along there; he'd have to cross the creek.

After a little while the visitor came across the creek and rode along the slope toward the ruined fort.

Coming in straight up, the man observed; but still he didn't show himself.

Halfway up to the house the horseman drew his rifle out of the saddle scabbard and laid it across his pommel, holding it that way with one hand as he approached without hurry.

The man lay in the brush and watched.

He saw that the rider was just a kid. Maybe 18, maybe 20. A leaned-down kid with no meat on him and a hungry narrow face under the brim of a pretentious black hat.

The horse went by not ten feet from the man's hiding place. Just beyond, the kid drew rein, not riding any closer to the fort.

"Hello the house. Anybody home?"

The man stood up behind him. "Right back here. Drop the rifle first. Then we'll talk."

The man was braced for anything; the kid might be a wild one. The man had the Bisley Colt cocked in his fist. The kid's head turned slowly until he picked up the man in the corner of his vision; evidently he saw and recognized the revolver because he let the rifle slide to the ground.

"Now the belt gun," the man said, and the kid stripped off his gunbelt and let it drop alongside the rifle. The kid eased his horse off to one side away from the weapons and the man said, "All right, you can speak your piece."

"Ain't rightly fair coming up from behind me like that," the kid said.

He had a surprisingly deep voice.

"Well you came calling on me with a rifle across your saddle-bow."

"Place like this, how do I know what to expect? Could be rattlers in there. Place could be crawling with road agents for all I know."

"Well, that's all right, son. You won't need your weapons. You want to come inside and share a bit of supper?"

The kid looked uncertainly at the man's Bisley revolver. The man walked over to the discarded weapons and picked them up. Then he uncocked the revolver and put it back in his waistband. He went up to the house and the woman came out onto the veranda and shaded her eyes to look at the visitor. She smiled a welcome, but when she glanced at the man he saw the knowledge in her face.

The kid had come to kill the man, right enough. All three of them knew it, but nobody said anything.

The kid ate politely; somebody had taught him manners. The woman said, to make conversation, "You hail from Tucson?"

"No, ma'am. Laramie, Wyoming."

"Long way off," the man said.

"I reckon."

After supper the three of them sat on the veranda. The sun was behind the house and they were in shadow; another ten minutes to sundown. The hard slanting light struck the face of Longshot Bluff and made the spire look like a fiery signal against the dark sky beyond it. The man got his pipe going to his satisfaction, broke the match, and contemplated the kid who had come to kill him. "How much they paying you for my scalp, son?"

"What?"

"The last one they sent, it was two thousand dollars they offered him."

"Mister, I ain't quite sure what you're talking about."

"That's a powerful grudge they're carrying, two thousand dollars' worth. It happened a long while back, you know."

The woman said, "But I suppose two thousand dollars looks like the world of money to a young man like you."

The man said, "It's not legal any more, you know, son. No matter what they told you. There was a fugitive warrant out on me from the state of Wyoming, but that was some years back. The statute of limitations expired three years ago."

"I'm sorry, mister, I just ain't tracking what you mean."

"The cattlemen up there were hiring range detectives like me to discourage homesteaders," the man explained. "This one cattleman had an eager kind of streak in him. I told him to keep out of the way but he had to mess in things. Got in the way of a bullet. My bullet, I expect, although I've never been whole certain about that.

"Anyhow, that cattleman's been in a wheelchair ever since. Accused me of backshooting him, said I'd sold out to the homestead crowd. It wasn't true, of course, but it's what he believes. All he does is sit in that wheelchair and brood over it. He's sent seven bounty men after me, one time or another. He just keeps sending them. Reckon he won't give it up till one of us dies of old age. You're number eight now. Maybe you want to think on that—think about the other seven that came after me, pretty good professionals some of them. I'm still here, son."

The kid just watched him, not blinking, no longer protesting innocence.

The man said, "That fellow in the wheelchair, how much did he offer you?"

The kid didn't answer that. After a moment the woman said, "You probably want the money for some good purpose, don't you, young fellow?"

"Ma'am, I expect anybody could find his own good purpose to turn money to if he had it."

"You got a girl back in Laramie, Wyoming?" she asked.

"Yes, ma'am."

"Fixing to marry her?"

"That's right, ma'am."

"On two thousand dollars you'd have a right good start," she said.

"That would be true, ma'am," the kid said with great courtesy.

"Well, I hope you make your way proper in the world," she said, "but you ain't likely to do that here. You do a sight of hunting, I imagine, from the look of that rifle you carry. You must have seen buck antelope square off a time or two. The young buck tries to get the better of the old buck, tries to displace him in the herd. Rarely happens. I expect you know that. The old buck knows all the tricks that the young buck still needs to learn. That's why you're setting on this porch now without a gun."

The man's pipe had gone out. He struck another match and indulged himself in the ritual of spreading the flame around the bowl. Then he said, "If you ain't ready to give it up, son, I'll take your weapons out there on the desert in the morning and then let you go out and get them and we'll finish this thing between us. If that's the way you want it."

The kid looked at him and uncertainty crept into his young face.

The man said, "The only weapon I own is this Bisley revolver here. Of course you may think you can outrange me with that forty-four-forty rifle of yours. You may think that, but I reckon as how you'd be mistaken."

The light was beginning to fade, but he still had another 15 or 20 minutes of light good enough for shooting. The wind had died; that was what he had waited for. He went inside the house and got the kid's rifle and brought it out onto the veranda. The kid watched him while the man worked the lever-action, jacking out the cartridges one by one until the rifle was empty.

Then the man picked up one of the cartridges off the floor and wiped it clean with his hand and chambered it into the rifle. He locked the breech shut and looked at the kid.

"Now I've put one load into this rifle of yours. I'm going to let you shoot it, if you like, but not at me. You can aim it down there toward the cliff. If I see that rifle start to swing toward me I'll just have to shoot you."

The kid, baffled, just stared at him.

The man pointed off toward the cliff. You could see the little ore cart down there; you could, if you had good eyesight, make out the two jugs perched on it.

"You see those jugs on the ore cart, son?"

"Yes, sir, if that's what they are."

"Half-gallon clay jugs. You think you can hit those with that rifle?"

The kid stood up and went to the rail of the veranda. He peered down the slope. "That's an awful long way off," he said, half to himself.

"Pret' near half a mile," the man agreed. "Six, seven hundred yards anyhow."

The kid said, "I don't know as how even Wild Bill Hickok could have made a shot like that, sir."

"Well, you can try it if you like."

"I don't see the point."

The man handed the rifle to the woman. Then he drew out his Bisley revolver and stepped over to the pillar that supported the veranda roof.

"I'll show you why," he said, and lifted his left arm straight out from the shoulder and braced his palm against the pillar. Then he twisted his body a little and set his feet firm, and holding the Bisley revolver in his right fist he lowered it until his two wrists were crossed, the left one supporting the right one—the shooter's-rest position. He cocked the revolver and fired it once, almost with careless speed.

Down below at the cliff all three of them plainly saw one of the clay jugs hurtle off its perch on the corner of the ore cart. The jug struck the rocky ground and shattered.

The kid's eyes, big and round, came around slowly to rest on the man. "Lordy. Seven hundred yards—with a *handgun?*"

The man cocked his Bisley revolver again and held it in his right hand pointed more or less at the kid. The woman walked behind the kid and held the rifle out over the railing, pointing it toward the cliff. She was proffering it to the kid. "Go ahead," she said. "You try."

Slowly the kid took the rifle from her. He was careful to make no sudden motions. He got down on one knee and braced his left forearm against the porch railing to steady his aim. He took his time. The man saw him look up toward the sky, trying to judge the elevation and the windage and the range. The kid adjusted the rear sight of the rifle twice before he snugged down to take serious aim.

Finally he was ready and the man saw the kid's finger begin to whiten on the trigger as he squeezed. The kid was all right, the man thought. Knew what he was doing. But then that had been clear from the start—when the kid hadn't tried something foolish at the moment when the man had taken him by surprise back there on the horse. The kid was wise enough to know you didn't fight when the other man had the drop.

The kid squeezed the trigger with professionally unhurried skill and the rifle thundered. The man was watching the cliff and saw the white streak appear on the rocks where the bullet struck.

"Not bad," the man said. "You only missed by about ten feet."

"Lordy," the kid said. He handed the empty rifle back to the woman.

Then the man took his position again and fired a single shot from his Bisley revolver.

They saw the remaining jug shatter.

The light began to fade. The man said, "I did that to show you the first one wasn't a fluke."

The kid swallowed. "I expect I'm kind of overmatched." He wiped his mouth. "I take it right kindly you did it this way. I mean you could've proved the same thing by using me instead of those jugs." He sat down slowly. "You was right. But that old man in the wheel-chair, he showed me a warrant. He said it was all fair and legal. He even showed me where it said dead-or-alive."

The woman said, "Likely he didn't show you the date on that warrant, though, did he?"

"I don't recollect that he did, no, ma'am."

The man said, "If you ask at the courthouse when you get home you'll find out those charges expired three years ago."

In the morning they watched the kid ride away to the north. The man packed his Bisley revolver away after he cleaned it. Then he took the woman's hand and they went down to the cliff to start the day's work.

The man picked up the shards of the broken jugs and tossed them on the tailings pile. "It's a good thing he's that young. If he'd been older he'd have known for a fact that you just can't make a shot that far with a handgun. But a fellow that young, you can trick him because he believes what he sees."

The woman smiled. "Well, it wasn't exactly a trick. You still had to aim rock-steady. And figure the wind."

"I waited until there wasn't no wind. If the air's moving you can't do a trick like that."

He'd set up for it four years ago because he'd known they'd keep coming after him. He'd been counting on the statute of limitations; he hadn't reckoned, at the time, on that old man being so obsessed that he'd keep sending bounty men forever. But the trick still worked.

He'd done it by figuring the shot in reverse. He'd made a little notch on the pillar of the veranda and that was where he aimed the revolver from. He'd taken aim at the left side of the spire on top of Longshot Bluff. Then he'd taken aim at the right side of it. Then he'd gone down the hill and marked the spots where the two bullets had struck. After that, all he had to do was set up his two targets on exactly those spots. If there wasn't any wind, all you had to do was aim at one side of the spire or the other. You'd hit the same spots every time.

It had fooled the kid, of course, because it hadn't occurred to the kid that there was a fixed aiming point. The kid had had to guess the drop of his bullet over a seven-hundred-yard range. He'd guessed pretty close, matter of fact, but it hadn't been close enough.

The man was pleased with it. Because all the time he'd been a gun-handler by profession he'd managed to do it without ever killing a man. He'd arrested a lot of them and he'd shot a few, but none of them fatally. He wasn't about to let a bitter old fool in a wheelchair make a killer out of him at this time of his life.

P. G. Wodehouse

Death at the Excelsior

The room was the typical bedroom of the typical boardinghouse, furnished, insofar as it could be said to be furnished at all, with a severe simplicity. In contained two beds, a pine chest of drawers, a strip of faded carpet, and a wash basin. But there was that on the floor which set this room apart from a thousand rooms of the same kind. Flat on his back, with his hands tightly clenched and one leg twisted oddly under him and with his teeth gleaming through his gray beard in a horrible grin, Captain John Gunner stared up at the ceiling with eyes that saw nothing.

Until a moment before, he had had the little room all to himself. But now two people were standing just inside the door, looking down at him. One was a large policeman, who twisted his helmet nervously in his hands. The other was a tall gaunt old woman in a rusty black dress, who gazed with pale eyes at the dead man. Her face was quite expressionless.

The woman was Mrs. Pickett, owner of the Excelsior boardinghouse. The policeman's name was Grogan. He was a genial giant, a terror to the riotous element of the waterfront, but obviously ill at ease in the presence of death. He drew in his breath, wiped his forehead, and whispered, "Look at his eyes, ma'am!"

Mrs. Pickett had not spoken a word since she had brought the policeman into the room, and she did not do so now. Constable Grogan looked at her quickly. He was afraid of Mother Pickett, as was everybody else along the waterfront. Her silence, her pale eyes, and the quiet decisiveness of her personality cowed even the tough old salts who patronized the Excelsior. She was a formidable influence in that little community of sailormen.

"That's just how I found him," said Mrs. Pickett. She did not speak loudly, but her voice made the policeman start.

He wiped his forehead again. "It might have been apoplexy," he hazarded.

Mrs. Pickett said nothing. There was a sound of footsteps outside, and a young man entered, carrying a black bag.

"Good morning, Mrs. Pickett. I was told that—good Lord!" The young doctor dropped to his knees beside the body and raised one of the arms. After a moment he lowered it gently to the floor and shook his head in grim resignation.

"He's been dead for hours," he announced. "When did you find him?"

"Twenty minutes back," replied the old woman. "I guess he died last night. He never would be called in the morning. Said he liked to sleep on. Well, he's got his wish."

"What did he die of, sir?" asked the policeman.

"It's impossible to say without an examination," the doctor answered. "It looks like a stroke, but I'm pretty sure it isn't. It might be a coronary attack, but I happen to know his blood pressure was normal, and his heart sound. He called in to see me only a week ago and I examined him thoroughly. But sometimes you can be deceived. The inquest will tell us."

He eyed the body almost resentfully. "I can't understand it. The man had no right to drop dead like this. He was a tough old sailor who ought to have been good for another twenty years. If you want my honest opinion—though I can't possibly be certain until after the inquest—I should say he had been poisoned."

"How would he be poisoned?" asked Mrs. Pickett quietly.

"That's more than I can tell you. There's no glass about that he could have drunk it from. He might have got it in capsule form. But why should he have done it? He was always a pretty cheerful sort of man, wasn't he?"

"Yes, sir," said the constable. "He had the name of being a joker in these parts. Kind of sarcastic, they tell me, though he never tried it on me."

"He must have died quite early last night," said the doctor. He turned to Mrs. Pickett. "What's become of Captain Muller? If he shares this room he ought to be able to tell us something."

"Captain Muller spent the night with some friends at Portsmouth," said Mrs. Pickett. "He left right after supper, and hasn't returned."

The doctor stared thoughtfully about the room, frowning.

"I don't like it. I can't understand it. If this had happened in India I should have said the man had died from some form of snake bite. I was out there two years, and I've seen a hundred cases of it. The poor devils all looked just like this. But the thing's ridiculous. How could a man be bitten by a snake in a Southampton waterfront boardinghouse? Was the door locked when you found him, Mrs. Pickett?"

Mrs. Pickett nodded. "I opened it with my own key. I had been calling to him and he didn't answer, so I guessed something was wrong."

The constable spoke, "You ain't touched anything, ma'am? They're always very particular about that. If the doctor's right and there's been anything up, that's the first thing they'll ask."

"Everything's just as I found it."

"What's that on the floor beside him?" the doctor asked.

"Only his harmonica. He liked to play it of an evening in his room. I've had some complaints about it from some of the gentlemen, but I never saw any harm, so long as he didn't play it too late."

"Seems as if he was playing it when—it happened," Constable Grogan said. "That don't look much like suicide, sir."

"I didn't say it was suicide."

Grogan whistled. "You don't think—"

"I'm not thinking anything—until after the inquest. All I say is that it's queer."

Another aspect of the matter seemed to strike the policeman. "I guess this ain't going to do the Excelsior any good, ma'am," he said sympathetically.

Mrs. Pickett shrugged.

"I suppose I had better go and notify the coroner," said the doctor.

He went out, and after a momentary pause the policeman followed. Constable Grogan was not greatly troubled with nerves, but he felt a decided desire to be where he could not see the dead man's staring eyes.

Mrs. Pickett remained where she was, looking down at the still form on the floor. Her face was expressionless, but inwardly she was tormented and alarmed. It was the first time such a thing as this had happened at the Excelsior, and, as Constable Grogan had suggested, it was not likely to increase the attractiveness of the house in the eyes of possible boarders. It was not the threatened pecuniary loss which was troubling her. As far as money was concerned, she could have lived comfortably on her savings, for she was richer than most of her friends supposed. It was the blot on the escutcheon of the Excelsior, the stain on its reputation, which was tormenting her.

The Excelsior was her life. Starting many years before, beyond the memory of the oldest boarder, she had built up a model establishment. Men spoke of it as a place where you were fed well, cleanly housed, and where petty robbery was unknown.

Such was the chorus of praise that it is not likely that much harm could come to the Excelsior from a single mysterious death, but Mother Pickett was not consoling herself with that.

She looked at the dead man with pale grim eyes. Out in the hallway the doctor's voice further increased her despair. He was talking to the police on the telephone, and she could distinctly hear his every word.

The offices of Mr. Paul Snyder's Detective Agency in New Oxford Street had grown in the course of a dozen years from a single room to an impressive suite bright with polished wood, clicking typewriters, and other evidences of success. Where once Mr. Snyder had sat and waited for clients and attended to them himself, he now sat in his private office and directed eight assistants.

He had just accepted a case—a case that might be nothing at all or something exceedingly big. It was on the latter possibility that he had gambled. The fee offered was, judged by his present standards of prosperity, small. But the bizarre facts, coupled with something in the personality of the client, had won him over. He briskly touched the bell and requested that Mr. Oakes should be sent in to him.

Elliott Oakes was a young man who both amused and interested Mr. Snyder, for though he had only recently joined the staff, he made no secret of his intention of revolutionizing the methods of the agency. Mr. Snyder himself, in common with most of his assistants, relied for results on hard work and common sense. He had never been a detective of the showy type. Results had justified his methods, but he was perfectly aware that young Mr. Oakes looked on him as a dull old man who had been miraculously favored by luck.

Mr. Snyder had selected Oakes for the case in hand principally because it was one where inexperience could do no harm, and where the brilliant guesswork which Oakes preferred to call his inductive reasoning might achieve an unexpected success.

Another motive actuated Mr. Snyder. He had a strong suspicion that the conduct of this case was going to have the beneficial result of lowering Oakes's self-esteem. If failure achieved this end, Mr. Snyder felt that failure, though it would not help the agency, would not be an unmixed ill.

The door opened and Oakes entered tensely. He did everything tensely, partly from a natural nervous energy, and partly as a pose. He was a lean young man, with dark eyes and a thin-lipped mouth, and he looked quite as much like a typical detective as Mr. Snyder looked like a comfortable and prosperous stockbroker.

"Sit down, Oakes," said Mr. Snyder. "I've got a job for you."

Oakes sank into a chair like a crouching leopard and placed the tips of his fingers together. He nodded curtly. It was part of his pose to be keen and silent.

"I want you to go to this address"—Mr. Snyder handed him an envelope—"and look around. The address is of a sailors' boarding-house down in Southampton. You know the sort of place—retired sea captains and so on live there. All most respectable. In all its history nothing more sensational has ever happened than a case of suspected cheating at halfpenny nap. Well, a man has died there."

"Murdered?" Oakes asked.

"I don't know. That's for you to find out. The coroner left it open. 'Death by Misadventure' was the verdict, and I don't blame him. I don't see how it could have been murder. The door was locked on the inside, so nobody could have got in."

"The window?"

"The window was open, granted. But the room is on the second floor. Anyway, you may dismiss the window. I remember the old lady saying there were bars across it, and that nobody could have squeezed through."

Oakes's eyes glistened. "What was the cause of death?" he asked.

Mr. Snyder coughed. "Snake bite," he said.

Oakes's careful calm deserted him. He uttered a cry of astonishment. "Why, that's incredible!"

"It's the literal truth. The medical examination proved that the fellow had been killed by snake poison—cobra, to be exact, which is found principally in India."

"Cobra!"

"Just so. In a Southampton boardinghouse, in a room with a door locked on the inside, this man was stung by a cobra. To add a little mystification to the limpid simplicity of the affair, when the door was opened there was no sign of any cobra. It couldn't have got out through the door, because the door was locked. It couldn't have got out of the window, because the window was too high up, and snakes can't jump. And it couldn't have got up the chimney, because there was no chimney. So there you have it."

He looked at Oakes with a certain quiet satisfaction. It had come to his ears that Oakes had been heard to complain of the infantile nature of the last two cases to which he had been assigned. He had even said that he hoped someday to be given a problem which should be beyond the reasoning powers of a child of six. It seemed to Mr. Snyder that Oakes was about to get his wish.

"I should like further details," said Oakes, a little breathlessly.

"You had better apply to Mrs. Pickett, who owns the boarding-house," Mr. Snyder said. "It was she who put the case in my hands. She is convinced that it is murder. But if we exclude ghosts, I don't see how any third party could have taken a hand in the thing at all. However, she wanted a man from this agency, and was prepared to pay for him, so I promised her I would send one. It is not our policy to turn business away."

He smiled wryly. "In pursuance of that policy I want you to go and put up at Mrs. Pickett's boardinghouse and do your best to enhance the reputation of our agency. I would suggest that you pose as a ship's chandler or something of that sort. You will have to be something maritime or they'll be suspicious of you. And if your visit produces no other results, it will, at least, enable you to make the acquaintance of a very remarkable woman. I commend Mrs. Pickett to your notice. By the way, she says she will help you in your in-vestigations."

Oakes laughed shortly. The idea amused him.

"It's a mistake to scoff at amateur assistance, my boy," said Mr. Snyder in the benevolently paternal manner which had made a score of criminals refuse to believe him a detective until the moment when the handcuffs snapped on their wrists. "Crime investigation isn't an exact science. Success or failure depends in a large measure on applied common sense and the possession of a great deal of special information. Mrs. Pickett knows certain things which neither you nor I know, and it's just possible that she may have some stray piece of information which will provide the key to the entire mystery."

Oakes laughed again. "It is very kind of Mrs. Pickett," he said, "but I prefer to trust to my own methods." Oakes rose, his face purposeful. "I'd better be starting at once," he said. "I'll send you reports from time to time."

"Good. The more detailed the better," said Mr. Snyder genially. "I hope your visit to the Excelsior will be pleasant. And cultivate Mrs. Pickett. She's worthwhile."

The door closed, and Mr. Snyder lighted a fresh cigar. Dashed young fool, he thought and turned his mind to other matters.

A day later Mr. Snyder sat in his office reading a typewritten report. It appeared to be of a humorous nature, for, as he read, chuckles escaped him. Finishing the last sheet he threw his head back and laughed heartily. The manuscript had not been intended by its author for a humorous effect. What Mr. Snyder had been reading was the first of Elliott Oakes's reports from the Excelsior. It read as follows:

"I am sorry to be unable to report any real progress. I have formed several theories which I will put forward later, but at present I cannot say that I am hopeful.

"Directly I arrived I sought out Mrs. Pickett, explained who I was, and requested her to furnish me with any further information which might be of service to me. She is a strange silent woman, who impressed me as having very little intelligence. Your suggestion that I should avail myself of her assistance seems more curious than ever now that I have seen her.

"The whole affair seems to me at the moment of writing quite inexplicable. Assuming that this Captain Gunner was murdered, there appears to have been no motive for the crime whatsoever. I have made careful inquiries about him, and find that he was a man of 55; had spent nearly 40 years of his life at sea, the last dozen in command of his own ship; was of a somewhat overbearing disposition, though with a fund of rough humour; he had travelled all over the world, and had been a resident of the Excelsior for about ten months. He had a small annuity, and no other money at all, which disposes of money as the motive for the crime.

"In my character of James Burton, a retired ship's chandler, I have mixed with the other boarders, and have heard all they have to say about the affair. I gather that the deceased was by no means popular. He appears to have had a bitter tongue, and I have not met one man who seems to regret his death. On the other hand, I have heard nothing which would suggest that he had any active and violent enemies. He was simply the unpopular boarder—there is always one in every boardinghouse—but nothing more.

"I have seen a good deal of the man who shared his room—another sea captain named Muller. He is a big silent person, and it is not easy to get him to talk. As regards the death of Captain Gunner he can tell me nothing. It seems that on the night of the tragedy he was away at Portsmouth. All I have got from him is some information as to Captain Gunner's habits, which leads nowhere.

"The dead man seldom drank, except at night when he would take some whisky. His head was not strong, and a little of the spirit was enough to make him semi-intoxicated, when he would be hilarious and often insulting. I gather that Muller found him a difficult room-mate, but he is one of those placid persons who can put up with anything. He and Gunner were in the habit of playing draughts together every night in their room, and Gunner had a harmonica which he played frequently. Apparently he was playing it very soon before he died, which is significant, as seeming to dispose of any idea of suicide.

"As I say, I have one or two theories, but they are in a very nebulous state. The most plausible is that on one of his visits to India—I have ascertained that he made several voyages there—Captain Gunner may in some way have fallen foul of the natives. The fact that he certainly died of the poison of an Indian snake supports this theory. I am making inquiries as to the move-ments of several Indian sailors who were here in their ships at the time of the tragedy.

"I have another theory. Does Mrs. Pickett know more about this affair than she appears to? I may be wrong in my estimate of her mental qualities. Her apparent stupidity may be cunning. But here again, the absence of motive brings me up against a dead wall. I must confess that at present I do not see my way clearly. However, I will write again shortly."

Mr. Snyder derived the utmost enjoyment from the report. He liked the substance of it, and above all he was tickled by the bitter tone of frustration which characterized it. Oakes was baffled, and his knowledge of Oakes told him that the sensation of being baffled was gall and wormwood to that high-spirited young man. Whatever might be the result of this investigation, it would teach him the virtue of patience.

He wrote his assistant a short note:

"Dear Oakes,

"Your report received. You certainly seem to have got the hard case which, I hear, you were pining for. Don't build too much on plausible motives in a case of this sort. Fauntleroy, the London murderer, killed a woman for no other reason than that she had thick ankles. Many years ago I myself was on a case where a man murdered an intimate friend because of a dispute about a bet. My experience is that five murderers out of ten act on the whim of the moment, without anything which, properly speaking, you could call a motive at all.

Yours very cordially,
Paul Snyder

P.S. I don't think much of your Pickett theory. However, you're in charge. I wish you luck."

Young Mr. Oakes was not enjoying himself. For the first time in his life the self-confidence which characterized all his actions seemed to be failing him. The change had taken place almost overnight. The fact that the case had the appearance of presenting the unusual had merely stimulated him at first. But then doubts had crept in and the problem had begun to appear insoluble.

True, he had only just taken it up, but something told him that, for all the progress he was likely to make, he might just as well have been working on it steadily for a month. He was completely baffled. And every moment which he spent in the Excelsior boardinghouse made it clearer to him that that infernal old woman with the pale eyes thought him an incompetent fool. It was that, more than anything, which made him acutely conscious of his lack of success.

His nerves were being sorely troubled by the quiet scorn of Mrs. Pickett's gaze. He began to think that perhaps he had been a shade too self-confident and abrupt in the short interview which he had had with her on his arrival.

As might have been expected, his first act, after his brief interview with Mrs. Pickett, was to examine the room where the tragedy had taken place. The body was gone, but otherwise nothing had been moved.

Oakes belonged to the magnifying-glass school of detection. The first thing he did on entering the room was to make a careful examination of the floor, the walls, the furniture, and the window sill. He would have hotly denied the assertion that he did this because it looked well, but he would have been hard put to it to advance any other reason.

If he discovered anything, his discoveries were entirely negative and served only to deepen the mystery. As Mr. Snyder had said, there was no chimney, and nobody could have entered through the locked door.

There remained the window. It was small, and apprehensiveness, perhaps, of the possibility of burglars had caused the proprietress to make it doubly secure with two iron bars. No human being could have squeezed his way through.

It was late that night that he wrote and dispatched to headquarters the report which had amused Mr. Snyder . . .

Two days later Mr. Snyder sat at his desk, staring with wide unbelieving eyes at a telegram he had just received. It read as follows:

HAVE SOLVED GUNNER MYSTERY. RETURNING. OAKES.

Mr. Snyder narrowed his eyes and rang the bell.

"Send Mr. Oakes to me directly he arrives," he said.

He was pained to find that his chief emotion was one of bitter annoyance. The swift solution of such an apparently insoluble problem would reflect the highest credit of the agency, and there were picturesque circumstances connected with the case which would make it popular with the newspapers and lead to its being given a great deal of publicity.

Yet, in spite of all this, Mr. Snyder was annoyed. He realized now how large a part the desire to reduce Oakes's self-esteem had played with him. He further realized, looking at the thing honestly, that he had been firmly convinced that the young man would not come within a mile of a reasonable solution of the mystery. He had desired only that his failure would prove a valuable educational experience for him. For he believed that failure at this particular point in his career would make Oakes a more valuable asset to the agency.

But now here Oakes was, within a ridiculously short space of time, returning to the fold, not humble and defeated, but triumphant. Mr. Snyder looked forward with apprehension to the young man's probable demeanor under the intoxicating influence of victory.

His apprehensions were well grounded. He had barely finished the third of the series of cigars which, like milestones, marked the progress of his afternoon, when the door opened and young Oakes entered. Mr Snyder could not repress a faint moan at the sight of him. One glance was enough to tell him that his worst fears were realized.

"I got your telegram," said Mr. Snyder.

Oakes nodded. "It surprised you, eh?" he asked.

Mr. Snyder resented the patronizing tone of the question, but he had resigned himself to be patronized, and managed to keep his anger in check.

"Yes," he replied, "I must say it did surprise me. I didn't gather from your report that you had even found a clue. Was it the Indian theory that turned the trick?"

Oakes laughed tolerantly. "Oh, I never really believed that preposterous theory for one moment. I just put it in to round out my report. I hadn't begun to think about the case then—not really think."

Mr Snyder, nearly exploding with wrath, extended his cigar case. "Light up and tell me all about it," he said, controlling his anger.

"Well, I won't say I haven't earned this," said Oakes, puffing away. He let the ash of his cigar fall delicately to the floor—another action which seemed significant to his employer. As a rule his assistants, unless particularly pleased with themselves, used the ashtray.

"My first act on arriving," Oakes said, "was to have a talk with Mrs. Pickett. A very dull old woman."

"Curious. She struck me as rather intelligent."

"Not on your life. She gave me no assistance whatever. I then examined the room where the death had taken place. It was exactly as you described it. There was no chimney, the door had been locked on the inside, and the one window was too high up. At first sight it looked extremely unpromising. Then I had a chat with some of the other boarders. They had nothing of any importance to contribute. Most of them simply gibbered. I then gave up trying to get help from the outside and resolved to rely on my own intelligence."

He smiled triumphantly. "It is a theory of mine, Mr. Snyder, which I have found valuable, that in nine cases out of ten remarkable things don't happen."

"I don't quite follow you there," Mr. Snyder interrupted.

"I will put it another way, if you like. What I mean is that the simplest explanation is nearly always the right one. Consider this case. It seemed impossible that there should have been any reasonable explanation of the man's death. Most men would have worn themselves out guessing at wild theories. If I had started to do that, I should have been guessing now. As it is—here I am. I trusted to my belief that nothing remarkable ever happens, and I won out."

Mr. Snyder sighed softly. Oakes was entitled to a certain amount of gloating, but there could be no doubt that his way of telling a story was downright infuriating.

"I believe in the logical sequence of events. I refuse to accept effects unless they are preceded by causes. In other words, with all due respect to your possibly contrary opinions, Mr. Snyder, I simply decline to believe in a murder unless there was a motive for it. The first thing I set myself to ascertain was—what was the motive for the murder of Captain Gunner? And after thinking it over and making every possible inquiry, I decided that there was no motive. Therefore, there was no murder."

Mr. Snyder's mouth opened, and he obviously was about to protest. But he appeared to think better of it and Oakes proceeded: "I then tested the suicide theory. What motive was there for suicide? There was no motive. Therefore, there was no suicide."

This time Mr. Snyder spoke. "You haven't been spending the last few days in the wrong house by any chance, have you? You will be telling me next that there wasn't any dead man."

Oakes smiled. "Not at all. Captain John Gunner was dead, all right. As the medical evidence proved, he died of the bite of a cobra. It was a small cobra which came from Java."

Mr. Snyder stared at him. "How do you know?"

"I do know, beyond any possibility of doubt."

"Did you see the snake?"

Oakes shook his head.

"Then, how in heaven's name—"

"I have enough evidence to make a jury convict Mr. Snake without leaving the box."

"Then suppose you tell me this. How did your cobra from Java get out of the room?"

"By the window," replied Oakes impassively.

"How can you possibly explain that? You say yourself that the window was too high up."

"Nevertheless, it got out by the window. The logical sequence of events is proof enough that it was in the room. It killed Captain Gunner there and left traces of its presence outside. Therefore, as the window was the only exit, it must have escaped by that route. Somehow it got out of that window."

"What do you mean—it left traces of its presence outside?"

"It killed a dog in the back yard behind the house," Oakes said. "The window of Captain Gunner's room projects out over it. It is full of boxes and litter and there are a few stunted shrubs scattered about. In fact, there is enough cover to hide any small object like the body of a dog. That's why it was not discovered at first. The maid at the Excelsior came on it the morning after I sent you my report while she was emptying a box of ashes in the yard. It was just an ordinary stray dog without collar or license. The analyst examined the body and found that the dog had died of the bite of a cobra."

"But you didn't find the snake?"

"No. We cleaned out that yard till you could have eaten your breakfast there, but the snake had gone. It must have escaped through the door of the yard, which was standing ajar. That was a couple of days ago, and there has been no further tragedy. In all likelihood it is dead. The nights are pretty cold now, and it would probably have died of exposure."

"But I just don't understand how a cobra got to Southampton," said the amazed Mr. Snyder.

"Can't you guess it? I told you it came from Java."

"How did you know it did?"

"Captain Muller told me. Not directly, but I pieced it together from what he said. It seems that an old shipmate of Captain Gunner's was living in Java. They corresponded, and occasionally this man would send the captain a present as a mark of his esteem. The last present he sent was a crate of bananas. Unfortunately, the snake must have got in unnoticed. That's why I told you the cobra was a small one. Well, that's my case against Mr. Snake, and short of catching him with the goods, I don't see how I could have made out a stronger one. Don't you agree?"

It went against the grain for Mr. Snyder to acknowledge defeat, but he was a fair-minded man, and he was forced to admit that Oakes did certainly seem to have solved the impossible.

"I congratulate you, my boy," he said as heartily as he could. "To be completely frank, when you started out, I didn't think you could do it. By the way, I suppose Mrs. Pickett was pleased?"

"If she was, she didn't show it. I'm pretty well convinced she hasn't enough sense to be pleased at anything. However, she has invited me to dinner with her tonight. I imagine she'll be as boring as usual, but she made such a point of it I had to accept."

For some time after Oakes had gone, Mr. Snyder sat smoking and thinking, in embittered meditation. Suddenly there was brought the card of Mrs. Pickett, who would be grateful if he could spare her a few moments. Mr. Snyder was glad to see Mrs. Pickett. He was a student of character, and she had interested him at their first meeting. There was something about her which had seemed to him unique, and he welcomed this second chance of studying her at close range.

She came in and sat down stiffly, balancing herself on the extreme edge of the chair in which a short while before young Oakes had lounged so luxuriously.

"How are you, Mrs. Pickett?" said Mr. Snyder genially. "I'm very glad that you could find time to pay me a visit. Well, so it wasn't murder after all."

"Sir?"

"I've been talking to Mr. Oakes, whom you met as James Burton," said the detective. "He has told me all about it."

"He told *me* all about it," said Mrs. Pickett dryly.

Mr. Snyder looked at her inquiringly. Her manner seemed more suggestive than her words.

"A conceited, headstrong young fool," said Mrs. Pickett.

It was no new picture of his assistant that she had drawn. Mr. Snyder had often drawn it himself, but at the present juncture it surprised him. Oakes, in his hour of triumph, surely did not deserve this sweeping condemnation.

"Did not Mr. Oakes's solution of the mystery satisfy you, Mrs. Pickett?"

"No."

"It struck me as logical and convincing," Mr. Snyder said.

"You may call it all the fancy names you please, Mr. Snyder. But Mr. Oakes's solution was not the right one."

"Have you an alternative to offer?"

Mrs. Pickett tightened her lips.

"If you have, I should like to hear it."

"You will—at the proper time."

"What makes you so certain that Mr. Oakes is wrong?"

"He starts out with an impossible explanation and rests his whole case on it. There couldn't have been a snake in that room because it couldn't have gotten out. The window was too high."

"But surely the evidence of the dead dog?"

Mrs. Pickett looked at him as if he had disappointed her. "I had always heard *you* spoken of as a man with common sense, Mr. Snyder."

"I have always tried to use common sense."

"Then why are you trying now to make yourself believe that something happened which could not possibly have happened just because it fits in with something which isn't easy to explain?"

"You mean that there is another explanation of the dead dog?" Mr. Snyder asked.

"Not *another*. What Mr. Oakes takes for granted is not an explanation. But there is a common-sense explanation, and if he had not been so headstrong and conceited he might have found it."

"You speak as if you had found it," said Mr. Snyder.

"I have." Mrs. Pickett leaned forward as she spoke, and stared at him defiantly.

Mr. Snyder started. "*You* have?"

"Yes."

"What is it?"

"You will know before tomorrow. In the meantime try and think it out for yourself. A successful and prosperous detective agency like yours, Mr. Snyder, ought to do something in return for a fee."

There was something in her manner so reminiscent of the schoolteacher reprimanding a recalcitrant pupil that Mr. Snyder's sense of humor came to his rescue. "We do our best, Mrs. Pickett," he said. "But you mustn't forget that we are only human and cannot guarantee results."

Mrs. Pickett did not pursue the subject. Instead, she proceeded to astonish Mr. Snyder by asking him to swear out a warrant for the arrest of a man known to them both on a charge of murder.

Mr. Snyder's breath was not often taken away in his own office. As a rule he received his clients' communications calmly, strange as they often were. But at her words he gasped. The thought crossed his mind that Mrs. Pickett might be mentally unbalanced.

Mrs. Pickett was regarding him with an unfaltering stare. To all outward appearances she was the opposite of unbalanced. "But you can't swear out a warrant without evidence," he told her.

"I have evidence," she replied firmly.

"Precisely what kind of evidence?" he demanded.

"If I told you now you would think that I was out of my mind."

"But, Mrs. Pickett, do you realize what you are asking me to do? I cannot make this agency responsible for the arbitrary arrest of a man on the strength of a single individual's suspicions. It might ruin me. At the least it would made me a laughingstock."

"Mr. Snyder, you may use your own judgment whether or not to swear out that warrant. You will listen to what I have to say, and you will see for yourself how the crime was committed. If after that you feel that you cannot make the arrest I will accept your decision. I know who killed Captain Gunner," she said. "I knew it from the beginning. But I had no proof. Now things have come to light and everything is clear."

Against his judgment Mr. Snyder was impressed. This woman had the magnetism which makes for persuasiveness.

"It—it sounds incredible." Even as he spoke, he remembered that it had long been a professional maxim of his that nothing was incredible, and he weakened still further.

"Mr. Snyder, I ask you to swear out that warrant."

The detective gave in. "Very well," he said.

Mrs. Pickett rose. "If you will come and dine at my house tonight I think I can prove to you that it will be needed. Will you come?"

"I'll come," promised Mr. Snyder.

Mr. Snyder arrived at the Excelsior and shortly after he was shown into the little private sitting room where he found Oakes, the third guest of the evening unexpectedly arrived.

Mr. Snyder looked curiously at the newcomer. Captain Muller had a peculiar fascination for him. It was not Mr. Snyder's habit to trust overmuch to appearances. But he could not help admitting that there was something about this man's aspect, something odd—an unnatural aspect of gloom. He bore himself like one carrying a heavy burden. His eyes were dull, his face haggard. The next moment the detective was reproaching himself with allowing his imagination to run away with his calmer judgment.

The door opened and Mrs. Pickett came in.

To Mr. Snyder one of the most remarkable points about the dinner was the peculiar metamorphosis of Mrs. Pickett from the brooding silent woman he had known to the gracious and considerate hostess.

Oakes appeared also to be overcome with surprise, so much so that he was unable to keep his astonishment to himself. He had come prepared to endure a dull evening absorbed in grim silence, and he found himself instead opposite a bottle of champagne of a brand and year which commanded his utmost respect. What was even more incredible, his hostess had transformed herself into a pleasant old lady whose only aim seemed to be to make him feel at home.

Beside each of the guest's plates was a neat paper parcel. Oakes picked his up and stared at it in wonderment. "Why, this is more than a party souvenir, Mrs. Pickett," he said. "It's the kind of mechanical marvel I've always wanted to have on my desk."

"I'm glad you like it, Mr. Oakes," Mrs. Pickett said, smiling. "You must not think of me simply as a tired old woman whom age has completely defeated. I am an ambitious hostess. When I give these little parties, I like to make them a success. I want each of you to remember this dinner."

"I'm sure I will."

Mrs. Pickett smiled again. "I think you all will. You, Mr. Snyder." She paused. "And you, Captain Muller."

To Mr. Snyder there was so much meaning in her voice as she

said this that he was amazed that it conveyed no warning to Muller. Captain Muller, however, was already drinking heavily. He looked up when addressed and uttered a sound which might have been taken for an expression of polite acquiescence. Then he filled his glass again.

Mr. Snyder's parcel revealed a watch charm fashioned in the shape of a tiny candid-eye camera. "That," said Mrs. Pickett, "is a compliment to your profession." She leaned toward the captain. "Mr. Snyder is a detective, Captain Muller."

He looked up. It seemed to Mr. Snyder that a look of fear lit up his heavy eyes for an instant. It came and went, if indeed it came at all, so swiftly that he could not be certain. "So?" said Captain Muller. He spoke quite evenly, with just the amount of interest which such an announcement would naturally produce.

"Now for yours, Captain," said Oakes. "I guess it's something special. It's twice the size of mine, anyway."

It may have been something in the old woman's expression as she watched Captain Muller slowly tearing the paper that sent a thrill of excitement through Mr. Snyder. Something seemed to warn him of the approach of a psychological moment. He bent forward eagerly.

There was a strangled gasp, a thump, and onto the table from the captain's hands there fell a little harmonica. There was no mistaking the look on Muller's face now. His cheeks were like wax, and his eyes, so dull till then, blazed with a panic and horror which he could not repress. The glasses on the table rocked as he clutched at the cloth.

Mrs. Pickett spoke. "Why, Captain Muller, has it upset you? I thought that, as his best friend, the man who shared his room, you would value a memento of Captain Gunner. How fond you must have been of him for the sight of his harmonica to be such a shock."

The captain did not speak. He was staring fascinated at the thing on the table. Mrs. Pickett turned to Mr. Snyder. Her eyes, as they met his, held him entranced.

"Mr. Snyder, as a detective, you will be interested in a curious and very tragic affair which happened in this house a few days ago. One of my boarders, Captain Gunner, was found dead in his room. It was the room which he shared with Mr. Muller. I am very proud of the reputation of my house, Mr. Snyder, and it was a blow to me that this should have happened. I applied to an agency for a detective, and they sent me a stupid boy, with nothing to recommend him except his belief in himself. He said that Captain Gunner had died by accident, killed by a snake which had come out of a crate of bananas. I knew better. I knew that Captain Gunner had been murdered. Are you listening, Captain Muller? This will interest you, as you were such a friend of his."

The captain did not answer. He was staring straight before him. as if he saw something invisible in eyes forever closed in death.

"Yesterday we found the body of a dog. It had been killed, as Captain Gunner had been, by the poison of a snake. The boy from the agency said that this was conclusive. He said that the snake had escaped from the room after killing Captain Gunner and had in turn killed the dog. I knew that to be impossible, for, if there had been a snake in that room it could not have made its escape."

Her eyes flashed and became remorselessly accusing. "It was not a snake that killed Captain Gunner. It was a cat. Captain Gunner had a friend who hated him. One day, in opening a crate of bananas, this friend found a snake. He killed it, and extracted the poison. He knew Captain Gunner's habits. He knew that he played a harmonica. This man also had a cat. He knew that cats hated the sound of a harmonica. He had often seen this particular cat fly at Captain Gunner and scratch him when he played. He took the cat and covered its claws with the poison. And then he left the cat in the room with Captain Gunner. He knew what would happen."

Oakes and Mr. Snyder were on their feet. Captain Muller had not moved. He sat there, his fingers gripping the cloth. Mrs. Pickett rose and went to a closet. She unlocked the door. "Kitty!" she called. "Kitty! Kitty!" A black cat ran swiftly out into the room. With a clatter and a crash of crockery and a ringing of glass the table heaved, rocked, and overturned as Muller staggered to his feet. He threw up his hands as if to ward something off. A choking cry came from his lips. "Gott! Gott!"

Mrs. Pickett's voice rang through the room, cold and biting. "Captain Muller, you murdered Captain Gunner!"

The captain shuddered. Then mechanically he replied, "Gott! Yes, I killed him."

"You heard, Mr. Snyder," said Mrs. Pickett. "He has confessed before witnesses."

Muller allowed himself to be moved toward the door. His arm in Mr. Snyder's grip felt limp. Mrs. Pickett stopped and took something from the debris on the floor. She rose, holding the harmonica.

"You are forgetting your souvenir, Captain Muller," she said.

H. R. F. Keating

Mrs. Craggs' Sixth Sense

It was a good thing that Mrs. Craggs had had her twinges. If she had not, and had not acted on them, the nasty little somthing-or-other that had developed just under the skin on her right slbow could not have been dealt with so easily; and more important, poor old Professor Partheman would have been in much worse trouble than he was. But twinges she did have, and the doctor she went to recommended a minor operation. With the consequence that Mrs. Craggs "did for" Professor Partheman that particular week on Wednesday and not on Thursday.

And so she set eyes on Ralph.

He was doing no more than mow the lawn in front of the professor's ground-floor flat and from time to time taking a boxful of clippings round to the compost heap behind the shrubbery. But that was enough for Mrs. Craggs.

"Excuse me for mentioning it, sir," she said to the professor as she tucked her wages into her purse, "but I would just like to say a word about that chap."

"What chap, Mrs. Craggs? I was not aware that we had discussed any chap."

The old professor was a bit spiky sometimes, but Mrs. Craggs liked working for him because, despite his great age, there he was always beavering away at his writing and papers, doing his job and no messing about. So she ignored the objection and went on with what she had to say.

"That feller what you've got in to mow your old bit of a lawn, sir."

"Ralph, Mrs. Craggs," said the professor. "A young man employed as domestic help over at Royal Galloway College and making a little extra on his day off. Now, what do you want to say about him?"

The professor glared, as if he already knew without realizing it that Mrs. Craggs had an adverse comment to make.

She took a good long breath.

"I don't think you ought to have him around, sir," she said. "I don't like the looks of him, and that's a fact."

"Mrs. Craggs," said the professor in the voice he had used to put down any number of uppish undergraduates, "that you do not 'like the looks' of Ralph may be a fact, but anything else you have said or implied about him most certainly is not. Now, do you know any facts to the young man's detriment?"

"Facts, I don't know, sir. But feelings I have. He'll do you now good and of that I'm certain sure."

"My dear good lady, are you really suggesting I should cease to offer the fellow employment just because of some mysterious feeling you have? What is it about his looks that you don't like, for heaves's sake?"

Mrs. Craggs thought. She had not up to that moment attempted to analyze her feeling. She had just had it. But overshelmingly.

After a little she managed to pin something down.

"I think it's the way he prowls, sir," she said. "Whenever he goes anywhere he prowls. Like an animal, sir. Like a—"

She searched her mind.

"A jaguar, sir. He prowls like one o' them jaguars. That's it."

"My dear Mrs. Craggs. You cannot really be telling me that all you have against the chap is the way he walks. It's too ridiculous."

But Mrs. Craggs was not so easily discouraged. She thought about the young gardener at intervals right up to the following Monday when she was next due at the professor's. She even was thinking about him during the minor operation which had been such a striking success. And when on the Monday she had been given her money she broached the subject again.

"That Ralph, sir. I hope as 'ow you've had second thoughts there."

"Second thoughts." The aged professor's parchment-white face was suffused with pinkness. "Let me tell you, my dear lady, I had no need for more than the swiftest of first thoughts. I have spent a lifetime dealing in facts, Mrs. Craggs, hard facts, and I'm scarcely likely to abandon them now. Not one word more, if you please."

Mrs. Craggs sighed. "As you like, sir."

But, though she said no more then, she made up her mind to do all that she could to protect the old professor from the jaguar she had seen prowling across hiw lawn carefully avoiding ever appearing to look in at the windows of the flat.

And, she thought, she had one way of perhaps obtaining some "facts." It so happened at that time that her friend of long standing, Mrs. Milhorne, was employed as a daily cleaner at Royal Galloway College. At the first oppotunity she paid her a visit at her home, though that was not unfortunately till the following Tuesday evening.

"Oh, yes, Ralph," said Mrs. Milhorne. "I always knew in my bones about him. Handsome he may have been, and sort of romantic, if you take my meaning, but I never tried to make up to 'im, no matter what they say."

"I'm sure you didn't, dear," said Mrs. Craggs, who knew her friend's susceptible nature. "But why do you go on about him as if he ain't there no more?"

"Because that's what he aidn't," said Mrs. Milhorne.

And then the whole story came out. Ralph had been dismissed about a fornight before, suspected of having brutally attacked a young Spanish maid at the college. The girl, Rosita by name, although battered about terribly and still actually off work, had refused to say who had caused her injuries. But, as Ralph had notoriously been attracted to her, no one really had had any doubt.

"'Spect he's back home now, wherever that is," said Mrs. Milhorne, and she sighed.

"No, he's not," Mrs. Craggs said. "I told you, dear. He's coming every Wednesday to mow old Professor Partheman's lawn, and the professor's got picture frames full of old coins, gold an' all. He's what's called one o' them new miserists. An' if that Ralph's just half o' what I think he is, he'll be planning to help himself there, 'specially now he's out of a job."

A red flush of excitement came up on Mrs. Milhorne's pallid face.

"We'll have to go to the rescue," she said. "Just like on telly. The United States Cavalry."

"Yes," said Mrs. Craggs. "Only when old Professor Partheman sees you a-galloping up, an' me come to that, you know what he'll do? He'll tell us to turn right roun' and gallop away again. Or he will unless we come waving somefacts on our little blue flags."

She stood considering.

"Rosita," she said at last. "She's got to be made to talk."

But since Rosita knew hardly a word of English and since she had obstinately persevered with her silence, Mrs. Craggs's plan seemed to run up against insuperable difficulties.

Only it was Mrs. Craggs's plan.

Introduced next morning to the room in which Rosita was resting, her fact still blotched with heavy bruises, Mrs. Craggs first gave her a heartwarming smile and then joined her in a nice cuppa, selecting from a plate of biscuits the sweetest and stickiest and pressing them on the Spanish girl with such hearty insistence that if the interview was to do nothing else it would at least add some ounces to Rosita's already deliciously buxom figure. But Mrs. Craggs had only just begun.

" 'Ere," she said, when she judged the moment ripe. "You know I works for an old professor?"

Rosita would hardly have understood this abruptly proffered piece of information had not Mrs. Craggs at the same time jumped to her feet and first mimed to a T the old professor, frail as a branch of dried twigs, and then had imitated herself brushing and dusting and polishing fit to bust.

"*Si, si,*" said the Spanish girl, eyes alight and dancing. "Work, *si, si.* Ol' man, *si, si.*"

"Ah, you're right, dear," Mrs. Craggs said. "But I ain't the only one what works fer 'im."

Another bout of miming.

"*Ah, si. Si. Jardinero.*"

"Yes," said Mrs. Craggs. "A gardener. Ralph."

And the vigor she put into saying the name sent at once a wave of pallor across the Spanish girl's plump and pretty face.

"*Ah, si,* Ralph."

"Yes, dear. You got it nicely. But, listen. That old prof, he's got a lot o' valu'ble coins in his study. His study, see."

In place of Mrs. Craggs there came a picture of an ancient scholar bent over his books, scribbling rapidly on sheet after sheet of paper and from time to time taking a rare and precious old coin and scrutinizing it with extraordinary care.

"*Ah, si.* He have *antigo dinero, si.*" And then suddenly a new expression swept over her face. "*Dios,*" she said. "Ralph!"

After that it was the work of only half a minute for Mrs. Craggs to be seated at the driving wheel of some vehicle capable of the most amazing speed, and then to reincarnate her picture of Professor Partheman and put onto his lips a stream of sound that could not have meant anything to anybody, but made it perfectly clear that the old man was a fluent speaker of Spanish. Rosita seized a coat and scarf and showed herself ready for instant departure.

"But, hurry," said Mrs. Craggs. "We ain't got much time to lose. That Ralph gets there by two o'clock."

They had not much time, but in theory they had enough. Buses from outside the college ran at twenty-minute intervals; the journey to the professor's took only half an hour or a little more, and it was only just 12:45.

But.

But bus services everywhere suffer from shortage of staff, and when they do they are apt simply to miss one particular run. The run missed that day was the one due to pass Royal Galloway College at 1:00 P.M. exactly. That need not have mattered. The 1:20 would bring them to within a couple of hundred yards of the professor's by 1:55 at the latest. And it arrived at the college on the dot. And in the words of its conductor it "suffered a mechanical breakdown" just five minutes later.

Mrs. Craggs posted herself plank in the middle of the road. In less than a minute a car pulled to a halt. An irate lady motorist poked her head out. Mrs. Craggs marched up to her.

"Life an' death," she said. "It may be a matter o' life an' death. We gotter get to Halliman's Corner before two o'clock."

The lady motorist, without a word, opened the car's doors. Mrs. Craggs, Mrs. Milhorne, and Rosita piled in. Once on the go, Mrs. Craggs explained in more detail. The lady motorist grew excited. But she was a lady who relied more on the feel of the countryside than on signposts or maps. And a quarter of an hour later all four had to admit they had no idea where they were.

"The telephone," suggested the lady motorist. "We shall have to go to a house and telephone your professor."

"No good," said Mrs. Craggs. "He don't never answer it when he's working. Rare old miracle he is like that. Ring, ring, ring, an' never a blind bit o' notice."

"I'd die out o' curiosity," put in Mrs. Milhorne.

"So would I, dear," said Mrs. Craggs. "But that ain't getting the United States Cavalry to the wagon train."

They resumed their progress then, eyes strained to catch the least sign of anything helpful. And it was Mrs. Craggs who spotted something.

"That old plastic sack on top o' that gatepost," she said. "I remembers it from the bus coming out. It's that way. That way."

The lady motorist, recognizing an infallible sign when she heard one, turned at once.

"We'll be there in five minutes," she shouted.

"Yes," answered Mrs. Craggs. "An' it's two minutes to two now."

There was a little argument about whose watch was right, but all agreed that two o'clock was bound to come before they reached their destination. And it did.

"Quick," said Mrs. Craggs, as at last they got to the familiar corner. "Up that way. We may not be too late. He may not've doen it yet."

But she could not see in her mind's eye that prowling jaguar carefully mowing the old professor's lawn before he struck. And she could see, all too clearly, the thornlike obstinate old man defending his property to the last. And she could see frail thorns, spiky though they might be, all too easily being crushed to splinters.

The car pulled up with a screech of brakes. Mrs. Craggs was out of it before it had stopped. She hurled open the gate. The graden was empty. Ominously empty. Mrs. Craggs tore across the unmown lawn like an avenging amazon. She burst into the professor's study.

The professor was sitting holding up an ancient coin, scrutinizing it with extraordinary care.

"Ralph!" Mrs. Craggs burst out. "Where's Ralph?"

Professor Partheman turned to her.

"Ah, yes, Ralph," he said. "Well, Mrs. Craggs, I happened to read in *The Times* this morning a most interesting article about research at Johns Hopkins University in America proving that women do have a particular skill in what is called nonverbal communication. Or, to put it in popular terms, their instinct is to be trusted. So with that fact at my disposal I decided to give credence to your—ahem—feeling and left a note on the gate telling Ralph I no longer required him. Yes, you can trust a woman's intuition, Mrs. Craggs. You can trust it for a fact."

"Yes, sir," said Mrs. Craggs.

Cornell Woolrich

Death Between Dances

Every Saturday night you'd see them together at the country-club dance. Together, and yet far apart. One sitting back against the wall, never moving from there, never once getting up to dance the whole evening long. The other swirling about the floor, passing from partner to partner, never still a moment.

The two daughters of Walter Brainard (widower, 52, stocks and bonds, shoots 72 at golf, charter member of the country club).

Nobody seeing them for the first time ever took them for sisters. It wasn't only the difference in their ages, though that was great enough and seemed even greater than it actually was. There was about twelve years' difference between them, and fifty in outlook.

Even their names were peculiarly appropriate. Jane, as plain as her name, sitting there against the wall, dark hair drawn severely back from her forehead, watching the festivities through heavy-rimmed glasses that gave her an expression of owlish inscrutability. And Sunny, dandelion-colored hair, blue eyes, a dancing sunbeam, glinting around the floor, no one boy ever able to hold her for very long (you can't make sunbeams stay in one place if they don't want to). Although Tom Reed, until just recently, had had better luck at it than the rest. But the last couple of Saturday nights he seemed to be slipping or something; he'd become just one of the second-stringers again.

Sunny was usually in pink, one shade of it or another. She favored pink; it was her color. She reminded you of pink spun-sugar candy. Because it's so good, and so sweet, and so harmless. But it also melts so easily . . .

One of them had a history, one hadn't. Well, at eighteen you can't be expected to have a history yet. You can make one for yourself if you set out to, but you haven't got it yet. And as for the history—Jane's—it wasn't strictly that, either, because history is hard-and-fast facts, and this was more of a formless thing, a whispered rumor, a half forgotten legend. It had never lived, but it had never died either.

Some sort of blasting infatuation that had come along and changed her from what she'd been then, at eighteen—the darling of the dance floors, as her sister was now—into what she was now: a wallflower, an onlooker who didn't take part. She'd gone away for a while around that time, and then she'd suddenly been back again.

From the time she'd come back, she'd been as she was now. That was all that was definitely known—the rest was pure surmise. Nobody had ever found out exactly who the man was. It was generally agreed that it wasn't anyone from around here. Some said there had been a quiet annulment. Some—more viperishly—said there hadn't been anything to annul.

One thing was certain. She was a wallflower by choice and not by compulsion. As far back as people could remember, anyone who had ever asked her to dance received only a shake of her head. They stopped asking, finally. She wanted to be left alone, so she was. Maybe, it was suggested, she had first met him, whoever he was, while dancing, and that was why she had no use for dancing any more. Then in that case, others wondered, why did she come so regularly to the country club? To this there were a variety of answers, none of them wholly satisfactory.

"Maybe," some shrugged, "it's because her father's a charter member of the club—she thinks it's her duty to be present."

"Maybe," others said, "she sees ghosts on the dance floor—sees someone there that the rest of us can't see."

"And maybe," still others suggested, but not very seriously, "she's waiting for him to come back to her—thinks he'll suddenly show up sometime in the Saturday-night crowd and come over to her and claim her. That's why she won't dance with anyone else."

But the owlish glasses gave no hint of what was lurking behind them; whether hope or resignation, love or indifference or hate.

At exactly 9:45 this Saturday, this Washington's Birthday Saturday, tonight, the dance is on full-blast; the band is playing an oldie, "The Object of My Affections," Number Twenty in the leader's book. And Jane is sitting back against the wall. Sunny is twinkling about on the floor, this time in the arms of Tom Reed, the boy who loved her all through high school, the man who still does, now, at this very moment—

She stopped short, right in the middle of the number, detached his arm from her waist, and stepped back from its half embrace.

"Wait here, Tom. I just remembered. I have to make a phone call."

"I no sooner get you than I lose you again."

But she'd already turned and was moving away from him, looking back over her shoulder now.

He tried to follow her. She laughed and held him back. A momentary flattening of her hands against his shirtfront was enough to do that. "No, you can't come with me. Oh, don't look so dubious. It's just to Martha, back at our house. Something I forgot to tell her when we left. You wouldn't be interested."

"But we'll lose this dance."

"I'll give you—I'll give you one later, to make up for it," she promised. "I'll foreclose on somebody else's." She gave him a smile, and even a little wink, and that held him. "Now, be a good boy and stay in here."

She made sure that he was standing still first. It was like leaving a lifesize toy propped up—you wait a second to make sure it won't fall over. Then she turned and went out into the foyer.

She looked back at him from there, once more. He was standing obediently stock-still in the middle of the dance floor like an ownerless pup, everyone else circling around him. She raised a cautioning index finger, shook it at him. Then she whisked from sight.

She went over to the checkroom cubbyhole.

"Will you let me have that now, Marie."

"Leaving already, Miss Brainard?" The girl raised a small overnight case from the floor—it hadn't been placed on the shelves, where it might have been seen and recognized—and passed it to her.

Sunny handed her something. "You haven't seen me go, though."

"I understand, Miss Brainard," the girl said.

She hurried out of the club with it. She went over to where the cars were parked, found a small coffee-colored roadster, and put the case on the front seat.

Then she got in after it and drove off.

The clubhouse lights receded in the indigo February darkness. The music got fainter, and then you couldn't hear it any more. It stayed on in her mind, though: still playing, like an echo.

> "The object of my affection
> Can change my complexion
> From white to rosy-red—"

The car purred along the road. She looked very lovely, and a little wild, her uncovered hair streaming backward in the wind. The stars up above seemed to be winking at her, as though she and they shared the same conspiracy.

After a while she took one hand from the wheel and fumbled in the glittering little drawstring bag dangling from her wrist.

She took out a very crumpled note, its envelope gone. The note looked as though it had been hastily crushed and thrust away to protect if from discovery immediately after first being received.

She smoothed it out now as best she could and reread it carefully by the dashboard light. A part of it, anyway.

"—There's a short cut that'll bring you to me even quicker, darling. No one knows of it but me, and now I'm sharing it with you. It will keep you from taking the long way around, on the main road, and risk being seen by anyone. Just before you come to that lighted filling station at the intersection, turn off, sharp left. Even though there doesn't seem to be anything there, keep going, don't be frightened. You'll pick up a back lane, and that'll bring you safely to me. I'll be counting the minutes—"

She pressed it to her lips, the crumpled paper, and kissed it fervently. Love is a master alchemist: it can turn base things to gold.

She put it back in her bag. The stars were still with her, winking. The music was still with her, playing for her alone.

"Every time he holds my hand
And tells me that he's mine."

Just before she came to that lighted filling station at the intersection, she swung the wheel and turned off sharp left into gritty nothingness that rocked and swayed the car.

Her headlights picked up a screen of trees and she went around to the back of them. She found a disused dirt lane there—as love had promised her she would—and clung to it over rises and hollows, and through shrubbery that hissed at her.

And then at last a little rustic lodge. A hidden secret place. Cheerful amber light streaming out to welcome her. Another car already there, offside in the darkness—his.

She braked in front of it. She took out her mirror, and by the dashboard light she smoothed her hair and touched a golden tube of lipstick lightly to her mouth. Very lightly, for there would be kisses that would take it away again soon.

She tapped the horn, just once.

Then she waited for him to come out to her.

The stars kept winking up above the pointed fir trees. Their humor was a little crueler now, as though someone were the butt of it. And in the lake that glistened like dark-blue patent leather down the other way, their winking still went on, upside down in the water.

She tapped her horn again, more heavily this time, twice in quick succession.

He didn't come out. The yellow thread outlining the lodge-door remained as it was; it grew no wider.

An owl hooted somewhere in the trees, but she wasn't afraid. She'd only just learned what love was; how should she have had time to learn what fear was?

She opened the car door abruptly and got out. Her footfalls crunched on the sandy ground that sloped down from here all the way to the lake. Silly, fragile sandals meant for the dance floor, their spike heels pecking into the crusty frosty ground.

She went up onto the plank porch, and there they sounded hollow. She knocked on the door, and that sounded hollow too. Like when you knock on an empty shell of something.

The door moved at last, but it was her own knock that had done it; it was unfastened. The yellow thread widened.

She pushed it back, and warmth and brightness gushed out, the night was driven to a distance.

"Hoo-hoo," she called softly. "You have a caller. There's a young lady at your door, to see you."

A fire was blazing in the natural-stone fireplace, gilding the walls and coppering the ceiling with its restless tides of reflection. There was a table, all set and readied for two. The feast of love. Yellow candles were twinkling on it; their flames had flattened for a moment, now they straightened again as she came in and closed the door behind her.

Flowers were on it in profusion, and sparkling, spindly-stemmed glasses. And under it there was a gilt ice pail, with a pair of gold-capped bottles protruding from it at different angles.

And on the wooden peg projecting from the wall, his hat and coat were hanging. With that scarf she knew so well dangling carelessly from one of the pockets.

She laughed a little, mischievously.

As she passed the table, on her way deeper into the long room, she helped herself to a salted almond, crunched it between her teeth. She laughed again, like a little girl about to tease somebody. Then she picked up a handful of almonds and began throwing them one by one against the closed bedroom-door, the way you throw gravel against a windowpane to attract someone's attention behind it.

Each one went *tick!* and fell to the floor.

At last, when she'd used up all the almonds, she gave vent to a deep breath of exasperation, that was really only pretended exasperation, and stepped directly up to it and knocked briskly.

"Are you asleep in there, or what?" she demanded. "Is this any way to receive your intended? After I come all the way up here—"

Silence.

A log in the fire cracked sharply. One of the gilt-topped bottles slumped lower in the pail, the ice supporting it crumbling.

"I'm coming in there, ready or not."

She flung the door open.

He was asleep. But in a distorted way, as she'd never yet seen anyone sleep. On the floor alongside the bed, with his face turned upward to the ceiling, and one arm flung over his eyes protectively.

Then she saw the blood. Stilled, no longer flowing. Not very old, but not new either.

She ran to him, for a second only, tried to raise him, tried to rouse him. And all she got was soddenness. Then after that, she couldn't touch him any more, couldn't go near him again. It wasn't him any more. He'd gone, and left this—this *thing*—behind him. This awful thing that didn't even talk to you, take you in its arms, hold you to it.

She didn't scream. Death was too new to her. She barely knew what it was. She hadn't lived long enough.

She began to cry. Not because he was dead, but because she'd been cheated, she had no one to take her in his arms now. First heartbreak. First love. Those tears that never come more than once.

She was still kneeling there, near him.

Then she saw the gun lying there. Dark, ugly, dangerous-looking. His, but too far across the room for him to have used it himself. Even she, dimly, realized that. How could it get all the way over there, with him all the way over here?

She began crawling toward it on hands and knees.

Her hand went out toward it, hesitated, finally closed on it, picked it up. She knelt there, holding it between both hands, staring at it in fascinated horror—

"Drop that! Put it down!"

The voice was like a whip across her face, stinging in its suddenness, its lashing sharpness. Then leaving her quivering all over, as an aftermath.

Tom Reed was standing in the doorway like a tuxedoed phantom.

Bare-headed, coatless, just as he'd left the dance floor and run out after her into the cold of the February night.

"You fool," he breathed with soft, suppressed intensity. "You fool, oh you little fool!"

A single frightened whimper, like the mewing of a helpless kitten left out in the rain, sounded from her.

He went over to her, for she was crouched there incapable of movement; he raised her in his arms, caught her swiftly to him, turned her away with a gesture that was both rough and tender at the same time. The toe of his shoe edged deftly forward and the gun slithered out of her sight somewhere along the floor.

"I didn't do it!" she protested, terrified. "I didn't! Oh, Tom, I swear—"

"I know you didn't," he said almost impatiently. "I was right behind you coming up here. I would have heard the shot and I didn't."

All she could say to that was, "Oh, Tom," with a shudder.

"Yes, 'oh, Tom,' after the damage is done. Why wasn't it 'oh, Tom' before that?" His words were a rebuke, his gestures a consolation that belied them. "I saw you leave and came right after you. Who did you think you were fooling, with your phone-call home? You blind little thing. I was too tame for you. You had to have excitement. Well, now you've got it." And all the while his hand stroked the sobbing golden-haired head against his shoulder. "You wanted to know life. You couldn't wait. Well, now you do. How do you like it?"

"Is this—?" she choked.

"This is what it *can* be like if you don't watch where you're going."

"I'll never—I'll never—oh, Tom, I'll never—"

"I know," he said. "They all say that. All the little, helpless purring things. After it's too late."

Her head came up suddenly, in renewed terror. "Oh, Tom, is it too late?"

"Not if I can get you back to that dance unnoticed—you've only been away about half an hour—" He drew his head back, still holding her in his arms, and looked at her intently. "Who was he?"

"I met him last summer when I was away. All of a sudden he showed up here. I never expected him to. He's only been here a few days. I lost my head, I guess—"

"How is it nobody ever saw him around here, even the few days you say he's been here? Why did he make himself so inconspicuous?"

"He wanted it that way, and I don't know—I guess to me it seemed more romantic."

He murmured something under his breath that sounded like, "Sure, at eighteen it would." Then aloud, and quite bitterly, he said, "What was he hiding from? Who was he hiding from?"

"He was going to—we were going to be married," she said.

"You wouldn't have been married," he told her with quiet scorn.

She looked at him aghast.

"Oh, there would have been a ceremony, I suppose. For how long? A week or two, a month. And then you'd come creeping back alone. The kind that does his courting under cover doesn't stick to you for long."

"How do you know?" she said, crushed.

"Ask your sister Jane sometime. They say she found that out once, long ago. And look at her now. Embittered for all the rest of her life. Eaten up with hate—"

He changed the subject abruptly. He tipped up her chin and looked searchingly at her. "Are you all right now? Will you do just as I tell you? Will you be able to—go through with this, carry it off?"

She nodded. Her lips formed the words, barely audible, "If you stay with me."

"I'm with you. I was never so with you before."

With an arm about her waist, he led her over toward the door. As they reached and passed it, her head stirred slightly on his shoulder. He guessed its intent, quickly forestalled it with a quieting touch of his hand.

"Don't look at him. Don't look back. *He isn't there. You were never here either*. Those are the two things you have to keep saying to yourself. We've all had bad dreams at times, and this was yours. Now wait here outside the door a minute. I've got things to do. Don't watch me."

He left her and went back into the room again.

After a moment or two she couldn't resist: the horrid fascination was too strong, it was almost like a hypnotic compulsion. She crept back to the threshold, peered around the edge of the door-frame into the room beyond, and watched with bated breath what he was doing.

He went after the gun first. Got it back from where he'd kicked it. Picked it up and looked it over with painstaking care. He interrupted himself once to glance down at the form lying on the floor, and by some strange telepathy she knew that something about the gun had told him it belonged to the dead man, that it hadn't been brought in from outside. Perhaps something about its type or size that she would not have understood; she didn't know anything about guns.

Then she saw him break it open and do something to it with deft fingers, twist or spin something. A cartridge fell out into the palm of his hand. He stood that aside for a minute, upright on the edge of the dresser. Then he closed up the gun again. He took out his own handkerchief and rubbed the gun thoroughly all over with it.

Each time she thought he was through, he'd blow his breath on it and steam it up, and then rub it some more. He even pulled the whole length of the handkerchief through the little guard where the trigger was, and made that click emptily a couple of times.

He worked fast but he worked calmly, without undue excitement, keeping his presence of mind.

Finally he wrapped the handkerchief in its entirety around the butt so that his own bare hand didn't touch it. Holding it in that way, he knelt down by the man. He took the hand, took it by the very ends, by the fingers, and closed them around the gun, first subtracting the handkerchief. He pressed the fingers down on it, pressed them hard and repeatedly, the way you do when you want to take an impression of something.

Then he fitted them carefully around it in a grasping position; even pushed one, the index-finger, through that same trigger guard. He watched a minute to see if the gun would hold that way on its own, without his supporting hand around the outside of the other. It did; it dipped a little, but it stayed fast. Then very carefully he eased it, and the hand now holding it, back to the floor, left them there together.

Then he got up and went back to the cartridge. He saw her mystified little face peering in at him around the edge of the door.

"Don't watch, I told you," he rebuked her.

But she kept right on, and he went ahead without paying any further attention to her.

He took out a pocketknife and prodded away at the cartridge with it until he had it separated into two parts. Then he went back to the dead man and knelt down by him. What she saw him do next was sheer horror.

But she had only herself to blame; he'd warned her not to look.

He turned the head slightly, very carefully, until he'd revealed the small, dark, almost neat little hole, where the blood had originally come from.

He took one half of the dissected cartridge, tilted it right over it, and shook it gently back and forth. As though—as though he were salting the wound from a small shaker. Her hands flew to her mouth to stifle the gasp this tore from her.

He thrust the pieces of cartridge into his pocket, both of them. Then he struck a match. He held it for a moment to let the flame steady itself and shrink a little. Then he gave it a quick dab at the gunpowdered wound and then back again.

There was a tiny flash from the wound. For an instant it seemed to ignite. Then it went right out again. A slightly increased blackness remained around the wound now; he'd charred it. This time a sick moan escaped through her suppressing hands. She turned away at last.

When he came out he found her at the far end of the outside room with her back to him. She was twitching slightly, as though she'd just recovered from a nervous chill.

She couldn't bring herself to ask the question, but he could read it in her eyes when she turned to stare at him.

"The gun was his own, or the user wouldn't have left it behind. I had to do that other thing. A gun suicide's always a contact wound. They press it hard against themselves. And with a contact wound there are always powder burns."

Then he said with strange certainty, "A woman did it."

"How do you—?"

"I found this in there with him. There must have been tears at first, and then later she dropped it when she picked up the gun."

He handed it to her. There wasn't anything distinctive about it—just a gauzy handkerchief. No monogram, no design. It could have been anyone's, anyone in a million. A faint fragrance reached her, invisible as a finespun wire but just as tenuous and for a moment she wondered at the scent.

Like lilacs in the rain.

"I couldn't leave it in there," he explained, "because it doesn't match the setup as I've arranged it. It would have shown that somebody was in there, after all." He smiled grimly. "I'm doing somebody a big favor, a much bigger favor than she deserves. But I'm not doing it for her, I'm doing it for you, to keep even a whisper of your name from being brought into it."

Absently she thrust the wisp of stuff into her own evening bag, where she carried her own, drew the drawstring tight once more.

"Get rid of it," he advised. "You can do that easier than I can. But not anywhere around here, whatever you do."

He glanced back toward the inside room. "What else did you touch
in there—besides the gun?"

She shook her head. "I just stepped in and—you found me."

"You touched the door?"

She nodded.

He whipped out his handkerchief again, crouched low on one knee,
and like a strange sort of porter in a dinner jacket scoured the
doorknobs on both sides, in and out.

"What about these? Did you do that?" There were some almonds
lying on the floor.

"I threw them at the door, like pebbles—to attract his attention."

"A man about to do what he did wouldn't munch almonds." He
picked them up, all but one which had already been stepped on and
crushed. "One won't matter. He could have done that himself," he
told her. "Let me see your shoe." He bent down and peered at the
tilted sole. "It's on there. Get rid of them altogether when you get
home. Don't just scrape it; they have ways of bringing out things
like that."

"What about the whole supper table itself? It's for two."

"That'll have to stay. Whoever he was expecting didn't come and
in a fit of depression aging Romeo played his last role, alone. That'll
be the story it tells. At least it'll show that no one *did* come. If we
disturb a perfect setup like that, we may prove the opposite to what
we're trying to."

He put his arm about her. "Are you ready now? Come on, here we
go. And remember: *you were never here. None of this ever happened.*"

A sweep of his hand behind his back, a swing of the door, and the
light faded away—they were out in the starry blue night together.

"Whose car is that?"

"My own. The roadster Daddy gave me. I had Rufus run it down
to the club for me and leave it outside after we all left for the dance."

"Did he check it?"

"No, I told him not to."

He heaved a sigh of relief. "Good. We've got to get them both out
of here. I'll get in mine. You'll have to get back into the one you
brought, by yourself. I'll lead the way. Stick to my treads, so you
don't leave too clear a print. It will probably snow again before they
find him, and that'll save us."

He went on ahead to his own car, got in, and started the motor.
Suddenly he left it warming up, jumped out again, and came back

to her. "Here," he said abruptly, "hang onto this until I can get you back down there again." And pressed his lips to hers with a sort of tender encouragement.

It was the strangest kiss she'd ever had. It was one of the most selfless, one of the nicest.

The two cars trundled away, one behind the other. After a little while the echo of their going drifted back from the lonely lake. And then there was just silence.

The lights and the music, like a warm friendly tide, came swirling around her again. He stopped her for a moment, just outside the entrance, before they went in.

"Did anyone see you leave?"

"Only Marie, the check girl. The parking attendant didn't know about the car."

"Hand me your lipstick a minute," he ordered.

She got it out and gave it to him. He made a little smudge with it, on his own cheek, high up near the ear. Then another one farther down, closer to the mouth. Not too vivid, faint enough to be plausible, distinct enough to be seen.

He even thought of his tie, pulled it a little awry. He seemed to think of everything. Maybe that was because he was only thinking of one thing: of her.

He slung a proprietary arm about her waist. "Smile," he instructed her. "Laugh. Put *your* arm around *my* waist. Act as if you really cared for me. We're having a giddy time. We're just coming in from a session in a parked car outside."

The lights from the glittering dance floor went up over them like a slowly raised curtain. They strolled past the checkroom girl, arm over arm, faces turned to one another, prattling away like a pair of grammar-school kids, all taken up in one another. Sunny threw her head back and emitted a paean of frivolous laughter at something he was supposed to have said just then.

The check girl's eyes followed them with a sort of wistful envy. It must be great, she thought, to be so carefree and have such a good time. Not a worry on your mind.

At the edge of the floor they stopped. He took her in his arms to lead her.

"Keep on smiling, you're doing great. We're going to dance. I'm going to take you once around the floor until we get over to where your father and sister are. Wave to people, call out their names as we pass them. I want everyone to see you. Can you do it? Will you be all right?"

She took a deep, resolute breath. "If you want me to. Yes. I can do it."

They went gliding out into the middle of the floor.

The band was back to Number Twenty in the books—the same song they had been playing when she left. It must have been a repeat by popular demand, it couldn't have been going on the whole time, she'd been away too long. What a different meaning it had now.

> "But instead I trust him implicitly
> I'll go where he wants to go,
> Do what he wants to do, I don't care—"

That sort of fitted Tom. That was for him—nobody else. Sturdy reliability. That was what you wanted, that was what you came back to, if you were foolish enough to stray from it in the first place. Sometimes you found that out too late—sometimes it took you a lifetime, it cost you your youth. Like what they said had happened to poor Jane ten or twelve years ago when she herself, Sunny, had been still a child.

But Sunny was lucky, she had found it out in time. It had only taken her—well, the interval between a pair of dance selections, played the same night, at the same club. It had only cost her—well, somebody else had paid the debt for her.

And so, it was back where it had begun. And as it had begun.

At exactly 10:55 this Saturday, this Washington's Birthday Saturday, the dance is still on full-blast; the band is playing "The Object of My Affections," Number Twenty in the leader's book. Jane is sitting back against the wall. And Sunny is twinkling about on the floor, once more in the arms of Tom Reed, the boy who loved her all through high school, the man who still does now at this very moment, the man who always will, through all the years ahead—

"Here are your people," he whispered warningly. "I'm going to turn you over to them now."

She glanced at them across his shoulder. They were sitting there, Jane and her father, so safe, so secure. Nothing ever happened to them. Less than an hour ago she would have felt sorry for them. Now she envied them.

She and Tom came to a neat halt in front of them.

"Daddy," she said quietly. And she hadn't called him that since she was fifteen. "Daddy, I want to go home now. Take me with you."

He chuckled. "You mean before they even finish playing down to the very last half note? I thought you never got tired dancing."

"Sometimes I do," she admitted wistfully. "And I guess this is one of those times."

He turned to his other daughter. "How about you, Jane? Ready to go now?"

"I've been ready," she said, "ever since we first got here, almost."

The father's eyes had rested for a moment on the telltale red traces on Tom's cheek. They twinkled quizzically, but he tactfully refrained from saying anything.

Not Jane. "Really, Sunny," she said disapprovingly. And then, curtly, to Tom: "Fix your cheek."

He went about it very cleverly, pretending he couldn't find it with his handkerchief for a minute. "Where? Here?"

"Higher up," said Jane. And this time Mr. Brainard smothered an indulgent little smile.

Sunny and Tom trailed them out to the entrance, when they got up to go. "Give me your spare garage key," he said in an undertone. "I'll run the roadster home as soon as you leave and put it away for you. I can get up there quicker with it than you will with the big car. I'll see that Rufus doesn't say anything; I'll tell him you and I were going to elope tonight and changed our minds at the last minute."

"He's always on my side anyway," she admitted.

He took a lingering leave of her by the hand.

"I have a question to ask you. But I'll keep it until next Saturday. The same place? The same time?"

"I have the answer to give you. But I'll keep that until next Saturday too. The same place. The same time."

She got in the back seat with her father and sister, and they drove off.

"It's beginning to snow," Jane complained.

Thanks, murmured Sunny, unheard, *Thanks*, as the first few flakes came sifting down.

Jane bunched her shoulders defensively. "It gets too hot in there with all those people. And now it's chilly in the car." She stifled a sneeze, fumbled in her evening bag. "Now, what did I do with my handkerchief?"

"Here, I'll give you mine," offered Sunny, and heedlessly passed her something in the dark, out of her own bag.

A faint fragrance, invisible as a finespun wire but just as tenuous. Like lilacs in the rain.

Jane raised it toward her nose, held it there, suddenly arrested. "Why, this *is* mine! Don't you recognize my sachet? Where'd you find it?".

Sunny didn't answer. Something had suddenly clogged her throat. She recognized the scent now. Lilacs in the rain.

"Where did you find it?" Jane insisted.

"Hattie—Hattie turned it over to me in the ladies' lounge. You must have lost it in there—"

"Why, I wasn't—" Jane started to say. Then just as abruptly she didn't go ahead.

Sunny knew what she'd been about to say. "I wasn't in there once the whole evening." Jane disliked the atmosphere of gossip that she imagined permeated the lounge, the looks that she imagined would be exchanged behind her back. Sunny hadn't thought quickly enough. But it was too late now.

Jane was holding the handkerchief pressed tight to her mouth. Just holding it there.

Impulsively Sunny reached out, found Jane's hand in the dark, and clasped it warmly and tightly for a long moment.

It said so much, that warm clasp of hands, without a word being said. It said: I understand. We'll never speak of it, you and I. Not a word will ever pass my lips. And thank you, thank you for helping me as you have, though you may not know you did.

Presently, tremulously, a little answering pressure was returned by Jane's hand. There must have been unseen tears on her face, tears of gratitude, tears of release. She was dabbing at her eyes in the dark.

Their father, sitting comfortably and obliviously between them, spoke for the first time since the car had left the club.

"Well, another Saturday-night dance over and done with. They're all pretty much alike—once you've been to one, you've been to them all. Same old thing week in and week out. Music playing, people dancing. Nothing much ever happens. They get pretty monotonous. Sometimes I wonder why we bother going every week, the way we do."

Patricia McGerr

Chain of Terror

*Selena Mead (now Mrs. Hugh Pierce), government agent extraor-
dinary, whose husband headed the secret security branch known
as Section Q, was in Jerusalem as a journalist, covering a story
for her magazine. Her intelligence adventures of the past tended
to make her "see spies and shadows everywhere" and to have an
intuitive "sense of foreboding." Then, in the shadow of Masada,
her intuition turned into fact, and the terror began . . .*

Detective: SELENA MEAD

Selena encountered Senator Stein in the lobby of the King David
hotel on what was to have been her last evening in Israel. She
had stopped at the desk to ask for messages when a familiar voice
called her name. Turning, she took a step forward to meet the tall
white-haired man who was hurrying toward her with arms outstretched.

"Selena, my dear, what a happy surprise!" He clasped both her
hands and gave her a hearty kiss on the cheek. "I had no idea you
were in Jerusalem. Is your husband with you?"

"No, this is a business trip," she explained, "and made on very
short notice. My magazine set up interviews with the prime minister
and several cabinet ministers. Then the Middle East correspondent
was hit by appendicitis. I was sent over in his place."

"A wise choice," he approved. "There's nothing for you to cover in
Washington after Congress adjourns."

"Only the White House and the Supreme Court," she replied with
a smile. "How about you? Is your trip business or pleasure?"

"Entirely pleasure. And paid for, every penny, out of my own
pocket." He shook an admonitory finger. "So don't you put me in one
of those exposés about Congressional junkets at taxpayers' expense.
Rachel and I are on holiday and I don't even intend to touch base

with our Embassy. And speaking of Rachel, she'll be as delighted as I am to see you. How much longer will you be here?"

"I fly home tomorrow. At least—" She turned round to pick up the message slips the clerk had placed on the counter and glanced at the one on top. "Oh, no!"

"Not bad news, I hope."

"Disappointing. I expected confirmation of my plane reservation. Instead they say there's nothing available until the next day."

"Then you can come with us tomorrow," the senator said. "I've rented a car and we plan to drive down into the Negev. We'll visit Masada and the Qumran caves, maybe swim in the Dead Sea. How does that sound?"

"Wonderful," she responded. "I'm almost glad there's no space on the plane."

They got an early start the next morning. Selena and Rachel Stein, in the back seat, exchanged news of mutual friends at home while the senator maneuvered the car through the traffic-clogged streets. There was a faint chill in the November air, but the sun was bright in an almost cloudless sky. They circled the walls of the old city and crossed the Kidron valley to reach the Jericho road.

In less than an hour signs of modern civilization were left behind as they drove into the Judean wilderness along the shore of the Dead Sea. From a capacious handbag Mrs. Stein brought out a map and a guidebook. Selena joined her in tracing their route and picking out points of historical or current interest along the way. Most of the land was hilly and rock-strewn, sparse in trees or other vegetation, but occasionally they passed an Israeli settlement where irrigation and hard work had made the desert bloom with fields of eggplant or tomatoes and orchards of date palm. The senator slowed the car while his wife pointed out the caves of Qumran where the Dead Sea scrolls had been discovered.

"We'll stop on the way back," he promised.

Ahead of them in the distance rose the mountains of Moab where, according to tradition, Moses was buried. Behind them rusting tanks recalled the 1967 war. Near the oasis of Ein Gedi, where David hid from Saul, they crossed the border from the West Bank of Jordan and were waved through a checkpoint by Israeli soldiers. Farther on the senator slowed again to call their attention to three tents of black goatskin which marked a Bedouin camp. Nearby, women and children on camels tended a small flock of sheep.

"Where are the men?" Mrs. Stein asked.

"In their tents, of course," her husband replied. "Drinking coffee and solving the problems of the universe."

"Sounds like a Senate Committee," she remarked.

It was then that Selena first noticed the dust-covered Fiat behind them. Since leaving Jerusalem they had passed a number of buses but few private vehicles. Now, with their car slowed to a sightseers' crawl, Selena expected the other car to pull out and pass. Instead it dropped back, widening the gap between them. When the senator accelerated, the Fiat also increased speed.

Are we being followed, she wondered, and immediately derided herself for an over-active imagination. That's what comes of working with an intelligence organization. I see spies and shadows everywhere. But I'm not on a Section Q assignment now and there's no cause for suspicion. The people in that car are no doubt tourists too and have the same reason we have to slow down at interesting places. A few minutes later they turned off the main highway to a narrower road that led to Herod's ancient fortress of Masada.

"Impressive, isn't it?" the senator said as he stopped in the parking lot near the great flat-topped mountain. "Remind me to fill up with gas when we finish here. The gauge shows nearly empty."

They left the automobile and walked past souvenir shops to the cable-car station. Soon, with a group of other visitors, they boarded a bright red car and were swiftly transported upward to a point near the summit. Looking down from the swaying car they could see a few energetic travelers starting the climb by way of the Snake Path.

Selena's eyes were drawn to the parking lot where a small car had pulled up beside the senator's. The Fiat again? And if so, what did it signify? Only that, like ourselves, they've come to view Masada. Shaking off a sense of foreboding, she turned back to Rachel who, guidebook in hand, was pointing out the restored walls of a Roman camp.

From the place where they left the cable car it was a short but steep walk up rocky steps to the summit. Sighting benches at the top, Mrs. Stein gave an exaggerated sigh of relief.

"Ah, good! We can sit down for a few minutes. That climb really wore me out."

But it was the senator who was breathing hard, his face flushed, and Selena suspected that his wife's pretense of exhaustion was meant to give him a chance to rest without an admission of weakness.

When they were seated the older woman drew from her bag another small book and read from it the story of Masada. The words took them back 19 centuries to the final revolt against Rome when Jewish zealots had captured this stronghold and held it for three years after the fall of Jerusalem. Surrounded at last by 10,000 Roman legionaries, the defenders—960 men, women, and children—chose to die by their own hands.

"I learned the speech of their leader Eleazar as a boy," the senator said, "though I've forgotten most of it." He closed his eyes, and bringing up snatches of memory he recited slowly, "Long ago we vowed never to serve the Romans nor anyone else but God. We were the first to revolt and we shall be the last to break off the struggle. Daybreak will end our resistance, but we are free to choose an honorable death with our loved ones. And I think it is God who has given us this privilege that we can die nobly and as free men."

"The site was excavated about fifteen years ago." Mrs. Stein turned to the last page. "And today, right where we're sitting, young Israeli soldiers come to receive their weapons and swear allegiance to the state and the flag with an oath that ends, 'Masada shall not fall again.' " She glanced sharply at her husband, saw that his breathing was steady, his color normal. "Well!" She closed the book and rose briskly to her feet. "I'm rested now. Let's see the sights."

There were many sights to see, starting with a series of rooms where food and wine were stored. Behind and in front of them as they made the circuit were many other tourists, most of them in bands of 20 or more led by a guide. They were on the upper terrace of Herod's palace when Mrs. Stein leaned close to Selena to whisper, "I think you have an admirer. Near the wall at your left. The young man in the yellow shirt."

Selena glanced in the direction indicated, then shook her head. "I've never seen him before."

"He keeps looking this way," Mrs. Stein told her. "I first noticed him when we came out of the synagogue. He was standing near the entrance, almost as if he were waiting for us."

"If he has his eye on either of you girls," the senator joked, "I can only say I admire his taste. But I think it's time we started down. I've worked up quite an appetite."

They descended from the mountain and ate a leisurely lunch in the restaurant at its base. They were starting back to the car when members of a tour group caught up with them.

"You're Senator Stein, aren't you?" one of the women asked. "See,

Rose, I told you that's who it was. You spoke to our sisterhood luncheon last year and—"

His wife and Selena walked on ahead, leaving him to shake the outstretched hands and answer questions.

"I hope this trip hasn't been too strenuous," Rachel looked back with a frown of concern. "It's so hard to keep him from overdoing."

"You're worried about him, aren't you? Is he ill?"

"Not really. Not if he's careful. He had a heart attack last spring. A mild one, so we were able to keep it out of the papers. The doctor said he'll be fine as long as he follows the rules. A proper diet. Plenty of sleep. No unusual exertion or excitement. It's the last part that's difficult. Dan's used to an active life. But he'll be seventy in a few weeks and he's promised me that when his term ends next year he won't run again."

They reached the car and stood beside it to wait for the senator. He had taken leave of the tour group and was crossing the parking lot when two young men came up behind him. One, Selena noted, was the man in the yellow shirt to whom her attention had been called on the upper terrace. As she watched they caught up with the senator, one moving to his left, the other to his right, so close that the three bodies were almost touching. The yellow-shirted one spoke and when Senator Stein replied, Yellow Shirt's arm went round his back so that he almost seemed to be supporting him. The senator's movements became mechanical, his body stiff, his legs leaden, as if each step was taken under duress.

"Something's wrong." Rachel Stein, alarmed, started forward. "Dan, aren't you feeling all right? What is it?"

"I'm all right, Rachel. Be calm."

There's a gun at his back, Selena thought. Instinctively she moved closer to the other woman and laid a restraining hand on her arm.

"Everybody get in the car," the yellow-shirted man said. His English was precise, the accent faintly British. "Be nice and quiet and nobody will get hurt."

Mrs. Stein shook off Selena's hand and continued her rush forward.

"Who are you?" she demanded. "What are you doing to my husband?"

She was about to throw herself on the spokesman when his companion stepped forward and, grasping her arm, twisted it behind her back to turn her fully around until she was again facing Selena. Tears started in her eyes but did not stop her angry protest. The senator hurled himself on his wife's assailant and the gun was for an instant visible in the second man's hand as he moved close to the entangled trio.

In that instant Selena weighed alternatives. To run for shelter behind the car and summon help by shouting? To take advantage of the gunman's distraction and try to seize his weapon? The restaurant was a long way off and a bus had moved in front of it, cutting off the view of the touring Americans, so the latter option seemed more practical. But as she poised to spring, the senator gave a low moan and sank to the ground.

"Pills," he gasped. "Pocket."

His wife broke free of the young man. He reached out to grab her again but was stopped by his partner.

"Don't hold her, Rahim. The old man needs help. You take care of the other one."

Rahim moved to Selena's side while Mrs. Stein dropped to her knees and quickly took a small bottle of pills from the senator's coat pocket. With trembling fingers she shook out a tiny pellet and placed it on his tongue, then cradled his head on her arm. Selena and the two men watched in silence until the senator opened his eyes and raised his head.

"I'm fine now, Rachel," he said. "No cause to worry."

"Then get in the car," Rahim ordered. "We've wasted enough time."

Selena moved to her friend's side, assisting her to rise, and she, in turn, gave a helping hand to her husband.

"Look at the old man, Abdul," Rahim said. "He's not in shape to drive."

"We'll have to change the plan," Abdul returned. His eyes fixed on Selena. "Can you handle the car?"

"I can drive," she answered. "But if it's money you want—"

"You think we're common robbers?" He drew himself up haughtily. "We are Palestinians and patriots. It is the man we've come for, not his money."

"Then take me." Strength had returned to the senator's voice. "And let the women go."

"Never, Daniel." Rachel clung tightly to his hand. "Whatever they do to you, they must do to me. I'll not be parted from you."

"Don't worry, lady. We'll keep you all together."

"My husband and I will go with you," she said firmly, "if you'll free our friend. Whatever your plans for us, she shouldn't be involved. She's not even Jewish."

"Then it's her bad luck she's traveling with you. We can't let her loose to call the police, can we? Come on, let's get out of here."

Soon they were all in the car. Rahim sat in back with the Steins as Selena took the wheel with Abdul at her side.

"I have a gun." He spoke matter-of-factly, without menace, as she started the engine. "My partner has a knife. If we need to use them, we will. But if everyone behaves with common sense, you will be treated honorably as prisoners of war. And if all goes well, you will be able to return home alive and unharmed in a very short time. Now, miss, please return to the main highway and then turn right."

Selena did as she was told. The tour bus, its passengers having boarded, followed them on the road leading from Masada. She tried to think of some way to signal them but too soon she reached the highway where, turning south, she watched in the rear-view mirror as the bus went in the opposite direction, back toward Jerusalem. Scanning the dashboard instruments, she confirmed the senator's earlier comment about needing gas. If this was to be a long journey, they'd have to stop and that might provide her with a chance to pass on a message. But for the moment she could only follow orders and keep driving.

It was a silent ride. The Steins exchanged a few words, cut off by Rahim's command to be quiet. Selena darted frequent glances from the road ahead to the instrument panel to see the kilometer numbers mount slowly upward while the needle on the gas gauge hovered near empty. If we do stop, she asked herself, how will I let the attendant know we're in trouble. They won't let me talk to him alone, that's certain. If it were like service stations at home, I could ask to use the restroom and write a note. But out here in the desert, there'll be nothing but a pump. And the man may be an Arab and in sympathy with our captors. But that will be our last chance to call for help, so when the time comes I must be ready.

"Slow down," Abdul broke in on her thoughts. "We're near our turnoff. Yes, here it is. Turn right."

The road to which he directed her was narrow and unpaved, hardly more than a trail. If they met another car, one of them would have to pull off to the side. But they met no one and passed no other signs of life. They were headed, it appeared, into a part of the desert that was isolated and uninhabited. The nearly empty gas tank was no longer a good omen. Running out of fuel here might inconvenience the Palestinians, but it would not improve the plight of their victims.

The suspense at any rate was soon ended. She had followed the trail for about ten minutes when she saw ahead, a few yards from the roadside, two goatskin tents. Standing beside them was a man in the flowing robes and headdress of a desert Arab.

"We've arrived," Abdul told her. "Stop the car."

She obeyed, noting as she did so that the needle on the gauge had passed the gauge-line indicating empty. They could probably have traveled only one or two kilometers farther. But that was no longer cause for hope. Instead it meant that, even if there was an opportunity, the car was useless as a means of escape.

The stranger approached and spoke through the window to Abdul. "Did everything go as planned?"

"Yes. Except that they took someone with them to Masada."

"So we have an extra guest. No problem." He opened the rear door with a bow that was almost courtly. "Senator Stein. Madame. Will you please alight?"

"Who are you?" the senator asked. "Why have you brought us here? What do you hope to gain from kidnaping three United States citizens?"

"A great deal." He answered the final question. "Our hospitality, I fear, is less than you are used to, but you will not have long to endure it. If you get out of the car, I will be pleased to introduce myself and, as far as possible, to satisfy your curiosity."

"It appears we have no choice." The senator climbed from the car, then leaned back to assist his wife. The others followed, forming an awkward group with the three Americans confronting the three Arabs.

"I am Hassan el-Fattah." The speaker was an imposing figure, taller and older than the other two and clearly the one in command. "I shall be your host for as long as it takes for the Jews to comply with our requests."

"So we're hostages," Senator Stein interpreted. "And you're members of a terrorist gang."

"Terrorists or freedom fighters." Hassan shrugged. "It depends, doesn't it, on who is speaking. We are not at war with you, Senator, and we will do our best to make you and your ladies comfortable. Abdul, move the car out of sight. And you, Rahim, can let our comrades know that the first step is accomplished."

The two young men moved quickly. Abdul got back in the car and drove it under an overhanging cliff while Rahim scurried into one of the tents. They must have a short-wave radio, Selena thought. If I can get to the transmitter when no one is watching, maybe I can send an S.O.S. But to whom? Even as the idea formed, she realized its absurdity. This isn't Citizen's Band land. I'd only reach the people with whom Rahim is communicating—a Palestinian command post. There has to be another way to get word to the outside world about what is happening to us.

There's a seven-hour time difference between Israel and Washington, so it was still morning when word was received at the White House that an American senator and his wife had been abducted. The price of their release, according to a message delivered to the American Embassy in Israel, was freedom for five Palestinians who had been jailed for a series of bombings in which nine Israelis had died.

The news, routinely circulated to all intelligence agencies, reached Hugh Pierce in his Georgetown studio. Section Q, the small secret security branch that he headed, was not directly involved, but it was asked to stay alert and contribute any relevant information. That his wife might be in danger did not occur to him. Selena's cable the night before had advised him of her delayed departure and he thought of phoning to tell her about the Steins. But she might take that as encouragement to stay and join in the search. Since he was unwilling to do anything that might delay her homecoming, he took no action but remained in his studio to await developments.

. At first there was hope, shared by the Israelis and Americans, that the message was a hoax. This was bolstered by inquiries at the King David Hotel from which it was learned that the Steins had set out in the morning on an all-day tour of the Dead Sea area. Tour agencies were checked until a guide was found who reported that several members of his group had actually spoken to Senator Stein after lunch at Masada. There was reassurance in the knowledge that, only a short time before the report of his kidnaping, he had been free and following his intended itinerary.

But it grew late and the Steins did not return to the hotel, and later still, friends whom they had invited to dinner had waited in vain in the lobby. Agents fanned out to question all members of the tour who had seen them at Masada. A couple riding in the front seat of the bus recalled following the senator's car back to the highway.

"But he wasn't driving," the woman volunteered. "You remember, Joe, there were three people in the back seat, a woman and two men. I'm sure one of them was Senator Stein. That thick crop of white hair couldn't belong to anyone else."

"That's right," Joe agreed. "We figured he must have a chauffeur."

The rental agency quickly refuted that guess. The senator had hired a car, not a driver, and the hotel porter confirmed that, when the party left the hotel that morning, the senator was at the wheel. So the conclusion was at last unavoidable. The Steins were at the mercy of terrorists and the government was faced with intolerable alternatives.

Even more disturbing to Hugh was information that was included in the report as a minor footnote. Several of the tourists said there were two women lunching with the senator. One they assumed was his wife, the other was much younger. The professional concern that Hugh had felt since the reports began was suddenly raised to white-hot anxiety. If Selena—no, it couldn't be—but she was in Jerusalem and at the same hotel—with a free day—and the Steins were old friends of Selena's parents.

With a hand that was barely steady, Hugh picked up the phone and put through a call to the King David. The wait seemed interminable, and when he was finally connected, the clerk's answers did nothing to quiet his fears. Selena was not in the hotel. The key was in her box, along with a teletype from the airline that had been received at 9:50 A.M. It appeared, therefore, that she had left the hotel soon after breakfast and had not yet returned.

"And in Jerusalem"—Hugh looked in despair at the bright sunshine streaming through his skylight—"in Jerusalem it's nearly midnight."

In the desert Hassan had provided his captives and his two associates with garments like those he was wearing. The road, he explained, led to a long abandoned archeological dig. Now nobody had reason to come within miles of the site. But in case anyone did, or if one of the low-flying Israeli patrol planes passed overhead, they would see a small Bedouin encampment, one of many that dotted the area. As long as they were properly costumed and stayed within specific boundaries, the captives were free to roam about or to rest in the smaller tent. It was, Selena realized, perfect camouflage. And to stifle any thought of flight, either Abdul or Rahim—the gun inconspicuous but not invisible—was at all times on guard.

At nightfall Abdul built a wood fire to heat a mixture of lamb chunks and rice which he ladled onto tin plates.

"Eat your fill," Hassan urged them. "We have rations and water for two days. Enough even"—he nodded to Selena —"for an unexpected guest."

"And after two days—" Selena ventured the question.

"We break camp," he said. "They have forty-eight hours to let our brothers go."

His tone was mild but his face, lit by the flickering flames, showed a fanatic determination that made it unnecessary to ask what would happen if the deadline was not met. It was not surprising that none of his guests had much appetite.

At bedtime a new complication appeared. It had been planned to put the Steins in the small tent and the Arabs in the larger one, which also contained the radio equipment. That left no place for Selena.

"I can sleep in the car," she suggested.

"Let both the ladies have the car," the senator said. "The cushions are softer than the ground and they'll be sheltered from the wind."

"But I'd rather stay with you," Mrs. Stein said.

"And let Selena be off by herself?" His quick glance at the other men was meaningful. "No, dear, that's not wise."

"I hope you're not so foolish as to think you can use the car to escape," Hassan said. "You would first need boards to lift the back wheels out of the sand. And of course one of us will be on watch all night. But if, for comfort, you choose the car as a sleeping place, I do not object."

So it was settled. Rachel Stein stretched out on the car's back seat while Selena curled up in the front. At ten o'clock she switched on the car radio and found an English-language news broadcast. The Israeli cabinet, they heard, had been called to an emergency meeting and would probably remain in session through the night to decide on a response to terrorists who held hostage an American senator, his wife, and an as-yet-unidentified female companion. The senator and the two women, according to the announcer, had last been seen when their car, driving away from Masada, had turned south on the road to Sodom.

"Sodom!" Mrs. Stein exclaimed. "That's appropriate. We couldn't be any harder to find if we had all turned to salt. My dear, I'm so sorry we got you into this."

"We're in it together," Selena answered. "What we need to find is a way out."

But as she lay awake, her mind busy, every avenue of escape seemed blocked. From time to time the sound of wood being placed

on the fire or the footsteps of someone walking near the car spoke
of their captors' unbroken vigil. Finally, from exhaustion, she slept.

When she woke, the fire was out and the camp dimly lighted by
the rising sun. She pulled herself upright in the seat and looked
back to see that Rachel was also awake. Rachel's carryall had yielded
another book which she was reading with the aid of a miniature
flashlight. She looked up to greet Selena.

"I'm sorry if my moving around disturbed you. You seemed so
peaceful."

"I hope you were able to get some sleep too."

"Enough." Her eyes went back to the book and she read aloud,
" 'The Lord is my light and my salvation, whom shall I fear? The
Lord is the stronghold of my life, of whom shall I be afraid?' "

"The Psalms?"

"Yes. I like to have them with me. Somewhere in here"—she
tapped the book's cover—"there are words of strength and solace for
every crisis."

They breakfasted on bread and dried fish and then began a long
stretch of waiting. Selena, covered from head to foot as a Bedouin
woman, roved restlessly about the camp, followed always by the
eyes of one of the Arabs. The Steins were more passive, staying close
together as if each drew comfort from the other's nearness.

In mid-morning Hassan came out of the communications tent to
tell them of a new development. The Israeli government had announced that they could not reach any decision without proof that
those making the demands had actually taken Senator Stein and
that he and his companions were alive and well.

"So they're ready to deal with us." Hassan was exultant. "You can
speak over our radio, Senator. Headquarters will put your voice on
tape and play it for the government. If all goes well, our brothers
will be in Damascus tonight and you can sleep in real beds. Is that
not good news?"

"No," the senator said. "I will not speak on your radio."

Hassan stared at him in surprise, then he said, "Nobody is asking
you to speak in support of our cause. All you have to say is that you
and the ladies are our prisoners and that you are well. That's true,
isn't it? And the sooner they hear you say so, the sooner we can all
go home."

"The Israelis won't give in to blackmail," the senator declared.
"They never have. They never will."

"Maybe not before," Hassan conceded. "But our side has never had a United States senator as a bargaining point. You're an important man and a popular one. How do you think the American public, and especially the other senators, will feel if the government here says they'd rather keep a few Palestinians in jail than save your life?"

"Those Palestinians," the senator snapped, "are murderers. If they're released, there'll be more bombs—and then more kidnapings to free the bombers—and on and on in an endless chain of terror. If you need my voice on your radio to convince the world that you have me, then perhaps I've found a way to stop you."

"At what cost, Senator?" Hassan asked. "You may be willing to die for Israel, but what about your wife and her friend? You talk to him, ladies. I'm sure you can persuade him to cooperate and save your lives."

Deliberately he walked away, out of earshot.

"You're right, Dan." Mrs. Stein reached for his hand. "They're counting on outside pressure to weaken Israel's resolve not to deal with terrorists. You must do nothing to help them."

"They won't deal, no matter what I do or say," he answered. "Asking for proof that we're alive—I'm sure that's just a way to gain time, to keep the negotiations open. The Israelis don't ransom hostages, they rescue them."

"Like at Entebbe." Eagerly Rachel seized the hope he held out. "Certainly it should be easier to pluck three people from an open space than it was to invade an airport guarded by soldiers in a hostile country."

"Much easier," Selena agreed. "If only they knew where we are."

"That's the rub," the senator said. "After we left Masada we vanished as if the earth had swallowed us up. I might even make their broadcast if there were some way to sneak in a clue to our location."

"Just say we're disguised as a sheik and his harem not far from the Dead Sea. Can you get that past the censor?"

"Not a chance," he replied. "But it makes an interesting fantasy."

Their spirits, Selena noted, seemed buoyed by the discussion. Although the hopelessness of their situation had not changed, the senator was no longer a passive figure. By refusing to speak, he had shown himself free to choose, to make a decision and hold to it, to take command of his fate.

"Well, Senator?" Hassan had come back to them. "Have you decided to listen to reason?"

"My position remains the same."

"And it won't change," his wife added.

"You are stupid!" Hassan exploded. "If we don't prove you're alive, your people will think you have already been killed. Then they will have no cause to deal with us."

"That's just how I see it."

"If they don't meet our terms, you will die." His gaze moved slowly around the circle. "All of you. Be sure you understand what you are doing. By refusing to cooperate, you commit suicide."

"And that"—Rachel echoed the words recited on the mountain top—"that can be an honorable death."

The midday meal was again a mixture of lamb and rice. Later Selena went to the car to tune in another news broadcast. She learned that there was no further word from the alleged kidnapers of Senator Stein, but Jerusalem and Washington were in constant consultation about what action to take. She learned also that her own identity had been established. But the announcer's final line was, to her, the most interesting.

"The husband of the third hostage, the well-known American artist Hugh Pierce, arrived today in Jerusalem to await news of his wife."

Hugh! Her heart bounded. Hugh was in Jerusalem. So short a distance away. Hugh would find them. She projected her thoughts northward as if she might, by willing it, force them into his mind. But that's insane. She brought herself back to reality. There was between them a depth of understanding that made them able to convey much in few words. But not, she thought wryly, in no words at all. If I'm to send a message to Hugh, I'll have to use means more substantial than telepathy.

She turned off the radio and weighed the possibilities. Then she left the car to join the Steins who were strolling arm in arm at the other end of the cliff. She asked Mrs. Stein if she might borrow her book of Psalms.

"Of course, dear. I left it in the car. I hope you'll find a verse to answer your need."

"I'm sure I shall." She returned to the car and began to read. A short time later she went to Hassan who was resting in the sun, his back against a rock outside the larger tent.

"I've been thinking." She sat down beside him. "The senator is determined not to help you. And Mrs. Stein agrees with him. Nothing will change their minds."

"There are ways to persuade people," he said darkly. "I think he would not like to see his wife hurt."

"Oh, no!" She drew back. "You wouldn't—you couldn't!"

"We do whatever is necessary for our cause. I am waiting now for instructions."

"But public opinion is important to your cause too. You've treated us kindly. I can report that to the world when we're free. I'm a journalist."

"I know. The radio told us who you are. Perhaps when you go back you will write that we are not monsters, that we fight only to regain our land."

"But when you threaten to hurt a helpless woman—"

"Her husband will be to blame, if he remains stubborn."

"There's another way. That's what I came to talk to you about. All you need is proof that the three of us are in your custody and well. So why not let me make a tape? I'll say what you want me to say—that Senator and Mrs. Stein and I are well and that you're taking good care of us. If you like, I'll even explain that I'm talking instead of the senator because he'd rather die than help you. People who know the kind of man he is will believe that. Then you'll have no need for his voice."

"Hmm." He frowned, thinking. "Yes, that may serve. I will pass on your proposal and see what the leader thinks. You wait."

In a few minutes he was back. "There is a difficulty," he told her. "The senator's voice is well-known. When he speaks, people recognize him. But if you make a tape, they cannot be sure if it is really you or someone else merely using your name."

"Ah, yes, I see." She did not add that if he had not raised that objection, she herself would have pointed it out to him. She remained silent, her eyes focused on the ground as if in deep thought. "But wait—" She looked up, brightening. "I have an idea. My husband is in Jerusalem. If I add a special message for him, one that he'll know can only come from me, that will solve the problem."

"What kind of message?"

"I often quote the Bible to him. There's one verse in particular that he'll associate with me."

"I will check."

Again he went into the tent. It was a long time before he returned, but when he did he was beaming his approval. "The leader is pleased that you will work with us," he told her. "He says to tell you that you will not be sorry. Now here is what you must say."

He handed her a slip of paper on which were written three short sentences. She was to identify herself, say that she and Senator and Mrs. Stein were well cared for by Palestinian patriots, and urge the government to save their lives by meeting the demands. "After that," he said, "you say the Bible verse that will make your husband certain it is you."

This time she went into the tent with him and sat quietly while he spun dials to renew radio contact with his headquarters. After a brief exchange in Arabic he handed her the microphone.

"Go ahead. They are ready to start the tape."

She read the message exactly as it was written, then added, "I heard on the radio that my husband is in Jerusalem. Please tell him that I quoted my favorite verse from the Psalms, 'The Lord is in his holy temple, his throne is in heaven. His eyes behold the children of men.' "

While government ministers held round-the-clock sessions at the Knesset, officers of an elite commando unit of the Israeli army met in the basement of a bank a few blocks away. They had planned and practised techniques for air and sea rescues from a wide variety of open and enclosed spaces—airfields and farms, offices, hotels, theaters, schools, houses—every conceivable place where hostages might be taken. But all these preparations were nullified by the total disappearance of the Steins and Selena. Known and suspected members of the Palestinian underground were under strict surveillance, but nothing was discovered. The demand for proof had been made on the chance that, in supplying it, the abductors might make a slip that would reveal their hiding place. But that was another dead end.

The tape bearing Selena's message had been played over the phone to the American ambassador who, in turn, made a tape that was passed to the commandos. Hugh, joining them in the basement, identified his wife's voice but scowled in bafflement as she recited her "favorite psalm." They played it several times, hoping to hear background noise that might furnish a clue. But there was nothing. Half of the 48 hours given in the original ultimatum had already elapsed.

"What I need," Hugh said suddenly, "is a rabbi."

The soldiers looked at him, startled, as if suspecting that he had cracked under the strain. But they acceded to his request for one more replay of the tape. He noted Selena's exact words, then went into an adjoining office to use the telephone.

"He may be right," the major commented. "There's not much left to do except pray."

But a short time later Hugh was back in the commando room and the atmosphere was dramatically changed. A large map hung on the wall and Hugh stood beside it with the officers clustered close to watch each movement of his pencil.

"Here—" He tapped the point at which the Masada road joined the main highway. "This is where they were last seen. We know from the tourists that they headed south. So we move along this route not less than eleven and not more than twelve kilometers." He measured carefully and put two dots on the map. "This is where they turned, either left or right."

"A left turn," a lieutenant commented, "would put them in the Dead Sea."

"Correct. So they went to the right. Not less than four or more than five kilometers." From the dots he drew parallel lines into the desert and then, checking his measurements with care, drew a square to enclose an area one kilometer in each direction. "That's where they are."

"We'll do an aerial rec," the major said. "and make sure."

"Be careful," Hugh warned. "If they guess they've been spotted, they may find another hole to hide in."

"We know our job," the Israeli answered. "We won't scare the birds. One pass with a wide telephoto lens will be enough. It will look like a routine desert patrol."

When the plane flew over, Selena was walking with Rachel Stein. She had told them at once about making the tape but had not explained her motive. It was possible that nothing would come of it and she did not want to arouse false hopes. Now Mrs. Stein, concerned that Selena might feel guilty, was trying to reassure her.

"Daniel and I both think you did the right thing," she said. "He couldn't help them. It would betray all his principles. But Israel doesn't mean to you what it does to us. And I was worried that they would use force on Dan, torture even. I don't know how long Dan could have held out. With his heart condition, he might—" She broke off, unwilling to complete the thought. "You spared us that, Selena, and I'm thankful. Also it should make the Arabs more friendly to you. In the end, if it comes to that, it may save your life."

"Oh, no! Mrs. Stein, that isn't why I made the tape."

"Of course not!" She was equally emphatic. "My dear, we know you too well to think that for one minute. But if it has that effect—well, it eases my mind to believe that whatever happens to us you'll survive. Daniel and I have lived a long time, the years have been full and happy for us. And there are worse ways to die than for a cause one believes in. But you're young and you were caught up in this by accident. We're to blame for your being here and if harm comes to you—ah, look!" She was distracted by the sound of an approaching plane. "Isn't there some way we can signal, let them know we're here?"

But the plane, staying high in the sky, had passed over them and was gone before she could finish the question.

In the commando room the series of pictures, greatly magnified, was spread out for inspection on a large table.

"A Bedouin family is great cover," the major said, "and all very authentic. Except for this." He pointed to a shiny surface near the ground close to the cliff. "What do you make it to be?"

"Something metal," his aide answered. "From the shape and location, I'd say it's the end of an auto bumper."

"So we've trapped our birds." The major smiled his satisfaction. "The pictures show five people. Three of ours, two of them."

"There may be one or two others out of sight," the aide suggested.

"Sitting ducks. We'll go in tonight, land behind this hill, and implement Plan D."

"There'll be a dangerous minute or two when we go over the hill," Hugh said. "If they hear us coming, they'll have time to grab one of the hostages to use as a shield."

"We're fast and silent in the dark," the major said. "Anyway, that's a risk we have to take."

"It's a risk we can minimize," Hugh countered. "My wife's tape said she has access to a radio. She told us where they are, so she's expecting us to mount a rescue. If I let her know exactly when we're coming, she'll figure a way to put space between them and their guards at the crucial moment. Can you arrange for me to put a message on every English-language newscast for the rest of the day?"

"Are you crazy?" the major asked. "Those fellows speak English. There's no way you can brief our people without tipping off the other side."

"You work out your strategy," Hugh reported, "and tell me the

exact hour and minute you start over the top. Then I'll get word to
my girl."

Selena waited impatiently for night to fall. Had Hugh, she wondered, understood her message? How and when would they act on
it? Surely not until after dark. Probably in the pre-dawn hours when
guards are least alert. By ten o'clock the women were in the car,
the senator was in his tent, and Hassan was keeping lonely vigil by
the campfire.

Again Selena switched on the radio. Most of the news was repe-
tition. Senator Stein and his party were still missing. The officials
were still debating. The public was demanding action.

Then came an announcement that quickened her pulse. "Hugh
Pierce, husband of one of the hostages, was interviewed this afternoon. Asked if he had any message for his wife, he replied, 'Only
this. Be brave, darling, and remember what the Psalmist said. 'You,
O Lord, are a shield about me, my glory and the lifter up of my
head.' "

"What a sweet thought." Mrs. Stein leaned over the back of the
seat to give Selena's shoulder a gentle pat. "I didn't know Hugh was
a religious man. But of course in times of trouble—"

"Yes," Selena concurred. "It makes a difference."

With the flashbulb sheltered to show no light outside the car, she
scanned the pages of the book of Psalms until she found the passage
Hugh had quoted.

"They're coming for us. We must be prepared."

"What shall we do?" Rachel asked.

"Our part is to be out of harm's way. This car is the safest place,
so you and I are all right. But we have to find a way to get the
senator in here with us without making them suspicious. There's
no hurry, though. We've several hours to think about it."

They discussed and made plans, discarded them and devised others, finally arrived at a firm arrangement. Then they were silent,
waiting. At midnight Abdul relieved Hassan. The fire burned low,
the camp was quiet. The hours dragged on, but neither of the women
slept. At last the luminous dial of Selena's watch showed 3:00 A.M.

"It's almost time," she whispered.

"I'm ready," Mrs. Stein replied. "Just tell me when to start."

She watched the second-hand sweep round.

3:01.

3:02.

"Now!" Selena said.

"Oh-o-oh!" Rachel broke the silence with a long drawn-out cry of pain. "Daniel, help me!"

"What's going on?" Abdul, dozing by the fire, sprang to his feet.

"Rachel, what is it?" The Senator burst from his tent but was caught and held back by Abdul.

"It's Mrs. Stein," Selena called across the open space. "Chest pains—her heart. Her husband has pills."

"Let him go to her, Abdul." Hassan came out of the other tent. "We don't want the old lady to die on us."

Released, the senator hurried toward the car. Mrs. Stein pushed open the back door.

"Rachel, what—"

"I'm all right, Dan. Get in. Hurry!"

He scrambled in beside her. Selena pulled the door shut, pressed down the lock. Hassan at a more leisurely pace was moving toward the car.

"What's this all about?" the senator asked. "Why—?"

Before he could say more there was a sound of movement on the hill to their right. A rock, dislodged by running feet, rolled to the bottom. Hassan whirled around, drawing his gun. Then a spotlight shone in his eyes, blinding him, and other lights illuminated the whole camp.

"Drop your guns," a voice out of the darkness ordered. "You're surrounded."

Hassan fired toward the light but an answering shot struck his arm and the gun fell to the ground. Abdul and Rahim were less militant. Within a few minutes the commandos were in the camp and had taken the three men prisoners. The Steins and Selena emerged from the car.

"Senator Stein?" The major introduced himself and his unit. "I hope you and the ladies are all right."

"We're fine, young man. And very grateful to you. That was a remarkable performance."

"Standard operating procedure," he replied. "There's a helicopter waiting to take you to Jerusalem."

Selena, spotting a familiar figure behind the major, had not listened to their exchange. Only when Hugh's arms were tightly around her was she able to release the emotion that she had, for 36 hours, held so tightly in check.

Later, riding in the helicopter, they reviewed what had happened.

"It was like a miracle!" Mrs. Stein exclaimed. "The way they suddenly swooped down and set us free. But what I don't understand"—she turned to Hugh—"how did you know where to find us?"

"Selena sent me a message."

"I watched the odometer while I was driving to the camp," Selena explained. "It showed a little over eleven kilometers south and about four west. When they let me tape a message, I added a verse from the Psalms."

"Psalm 11, verse 4," Hugh said. "As soon as a Bible scholar identified the passage, I had the numbers I needed."

"And the quotation Hugh sent back—Psalm 3, verse 4—told me when to expect them."

"Then the commandos," Hugh concluded, "did the rest. It was a by-the-book rescue operation."

"Exactly," Selena echoed. "Rescue by the Book."

Michael Gilbert

The Sark Lane Mission

In which Detective Sergeant Petrella is offered a most serious narcotics investigation—a case involving "an international crowd who are calculating their profits in the millions," and even more frightening, "who must be responsible, directly or indirectly, for hundreds of deaths a year," and to whom—a fact that Petrella must weigh carefully—"a single life is not of great importance" . . . a superlative example of Mr. Gilbert's police-procedural novelets . . .

Detective· SERGEANT PETRELLA

"You're wanted down at Central," said Gwilliam. "They want to have a little chat with you about your pension."

"My pension?" said Detective Sergeant Petrella. Being nearer 20 than 30, pensions were not a thing which entered much into his thoughts. "You're sure it's not my holiday? I've been promised a holiday for eighteen months."

"Last time I saw the pensions officer," said Gwilliam, "he said to me, 'Sergeant Gwilliam, it's a dangerous job you're doing.' It was the time I was after that Catford dog-track shower and I said, 'You're right, there, my boy.' 'Do you realize, Sergeant,' he said to me, 'that every year for the past ten years one hundred and ninety policemen have left the force with collapsed arches? And this year we may pass the two hundred mark. We shall have to raise your insurance contributions.' "

Petrella went most of the way down to Westminster by bus. It was a beautiful morning, with spring breaking through all round. Having some time in hand he got off the bus at Piccadilly, walked down St. James's, and cut across the corner of the park.

It was a spring which was overdue. They had had a dismal winter. In the three years he had been in Q Division, up at Highside, he could not remember anything like it. The devil seemed to have got among the pleasant people of North London.

161

First, an outbreak of really nasty hooliganism, led, as he suspected, by two boys of good family; but he hadn't been able to pin it on them. Then the silly business of the schoolgirl shoplifting gang. Then the far-from-silly, the dangerous and tragic matter of Cora Gwynne.

Gwynne was the oldest by several years of the Highside detectives. He was a quiet but well-liked man, and he had one daughter, Cora, who was 17. Six months before, Cora had gone. She had not disappeared; she had departed, leaving a note behind her saying that she wanted to live her own life. "Whatever that means," Gwynne had said to Haxtell.

"Let her run," Haxtell had replied. "She'll come back."

He was right. She came back at the end of the fifth month, in time to die. She was full of cocaine, and pregnant.

Petrella shook his head angrily as he thought about it. He stopped to look at the crocuses which were thick in the grass. A starved-looking sparrow was trying to bolt a piece of bread almost as large as itself. A pigeon sailed smoothly down and removed it.

Petrella walked on, up the steps into King Charles Street, across Whitehall, and under the arch into New Scotland Yard. He was directed to the office that dealt with pensions, allotted a wooden chair, and told to wait. At eleven o'clock a messenger brought in a filing tray with six cups of tea on it, and disappeared through a swing door in the partition. Since the tray was empty when he returned, Petrella deduced that there must be at least six people devoting attention to the pensions of the Metropolitan Police and he hoped one of them would soon devote some attention to him.

He became aware that the messenger had halted opposite him.

"You Sergeant Pirelli?" he said.

"That's right," said Petrella. He had long ago given up correcting people about his name.

"C.I.D., Q Division?"

"Ten out of ten."

"Whassat?"

"I said you're quite right."

"I'll tell 'em you're here," said the messenger.

Five minutes later a cheerful-looking girl arrived and said, "Sergeant Petrella? Would you come with me, please?"

His opinion of the Pensions Section became a good deal more favorable. Any department that employed a girl with legs like that must have some good in it.

So engrossed was he in this speculation that it did not, at first, occur to him to ask where they were going. When they reached and pushed through a certain swing door on the first floor, he stopped her.

"You've got it wrong," he said. "This is where the top brass works. If we don't look out we shall be busting in on the Assistant Commissioner."

"That's right," said the girl.

She knocked on one of the doors on the south side of the corridor, then opened it without waiting for an answer, and said, "I have Sergeant Petrella here for you."

He advanced dazedly into the room. He had been there once before, and he knew that the gray-haired man behind the desk was Assistant Commissioner Romer, of the C.I.D., a man who, unlike some of his predecessors, had not come to his office through the soft byways of the legal department, but had risen from the bottom-most rung of the ladder, making enemies at every step, until finally he had found himself at the top; and when, there being no one left to fight, he proved himself a departmental head of exceptional ability.

In a chair beside the window he noted Superintendent Costorphine, who specialized in all matters connected with narcotics. He had worked for him on two previous occasions and had admired him, although he could not love him.

Romer said in a very friendly voice, "Sit down, will you, Sergeant. This is going to take some time. You know Costorphine, don't you? I'm sorry about this cloak-and-dagger stuff, but you'll understand better when I explain what it's about, and what we're going to ask you to do. And when I say 'ask' I mean just that. Nothing at all that's said this morning is anything approaching an order. It's a suggestion. If you turn it down, no one's going to think any the worse of you. In fact, Costorphine and myself will be the only people who will even know about it."

Assuming a cheerfulness which he was far from feeling, Petrella said, "You tell me what you want me to do, sir, then I can tell you if I want to run away."

Romer nodded at Costorphine, who said in his schoolmasterly voice, "Almost a year ago we noted a new source of entry of cocaine into this country. Small packets of it were taken from distributors *inside* the country. It was never found in large quantities, and we never found how it got in.

"Analysis showed it to be Egyptian in origin. It also showed quite appreciable deposits of copper. It is obviously not there as the result of any part of the process of manufacture, and it is reasonable to suppose that it came there during some stage in shipment or entry.

"Once the source had been identified, we analyzed every sample we laid hands on, and it became clear"—Costorphine paused fractionally, not for effect; he was a man who had no use for effects, but because he wished to get certain figures clear in his own head—"that rather over half of the total intake of illicit cocaine coming into this country was coming under this head. And that the supply was increasing."

"And along with it," said Romer, "were increasing, at a rate of geometrical progression, most of the unpleasant elements of criminal activity with which we have to deal. Particularly among juveniles. I've had some figures from America which made my hair stand on end. We're not quite as bad yet, but we're learning."

Petrella could have said, "There's no need to tell me. I knew Cora Gwynne when she was a nice friendly schoolgirl of fourteen, and I saw her just before she died." But he kept quiet.

Romer went on, "I suppose if youth thinks it may be blown to smithereens inside five or ten years by some impersonal force pressing a button, it's predisposed to experiment. I don't know. Anyway, you'll understand why we thought it worth bringing down a busy Detective Sergeant from Q Division.

"Now, I'm going to give you some facts. We'll start, as our investigators started about nine months ago, with a gentleman named Batson. Mr. Batson is on the board of the Consort Line, a company which owns and runs three small cargo steamers: the *Albert Consort*, the *William Consort*, and the *Edward Consort*—steamers which run between various Mediterranean ports, Bordeaux, and London."

When Romer said, "Bordeaux," Petrella looked up at Costorphine, who nodded.

"Bordeaux, but not the racket you're thinking of," he said. "We've checked that."

"Batson," went on Romer, "is not only on the board of the Consort Line. It has been suggested that he *is* the board. But one thing about him is quite certain. Whatever his connection with this matter he, personally, takes no active part. He neither carries the stuff nor has any direct contact with the distributors. But I think that, at the end of the day, the profit goes to him.

"That being so, we looked carefully at his friends, and the one who caught our eye was Captain Cree. Ex-captain now, since he has retired from the services of the Consort Line, he lives in considerable affluence in a house at Greenwich. He maintains a financial interest in the *Consorts* through his friend, Mr. Batson, and acts as chandler and shore agent for them—finds them crews and cargoes, and buys their stores.

"All of which might add up, in cash, to a nice house at Greenwich, but wouldn't really account for"—Romer ticked them off on his fingers—"two personal motor cars, with a chauffeur bodyguard to look after the same, a diesel-engined tender called *Clarissa* based on Wapping, with a whole-time crew of three and, in addition to all these, a large number of charitable and philanthropic enterprises, chiefly among seamen and boys in the dockside area."

"He sounds perfectly terrible," said Petrella.

"Such a statement, made outside these four walls," said Romer, "would involve you in very heavy damages for defamation. Captain Cree is a respectable, and a respected, citizen. One of his fondest interests is the Sark Lane Mission."

"The Sark Lane—"

"The name is familiar to you? It should be. The Mission was one of the first in Dockland, and it was founded by your old school."

"Of course. I remember now. We used to have a voluntary subscription of five shillings taken off us on the first day of every term. I don't think anyone took any further interest in it."

"I should imagine that one of the troubles of the Sark Lane Mission is that people have not taken enough interest in it. The Missioner for the last twenty-five years has been a Mr. Jacobson. A very good man in his way and, in his early years, energetic and successful. He retired last month, at the age of seventy-five.

"I should imagine that for the last ten years his appearances at the Mission have been perfunctory. The place has really been kept going by an old ex-naval man named Batchelor—and by the regular munificence of Captain Cree."

"I see," said Petrella. But he felt that there must be something more to it than that.

"The appointment of the Missioner lies with the School Governors, but they act on the recommendation of the Bishop of London. Sometimes the post is filled by a clergyman. Sometimes not. On this occasion the recommended candidate was the Reverend Freebone."

"Philip Freebone!"

"The present incumbent of the Church of St. Peter and St. Paul, Highside. You know him, I believe?"

"Very well indeed. He started up at Highside as curate, and when the incumbent died he was left in charge. I can't imagine anyone who would do the job better."

"I can," said Romer.

When he had got over the shock, Petrella did not pretend not to understand him.

"I don't think I could get away with it, sir," he said. "Not for any length of time. There'd be a hundred things I'd do wrong."

"I'm not suggesting that you should pose as a clergyman. You could go as *Mr.* Freebone. You've had some experience with youth clubs, I believe."

"For a few months before I joined the police, yes. I wasn't very successful."

"It may have been the wrong sort of club. I have a feeling you're going to be very successful in this one."

"Has Freebone been told?"

"He knows that he's got the job. He hasn't been told of the intended—er—rearrangement."

"I think you may have some difficulty there. Phil's one of the most obstinate people I know."

"I will have a word with his Bishop."

"I am afraid clergymen do not always do what their Bishops tell them these days," remarked Costorphine.

"This isn't a job on which we can afford to make a second mistake," continued Romer.

Petrella looked up.

"We got a man into the Consort Line about six months ago. It took some doing but we managed it without, as far as we know, arousing any suspicions. He was engaged as an ordinary seaman, under the name of Mills. He made voyages on all three of the ships, and gave us very full but absolutely negative reports. He was on his way home a fortnight ago in the *Albert Consort*, and was reported as having deserted ship at Marseilles."

"And hasn't been seen since?"

"He's been seen," said Romer. "The French police found him in the foothills behind Marseilles two days ago. What was left of him. He'd been tortured before he was killed."

"I see," said Petrella.

"I'm telling you this so that, if you go in at all, you go in with your eyes wide open. This is an international crowd, who are calculating their profits in the millions. And who must be responsible, directly and indirectly, for hundreds of deaths a year. A single life is not of great importance."

"No," said Petrella. "I can quite see that . ."

A fortnight later the new Missioner came to the Sark Lane Mission. This was a rambling, two-story, yellow brick building in the style associated, through the East End, with temperance and good works.

The street doors opened into a small lobby in which a notice said, in startling black letters, WIPE YOUR FEET. Someone had crossed out FEET and hopefully substituted a different part of the body. On the left of the lobby was a reception office, which was empty.

Beyond, you went straight into the main Mission room, which rose the full two-story height of the building and looked like a drill hall half-heartedly decorated for a dance. Dispirited red and white streamers hung from the iron cross-bars which spanned the roof. A poster on the far wall bore the message, in cotton wool letters, "*How will you spend Eternity?*"

At the far end of the hall three boys were throwing darts into a board. Superficially they all looked alike, with their white town faces, their thick dark hair, and their general air of having been alive a lot longer than anyone else.

When, later, Mr. Freebone got to know them, he realized that there were differences. The smallest and fattest was a lazy but competent boy called Ben. The next in height and age was Colin, a dull boy of 15, who came to life only on the football field; but for football he had a remarkable talent, a talent which was already attracting the scouts from the big clubs, and was one day to put his name in the headlines.

The oldest and tallest of the boys was called Humphrey, and he had a long solemn face with a nose which started straight and turned to the right at the last moment, and a mouth like a crocodile's. It was not difficult to see that he was the leader of the three.

None of them took the slightest notice of Mr. Freebone as he padded across the scarred plank flooring to watch them.

In the end he said, "You're making an awful mess of that, aren't you?" He addressed this remark to the fat boy. "If you want fifteen and end on a double it's a waste of time going for one."

The boy gaped at him. Mr. Freebone took the darts from him and threw them. First a single three, then, at the second attempt, a double six.

"There you are, Ben," said the tall boy. "I told you to go for three." He transferred his gaze to Mr. Freebone. "You want Batchy?" he said.

"Batchy?" said Mr. Freebone. "Now who, or what, would that be?"

"Batchy's Batchelor."

This was even more difficult, but in the end he made it out. "You mean the caretaker. Is his name Batchelor?"

"'Sright. You want him, you'll find him in his room." He jerked his head toward the door at the far end of the building.

"Making himself a nice cupper," said Ben. "I once counted up how many cuppers Batchy drinks in a day. Guess how many? Seventeen."

"I'll be having a word with him soon, I expect," said Mr. Freebone. "Just for the moment I'm more interested in you. I'd better introduce myself. My name's Freebone. I'm the new Missioner."

"What's happened to old Jake?" said Ben. "I thought we hadden seen him round for a bit. He dead?"

"Now that's not nice, Ben," said the tall boy. "You don't say, 'Is he dead?' Not when you're talking to a clergyman. You say, 'Has he gone before?' "

"Clergyman or not," said Mr. Freebone, "I shouldn't use a ghastly expression like that. If I meant dead, I'd say dead. And Mr. Jacobson's not dead, anyway. He's retired. And I've got his job. Now I've told you all about me, let's hear about you. First, what are your names?"

The boys regarded him warily. The man-to-man approach was not new to them. In their brief lives they had already met plenty of hearty young men who had expressed a desire to lead them onward and upward to better things.

In the end it was Humphrey who spoke. "I'm Humphrey," he said. "The thin one's Colin. The fat one's Ben. You like to partner Ben we'll play 301 up, double in, double out, for a bob a side."

"Middle for diddle," said Mr. Freebone.

At the end of the third game, at which point Mr. Freebone and Ben were each richer by three shillings, Humphrey announced without rancor that he was skinned and would have to go home and get some more money. The others decided to pack it up, too.

"I hope we'll see you here this evening," said the new Missioner genially, and went in search of the resident caretaker, Batchelor, whom he found, as predicted, brewing tea in his den at the back of the hall.

He greeted the new Missioner amiably enough.

"You got lodgings?" he said. "Mr. Jacobson lived up at Greenwich and came down every day. Most days, that is."

"I'm going to do better than that," said Mr. Freebone. "I'm going to live here."

"*Live* here? *Here?*"

"Why not? I'm told there are two rooms up there."

"Well, there *are* two rooms at the back. Gotter nice view of tne factory. It's a long time since anyone lived in 'em."

"Here's someone going to start," said Mr. Freebone.

"There's a piler junk in 'em."

"If you'll lend me a hand, we'll move all the junk into one of the rooms for a start. I've got a camp bed with my luggage."

Batchelor gaped at him.

"You going to sleep here *tonight?*" he said.

"I'm going to sleep here tonight and every night," said Mr. Freebone happily. "I'm going to sleep here and eat here and live here, just as long as they'll have me."

The next week was a busy one.

As soon as Batchelor saw that the new Missioner was set in his intention and immovable in his madness, he made the best of it, and turned to and lent a hand.

Mr. Freebone scrubbed and Batchelor scrubbed. Windows were opened which had not been opened in living memory. Paint arrived by the gallon.

Almost everyone fancies himself as a decorator, and as soon as the boys grasped that an ambitious program of interior decoration was on foot, they threw themselves into it with zeal. One purchased a pot of yellow paint, and painted, before he could be stopped, the entire outside of the porch.

Another borrowed a machine from his employer without his employer's knowledge and buffed up the planks of the main room so hard there was soon very little floor left. Another fell off the roof and broke his leg.

Thus was inaugurated Mr. Freebone's Mission at Sark Lane, a Mission which in retrospect grew into one of the oral traditions of the East End, until almost anything would be believed if it was prefaced with the words, "When ol' Freebone was at Sark Lane."

It was not, as his charges were quick to remark, that he was a particularly pious man, although the East End is one of the few places where saintliness is estimated at its true worth. Nor that he interested himself, as other excellent missioners had done, in the home life and commercial prospects of the boys in his care. It was simply that he lived in, with, and for the Mission. That, and a certain light-hearted ingenuity, allied to a curious thoroughness in the carrying out of his wilder plans.

The story will someday be told more fully of his Easter Scout Camp, a camp joined, on the first night, by three strange boys whose names had certainly not been on the original roll, and who turned out to be runaways from a Borstal institution—to whose comforts they hastily returned after experiencing, for a night and a day, the vigorous hospitality of the Sark Lane Scout Troop.

Nor would anyone who took part in it lightly forget the Great Scavenger Hunt which culminated in the simultaneous arrival at the Mission of a well-known receiver of stolen goods and the Flying Squad; or the Summer Endurance Test in the course of which a group of contestants set out to swim the Thames in full clothes and ended up in a debutante's Steamer Party. In which connection Humphrey claimed to be one of the few people who has danced, dripping wet, with a Royal personage.

Captain Cree turned up about a month after Mr. Freebone's arrival. The first intimation that he had a visitor was a hearty burst of bass laughter from the clubroom. Poking his head round the door he saw a big heavy figure, the upper half encased in a double-breasted blue jacket with brass buttons, the lower half in chalk-striped flannel trousers. The face that slewed round as he approached had been tanned by the weather to a deep russet and then transformed to a deeper red by some more cultivated alchemy.

"Mussen shock the parson," said Captain Cree genially. "Just showing the boys some pictures the Captain of the *William* picked up at Port Said on his last trip. You're Freebone, arnchew? I'm pleased to meet you."

He pushed out a big red hand, grasped Mr. Freebone's, and shook it heartily.

"I've heard a lot about you," said Mr. Freebone.

"Nothing to my credit, I bet," said Captain Cree, with a wink at the boys.

"I know that you're a very generous donor to the Mission," said Mr. Freebone, "and you're very welcome to come and go here as you like."

Captain Cree looked surprised. It had perhaps not occurred to him that he needed anyone's permission to come and go as he liked. He said, "Well, I call that handsome. I got a bit of stuff for you outside. The *William* picked it up for me in Alex. I've got it outside in the station wagon. You two nip out and give my monkeys a hail and we'll get it stowed."

Humphrey and Ben departed, and returned escorting two sailors, dressed in blue jerseys, with the word *Clarissa* in red stitching straggling across the front.

"Dump 'em in there, David," said Captain Cree to the young black-haired sailor. "There's a half gross of plimsolls, some running vests, a couple of footballs, and two pairs of foils. You put them down, Humphrey. I'm giving 'em to the Mission, not to you. Where'd you like 'em stowed?"

"In the back room, for the moment, I think ' said Mr. Freebone. "Hey—Batchelor."

"Old Batchy still alive?" said Captain Cree. "I thought he'd have drunk himself to death long ago. How are you, Batchy?"

"Fine, Captain Cree, fine, thank you," said the old man, executing a sketchy naval salute.

"If you've finished stewing up tea for yourself, you might give a hand to get these things under hatches. You leave 'em out here a moment longer, they'll be gone. I know these boys."

When the Captain had left, Mr. Freebone had a word with Humphrey and Ben, who were now his first and second lieutenants in most club activities.

"He's given us a crate of stuff," said Humphrey.

"Crates and crates," agreed Ben. "Footballs, jerseys, dart boards. Once he brought us a couple of what's-its—those bamboo things—you know, with steel tips. You throw 'em."

"Javelins?"

"That's right. *They* didn't last long. Old Jake took 'em away after Colin threw one at young Arthur Whaley."

"Who were the sailors?"

"The big one, he's Ron Blanden. He used to be a boy round here. The other one's David," Ben explained. "He'd be off one of the ships. Old Cree gets boys for his ships from round here, and when they've done a trip or two, maybe he gives 'em a job on the *Clarissa*. That's his own boat."

"I see," said Mr. Freebone.

"He offered to take me on, soon as I'm old enough," said Humphrey.

"Are you going to say yes?"

Humphrey's long face creased into a grin. "Not me," he said. "I'm keeping my feet dry. Besides, he's a crook."

"He's a what?"

"A crook."

"He can't just be *a* crook," said Mr. Freebone patiently. "He must be some sort of crook. What does he do?"

"I dunno," said Humphrey. "But it sticks out he's a crook, or he wouldn't have so much money. Eh, Ben?"

Ben agreed this was correct. He usually agreed with Humphrey.

Later that night Mr. Freebone and Batchelor sorted out the new gifts. The foils were really nice pairs, complete with masks and gauntlets. Mr. Freebone, who was himself something of a swordsman, took them up to his own room to examine them at leisure. The gym shoes were a good brand, with thick rubber soles. They should be very useful. Boys in these parts wore gym shoes almost all day.

"We usually wash out the vests and things," said Batchelor. "You know what foreigners are like."

Mr. Freebone approved the precaution. He said he knew what foreigners were like. Batchelor said he would wash them through next time he had a boil-up in his copper . . .

A fortnight later—in the last week of May—the officer on the monitored telephone in the basement at New Scotland Yard received a call. The call came at six o'clock in the evening, and the caller announced himself as Magnus.

The officer said, "Count five slowly, please. Then start talking." He put out his hand and pressed down the switch. The tape recorder whirred softly as the man at the other end spoke. Later that evening Romer came down to the Yard and listened to the playback. The voice came, thin and resonant, but clear.

"Magnus here. This is my first report. I've settled into my new job. I feel little real doubt that what we suspect is correct but it's difficult to see just how the trick is pulled.

"The *Clarissa* meets all incoming *Consorts*. She takes out miscellaneous stores and usually fetches back a load of gear for the Mission. It must be the best equipped outfit in London. The customs experts give the stuff the magic-eye treatment before it's put on the *Clarissa*, and I've managed to look through most of it myself. Once it's in the Mission it's handed straight over to the boys, so it's a bit difficult to see how it could be used as a hiding place.

"Cocaine's not bulky, I know; but I gather the quantities we're looking for are quite considerable. I have a feeling this line in sports goods might be a big red herring. Something to take our eye off the real job.

"Carter, the mate of the *Clarissa*, is, I think, an ex-convict. His real name is Coster, and he's been down a number of times for larceny and aggravated assault. He carries a gun. Nothing known about the crew.

"Captain Cree"—here the tape gave a rasping scratch—"Sorry. That was me clearing my throat. As I was saying, Captain Cree's a smart operator. I should think he makes a good bit on the side out of his chandlering, but not nearly enough to account for the style he lives in. You'd imagine a man like him would keep a little woman tucked away somewhere, wouldn't you? But I never heard any whisper about the fair sex. A pity. We might get a woman to talk. That's all for now."

The weather was hot and dry that summer, and through July and August increasing supplies of illicit cocaine continued to dribble into London as water through a rotten sluice gate; and the casualty figures and the crime graphs climbed, hand in hand with the mercury in the thermometer. Superintendent Costorphine's face grew so long and so bleak that Romer took to avoiding him. For all the comfort he could give him was that things would probably get worse before they got better.

At Sark Lane, Mr. Freebone was working an eighteen-hour day. Added to his other preoccupations was an outbreak of skin disease. The boys could not be prevented from bathing in the filthy reaches and inlets of the Thames below Tower Bridge.

When he could spare a minute from his routine work he seemed to cultivate the company of the crew of the *Clarissa*. Carter was surly and unapproachable, but the boys were pleasant enough. Ron Blanden was a burly fair-haired young man of 20. He had ideas beyond the river and talked of leaving the *Clarissa* and joining the Merchant Navy.

David, the young black-haired one, seemed to be a natural idler, with few ideas beyond taking life easy, picking up as much money as he could, and dressing in his smartest clothes on his evenings off. He once told Mr. Freebone that he came from Scotland, but his eyes and hair suggested something more Mediterranean in origin. There was a theory that he had been in bad trouble once, in his early youth, and was now living it down.

Mr. Freebone had no difficulty, in time, in extracting the whole of the candid Ron Blanden's life story, but David, though friendly, kept his distance. All he would say—and this was a matter of record—was that he had made one trip on the *Albert Consort* that April, and had then been offered a job by Captain Cree which he had accepted.

"I don't like that David," said Batchelor one evening.

"Oh? Why?" said Mr. Freebone.

"He's a bad sort of boy," said Batchelor. "I've caught him snooping round this place once or twice lately. Fiddling round with the sports kit. I soon sent him packing."

"Hm," said Mr. Freebone. He changed the subject somewhat abruptly. "By the way, Batchelor, there's something I've been meaning to ask you. How much do we pay you?"

"Four pounds a week, and keep."

"And what does Captain Cree add to that?"

The old man stirred in his chair and blinked. "Who said he added anything?"

"I heard it."

"He pays me a pound or two, now and then. Nothing regular. I do jobs for him. Anything wrong with that?"

Magnus had fallen into the routine of reporting at the appointed hour on every second Wednesday. Toward the end of September his message was brief and contained a request. "Could you check up on the old boy who acts as caretaker at the Mission? He calls himself Batchelor and claims to be ex-R.N. I don't believe that's his real name and I don't believe he was ever in the Navy. Let me know through the usual channels and urgently."

Costorphine said to Romer, "Something's brewing down there. My contacts all tell me the same story. The suppliers are expecting a big autumn run."

Romer made a small helpless gesture. "And are we going to be able to stop it?" he asked.

"We can always hope," said Costorphine. "I'll find out about that man Batchelor. Jacobson will know something about him. He took him on, I believe."

It was a week later that Humphrey said to Mr. Freebone, apropos of nothing that had gone before, "He's a character, that David, all right."

"What's he up to now?" said Mr. Freebone, between gasps, for he was busy blowing up a batch of new footballs.

"Wanted to cut me in on a snide racket."

Mr. Freebone stopped what he was doing, put the football down, and said, "Come on. Let's have it."

"David told me he can get hold of plenty of fivers. Good-looking jobs, he said. The *Clarissa* picks 'em up from the Dutch and German boats. He had some story they were a lot the Gestapo had printed during the war. Is that right?"

"I believe they did. But they'd be the old white sort."

"That's right. That's why he wanted help passing 'em. If he turned up with a lot of 'em, it'd look suspicious. But if some of us boys helped him—"

In a rage Mr. Freebone sought out Captain Cree, who listened to him with surprising patience.

"Half those lads are crooks," he said, when the Missioner had finished. "You can't stop it."

"I'm not going to have your crew corrupting my boys," said Mr. Freebone. "And I look to you to help me stop it."

"What do you want me to do? Sack David?"

Mr. Freebone said, "I don't know that that would do a lot of good. But he's not to come near the Mission."

"I'll sort him out," said the Captain. He added, "You know, what you want's a holiday. You've had a basinful of us since you came, and you haven't had a day off in six months that I can see."

"As a matter of fact," said Mr. Freebone, "I was thinking of taking a long weekend soon."

"You do that," said the Captain. "Tell me when you're going and I'll keep an eye on the place for you myself."

He sounded almost paternal.

"This is report number thirteen," said the tape-recorded voice of Magnus. "I hope that doesn't make it unlucky. I had a narrow escape the other day, but managed to ride the Captain off. I'm bound to say that, in my view, things are coming to a head. Just how it's going to break I don't know, but some sort of job is being planned for next weekend. Cree and Carter have been thick as thieves about it.

"Talking about thieves, I was glad to hear that my hunch about Batchelor was correct, and that he had been inside. There's something about an old lag that never washes off. It was interesting, too, that he worked at one time in a chemist's shop and had done a bit of dispensing in his youth. All he dispenses openly now are cups of vile tea. That's all for now. I hope to be on the air again in a fort-night's time with some real news for you."

Costorphine said, "That ties in with what I'd heard. A big con-signment, quite soon."

"We'd better put the cover plan into operation," said Romer.

"You've got two police boats on call. Whistle them up now."

"A police launch would be a bit outgunned by the *Clarissa*. I've arranged a tie-up with the Navy. There's a launch standing by at Greenwich. We can have her up when we want her. Only we can't keep her hanging about for long—she's too conspicuous.

"I've got an uneasy feeling about this," said Romer. "They're not fools, the people we're dealing with. They wouldn't walk into any-thing obvious."

"Do you think Petrella—?"

"You've got to admit he's been lucky," said Romer. "It was luck that the job was going, and luck that we managed to get it for him. And he's done very well, too. But luck can't last forever. It only needs one person to recognize him—one criminal he's ever had to deal with, and he must have had hundreds through his hands in the last few years."

"He'll be all right," said Costorphine. "He's a smart lad."

"I'm superstitious," said Romer. "I don't mean about things like black cats and ladders. I mean about making bargains with fortune. You remember when we were talking about this thing in here, way back in March, I said something about a single life not being im-portant. It might be true; but I wish I hadn't said it, all the same."

Costorphine confided to his wife that night, "It's the first time I've ever seen the old man jumpy. Things must be bad. Perhaps the politicians are after him."

That Saturday night there were about two dozen boys in the club-room of the Mission, and it says a lot for the enthusiasm engendered by Mr. Freebone that there was anyone there at all, for if ever there was a night for fireside and television this was it. The wind had started to get up with the dusk and was now blowing in great angry gusts, driving the rain in front of it.

At half-past four Captain Cree, faithful to his promise, had come up to keep an eye on things in the Missioner's absence. There had been nothing much for him to do, and he had departed for the dock where the *Clarissa* lay. Now, through the dark and the rain, he drove his big station wagon carefully back, once more, through the empty streets, and maneuvered it into the unlighted cul-de-sac beside the Mission Hall.

Carter, a big unlovely lump of a man, was sitting beside him, smoking one of an endless chain of cigarettes. This time Captain Cree did not trouble with the front entrance. There was a small side door, which gave onto a dark lobby. Out of the lobby bare wooden stairs ran up to Mr. Freebone's bedroom; on the far side a door opened through to Batchelor's sanctum.

Captain Cree stood in the dark empty lobby, his head bent. He was listening. Anyone glimpsing his good-natured red face at that particular moment might have been shocked by the expression on it.

At the end of a full minute he relaxed, went back to the street door, and signaled to Carter. The back of the station wagon was opened and the first of four big bales was lifted out and humped indoors. The bolt of the outer door was shot.

Batchelor was waiting for them. Everything about him showed that he, too, knew that some crisis was impending.

"You locked the door?" said Captain Cree. He jerked his head at the door which led into the Mission Hall.

"Of course I locked it," said Batchelor. "We don't want a crowd of boys in here. How many have you got?"

"Four," said Carter. He was the coolest of the three.

"We'll do 'em all now," said Captain Cree. "It'll take a bit of time, but we won't get a better chance than this. When's *he* coming back?" An upward jerk of his head indicated that he was talking about the occupant of the back attic.

"Sunday midday, he said. Unless he changed his mind."

"He'd better not change it," said Carter.

He helped Batchelor to strip the thick brown-paper wrapping from one of the bales. As the covering came away the contents could be seen to be woolens, half a gross of thick woolen vests. In the second there was half a gross of long pants. Gray socks in the third. Gloves and balaclava helmets and scarves in the fourth.

Carter waddled across to the enormous gas-operated copper in the corner and lifted the lid. A fire had been lit under it earlier in the afternoon and was now glowing red; the copper was full of clean hot water.

What followed would have interested Superintendent Costorphine intensely. He would have realized how it is possible to bring cocaine into the country under the noses of the smartest customs officials, and he would have appreciated just why those samples might contain minute traces of copper.

The three men worked as a team, with the skill born of long practise. Carter dumped the woolens by handfuls in the copper. Captain Cree took them out and wrung each one carefully into a curious contraption which Batchelor had pulled from a closet. Basically this was a funnel, with a drip tray underneath. But between funnel and tray was a fine linen gauze filter. And as the moisture was wrung from each garment a grayish sediment formed on the filter.

When the filter was so full that it was in danger of becoming clogged the Captain called a halt. From a suitcase he extracted an outsize thermos bottle, and into it, with the greatest possible care, he deposited the gray sediment.

It took them over an hour to go through the first three packages. During this time the water in the copper had itself been emptied and filtered, and the copper refilled. Twice during this time a boy had rattled on the door that led into the hall and Batchelor had shouted back that he was busy.

"Tip the last lot in," said the Captain, "and be quick about it." They were all three sweating. "We don't want anyone busting in on us now."

He had never handled such a large quantity before. The third bottle was in use. Two were already full. He had his back to the door leading to the lobby and none of them heard or saw it open.

"What on earth are you all up to?" said Mr. Freebone.

The three men swung round in one ugly savage movement. The plastic cap of the bottle fell from Captain Cree's hand and rolled across the floor.

"What is it—washing day?"

There was a silence of paralysis as Mr. Freebone walked across the room and peered down into the bottle. "And what's this stuff?"

"What—where have you come from?" said Captain Cree hoarsely.

"I've been up in my room, writing," said Mr. Freebone. "I changed my mind and came back. Do I have to ask your permission?" He extended one finger, touched the gray powder in the bottle, and carried his finger to his lips.

Then Carter hit him. It was a savage blow, delivered from behind, with a leather-covered sap, a blow which Mr. Freebone neither saw nor heard.

They stared at him.

"You killed him?" said Batchelor.

"Don't be a damned fool," said Carter. He looked at Captain Cree. The same thought was in both their minds.

"We shall want some rope," he said. "Have you got any?"

"I don't know—"

"Go on. Get it."

It took five minutes to truss up Mr. Freebone. He was showing no signs of life, even while they manhandled him out and dumped him in the back of the station wagon.

Captain Cree seemed to have recovered his composure.

"You stay here and watch him," he said to Carter.

"Are we going to gag him?"

"I think that would be a mistake," said the Captain. "Leave too many traces." They looked at each other again. The thought was as clear now as if it had been spoken. "If he opens his mouth hit him again."

Carter nodded, and the Captain disappeared into the building. In half an hour the job was finished and he came out carrying a suitcase.

"Not a blink," said Carter.

The Captain placed the suitcase carefully in the back of the car, where it rested on the crumpled body of Mr. Freebone. Then he climbed into the driving seat, backed the car out, and started on the half-mile drive to Pagett's Wharf, where the *Clarissa* lay.

The wind, risen almost to gale force, was flogging the empty streets with its lash, part rain, part hail, as the big car nosed its way slowly across the cobbles of the wharf.

Captain Cree turned off the lights and climbed out, followed by Carter. Twenty yards away, in the howling wilderness of darkness, a single riding light showed where the *Clarissa* bumped at her moorings. At their feet the river slid past, cold and black.

The Captain said into Carter's ear, "We'll take the rope off him first. I put 'em on over his clothes so they won't have left much mark. If he's found, what's to show he didn't slip and knock his head going in?"

"*If* he's found," said Carter.

Back at the Mission, Batchelor was facing a mutiny.

"What've you been up to, locked in here all evening?" said Humphrey. "That was the Captain's car in the alley, wasn't it?"

"That's right," said Ben.

"And what've you done with Mr. Freebone?"

"He ent here," said Batchelor. "And you can get out of my room too, all of you."

"Where is he?"

"He went away for the weekend. He'll be back tomorrow."

As soon as he had said this, Batchelor realized his mistake.

"Don't be soft," said Humphrey. "He came back after tea. We saw him. Pop upstairs, Ben, and see if he's in his room."

"You've got no right—" said Batchelor. But they were past taking any notice of what he said.

"And what were you doing with all those clothes?" He pointed at the sodden pile in the corner. "Is this washing night or something?"

Batchelor was saved answering by the reappearance of Ben. "He's been there," he said. "The light's on. And there's a letter on the table he was finishing writing. *And* his raincoat's there."

"He wouldn't go out without a coat," said Humphrey. "Not on a night like this. He's been took."

Here Batchelor made his second mistake. He broke for the door. Several pairs of hands caught him and threw him back ungently into the chair. For the moment, after the scuffle, there was silence and stillness.

Then Humphrey said, "I guess they were up to something. And I guess Mr. Freebone came back when he wasn't expected. And I guess the Captain and Carter and that lot have picked him up."

"So that's all you can do, guess," said Batchelor viciously. But the fear in his voice could be felt.

"All right," said Humphrey calmly. "Maybe I'm wrong. You tell us." Batchelor stared at him. Humphrey said, "Is that water hot, Ben?"

Ben dipped the tip of his finger in and took it out again quickly.

Humphrey said, "Either you talk or we hold you head-down in that."

It took six of them to get him halfway across the floor. Batchelor stopped cursing and started to scream. When his nose was six inches away from the water he talked.

"Pagett's Wharf," said Humphrey. "All right. We'll lock him up in here. If he's lying to us, we'll come back and finish him off afterwards."

"How do we get there?" said one of the boys.

"Night like this," said Humphrey, "the quickest way to get anywhere's to run."

The pack streamed out into the howling darkness.

In the big foredeck cabin of the *Clarissa*, Captain Cree was giving some final instructions to Carter when he heard the shout. Carter jumped across to the cabin door and pulled it open.

"Who's out there?" said the Captain.

"Ron's on deck," said Carter. "David's ashore somewhere."

"Who was that shouted?"

"It sounded like Ron," said Carter.

This was as far as he got. The next moment a wave of boys seemed to rise out of the darkness. Carter had time to shout before something hit him, and he went down.

The attack passed into the cabin. Captain Cree got his hand to a gun, but he had no time to fire it. Humphrey, swinging an iron bar which he had picked up on deck, broke Cree's arm with a vicious side swipe. The gun dropped from his fingers.

"Pull him in," said Humphrey. "Both of them."

Captain Cree, his right arm swinging loosely in front of him, his red face mottled with white, held himself up with his sound hand on the table.

Carter lay on the floor at his feet, and Ben kicked him, as hard and as thoughtlessly as you might kick a football. The boys had tasted violence and victory that night, and it had made them drunker than any strong drink.

"There's one thing can keep you alive," said Humphrey. "And that's Mr. Freebone. Where is he?"

For a count of ten there was silence. The Captain's mouth worked, but no sound came out of it.

Almost gently Humphrey said, "So you dropped him in the river. He's going to have three for company. Right?"

That was right. That was the way things were done in the land of violence and hot blood. Humphrey swung his iron bar delicately.

"You can't," said the Captain. "You can't do it. I'll tell you everything. I'll do what you like. There's ten thousand pounds' worth of cocaine in that suitcase. It's yours for the taking."

"We'll pour it in after you," said Humphrey. "It'll be useful where you're going."

"You can't do it—"

"Who's stopping us?"

"I am," said a voice from behind them. The third member of the *Clarissa's* crew, David, stepped through the door into the cabin.

He was drenched with rain and out of breath from running; but there was something about him which held all their eyes.

"How—"

"It'll save a lot of time and trouble," said David, "if I tell you that I'm a police officer. My name, not that it matters, is Petrella. I'm a Sergeant in the plainclothes branch, and I'm taking these three men into custody."

"But," said Humphrey, "they've killed Mr. Freebone."

"They meant to kill him," said Petrella. "No doubt of it. But there've been two police launches lying off this wharf ever since dusk, and one of them picked him up. He's at Leman Street Police Station, and from what he's told me we've got more than enough to send both these men away for life. So don't let's spoil a good thing now."

There was a bump at the side of the boat as the River Police tender hitched on alongside. The first man into the cabin was Superintendent Costorphine, looking like a bedraggled crow. He pounced on the suitcase.

"Three months' supply for London," said Petrella. "It'll need a bit more drying out, but it's all there . . ."

Later Petrella found Philip Freebone propped up on pillows in St. George's Hospital, where he had been taken under protest and deposited for the night.

"There's nothing wrong with me," he said. "I'd just as soon be back in my bed at the Mission. There's a lot to do. I shall have to find a replacement for Batchelor."

"Are you going on with that job?"

Freebone looked surprised. "Of course I am," he said. "I've enjoyed it. I knew I would. That's why I wouldn't let you do it."

"The trouble is," said Petrella, "that you've set yourself too high a standard. The boys will never have another night like tonight as long as they live. Do you realize that if I hadn't turned up, they really were going to knock Captain Cree off and put him and Carter over the side?"

"Yes, I expect they would." Freebone thought about it and added, "It's rather a compliment, really, isn't it? What are you going to do now, Patrick?"

"Take a holiday," said Detective Sergeant Petrella. "A good long holiday."

Ruth Rendell

The Strong and the Weak

A tale of two sisters named May and June because they were born in those months—a tale of hate and love, of misery and happiness, of despair and hope . . . Ruth Rendell is masterly at this kind of story—she feels the heartbeats of her characters, and she can make you feel them too. Reading one of her stories is like having your finger on someone's pulse . . .

Their parents named them May and June because their birthdays occurred in those months. A third sister, an April child, had been christened Avril but she had died. May was like the time of year in which she had been born, changeable, chilly and warm by turns, sullen and yet to know and show a loveliness which could not last.

In the 1930s, when May was in her twenties, it was still important to get one's daughters well married, and though Mrs. Thrace had no anxieties on that score for sunny June, she was less sanguine about May. Her older daughter was neither pretty nor graceful nor clever, and no man had ever looked at her twice. June, of course, had a string of admirers.

Then May met a young lawyer at a *thé dansant*. His name was Walter Cheney, he was extremely good-looking, his father was wealthy and made him a generous allowance, and there was no doubt he belonged in a higher social class than that of the Thraces. May fell passionately in love with him, but no one was more surprised than she when he asked her to marry him.

The intensity of May's passion frightened Mrs. Thrace. It wasn't quite "nice." The expression on May's face while she awaited the coming of her fiancé, her ardor when she greeted him, the hunger in her eyes—that sort of thing was all very well in the cinema, but unsuitable for a customs officer's daughter in a genteel suburb.

For a brief period she had become almost beautiful. "I'm going to marry him," she said when cautioned. "He wants me to love him, doesn't he? He loves me. Why shouldn't I show my love?"

June, who was clever as well as pretty, was away at college, training to be a schoolteacher. It had been considered wiser, long before Walter Cheney had appeared, to keep May at home. She had no particular aptitude for anything, and she was useful to her mother about the house. Now, of course, it turned out that she had an aptitude for catching a rich, handsome, and successful husband. Then, a month before the wedding, June came home for the summer holidays.

It was all very unfortunate, Mrs. Thrace said over and over again. If Walter Cheney had jilted May for some other girl, they would have been bitterly indignant, enraged even, and Mr. Thrace would have felt old-fashioned longings to apply a horsewhip. But what could anyone say or do when Walter transferred his affections from the older daughter to the younger?

May screamed and sobbed and tried to attack June with a knife. "We're all terribly sorry for you, my darling," said Mrs. Thrace, "but what can we do? You wouldn't marry a man who doesn't love you, would you?"

"He does love me, he does! It's just because she's pretty. She's cast a spell on him. I wish she was dead and then he'd love me again."

"You mustn't say that, May. It's all very cruel to you, but you have to face the fact that he's changed his mind. Isn't it better to find out now than later?"

"I would have had him," insisted May.

Mrs. Thrace blushed. She was shocked to the core.

"I shall never marry now," said May. "She's ruined my life and I shall never have anything ever again."

Walter and June were married, and Walter's father bought them a house in Surrey. May stayed at home, being useful to her mother. The war came. Walter went straight into the army, became a captain, then a major, finally a colonel. May also went into the army, where she remained a private for five years, working in some catering department. After that there was nothing for her to do except to go home to her parents once more . . .

May never forgave her sister.

"She stole my husband," she would remind her mother.

"He wasn't your husband, May."

"As good as. You wouldn't forgive a thief who came into your house and stole the most precious thing you had or were likely to have."

"We're told to forgive those who trespass against us, as we hope to be forgiven."

"I'm not religious," said May, and on those occasions when the Cheneys came to the Thrace home she took care to be absent. But she knew all about them—all, that is, except one thing.

Mr. and Mrs. Thrace were most careful never to speak of June in May's presence, so May listened outside the door, and she secretly read all June's letters to her mother. Whenever Walter's name was mentioned in a letter, or spoken, she winced and shivered with the pain of it. She knew that they had moved to a larger house, that they were building up a collection of fine furniture and valuable paintings. She knew where they went for their holidays and what friends they entertained. But what she was never able to discover was how Walter felt about June.

Had he ever really loved her? Had he repented of his choice? May thought that perhaps, after the first flush of infatuation was over, he had come to long for May as much as she longed for him. Since she never saw them, she could never know, for, however he might feel, Walter couldn't leave June. When you have done what he had done—what June had made him do—you can't change again. You have to stick it out till death.

It comforted May—it was perhaps the only thing that kept her going—to convince herself that Walter regretted his bargain. If there had been children—what the Victorians called pledges of love . . . Sometimes, after a letter had come from June, May would see her mother looking particularly pleased and satisfied. And then, shaking with dread, May would read that letter, terrified to learn that June was pregnant. But Mrs. Thrace's pleasure and satisfaction must have come from some other source, from some account of Walter's latest *coup* in court or June's latest party, for no children came and now June was past 40.

Trained for nothing, May worked as a canteen supervisor in a women's hostel. She continued to live at home until her parents died. Their deaths took place within six months, Mrs. Thrace dying in March and her widower in August. And that was how it happened that May saw Walter again.

At the time of her mother's cremation, May was ill in bed with a virus infection and unable to attend. But she had no way of avoiding her father's funeral. When she saw Walter come into the church, a faintness seized her and she pushed against the pew rail, trembling. She covered her face with her hands to make it seem as if she were praying, and when at last she took them away Walter was beside her.

He took her hand and looked into her face. May's eyes met his, which were as blue and compelling as ever, and she saw with anguish that he had lost none of his good looks, but had become only more distinguished-looking. She would have liked to die then, holding his hand and gazing into his face.

"Won't you come and speak to your sister, May?" said Walter in the rich deep voice which charmed juries, struck terror into the hearts of witnesses, and won women. "Shall we let bygones be bygones on this very sad day?"

May shivered. She withdrew her hand and marched to the back of the church. She placed herself as far away from June as she could, but not too far to observe that it was June who took Walter's arm as they left and not Walter who took June's; that it was June who looked up at Walter for comfort while his face remained grave and still; that it was June who clung to him while he merely permitted the clinging. It couldn't be that he was behaving like that because she, May, was there. He must hate and despise June, as May, with all her heart, still hated and despised her sister.

But it was at a funeral that they were reconciled.

May learned of Walter's death by reading an announcement of it in a newspaper. And the pain of it was as great as the one she had suffered when her mother had told her he wanted to marry June. She sent flowers, an enormous wreath of snow-white roses that cost her half a week's wages. And of course she would go to the funeral, whether June wanted her there or not.

Apparently June did want her. Perhaps she thought the roses were for the living bereaved and not for the dead. She came up to May and put her arms round her, laying her head against her sister's shoulder in misery and despair.

May broke their long silence. "Now you know what it's like to lose him."

"Oh, May, May, don't be cruel to me now! Don't hold that against me now. Be kind to me now, I've nothing left."

So May sat beside June, and after the funeral she went back to the house where June had lived with Walter. In saying she had nothing left, June had presumably been referring to emotional rather than material things. Apart from certain stately homes she had visited on tours, May had never seen anything like the interior of that house.

"I'm going to retire next month," May remarked, "and then I'll be living in what they call a flatlet—one room and a kitchen."

Two days later a letter came from June:

"Dearest May: Don't be angry with me for calling you that. You have always been one of my dearest, in spite of what I did and in spite of your hatred of me. I can't be sorry for what I did because so much happiness came of it for me, but I am truly, deeply sorry that you were the one who suffered. And now, dear May, I want to try to make up to you for what I did, though I know I can never really do that, not now, not after so long.

"You said you were going to retire and wouldn't be living very comfortably. Will you come and live with me? You can have as many rooms in this house as you want—you are welcome to share everything with me. You will know what I mean when I say I feel that would be just. Please make me happy by saying you forgive me and will come. Always your loving sister, June."

What did the trick was June saying it would be just. Yes, it would be justice if May could now have some of those good things which were hers by right and which June had stolen from her along with her man. She waited a week and then she wrote:

"Dear June: What you suggest seems a good idea. I have thought about it and I will make my home with you. I have very little personal property, so moving will not be a great bother. Let me know when you want me to come. It is raining again here and very cold. Yours, May."

There was nothing, however, in the letter about forgiveness.

And yet May, sharing June's house, was almost prepared to forgive. For she was learning at last what June's married life had been.

"You can talk about him if you want to," May had said hungrily on their first evening together. "If it's going to relieve your feelings, I don't mind."

"What is there to say except that we were married for forty years and now he's dead?"

"You could show me some of the things he gave you." May picked up ornament after ornament, gazed at paintings. "Did he give you that? What about this?"

"They weren't presents. I bought them or he did."

May couldn't help getting excited. "I wonder you're not afraid of

burglars. This is a proper Aladdin's Cave. Have you got lots of jewelry too?"

"Not much," said June uncomfortably.

May's eyes were on June's engagement ring, a poor thing of diamond chips in nine-carat gold, far less expensive than the ring Walter had given his first love. Of course she had kept hers, and Walter,
though well off even then, hadn't been rich enough to buy a second
magnificent ring within six months of the first—not with all the
expenses of furnishing a new home. But later, surely . . . ?

"I should have thought you'd have an eternity ring."

"Marriage doesn't last for eternity," said June.

May could tell June didn't like talking about it. June even avoided
mentioning Walter's name, and soon she put away the photographs
of him which had stood on the piano and on the drawing-room mantelpiece. May wondered if Walter had ever written any letters to his
wife. They had seldom been parted, of course, but it would be strange
if June hadn't received a single letter from him in 40 years.

So the first time June went out alone, May tried to open her desk.
It was locked. The drawers of June's dressing table disclosed a couple
of birthday cards with *Love from Walter* scrawled hastily on them,
and the only other written message from her husband June had
considered worth keeping May found tucked into a cookbook in the
kitchen. It was a note written on the back of a bill, and it read:
Baker called. I ordered a large white bread for Saturday.

That night May reread the two letters she had received from
Walter during their engagement. Each began "Dearest May." She
hadn't looked at them for 40 years—she hadn't dared—but now she
read them with calm satisfaction.

"Dearest May: This is the first love letter I have ever written. If
it isn't much good you must put it down to lack of practise. I miss
you a lot and rather wish I hadn't told my parents I would visit
them on this holiday . . ."

And "Dearest May: Thanks for both your letters. Sorry I've taken
so long to reply, but I feel a bit nervous that my letters don't match
up to yours. Still, with luck, we soon shan't have to write to each
other because we shan't be separated. I wish you were here with
me . . ."

Poor Walter had been reticent and shy, unable to express his
feelings on paper or by word of mouth. But at least he had written
love letters to *her* and not notes about loaves of bread. May decided
to start wearing her engagement ring again—on her little finger,

of course, because she could no longer get it over the knuckle of her ring finger. If June noticed, she didn't comment on it.

"Was it you or Walter who didn't want children?" May asked one day.

"Children just didn't come."

"Walter *must* have wanted them. When he was engaged to me we talked of having three."

June looked upset, but May could have talked of Walter all day long. "He was only sixty-five," she said. "That's young to die these days. You never told me what he died of."

"He needed an operation," said June, "and never regained consciousness."

"Just like mother," said May. Suppose June had had an incurable disease and had died—what would have happened then? Remembering Walter's tender look and strong handclasp at her father's funeral, May thought he would have married her. She twisted the ring on her little finger. "You were almost like a second wife, weren't you? It must have been a difficult position."

"I'd much rather not talk about it," said June, and with her handkerchief to her eyes, she left the room.

May was happy. For the first time in 40 years she was happy. She busied herself about the house, caring for June's things, dusting and polishing, pausing to look at a painting and reflecting that Walter must have often paused to look at it too. Sometimes she imagined him sitting in this chair or standing by that window, his heart full of regret for what he might have had with May. And she thought how, while he had been longing for her, she, far away, had been crying for him. She never cried now, though June did, often.

"I'm an old fool. I can't help giving way," June sobbed. "You're strong, May, but I'm weak and I miss him so."

"Didn't I miss him?"

"He was always fond of you. It upset him a lot to think you were unhappy. He often talked about you." June looked at her piteously. "You *have* forgiven me, haven't you, May?"

"As a matter of fact, I have," said May. She was a little surprised at herself. But, yes, she had forgiven June. "I think you've been punished for what you did." A loveless marriage, a husband who talked constantly of another woman . . .

"I've been punished," said June, and she put her arms round May's neck.

The strong and the weak. May recalled that when a movement

downstairs woke her in the middle of one night. She heard footsteps and a wrenching sound as of a door being forced. It was the burglar she had always feared and had warned June about, but June would be cowering in her room now, terrified, incapable of taking any action.

May put on her dressing gown and went down the passage to June's room. The bed was empty. She looked out of the window, and the moonlight showed her a car parked on the gravel driveway that led to the lane. A yellower, stronger light streamed from the drawing-room window. A shiver of fear went through her, but she knew she must be strong.

Before she reached the head of the stairs she heard a violent crash as of something heavy yet brittle hurled against a wall. There was a cry from below, then footsteps running. May got to the stairs in time to see a slight figure rush across the hall and slam the front door behind him. The car started up.

In his wake he had left a thin trail of blood. May followed the blood trail into the drawing room. June stood by her desk which had been torn open and all its contents scattered onto the table. She was trembling, tearful, and laughing with shaky hysteria, pointing to the shards of cut glass that lay everywhere.

"I threw the decanter at him. I hit him and cut his head and he ran."

May went up to her. "Are you all right?"

"He didn't touch me. He pointed that gun at me when I came in, but I didn't care. I couldn't bear to see him searching my desk, getting at all my private things. Wasn't I brave? He didn't get away with anything but a few pieces of silver. I hit him and then he heard you coming and he panicked. Wasn't I brave, May?"

But May wasn't listening. She was reading the letter which lay open and exposed on top of the papers that the burglar had pulled out of the desk. Walter's handwriting leaped at her, weakened though it was, enfeebled by his last illness. "My darling love: It is only a minute since you walked out of the hospital room, nevertheless I must write to you. I can't resist an impulse to write now and tell you how happy you have made me in all the beautiful years we have been together. If the worst comes to the worst, my darling, and I don't survive the operation, I want you to know you are the only woman I ever loved . . ."

"I wouldn't have thought I'd have had the courage," said June, "but perhaps the gun wasn't loaded. He was only a boy. Would you call the police, please, May?"

"Yes," said May. She picked up the gun.

The police arrived within 15 minutes. They brought a doctor with them, but June was already dead, shot through the heart at close range.

"We'll get him, Miss Thrace, don't you worry," said the Inspector. "It was a pity you touched the gun, though. Did it without thinking, I suppose?"

"It was the shock," said May. "I've never had a shock like that, not in the last forty years."

Thomas Walsh

The Dead Past

Thomas Walsh is at his best when he views crime as a human equation. He understands the people involved—the guilty, the innocent, and those caught in the mesh of circumstances. Young Ned McKestin was caught in such a web—a web he had helped spin himself. But now others were caught with him. Now there were Kate and the baby for Ned to worry about . . .

But never once was it a dead past, not even years later, for Ned McKestin. After it happened he told Kate and Uncle Gerry the whole story, being that honest with them, but no one else. He had done it, after all. Therefore it was right that he, and he alone, should bear the burden of it. And so he did. He bore it silently, never once able to completely force it out of his mind, not even after three or four years had gone by, and then five, and then six.

He carried it by himself all that time, and his sole comfort was a feeling that he now understood the big secret of human life. To be a straight decent man one simply established straight decent habits. There it was, as simple as that. Then why did he go on worrying and worrying about it?

Yet he did. Occasionally at night, when he found himself tossing restlessly hour after hour; now and again during work hours at the store with Uncle Gerry; but here and there, every so often, he would sense that the dead past was beginning to darken and close in around him, biding its time. Very stupid. How long were the odds now that he would ever see Preston Ruby or Dandy Jack O'Hara again? Yet still . . .

Still. "What's the matter?" Kate sometimes would demand of him. "You seem awfully quiet tonight, Ned. What's wrong?"

"No, no," Ned would insist, managing to slip a reassuring arm around her shoulders. "Nothing at all, Kate. I'm just the original quiet man, maybe. I feel fine."

Because his shadow was not her problem. It was Ned's, and Ned deserved it, and could only do the best he could to live with it. Why was it impossible, however, to feel that the dead past was over and done with for him? Why did he have to have the silly idea that somehow, somewhere, even now, it still waited for him? At 24 he knew at last what really mattered to him, and what did not. The important thing was to concentrate on his new life.

And in the year 1975 the new life became more wonderful than ever. Uncle Gerry retired to the Florida Keys with Aunt Mamie and his fishing tackle and left Ned in complete charge at G. G. McKestin & Company, as a third partner.

"I've got enough," Uncle Gerry said to him that night, "and you've earned what I'm giving you, Ned. You've done better than I ever expected up here. You've settled down, thank God, and there won't be a worry in the world for me with you running things. I'm depending on you. You're the best man I ever had in the store."

And Ned was. He had great manual ability at driving a car, and as a handyman at odd jobs around the house, and at fixing almost anything in the electrical line. So by the time Uncle Gerry retired, the firm of G. G. McKestin, TV Sales and Service, 36 Main Street, was one of the biggest and best of its kind in the whole North Country. For 30 years Uncle Gerry had worked day and night to give it the most trustworthy reputation possible, and in the spring of 1975 Ned's one-third interest meant all clear sailing ahead. He and Kate had it made.

"Oh, golly," Kate said, after hugging Uncle Gerry half breathless. "I never had any desire to be rich, Ned. All I ever wanted was to have you and maybe three or four kids. There's only one thing I'd like. Do you suppose we could have our own house now?"

Because Kate had always been a great one for their own house. Until then they had lived in a small apartment over the store, where Ned had often caught her sighing wistfully at night at pictures in home magazines of the newest and most modern in kitchen equipment, or the latest fashion in bathroom fixtures. So that year they got their own house, building it in the woods out of town near the lower lake, with a spectacular view of Whiteface Mountain in back, and he and Kate had never been so happy.

They had a wonderful summer—almost every week there were cookouts or picnics with friends, or swimming and boating off their own dock—and after Christmas, Kate discovered radiantly that she was pregnant. But there were a few complications about a blood factor, and in the end, on the local doctor's advice, Ned took her down to Albany Medical Center when her time came. A few days later she had a fine healthy boy, no problems at all, and driving home to Martinsville that night, 150 miles north, Ned felt wonderfully exuberant.

He got back about ten o'clock and, still too excited to sleep, mixed a mild Scotch for himself in the kitchen. Just as he was taking his first sip the front doorbell rang. That time, when it turned out to be the dead past in brute fact, there was no premonition of any kind. A neighbor, Ned thought, wanting to hear how Kate had made out down in Albany; and with the drink in his hand and a huge happy grin on his lips, Ned walked out to the front door.

But it was not a neighbor who had seen his kitchen light on and had stopped off to hear the good news. Instead, dapper as ever, it was Dandy Jack O'Hara.

Ned stood frozen, his grin dead on his lips, and Dandy Jack allowed himself a moment of maliciously covert triumph.

"Well, what do you know?" Dandy Jack drawled, studying with his foxily wizened face and cunningly observant gray eyes the front hall behind Ned. "Sure enough. Nobody but the kid himself. Long time no see, kid. How you been?"

And he did not wait for Ned to ask him inside. He came in, at once establishing the authority between them, removed a dark green Borsalino hat with a negligent sweep of his right arm and tossed it onto the hall table.

"And you know something else?" he went on, glancing at the antique wall mirror with the gold eagle on it, at the soft green carpeting, and at the beautifully waxed old drum table with the big porcelain bowl of fresh flowers. "What a great layout you got, kid. Everything you'd ever want, eh? Guess you did all right for yourself. But how long has it been, anyway? Five or six years, ain't it?"

Ned closed the front door. He closed it numbly, one breathless catch of the heart in him, and with his ears ringing. But Dandy Jack, elegant gold sweater with a knitted white scarf at the throat, red-and-brown houndstooth slacks, and highly polished English brogues, paid no attention at all to the lack of welcome for him.

"Funny how things happen," he remarked, slipping a cigarette out of his monogrammed gold case. "Like tonight. I'm in a taproom downtown just to kill a little time, and a guy on the next stool asks the bartender if he heard how Ned McKestin's wife was getting along down in Albany. Now that's kind of an exceptional name, kid—Ned McKestin. But you know me. I start asking a question here and there to see if you're the same guy I once knew. And what do you know? You turn out to be the same Ned McKestin, all right. The kid himself. You know Preston and me often wondered what the hell ever happened to you."

Ned had to clear his throat. It felt dry as desert sand.

"Nothing much," he got out. "I did what you and Ruby did, that's all. I got out as fast and far as I could, Dandy. I bummed rides up here to an uncle I have "

"Yeah, who wouldn't?" Dandy Jack said, still studying Ned with his mockingly observant gray eyes. "Matter of fact, Preston and me got to hell and gone all the way out to the coast. No sense hanging around for trouble, the way we saw it. Got another drink in the house?"

"In the kitchen," Ned told him. "This way, Dandy."

But he was still numb, although with a slight pressing pain making itself felt at the back of his skull. Yet maybe there was nothing at all to worry about, he tried to convince himself. Why should there be? A couple of old friends meeting unexpectedly and exchanging the news with each other. No need to push the panic button. Best that he take this meeting between them just as casually as Dandy Jack was taking it.

"But it looks," Dandy Jack said, noting with approval the glistening new stove and refrigerator in the kitchen, and the alcove near the back door with the new washer and dryer, "you've done a lot better for yourself than me and Preston. We've had to scamper. I mean, a layout like this, and you married and settled down and all. What's wrong with your wife, kid?"

Ned told him, pouring out his drink.

"Well, well, well," Dandy Jack murmured. "How sweet it is. A real family man, eh? Great. But how about showing me around the house now? Like to see how you did for yourself. Come on, kid. Give me the grand tour."

So Ned showed him the whole place, upstairs and down—the basement clubroom, the basement garage with the automatic electric door. But the very odd feeling he had while doing so was that it was not Ned and Kate McKestin's new house any more. Something had happened. Something had moved in. It seemed that it was Dandy Jack's house now, and Preston Ruby's.

Back in the kitchen again, Dandy Jack settled himself comfortably and began talking about old times. It was half an hour later before he got up and reached for the Borsalino hat.

"Seem kind of nervous," he remarked casually, "but don't be. Way out in the woods here, who the hell ever saw me come in? See what I mean, kid? Mum's the word. I'm just up here for a couple of days on a little scouting trip, as you might call it. Leaving first thing tomorrow morning."

Ned followed him out to the hall, the pressure noticeably tightening around the back of his skull. He attempted to make his next question very casual.

"Oh? A little scouting trip, Dandy?"

"Well, yeah," Dandy Jack said, daintily wiping off his fingers with an immaculate linen handkerchief. "Only looking around, that's all. Just in case. But of course there's no telling when lightning could strike. You keeping clean?"

"Ever since," Ned told him tightly, to get everything clearly understood between them. "The straight and narrow, Dandy. My first and last experience. Never again."

"Atta boy," Dandy told him, with another slyly covert grin on his lips. "Nothing like it, they tell me. Still, though—we were all damned lucky to get out of it that time, weren't we? Or all of us but Rod Connihan. He's the one bought it, eh?"

Ned had opened the door, but without putting on the porch light. It was a clear frosty night with a lot of stars, but very dark off in the woods. And suddenly, against the dark, like a confused movie montage, Ned could see himself six years ago at the steering wheel of a big Buick, with Preston Ruby and Dandy Jack darting out to him from the bank entrance. Behind them, crawling and scrambling horribly, was Rod Connihan, blood all over one leg of his gray trousers.

Then more shots had rung out in the blazing stillness that seemed to have frozen all around Ned, and Connihan had sprawled full length on the pavement, at the same time dropping the bag in his hands. "Don't," Ned could hear again, and in the most breathless and anguished tones he had ever heard, "Wait a minute. Give me a hand, fellow! Don't leave me!"

But there was one more shot from inside the bank door, with Connihan jerking forward at it, and then lying rigidly still. It was only Ned who attempted to get out of the car to him, but Preston Ruby had knocked him back with a savage thrust of his right arm. "Get out of here!" Dandy Jack had begun yelling. "They got him, you damned fool. Start driving the car!"

Six years ago—and Ned was only 18.

But now Dandy Jack, out on the porch steps, turned for one more moment.

"Well, all the best," he said. "Sincere good wishes, kid—like all the postcards have it. I'll only tell Preston I saw you, but that's all. And you know what? I kind of got an idea he's going to be pretty damned glad to hear."

Alone then in the front hall, Ned leaned back against it with his eyes closed and his hands behind him. He remembered himself at 18, all alone on the city streets after his parents had died, and how that Ned had thought Connihan and Dandy Jack were just about the greatest guys in the world. They fed him, gave him a few dollars now and again, took him around—and in return he had fixed up cars for them, a lot of cars that he never inquired about, and had run their errands.

"Might have a driving job for you tomorrow," Connihan had told him one night. "You're some jockey, kid. Just love the way you can cut around a corner slick as a whistle at seventy or seventy-five. How about it?"

"Well, sure," young Ned had replied earnestly. "Of course, Rod. Where are we going to go?"

"Let you know," Rod had told him, winking brightly. "Couple of things to arrange first. Just bring the car around here right after breakfast, that's all. I got the idea it's going to go easy as pie for us."

But it had not gone easy as pie, or not for dead Rod. And alone in the hall now, still with the ugly nausea in him, Ned once more had that bad feeling in him. Somehow not his own house any more; and most likely, if he could be useful in any way to Preston Ruby, not even his own life any more.

Later on, sitting on the edge of his bed and staring off into the dark woods, Ned kept thinking about the last remark that Dandy Jack had made to him. "Pretty damned glad to hear," Ned remembered. "I'll tell Preston. I'll tell Preston, kid. I'll tell Preston."

Two days later Ned went down to Albany again, to see Kate and the baby, who were just fine although the doctor wanted her to stay on a few more days for another couple of tests. Ned did not tell her anything about Dandy Jack, however; his problem. Instead he was very cheerful with her, forcing himself; but he went out of her room finally a bit paler than usual, and with his heart heavy in him.

The thing would happen, Ned felt, just as he had always known it would happen. He had too much now, and had got it too easily.

He would have to pay. When? How? Those were the only questions. For six years he had not known in what way it would happen, but he had known it would. The dead past was closing in. Preston Ruby had found him

And that conviction was perfectly correct. It happened that night. It happened in the slight drizzle down in the parking lot, when he saw two men waiting by the car for him. The one in the trench coat and the dapperly slanted Borsalino was Dandy Jack. The one beside him was Preston Ruby.

"Thought we might run into you here," Dandy Jack began affably. "Even waited around till ten o'clock last night, Ned. Look. Preston and I thought you might like to give us a ride with you back to Martinsville. Seems like we got a little unfinished business up there. How about it?"

Ruby said nothing. He did not even bother to say hello. But then he always stuck to the bare essentials in conversation, as Ned knew. Dark hat and overcoat; dark glasses; undersized, very quick body, quick as light when required; calm and narrow white face.

"Well, I don't know," Ned began painfully. "The car's not running too hot. I'd hate it if—"

It was time for the essentials, apparently. Ruby reached over for the car door, opened it and gestured.

"Not asking you," Ruby said. "Telling you. Get in."

And Ned got in. Nothing else for it. Dandy Jack sat in front with him, and Ruby behind. When he spoke again, Ned's voice was a lot weaker and jumpier than he wanted it to be.

"What do you want to go back to Martinsville for?" he asked them. "What's the business?"

"Wait'll you hear," Dandy Jack said, in the same cheerfully persuasive manner of Rod Connihan six years ago. "Easiest thing in the world, kid. Just like old times for all three of us. Preston and I decided that maybe we'd like to board with you for a few days. Little company, see—you being alone in the house and all. Feed us real good and we might even throw you a couple of grand when it's all over. Fair enough?"

Ned took the Northway turn without answering, but it seemed to be time for essentials there too. Ruby stirred.

"Keep it right at fifty," he ordered. "We don't want no trouble with the cops."

"Yeah," Dandy Jack agreed. "We wouldn't like to get stopped by one of them troopers, kid. Your interests, understand? This way nobody's going to know we're in the car with you, just as nobody's going to know when you get us back to Martinsville tonight, either. So there ain't a thing for you to worry about, not a thing. You're all covered. All anyone knows but you, me and Preston could be up on the moon."

"Covered on what?" Ned asked grimly, discovering that his hands had become clammy. There was not only Ned McKestin to think about now. There were Kate and the baby. It was necessary to get hold of himself. The thing had happened.

"On the favor we want you to do for us," Dandy Jack said. "It's this way, see? I hear tell a lot of prominent people live in those big camps off in the woods in your neighborhood, all around the upper lake. Saw some of them the other day when I took a ride. Biggest and best one you can't even see from the road—too private. Forest Ridge, it's called. Mrs. James Devereux Murchison."

Ruby said nothing at all in the back seat—not time yet.

"And that old biddy," Dandy Jack murmured almost reverently, "has just about everything there is, the way I get it. Place in Palm Beach, in New York, in Paris, France, in Washington, and the swellest summer camp in the whole country just about a mile and a half from where you live. Paced it off the other afternoon, just to be sure. She invites people and they get flied in there on her private plane. Land on the lake, then go up the mountain on her own private elevator. Built right into it—saw it myself that afternoon, the whole thing. And three chefs, Preston, did I tell you? Meat chef, salad chef, pastry chef. Maybe thirty or thirty-five in help, but only one watchman. Only one watchman, kid. Kind of careless, huh?"

Fifty miles steady on the speedometer, Ned saw; just as ordered. A bad sign? He struggled to rouse himself.

"Yes, I've heard about it," he said. "Never saw it, though. Quite a place, eh?"

"Just lemme tell you," Dandy Jack said, pressing the most companionable of hands on Ned's right knee and squeezing in gently. "You wouldn't believe, kid. A big main house where they all go for their meals, the old biddy and her friends, and then a lot of little guest cottages all over the grounds, so everybody can be in his own place when he wants to be. Met a fellow down in New York who worked there a couple of years ago, and what he says is that the old lady herself lives in one of them guest cottages, of course the nicest one, when she's in residence, which I found out she is now. You can see her cottage right at the edge of the mountain overlooking the lake. Wonderful view from there. That's where she sleeps. Nobody else in her cottage, either. Not even a maid.

"So this guy brings her breakfast in bed one morning when her personal maid is sick, and just as he walks in with the tray she's opening a big wall safe back of some hangings. Holy smoke, he says. Like a damn jewelry store. Rings and necklaces and brooches, and whatever the hell else you can think of. Dough, even—nice fresh packets of it right from the bank.

"I see this guy around for three or four days maybe, treating him like he's the greatest guy in the world, and little by little coaxing the whole story out of him, and then I come up here to check it out for myself. Of course I never tell him my right name and after the three or four days he never sees me again. So don't worry about that part—no connection at all the way I foxed that dumb jerk. You following all this?"

Ned said nothing. Ruby said nothing. Dandy Jack inched forward and tightened his affectionate pressure on Ned's knee.

"So there it is, understand? Why keep all that dough in one pocketbook, kid? Why not spread it around? Who the hell is she to have a setup like that all to herself? Only one thing—how to get away afterwards. Damned easy to block off all the roads up in this part of the state, and to check every car that tries to get in or out for the next week. That was what Preston and me really had to figure out. But of course when I met you, and saw the kind of setup you had established for us—"

"Perfect," Ruby cut in, his dark glasses dangling wearily from his right hand, as if he had become just a little impatient with all this talk. "We don't have to try to get away afterwards. You put us up. When we get back tonight, you drive into your cellar garage before we even get out of the car, so who sees anything? Who can even guess we're inside with you? After the caper we make sure we've got a clean hour or so to get back to your place, to that basement clubroom of yours Jack told me about. We're quiet as mice in there, we pull down the shades, you don't invite anybody out to your house—and nobody ever knows a damned thing about it. How can they? So what's your complaint, McKestin?"

"Oh, he's in with us," Dandy Jack said. "He ain't a damned dummy, Preston. The kid's all right. When they stop watching the roads, which he can find out easy for us, he drives his pickup truck down to Albany on business, with a couple of big busted television sets in back—just the cabinets, though, and you and I squeezed inside them all the way down. It's like a dream, I tell you. It's all there right in our hands, kid. Don't you see?"

"G. G. McKestin and Company," Ruby murmured, swinging the dark glasses in his hand—almost happily for Preston Ruby. "Thirty-six Main Street, Sales and Service. I think it's all there, Jack. What else could we want?"

Ned took one hand off the steering wheel and wiped his mouth.

"But maybe she won't tell you how to open the safe," was all he could think of saying. "And you couldn't blow it, not with thirty or forty servants around. If you even tried—"

"Kid, kid," Dandy Jack said, with the foxy little smile on his lips. "She'll tell Preston. In about ten seconds she'll be damned glad to tell him. I give you my word."

Yes, very probably, Ned had to admit. Mrs. James Devereux Murchison, who looked like a nice ordinary old lady, absolutely no side to her. Once or twice he had seen her on the Martinsville streets, and once she had bought three television sets for the servants from G. G. McKestin. She had a nasal but rather pleasant New England twang, and had looked just like an old farmwife to Ned.

But what would she look like in that isolated cottage of hers when Ruby and Dandy Jack got through? Ned found himself wincing, not wanting even to think of it. Suppose she tried to scream or to make a fight of it? He felt the whole top of his scalp crawling.

"No," he heard himself get out breathlessly. "I don't care how easy it is. I won't do it for you! I was only a kid with Rod Connihan that time, and he didn't even explain first what you were going to do. I told Dandy the other night. I'm through with that business. I've got a wife and a child now. I won't do it!"

In the back seat Ruby whistled *Night and Day* very softly to himself. Dandy Jack chuckled.

"Look," he said. "Look, kid, with what we know about you, you figure you got any kind of a choice? Then figure again. Use your head. We're including you in."

And that night, trying uselessly to think of a way out, with Ruby and Dandy Jack quiet as quiet down in the basement clubroom, Ned realized he was in beyond question. It was not necessary for Preston Ruby even to threaten him. Why waste words? Ned was intelligent enough to see for himself. He had a wife and a child now and a new life—so he had a lot to protect. And Ruby was not a man to be moved by any consideration if you got in his way or spoiled his plans. That

attempted bank robbery down in New York City might be still unsolved, but of course the police had the case still open. And just one
anonymous phone call identifying the man who had driven the get-
away car that day . . .

No, they had him. And he did not have them. He had been foolish
enough, not knowing until too late what he was in for, to leave his
fingerprints all over the steering wheel of that abandoned Buick;
but they had not left a print. He could still be identified through
the fingerprints, identified beyond question. But they could not. And
the testimony of an accomplice in crime, Ned had read somewhere,
would not be accepted in court without corroborating evidence.

No, Ruby had thought out that part too. There was not a hole
anywhere, and Ned had no choice. He would do exactly as they
ordered or Ruby and Dandy Jack would turn him in. And then what?
Five or ten years in jail probably; G. G. McKestin & Company, after
all Uncle Gerry had done for him, would never be trusted or patronized again; and Kate and the baby would be left to fend for
themselves. The dead past . . .

He heard, smoking silently, two o'clock chime out from the Town
Hall belfry; three o'clock; four. It was no use—nothing came to him,
nothing at all. The dead past was back again, blacker and more
ominous than ever. He had to accept it. Ned McKestin was caught.

Next morning he was making early coffee for himself in the
kitchen when the basement door opened and dark glasses and a
narrow calm face—Ruby had always been troubled with bad
eyes—looked out at him.

"Think it all out yet?" Ruby inquired softly. "Made up your mind,
McKestin?"

Ned, his jaws clamped, kept his two hands on the coffee pot. That
was advisable. He wanted to use them at this moment more than
he ever had in his life.

"Not yet," he muttered. "Not decided yet, Ruby."

"No?" Ruby said, a faint chilly smile on his lips, so obviously
knowing better; just pushing the pin. "Then take your time. Go to
the store today, do what you always do, and watch your step. Now
bring down some coffee for Jack and me, and don't forget to lock
everything up here tight as a drum when you leave. We wouldn't
like any visitors, McKestin. We want things just as they are."

All that day Ned sat numbly in his small cubbyhole of an office
at G. G. McKestin's, but late in the afternoon, again with set jaws,

he took Uncle Gerry's big old .38 revolver out of his desk. There was even more than Ned McKestin and his family to worry about. There was the safety of that one watchman out at Forest Ridge and the physical well-being of a nice old lady named Mrs. James Devereux Murchison. Nobody knew who was in the house with Ned now, in view of the care with which Preston had thought out the whole business. Good.

There was a spade in the basement and a lot of dark empty woods back of the house. Ned McKestin did not want to do anything like that. But if Ruby and Dandy Jack forced him to the last step . . .

But could he actually bring himself to do it? To shoot down two men, even men like Ruby and Dandy Jack, shoot them like caged rats? No, that would mean the dark past would be with him forever. Impossible. What else then? How to manage it?

Nothing came to him until he was closing the store and saw old Charlie Burger walking past on the other side of the street. Ned stopped off at the supermarket for a carton of cigarettes, then made one brief call in the pay-phone booth. It was not even necessary to disguise his voice. It seemed to him that he would never have recognized it himself. "But who's this?" Charlie Burger demanded. "And how do I know that you're not just—"

Ned hung up. He wiped his mouth shakily, the .38 still heavy in his coat pocket, and drove home. But it was a silent meal down in the basement clubroom that night, just bread and butter, hot dogs and baked beans. Then, with television on, Ruby sat there. Ned sat there. Dandy Jack sat there. Yet undoubtedly there built up a certain tension in the air: zero hour. Which meant tonight, Ned told himself, and probably late tonight, without even the least warning to him. Much better that way, Ruby would have decided. Then early tomorrow they would confront him with the *fait accompli*. And what could Ned McKestin do about it? Nothing at all. Just go back to the dead past.

About ten o'clock he went up to bed, making a bit of noise in the bathroom, then slamming the bedroom door to let them hear; but after that, very quietly in stockinged feet, he tiptoed down. He was still sitting motionless in his dark kitchen, the .38 out in plain view on his knee, when the basement door opened noiselessly and Ruby and Dandy Jack came out. It was three o'clock then, and Ned deliberately raised the .38 so that they could see it. Preston Ruby stopped dead, and behind him Dandy Jack gawked.

"Now I'm going to tell you what to do," Ned gritted. "Tell you exactly. You're going to take my car and drive down to Albany tonight without a care in the world. I've got something to say. You're not going on with this thing. You can't. Because I've—"

"Now, kid," Dandy Jack said, wetting his lips. "Don't start to act up, will you? Preston and I might be willing to cut you in for a full third, say. Could be a hundred grand right in your pocket. What the hell's the matter with you? Why can't you see the thing?"

Ruby said nothing at all; thinking it out, Ned understood, in the Ruby manner. What Ned forgot momentarily, however, was how quick Ruby could be when he once decided to act. Now his head jerked around and he jumped back, as if in blind panic, for the basement door.

"Who's that?" Ruby cried out. "What are you trying to do here, McKestin? Who's out in your back porch?"

And Ned turned to look. It was altogether instinctive, and of course altogether stupid. Behind him there came the impression that something whizzed in the air, whizzed fast and venomously, and he turned back just in time to get the kitchen hammer, the one Kate always hung up on the basement door, across the top of his head. When he fell under it, Ruby was quick as light once more, and Dandy Jack moved in savagely from the other side.

"No, wait," Ned wanted to say. "You don't understand, Ruby. I'm trying to warn you! I called the town police chief this afternoon and he's waiting for you out at Forest Ridge right now. If you show up there, his men will shoot you down like a couple of mad dogs. Listen to me!"

But it came out in a confused shout, and Ruby, getting hold of the .38, slashed down calmly but grimly with it. The last thing Ned remembered was Ruby's face over him and the .38 smashing . . .

When he came to, he was lying face down on the coolness of the linoleum floor, and the illuminated kitchen clock showed him that a half hour had passed. For some reason, Ned understood, it was a very important half hour. But why?

He lay dazedly, trying to think. At last he managed to push himself up, shaking his head, then realized that half an hour was long enough to cut through the empty woods and run over the little bridge on Conklin Creek to the Murchison place. Dandy Jack and Preston Ruby could be out there by now. They might already have knocked out the night watchman, or killed him. But wait—wait a minute! If Chief of Police Burger had paid attention to Ned's anonymous phone call this afternoon—

Distantly, in the direction of Forest Ridge, there was a flurry of gunshots. The last few sounded deliberate, final. Ned whispered a few low words, rested against Kate's kitchen stove, and closed his eyes.

There were no more shots. But presently, from the direction of Forest Ridge once more, he could dimly hear men shouting . . .

"But I guess they never counted on somebody like Old Charlie," little Jack Holleran exulted shrilly the next morning. He was the stock boy at G. G. McKestin's, and now he danced around Ned excitedly. "Two guys, Ned. Seems like they kept shooting and shooting when he tried to warn them, and the one little guy, quick as a cat, winged Harry Johansson in the right shoulder. But Old Charlie had his rifle out and they say he can knock the spots off a playing card at a hundred yards. You hear anything yet?"

Ned, a strange pale smile on his lips, nodded. All night he had been waiting motionless in the shadows of his dark kitchen for Old Charlie to ring his front doorbell. He had not known what the delay meant. He could not imagine.

"So he caught them, Jack? Where are they now?"

"Walter Engstrom's funeral parlor," Jack crowed. "I just stole a peek at them in the back room. After they shot Harry, they both got it smack through the head, the damned fools. Dead as doornails, both of 'em!"

Ned went into his cubbyhole and sat down numbly. He had thought that when he told them about Chief Burger they would have no other recourse but to do as he said—to get out of town right away. He had tried to warn them, but they had not let him. So now . . .

He covered his eyes with both hands. But after a few moments, steady as rock now, he took three deep breaths, reached out for his desk telephone, and called Kate. At long last the past was dead.

Edgar Wallace

A More-or-Less Crime

April 1, 1975 marked the 100th anniversary of Edgar Wallace's birth. To celebrate the centenary there were BBC TV programs on Wallace's life, considerable radio and press coverage, and reissues of some of his books—according to Penelope Wallace, his daughter, about 50 Edgar Wallace titles are still in print and selling well. And to commemorate the Edgar Wallace centenary, though belatedly, Ellery Queen's Mystery Magazine brought you an Edgar Wallace story never before published in the States—a tale told by the "Sooper" involving "a real bit of detective work." As always in Mr. Wallace's stories, you will find his smooth, easy style and his quietly persuasive economy of characterization . . .

Detective: SUPERINTENDENT MINTER

"It's a strange thing," said Superintendent Minter, "that when I explain to outsiders the method and system of criminal investigation as practiced by the well-known academy of arts at Scotland Yard, they always seem a bit disappointed.

"I've shown a lot of people over the building, and they all want to see the room where the scientific detectives are looking at mud stains through microscopes, or putting cigar ash in test tubes, or deducting or deducing—I don't know which is the right word—from a bit of glue found in the keyhole that the burglar was a tall dark man who drove a gray touring car and had been crossed in love.

"I believe there are detectives like that. I've read about 'em. When you walk into their room or bureau or boudoir, as the case may be, they give you a sharp penetrating look from their cold gray eyes and they say, 'You came up Oxford Street in a motorbus; I can smell it. You had an argument with your wife this morning; I can see the place where the plate hit you. You're going on a long journey across water; beware of a blue-eyed waitress—she bites.'

"I believe that the best way to detect a man who's committed a crime is to see him do it. It isn't necessary even to see him do it. In nine cases out of ten the right man will come along sooner or later and tell you he did it, and what he did it with.

"Most criminals catch themselves. And I'll tell you why. Not nine out of ten, but ninety-nine out of every hundred of these birds of paradise don't know where to stop, and as they don't know where to stop they stop halfway. I've never met a crook who was a whole hogger and could carry any job he started to a clean and tidy finish. There never was a burglar who didn't leave something valuable behind, but that's understandable, for burglars are the most nervous criminals in the world. They lose heart halfway through and there's a lot of people like 'em. As Mr. Rudyard Kipling, the well-known poet, says: 'All along of doing things/Rather more or less.'

"The most interesting more-or-less crime I ever saw was the Bidderley Hall affair. Bidderley Hall is a country house in the Metropolitan Police area—right on the edge of T Division near Staines. It was an old Queen Anne house—it's been pulled down lately—standing in a ten-acre park, and it was owned by a gentleman named Costino—Mr. Charles Costino. He was a rich man, having inherited about half a million from his brother Peter.

"In the beginning Peter was rich and Charles was poor. Peter boozed but Charles never got happy on anything stronger than barley water. Charles was artistic and knew a lot about the Old Masters; he never bought any but he knew about 'em. His brother Peter knew nothing except that two pints made a quart and two quarts made you so that you weren't responsible for your actions.

"As a matter of fact, he was a bit of a bad egg, Peter was—gave funny parties at his home in Eastbourne and was pinched once or twice for being tight when in charge of a motorcar.

"One morning the coast guard found Peter's car at the foot of a two-hundred-foot cliff, smashed to blazes. They never found Peter. The tide was pretty high when his car went over—about three in the morning, according to a revenue boat that saw the lights; and after a time Charles got leave to presume Peter's death and took over all that Peter had left of a million.

"I saw Peter once. He was one of those blue-faced soakers who keep insurance companies awake at night.

"It was a grand bit of luck for Charles, who had this old house on his hands and found it a bit difficult to pay the taxes.

"When he came into money, Charles didn't live much better than when he was poor. The only time he broke out was when he took in a man-of-all-work, who was butler, footman, valet, and fed the chickens. In a way it was not a good break, as I could have told him if I had only known him at the time.

"Mr. Costino, it seems, had had an old lady looking after him—I forget her name, but anyway it doesn't matter. She'd been in the family for four generations, and she either left to better herself or died. Whatever she did she bettered herself.

"Anyway, Mr. Charles Costino was without a servant. He only lived in four rooms of the house since he came into the money and there wasn't much cleaning to be done, but he did have a bit of silver to clean, and there were the chickens to look after. The silver used to be locked in a cupboard in the dining room and was pretty valuable, as I happen to know.

"Now, the new man he employed was named Simon. He's no relation to anybody you know, and I very much doubt whether that was his real name at all. He was a graduate of the University of Dartmoor where he had spent three happy years at the taxpayers' expense. I knew him as well as the back of my right hand.

"One day, by accident, I was passing through the Minories and I saw Simon come out of a shop that buys a bit of other people's silver now and again, so I pulled him up. According to his story, he had been to this pawnbroker's shop to buy a ring for his young lady, but they didn't have one to fit. I know most of the young ladies Simon has promised to marry—they've all been through my hands at one time or another—but I've never met one that he bought anything for, except a bit of sticking plaster. So I took him back to the shop, and the fence blew it and showed me the silver Mr. Simon had parted with.

"It was not in my division at all and perhaps I had no right to interfere. To tell you the truth, the Divisional Inspector was a bit nasty about it afterwards, but what made it all right for me was when Simon said it was a cop and volunteered to come back with me to Staines.

"He didn't want any trouble and he told me he was tired of working for Mr. Costino and would be glad to get back amongst the boys at the dear old college. He said he had sold four pieces and had six hidden in the house ready to bring away.

" 'Costino wouldn't notice them going,' he said. 'He's soused half the time and the other half he's in delirium tremens.'

"It was news to me, because I didn't know that Costino drank.

"We drove from the station to the house in a cab and on the way there Simon told me how slick he'd had to be to get the stuff out of the house at all. Apparently he slept in a room over a stable, some distance from the house but on the grounds. Nobody slept in the house but Charles Costino.

"We drove up to the Hall—and a miserable-looking building it was. I think I told you it was a Queen Anne house. Queen Anne is dead and this house was ready to pop off at any minute. None of the windows was clean, except a couple on the ground floor. It took us a quarter of an hour to wake up Costino and even then he only opened the door on the chain and wouldn't have let us in, but he recognized me.

"I have never seen such a change in a man. The last time I saw him he was a quiet sober feller and his idea of a happy evening was to drink lemonade and listen to the radio. Now he was the color of a bad lobster. He stared at Simon, and when I told him what the man had told me, Charles sat down in a chair and turned gray—well, it wasn't gray, but a sort of putty color.

"After a bit he said, 'I'd like to speak to this man. I think I can persuade him to tell me the truth.'

"I don't like people coming between me and my lawful prey, but I humored him, and he took Simon into the other corner of the room and talked to him for a long time in an undertone.

"When he finished he said, 'I think this man has made a mistake. There are only four pieces of silver stolen, and those are the four pieces he has sold. I can tell you in a minute.'

"With that he unlocked the door of a high cupboard. It was so crowded with silver that it was impossible for any man to count the stuff that was in it. But he only looked at it for a minute and then he said, 'Quite right. Only four pieces are missing.'

"So far as I was concerned it didn't matter to me whether it was four or ten, so long as he gave me enough for a conviction. It was not my business to argue the point. I took Simon down to the cooler and I could tell something had happened, because he was not his normal bright and cheery self. Usually when you take an old con to the station he is either telling you what he's going to do when he comes out to your heart, lungs and important blood vessels, or else he's all friendly and jolly. But Simon said nothing and sort of looked dazed and surprised. He was hardly recovered the next morning when I met him at the police court and got my remand.

"It was a very simple case. It came at the Sessions, and Mr. Costino went into the box and said Simon was one of the best servants that had ever blown into a country house. You expect perjury at the Assizes but not that kind of perjury. But that was his business.

"Anyway, Costino made such a scene about what a grand fellow Simon was, how he fed the chickens so regular that they followed him down the street, that Simon got off with six months, and that, so far as I was concerned, was the end of it till it came my turn to take him in again.

"About seven months after this I was on duty on the Great West Road, watching for a stolen motorcar. It was one of those typical English summer days you read about—raining cats and dogs, with a cold north wind blowing—and I was getting a bit fed up with waiting when I saw a car coming along following a course that a yachtsman takes when he is tacking into the breeze.

"The last tack was against an iron lamp standard, which smashed the radiator and most of the glass, but it didn't apparently kill the driver, for he opened the door and staggered out. I had only to look at him to see that he had about twenty-five over the eight.

"My first inclination was to hand him over to my sergeant on a charge of being drunk while driving. It would mean a lot of bother, because if he had plenty of money he'd produce three Harley Street doctors and fourteen independent witnesses to prove that the only thing he'd drunk since yesterday morning was a small glass of cider diluted with tonic water.

"I was deciding whether or not to pinch him when I recognized him. It was Simon.

" 'Hello!' I said. 'How long is it since *you* came out of the home for dirty dogs?'

"He didn't know me at first, and I oughtn't to have known him at all, because he was beautifully dressed, with a green tie and a brown hat, and a bunch of forget-me-nots in his buttonhole, not that anybody who had ever put their lamps on this dial would ever forget him. I asked him if it was his car, and he admitted it was.

"While I was talking to him one of my men came up and told me that they had stopped the stolen car about a hundred yards down the road, so I was able to devote myself to my little friend.

"We helped him along and got him into the substation round the corner. He was, so to speak, flush with wine. He got over his shock and began to talk big, flash his money about, and gradually, as he recognized the old familiar surroundings—the sergeant's desk and the notice on the wall telling people not to spit on the floor—he saw he was in the presence of law and order and it gradually dawned on him that I was me.

" 'What bank have you been robbing?' says I.

"He laughed in my face. 'Costino gave it all to me for saying that I only pinched four bits of silver.'

"He started to laugh again and stopped. I have an idea that in the thing he called his mind he realized he had said too much. Anyway, he wouldn't say any more. We took his money away from him, counted it, and put him in a nice clean cell.

"Now I am not a man who is easily puzzled. Things in life are too straightforward for anybody to have anything to puzzle about, but this certainly got me thinking. Costino must have given him the best part of a thousand pounds to admit that he had stolen only four pieces of silver. Now why did he do that?

"I thought it out. At about eleven o'clock that night I said to my sergeant, 'Let's go and do a real bit of detective work.'

"I drove him down in my car to the road in front of Bidderley Hall. We parked the car in the drive, just inside the old gates, and walked up to the house. The rain was pelting down. I don't remember a worse night. The wind howled through the trees and gave me one of those bogey feelings I haven't had since I was a boy.

"When we got up to the house, we made a sort of reconnaissance. All the windows were dark; there was no sign of life; if there had been any sound we couldn't have heard it anyway. We went all round trying to find a way in, and just as we got back to the front of the house one of the worst thunderstorms I can remember started up without any warning.

"My sergeant was all for knocking up Mr. Costino and putting the matter to him plump and plain, but I saw all sorts of difficulties and my scheme was to pretend that we found a window open and being good policemen and not being able to make Costino hear, we had got in through the window and had a look round. There was only one place possible, we decided, and that was a window on a small balcony at the back of the house.

"We searched round and found a ladder, and put it against the balcony. I went up first and I had just put my leg over the parapet and was facing the window when there came a blinding flash of lightning that made my head spin. It was one of those flashes of lightning that seem to last two or three seconds, and in the light of it, as plain as day, I saw right in front of me, staring through the window, a horribly white face with a long untidy beard.

"I was so startled I nearly dropped back. I called my sergeant up the ladder. I wasn't afraid, but I wanted somebody with me. I don't know whether you have ever had that feeling. Two can be frightened to death better than one.

"I told him just what I had seen, and then I got my pocket lamp and flashed it into the room. As far as I could see through the dirty window the room was empty. Between the window and the room was a set of iron bars. They weren't very thick; they looked like the kind put up in West End houses so that children can't escape from a nursery when the room catches fire.

"We got the window open. The sergeant and I not only bent the bars, but we bent the whole frame. It was not very securely fastened—a bit of carpentry work done by a plumber.

"There was no furniture in the room. It was thick with dust. On the wall was a picture hanging cockeyed. The door was open and we went on and found a landing and a narrow flight of stairs leading down. But the curious thing about those stairs was that they didn't stop on the ground floor. In fact, there was no door opening until we got to the basement. There had been a door on the ground floor, but it had been bricked up.

"We were going down the last flight of steps when we heard a door bang and the sound of a bolt being shot. When we got to the basement level we found a door. It was shut, and we couldn't move it. I could find nothing on the stairs in the light of my lamp except evidence that somebody was in the habit of going up and down.

"When I went back up to the room with the balcony and examined the bars we had bent, I made rather an interesting discovery. Three of the screws on the lower left-hand corner had been taken out, and they had been taken out with a jagged top of a sardine tin. We found the 'opener' lying on the floor. It must have taken a long time to loosen those screws, for one of the screwholes was quite dark, and must have been exposed for months.

"There were two courses left to us: one was to come the next day with an official search warrant, which no magistrate would grant on the information we had; and the other was to go round and wake up Costino and ask him to let us go through the house. But there was a good reason for not doing that.

"I took off my shoes and went down the stairs in my stockinged feet, with my sergeant behind me. We crept up to the door and listened. For a little time I heard nothing, partly because the thunder was still turning the house into a drum, and partly because we could not quite tune in. But after a while I heard a man breathing very quickly, like somebody who had been running.

"We waited for a quarter of an hour and then another quarter of an hour. It seemed like a week. And then we heard the bolt being very gently pushed back. A man on the other side of the door opened it an inch. In another second I was through. He ran like the wind along the cellar and was just reaching another door when I grabbed him. He fought like six men, but we got him down.

"And then he said, 'Don't kill me, Charles. I'll give you half of the money.'

"And that was all I wanted to know.

"We pulled him up and sat him on an old box, and I explained that we were just innocent police officers, that we very seldom kill anybody except under the greatest provocation, and after a while we got Mr. Peter Costino calm, and he told us how his brother had come down to Eastbourne to see him and borrow some money, and how Charles got him drunk and intended driving him and the car over the cliff.

"Peter wouldn't have known this but his brother told him afterwards. Charles had lost heart and let the car go over by itself, then brought Peter back to Bidderley Hall, and shut him up in the cellar. Peter didn't know very much about it till he woke up the next morning and found himself a prisoner, and after two years of this kind of life he got more or less reconciled, especially as he was allowed to go up to the room with the balcony. It was the only bit of the world he was allowed to see, and then only at nights.

"That's the trouble with criminals—they never go the whole hog. Charles didn't have the nerve to kill his brother. He just locked him up. He got the house and half a million pounds, but he got about two million worries. Those two years made Peter a sober man and turned Charles into a drunkard. Peter might have eventually died in this cellar if Mr. Charles Costino hadn't given Simon a thousand quid to keep his mouth shut about the silver he had stolen and hidden in the house. Charles was in mortal terror that we would search the house for the missing silver, and if we had searched the house we'd have found Peter.

"Charles is in Dartmoor now. So is Simon. He got a lagging for a big smash-and-grab raid, and drew five years. From what I've heard, he and Charles are quite good friends. The last I heard of Charles he was painting angels in the prison chapel. As I say, he was always a bit artistic."

E. X. Ferrars

The Rose Murders

*"The dangerous rage that had possessed him only a few times in
his life had exploded like fireworks in his brain"* . . .

It was on the day that Mrs. Holroyd refused Mr. Pocock's offer of
marriage that he first thought of murdering her.

The rejection, so gently and kindly put but so utterly unexpected,
filled him first with astonishment, so that he felt as if he had tripped
over something uneven in his path and fallen flat on his face, and
then with a searing rage.

For a wild moment he wanted to clasp his hands around her slender neck and squeeze the life out of her. But after that flare of hatred
came intense fear. He had made up his mind, after his last murder,
never to kill again.

On that occasion he had escaped arrest only by the skin of his
teeth and he knew that the police still believed he was guilty, although they had never had enough evidence to bring a charge
against him. That had been largely because of Lucille's passion for
cleanliness. She had polished and washed and scrubbed everything
in her little flat at least twice a week, so that the police, in their
investigation, had not been able to find a single one of Mr. Pocock's
fingerprints.

Dear Lucille. He remembered her still with a kind of affection,
partly because she had cooperated so beautifully in her own death.
Except, of course, for that business of the roses. It was the love she
had had for roses and the pleasure it had given him to bring them
to her from his own little garden that had almost destroyed him.

There had been no complications like that about his first murder.
Almost no drama either. He had nearly forgotten why he had committed it. Alice had been a very dull woman. He could hardly recollect her features. However, it had happened one day that she told
him in her flat positive way that she did not believe a word he had
told her about his past life, that she was sure he had never been an
intelligence officer during the war, that he had never been para-
chuted into occupied France, that he had never been a prisoner of

214

the Nazis and survived hideous tortures at their hands—in all of which she had been perfectly correct; and really the matter had been of very little importance, but her refusal to share his fantasies had seemed to him such a gross insult that for a few minutes it had felt impossible to allow her to go on living.

Afterward he had walked quietly out of the house, and it had turned out that no one had seen him come or go, and her death had become one of the unsolved mysteries in the police files. There had been a certain flatness about it, almost of disappointment.

But in Lucille's case it had been quite different. For one thing, he had been rather fond of her. She had been an easy-going woman, comfortable to be with, and she had never expected gifts other than the flowers he brought her. But one day when he had happened to say how much he wished she could see them growing in his glowing flowerbeds, but that the anxious eye of his invalid wife, who would suffer intensely if she even knew of Lucille's existence, made this impossible, she had gone into fits of laughter.

She had told him there was no need for him to tell a yarn like that to her of all people, and he had realized all of a sudden that she had never believed in the existence of any frail, lovely, dependent wife to whom he offered up the treasure of his loyalty.

The dangerous rage that had possessed him only a few times in his life had exploded like fireworks in his brain. It had seemed to him that she was mocking him not merely for having told her lies that had never deceived her, but for having tried to convince her that any woman, even a poor invalid, could ever love him enough to marry him. His hands, made strong by his gardening, although they were small and white, had closed on her neck, and when he left her she had been dead.

By chance he had left no fingerprints in her flat that day. But he had been seen arriving by the woman who lived in the flat below Lucille's. Meeting on the stairs on his way up, he and the woman, an elderly person in spectacles, had even exchanged remarks about the weather, and it turned out that she had taken particular notice of the bunch of exquisite Kronenbourgs he had been carrying.

The rich velvety crimson of the blooms and the soft gold of the undersides of the petals and their delicious fragrance had riveted her attention, a fact which at first he had thought would mean disaster for him, but which actually had been extraordinarily fortunate. For afterward she had been able to describe the roses minutely, but had given a most inaccurate description of the man who had been carrying them, and in the lineup in which he had been compelled to take part when the police had been led to him by a telephone number scrawled on a pad in Lucille's flat, the woman had picked out the wrong man.

So the police had had no evidence against him except for the telephone number and the rose bush in his garden. But half a dozen of his neighbors, who had imitated him when they had seen the beauty of that particular variety of rose, had Kronenbourgs in their gardens too, and so Lucille's murder, like Alice's, had remained an unsolved mystery.

Yet not to the police. Mr. Pocock was sure of that and sometimes the thought that he might somehow betray himself to them, even now after two years, that he might drop some word or perform some thoughtless action, though heaven knew what could do him any damage after all this time, made terror stab like a knife into his nerves. He would never kill again, of that he was certain.

But that was before Mrs. Holroyd refused to marry him.

It had taken him a long time to convince himself that marriage to her would be a sound idea, even though he was certain she had been pursuing him ever since she had come to live in the little house next door to his. She was a widow and she believed him to be a widower, and she often spoke to him of her loneliness since her husband's sudden death and sympathized with Mr. Pocock because of his own solitary state.

She admired his garden and took his advice about how to lay out her own, was delighted with the gifts of flowers he brought her, and when he was ill with influenza she did his shopping for him, cooked him tempting meals, and changed his books at the library. And she had let him know, without overstressing it, that her income was ample.

"I'm not a rich woman," she had said, "but thanks to the thoughtfulness of my dear husband, I have no financial worries."

So it seemed clear to Mr. Pocock that Mrs. Holroyd's feelings were not in doubt and that it was only his own which it was necessary for him to consider. Did he want marriage? Would he be able to endure the continual company of another person after all his years of comfortable solitude? Would not the effort of adapting his habits to fit those of someone else be an extreme irritation?

Against all that, he was aging and that bout of influenza had shown him how necessary it was to have someone to look after him. And marrying Mrs. Holroyd might actually be financially advantageous instead of very expensive, as it would be to employ a full-time housekeeper. She was a good-looking woman too, for her age, and an excellent cook. If he wanted a wife, he could hardly do better.

Of course, she had certain little ways which he found hard to tolerate. She liked to sing when she was doing her housework. If he had to listen to it in his own house, instead of softened by distance, it would drive him mad. She chatted to all the neighbors, instead of maintaining a courteous aloofness, as he did. And she had a passion for plastic flowers. Every vase in her house was filled with them, with a total disregard for the seasons, her tulips and daffodils blooming in September and her chrysanthemums in May.

She always thanked him with a charming lighting up of her face for the flowers he brought her, but he was not really convinced she could distinguish the living ones from the lifeless imitations. But no doubt with tact he would be able to correct these small flaws in her. On a bright evening in June he asked her to marry him.

She answered, "Oh, dear Mr. Pocock, how can I possibly tell you what I feel, I am so touched, so very honored! But I could never marry again. It would not be fair to you if I did, for I could never give my heart to anyone but my poor Harold. And our friendship, just as it is, is so very precious to me. I think we are wonderfully fortunate, at our age, to have found such a friendship. To change anything about it might only spoil it. So let us treasure what we have, won't that be wisest? What could we possibly give to each other more than we already do?"

He took it with dignity and accepted a glass of sherry from her. What made the occasion peculiarly excruciating for him was his certainty that she had known he was going to propose marriage and had her little speech already rehearsed. It disgusted him to discover that all her little kindnesses to him had simply been little kindnesses that had come from the warmth of her heart and not from desire to take possession of him.

Looking at her, with her excellent sherry tasting like acid in his mouth, he was suddenly aware of the terrible rage and hatred that he had not felt for so long. However, he managed to pat her on the shoulder, say that of course nothing between them need be altered, and go quietly home.

The most important thing for the moment, it seemed clear to him, was not to let her guess what her refusal had done to him. She must never be allowed to know what power she had to hurt him. Everything must appear to be as it had been in the past. In fact their relationship was poisoned forever, but to save his pride this must be utterly hidden from her. Two days later he appeared on her doorstep, smiling, and with a beautiful bunch of Kronenbourgs for her.

She exclaimed over them with extra-special gladness and there was a tenderness on her face that he had never seen there before. She was so happy, he thought, to have humiliated him at apparently so little cost to herself. Tipping some plastic irises and sprays of forsythia out of one of the vases in her sitting room, she went out to the kitchen to fill the vase with water, brought it back, and began to arrange the roses in it.

Up to that moment he had not really intended to murder her. He would find some way of making her suffer as she was making him suffer, but when his hands went out to grasp her neck and he saw at first the blank astonishment on her face before it changed to terror, he was almost as surprised and terror-stricken as she was. When she fell to the floor at his feet in a limp heap and he fled to the door, he was shaking all over.

But then he remembered something. The Kronenbourgs. Once before they had almost destroyed him. This time he would not forget them and leave them behind. Turning back into the room, he snatched the roses from the vase, jammed the plastic flowers back into it, and only pausing for a moment at the front door to make sure the street was empty, made for his own house.

Inside, he threw the roses from him as if they carried some horrible contagion and for some time left them lying where they had fallen, unable to make himself touch them. How mad he had been to take them to the woman, how easily fatal to him they could have been.

He drank some whiskey and smoked several cigarettes before he could force himself to pick the roses up and put them in a silver bowl which he placed on a bookcase in his sitting room. They looked quite normal there, not in the least like witnesses against him. It was very important that everything should look normal.

The next morning, when two policemen called on him, he was of course prepared for them and felt sure that his own behavior was quite normal. But he was worried by a feeling that he had met one of them before. The man was an inspector who now told Mr. Pocock that the body of his neighbor had been discovered by her daily woman, then went on to ask him when he had seen the dead woman last and where he had spent the previous evening.

He supposed that such questions were inevitable, but he did not like the way, almost mocking, that the man looked at him. But standing there, looking at the roses in the silver bowl, the inspector remarked admiringly, "Lovely! Kronenbourgs, aren't they?"

"Yes," Mr. Pocock said, "from my garden."

"I've got some in my own garden," the inspector said. "There's nothing to compare with a nice rose, is there? Now your neighbor doesn't seem to have cared for real flowers. She stuck to the plastic kind. Less trouble, of course. But a funny thing about her, d'you know, she kept some of them in water? Some irises and forsythia, they were in a vase full of water, just as if they were real. That's carrying pretense a bit far, wouldn't you say, Mr. Pocock?

"Unless there'd been some real flowers there first like, say, your roses. You'd a way of giving her flowers, hadn't you, Mr. Pocock? That's something she told the neighbors. But really you ought to have learned better by now than to take them with you when you're going out to do murder."

Lawrence Block

Gentlemen's Agreement

We welcome Lawrence Block to the ever-growing family of EQMM contributors. Mr. Block has a style and humor all his own, and this story is a "chip off the old Block"—of a burglar and a businessman and what came of their unexpected meeting ...

The burglar, a slender and clean-cut chap just past 30, was rifling a drawer in the bedside table when Archer Trebizond slipped into the bedroom. Trebizond's approach was as catfooted as if he himself were the burglar, a situation which was manifestly not the case. The burglar never did hear Trebizond, absorbed as he was in his perusal of the drawer's contents, and at length he sensed the other man's presence as a jungle beast senses the presence of a predator.

The analogy, let it be said, is scarcely accidental.

When the burglar turned his eyes on Archer Trebizond his heart fluttered and fluttered again, first at the mere fact of discovery, then at his own discovery of the gleaming revolver in Trebizond's hand. The revolver was pointed in his direction, and this the burglar found upsetting.

"Darn it all," said the burglar, approximately, "I could have sworn there was nobody home. I phoned, I rang the bell—"

"I just got here," Trebizond said.

"Just my luck. The whole week's been like that. I dented a fender on Tuesday afternoon, overturned my fish tank the night before last. An unbelievable mess all over the carpet, and I lost a mated pair of African mouthbreeders so rare they don't have a Latin name yet. I'd hate to tell you what I paid for them."

"Hard luck," Trebizond said.

"And just yesterday I was putting away a plate of fettucine and I bit the inside of my mouth. You ever done that? It's murder, and the worst part is you feel so stupid about it. And then you keep biting it over and over again because it sticks out while it's healing.

220

At least I do." The burglar gulped a breath and ran a moist hand over a moister forehead. "And now this," he said.

"This could turn out to be worse than fenders and fish tanks," Trebizond said.

"Don't I know it. You know what I should have done? I should have spent the entire week in bed. I happen to know a safecracker who consults an astrologer before each and every job he pulls. If Jupiter's in the wrong place or Mars is squared with Uranus or something he won't go in. It sounds ridiculous, doesn't it? And yet it's eight years now since anybody put a handcuff on that man. Now who do you know who's gone eight years without getting arrested?"

"I've never been arrested," Trebizond said.

"Well, you're not a crook."

"I'm a businessman."

The burglar thought of something but let it pass. "I'm going to get the name of his astrologer," he said. "That's just what I'm going to do. Just as soon as I get out of here."

"If you get out of here," Trebizond said. "Alive," Trebizond said.

The burglar's jaw trembled just the slightest bit. Trebizond smiled, and from the burglar's point of view Trebizond's smile seemed to enlarge the black hole in the muzzle of the revolver.

"I wish you'd point that thing somewhere else," he said nervously.

"There's nothing else I want to shoot."

"You don't want to shoot me."

"Oh?"

"You don't even want to call the cops," the burglar went on. "It's really not necessary. I'm sure we can work things out between us, two civilized men coming to a civilized agreement. I've some money on me. I'm an openhanded sort and would be pleased to make a small contribution to your favorite charity, whatever it might be. We don't need policemen to intrude into the private affairs of gentlemen."

The burglar studied Trebizond carefully. This little speech had always gone over rather well in the past, especially with men of substance. It was hard to tell how it was going over now, or if it was going over at all. "In any event," he ended somewhat lamely, "you certainly don't want to shoot me."

"Why not?"

"Oh, blood on the carpet, for a starter. Messy, wouldn't you say? Your wife would be upset. Just ask her and she'll tell you shooting me would be a ghastly idea."

"She's not at home. She'll be out for the next hour or so."

"All the same, you might consider her point of view. And shooting me would be illegal, you know. Not to mention immoral."

"Not illegal," Trebizond remarked.

"I beg your pardon?"

"You're a burglar," Trebizond reminded him. "An unlawful intruder on my property. You have broken and entered. You have invaded the sanctity of my home. I can shoot you where you stand and not get so much as a parking ticket for my trouble."

"Of course you can shoot me in self-defense—"

"Are we on *Candid Camera*?"

"No, but—"

"Is Allen Funt lurking in the shadows?"

"No, but I—"

"In your back pocket. That metal thing. What is it?"

"Just a pry bar."

"Take it out," Trebizond said. "Hand it over. Indeed. A weapon if I ever saw one. I'd state that you attacked me with it and I fired in self-defense. It would be my word against yours, and yours would remain unvoiced since you would be dead. Whom do you suppose the police would believe?"

The burglar said nothing. Trebizond smiled a satisfied smile and put the pry bar in his own pocket. It was a piece of nicely shaped steel and it had a nice heft to it. Trebizond rather liked it.

"Why would you want to kill me?"

"Perhaps I've never killed anyone. Perhaps I'd like to satisfy my curiosity. Or perhaps I got to enjoy killing in the war and have been yearning for another crack at it. There are endless possibilities."

"But—"

"The point is," said Trebizond, "you might be useful to me in that manner. As it is, you're not useful to me at all. And stop hinting about my favorite charity or other euphemisms. I don't want your money. Look about you. I've ample money of my own—that should be obvious. If I were a poor man you wouldn't have breached my threshold. How much money are you talking about, anyway? A couple of hundred dollars?"

"Five hundred," the burglar said.

"A pittance."

"I suppose. There's more at home but you'd just call that a pittance too, wouldn't you?"

"Undoubtedly." Trebizond shifted the gun to his other hand. "I told you I was a businessman," he said. "Now if there were any way in which you could be more useful to me alive than dead—"

"You're a businessman and I'm a burglar," the burglar said, brightening.

"Indeed."

"So I could steal something for you. A painting? A competitor's trade secrets? I'm really very good at what I do, as a matter of fact, although you wouldn't guess it by my performance tonight. I'm not saying I could whisk the Mona Lisa out of the Louvre, but I'm pretty good at your basic hole-and-corner job of everyday burglary. Just give me an assignment and let me show my stuff."

"Hmmmm," said Archer Trebizond.

"Name it and I'll swipe it."

"Hmmmm."

"A car, a mink coat, a diamond bracelet, a Persian carpet, a first edition, bearer bonds, incriminating evidence, eighteen and a half minutes of tape—"

"What was that last?"

"Just my little joke," said the burglar. "A coin collection, a stamp collection, psychiatric records, phonograph records, police records—"

"I get the point."

"I tend to prattle when I'm nervous."

"I've noticed."

"If you could point that thing elsewhere—"

Trebizond looked down at the gun in his hand. The gun continued to point at the burglar.

"No," Trebizond said, with evident sadness. "No, I'm afraid it won't work."

"Why not?"

"In the first place, there's nothing I really need or want. Could you steal me a woman's heart? Hardly. And more to the point, how could I trust you?"

"You could trust me," the burglar said. "You have my word on that."

"My point exactly. I'd have to take your word that your word is good, and where does that lead us? Up the proverbial garden path, I'm afraid. No, once I let you out from under my roof I've lost my advantage. Even if I have a gun trained on you, once you're in the open I can't shoot you with impunity. So I'm afraid—"

"No!"

Trebizond snrugged. "Well, really," he said. "What use are you?

What are you good for besides being killed? Can you do anything besides steal, sir?"

"I can make license plates."

"Hardly a valuable talent."

"I know," said the burglar sadly. "I've often wondered why the state bothered to teach me such a pointless trade. There's not even much call for counterfeit license plates, and they've got a monopoly on making the legitimate ones. What else can I do? I must be able to do something. I could shine your shoes, I could polish your car—"

"What do you do when you're not stealing?"

"Hang around," said the burglar. "Go out with ladies. Feed my fish, when they're not all over my rug. Drive my car when I'm not mangling its fenders. Play a few games of chess, drink a can or two of beer, make myself a sandwich—"

"Are you any good?"

"At making sandwiches?"

"At chess."

"I'm not bad."

"I'm serious about this."

"I believe you are," the burglar said. "I'm not your average wood-pusher, if that's what you want to know. I know the openings and I have a good sense of space. I don't have the patience for tournament play, but at the chess club downtown I win more games than I lose."

"You play at the club downtown?"

"Of course. I can't burgle seven nights a week, you know. Who could stand the pressure?"

"Then you *can* be of use to me," Trebizond said.

"You want to learn the game?"

"I know the game. I want you to play chess with me for an hour until my wife gets home. I'm bored, there's nothing in the house to read, I've never cared much for television, and it's hard for me to find an interesting opponent at the chess table."

"So you'll spare my life in order to play chess with me."

"That's right."

"Let me get this straight," the burglar said. "There's no catch to this, is there? I don't get shot if I lose the game or anything tricky like that, I hope."

"Certainly not. Chess is a game that ought to be above gim-mickry."

"I couldn't agree more," said the burglar. He sighed a long sigh.

"If I didn't play chess," he said, "you wouldn't have shot me, would you?"

"It's a question that occupies the mind, isn't it?"

"It is," said the burglar.

They played in the front room. The burglar drew the white pieces in the first game, opened king's pawn, and played what turned out to be a reasonably imaginative version of the Ruy Lopez. At the sixteenth move Trebizond forced the exchange of knight for rook, and not too long afterward the burglar resigned.

In the second game the burglar played the black pieces and offered the Sicilian Defense. He played a variation that Trebizond wasn't familiar with. The game stayed remarkably even until in the end game the burglar succeeded in developing a passed pawn. When it was clear that he would be able to queen it, Trebizond tipped over his king, resigning.

"Nice game," the burglar offered.

"You play well."

"Thank you."

"Seem's a pity that—"

His voice trailed off. The burglar shot him an inquiring look. "That I'm wasting myself as a common criminal? Is that what you were going to say?"

"Let it go," Trebizond said. "It doesn't matter."

They began setting up the pieces for the third game when a key slipped into a lock. The lock turned, the door opened, and Melissa Trebizond stepped into the foyer and through it to the living room

Both men got to their feet. Mrs. Trebizond advanced, a vacant smile on her pretty face. "You found a new friend to play chess with. I'm happy for you."

Trebizond set his jaw. From his back pocket he drew the burglar's pry bar. It had an even nicer heft than he had thought. "Melissa," he said. "I've no need to waste time with a recital of your sins. No doubt you know precisely why you deserve this."

She stared at him, obviously not having understood a word he had said to her, whereupon Archer Trebizond brought the pry bar down on the top of her skull. The first blow sent her to her knees. Quickly he struck her three more times, wielding the metal bar with all his strength, then turned to look into the wide eyes of the burglar.

"You've killed her," the burglar said.

"Nonsense," said Trebizond, taking the bright revolver from his pocket once again.

"Isn't she dead?"

"I hope and pray she is," Trebizond said, "but I haven't killed her. *You've* killed her."

"I don't understand."

"The police will understand," Trebizond said, and shot the burglar in the shoulder. Then he fired again, more satisfactorily this time, and the burglar sank to the floor with a hole in his heart.

Trebizond scooped the chess pieces into their box, swept up the board, and set about the business of arranging things. He suppressed an urge to whistle. He was, he decided, quite pleased with himself. Nothing was ever entirely useless, not to a man of resources. If fate sent you a lemon you made lemonade.

Harry Kemelman

The Nine Mile Walk

I had made an ass of myself in a speech I had given at the Good Government Association dinner, and Nicky Welt had cornered me at breakfast at the Blue Moon, where we both ate occasionally, for the pleasure of rubbing it in. I had made the mistake of departing from my prepared speech to criticize a statement my predecessor in the office of district attorney had made to the press. I had drawn a number of inferences from his statement and had thus left myself open to a rebuttal which he had promptly made and which had the effect of making me appear intellectually dishonest. I was new to this political game, having but a few months before left the Law School faculty to become the Reform Party candidate for district attorney. I said as much in extenuation, but Nicholas Welt, who could never drop his pedagogical manner (he was Snowdon Professor of English Language and Literature), replied in much the same tone that he would dismiss a request from a sophomore for an extension on a term paper, "That's no excuse."

Although he is only two or three years older than I, in his late forties, he always treats me like a school master hectoring a stupid pupil. And I, perhaps because he looks so much older with his white hair and lined, gnomelike face, suffer it.

"They were perfectly logical inferences," I pleaded.

"My dear boy," he purred, "although human intercourse is well nigh impossible without inference, most inferences are usually wrong. The percentage of error is particularly high in the legal profession where the intention is not to discover what the speaker wishes to convey, but rather what he wishes to conceal."

I picked up my check and eased out from behind the table.

"I suppose you are referring to cross-examination of witnesses in court. Well, there's always an opposing counsel who will object if the inference is illogical."

"Who said anything about logic?" he retorted. "An inference can be logical and still not be true."

He followed me down the aisle to the cashier's booth. I paid my check and waited impatiently while he searched in an old-fashioned change purse, fishing out coins one by one and placing them on the

227

counter beside his check, only to discover that the total was insufficient. He slid them back into his purse and with a tiny sigh extracted a bill from another compartment of the purse and handed it to the cashier.

"Give me any sentence of ten or twelve words," he said, "and I'll build you a logical chain of inferences that you never dreamed of when you framed the sentence."

Other customers were coming in, and since the space in front of the cashier's booth was small, I decided to wait outside until Nicky completed his transaction with the cashier. I remember being mildly amused at the idea that he probably thought I was still at his elbow and was going right ahead with his discourse.

When he joined me on the sidewalk I said, "A nine-mile walk is no joke, especially in the rain."

"No, I shouldn't think it would be," he agreed absently. Then he stopped in his stride and looked at me sharply. "What the devil are you talking about?"

"It's a sentence and it has eleven words," I insisted. And I repeated the sentence, ticking off the words on my fingers.

"What about it?"

"You said that given a sentence of ten or twelve words—"

"Oh, yes." He looked at me suspiciously. "Where did you get it?"

"It just popped into my head. Come on now, build your inferences."

"You're serious about this?" he asked, his little blue eyes glittering with amusement. "You really want me to?"

It was just like him to issue a challenge and then to appear amused when I accepted it. And it made me angry.

"Put up or shut up," I said.

"All right," he said mildly. "No need to be huffy. I'll play. Hmm, let me see, how did the sentence go? 'A nine-mile walk is no joke, especially in the rain.' Not much to go on there."

"It's more than ten words," I rejoined.

"Very well." His voice became crisp as he mentally squared off to the problem. "First inference: the speaker is aggrieved."

"I'll grant that," I said, "although it hardly seems to be an inference. It's really implicit in the statement."

He nodded impatiently. "Next inference: the rain was unforeseen, otherwise he would have said, 'A nine-mile walk in the rain is no joke,' instead of using the 'especially' phrase as an afterthought."

"I'll allow that," I said, "although it's pretty obvious."

"First inferences should be obvious," said Nicky tartly.

I let it go at that. He seemed to be floundering and I didn't want to rub it in.

"Next inference: the speaker is not an athlete or an outdoors man."

"You'll have to explain that one," I said.

"It's the 'especially' phrase again," he said. "The speaker does not say that a nine-mile walk in the rain is no joke, but merely the walk—just the distance, mind you—is no joke. Now, nine miles is not such a terribly long distance. You walk more than half that in eighteen holes of golf—and golf is an old man's game," he added slyly. I play golf.

"Well, that would be all right under ordinary circumstances," I said, "but there are other possibilities. The speaker might be a soldier in the jungle in which case nine miles would be a pretty good hike, rain or no rain."

"Yes," and Nicky was sarcastic, "and the speaker might be one-legged. For that matter, the speaker might be a graduate student writing a Ph.D. on humor and starting by listing all the things that are not funny. See here, I'll have to make a couple of assumptions before I continue."

"How do you mean?" I asked, suspiciously.

"Remember, I'm taking this sentence in vacuo, as it were. I don't know who said it or what the occasion was. Normally a sentence belongs in the framework of a situation."

"I see. What assumptions do you want to make?"

"For one thing, I want to assume that the intention was not frivolous, that the speaker is referring to a walk that was actually taken, and that the purpose of the walk was not to win a bet or something of that sort."

"That seems reasonable enough," I said.

"And I also want to assume that the locale of the walk is here."

"You mean here in Fairfield?"

"Not necessarily. I mean in this general section of the country."

"Fair enough."

"Then, if you grant those assumptions, you'll have to accept my last inference that the speaker is no athlete or outdoors man."

"Well, all right, go on."

"Then my next inference is that the walk was taken very late at night or very early in the morning—say, between midnight and five or six in the morning."

"How do you figure that one?" I asked.

"Consider the distance, nine miles. We're in a fairly well-populated section. Take any road and you'll find a community of some sort in less than nine miles. Hadley is five miles away, Hadley Falls is seven and a half, Goreton is eleven, but East Goreton is only eight and you strike East Goreton before you come to Goreton. There is local train service along the Goreton road and bus service along the others. All the highways are pretty well traveled. Would anyone have to walk nine miles in a rain unless it were late at night when no buses or trains were running and when the few automobiles that were out would hesitate to pick up a stranger on the highway?"

"He might not have wanted to be seen," I suggested.

Nicky smiled pityingly. "You think he would be less noticeable trudging along the highway then he would be riding in a public conveyance where everyone is usually absorbed in his newspaper?"

"Well, I won't press the point," I said brusquely.

"Then try this one: he was walking towards a town rather than away from one."

I nodded. "It is more likely, I suppose. If he were in a town, he could probably arrange for some sort of transportation. Is that the basis for your inference?"

"Partly that," said Nicky, "but there is also an inference to be drawn from the distance. Remember, it's a *nine*-mile walk and nine is one of the exact numbers."

"I'm afraid I don't understand."

That exasperated schoolteacher look appeared on Nicky's face again. "Suppose you say, 'I took a ten-mile walk' or 'a hundred-mile drive'; I would assume that you actually walked anywhere from eight to a dozen miles, or that you rode between ninety and a hundred and ten miles. In other words, *ten* and *hundred* are round numbers. You might have walked *exactly* ten miles or just as likely you might have walked *approximately* ten miles. But when you speak of walking *nine* miles, I have a right to assume that you have named an exact figure. Now, we are far more likely to know the distance of the city from a given point than we are to know the distance of a given point from the city. That is, ask anyone in the city how far out Farmer Brown lives, and if he knows him, he will say, 'Three or four miles.' But ask Farmer Brown how far he lives from the city and he will tell you. 'Three and six-tenths miles—measured it on my speedometer many a time.' "

"It's weak, Nicky," I said.

"But in conjunction with your own suggestion that he could have arranged transportation if he had been in a city—"

"Yes, that would do it," I said. "I'll pass it. Any more?"

"I've just begun to hit my stride," he boasted. "My next inference is that he was going to a definite destination and that he had to be there at a particular time. It was not a case of going off to get help because his car broke down or his wife was going to have a baby or somebody was trying to break into his house."

"Oh, come now," I said, "the car breaking down is really the most likely situation. He could have known the exact distance from having checked the mileage just as he was leaving the town."

Nicky shook his head. "Rather than walk nine miles in the rain, he would have curled up on the back seat and gone to sleep, or at least stayed by his car and tried to flag another motorist. Remember, it's nine miles. What would be the least it would take him to hike it?"

"Four hours," I offered.

He nodded. "Certainly no less, considering the rain. We've agreed that it happened very late at night or very early in the morning. Suppose he had his breakdown at one o'clock in the morning. It would be five o'clock before he would arrive. That's daybreak. You begin to see a lot of cars on the road. The buses start just a little later. In fact, the first buses hit Fairfield around 5:30. Besides, if he were going for help, he would not have to go all the way to town—only as far as the nearest telephone. No, he had a definite appointment, and it was in a town, and it was for some time before 5:30."

"Then why couldn't he have got there earlier and waited?" I asked. "He could have taken the last bus, arrived around one o'clock, and waited until his appointment. He walks nine miles in the rain instead, and you said he was no athlete."

We had arrived at the Municipal Building where my office is. Normally, any arguments begun at the Blue Moon ended at the entrance to the Municipal Building. But I was interested in Nicky's demonstration and I suggested that he come up for a few minutes.

When we were seated I said, "How about it, Nicky, why couldn't he have arrived early and waited?"

"He could have," Nicky retorted. "But since he didn't, we must assume that he was either detained until after the last bus left or that he had to wait where he was for a signal of some sort, perhaps a telephone call."

"Then according to you, he had an appointment sometime beteen midnight and 5:30—"

"We can draw it much finer than that. Remember, it takes him four hours to walk the distance. The last bus stops at 12:30 A. M. If he doesn't take that, but starts at the same time, he won't arrive at his destination until 4:30. On the other hand, if he takes the first bus in the morning, he will arrive around 5:30. That would mean that his appointment was for sometime between 4:30 and 5:30."

"You mean that if his appointment were earlier than 4:30, he would have taken the last night bus, and if it were later than 5:30, he would have taken the first morning bus?"

"Precisely. And another thing: if he were waiting for a signal or a phone call, it must have come not much later than one o'clock."

"Yes, I see that," I said. "If his appointment is around five o'clock and it takes him four hours to walk the distance, he'd have to start around one."

He nodded, silent and thoughtful. For some queer reason I couldn't explain, I didn't feel like interrupting his thoughts. On the wall was a large map of the county and I walked over to it and began to study it.

"You're right, Nicky," I remarked over my shoulder, "there's no place as far as nine miles away from Fairfield that doesn't hit another town first. Fairfield is right in the middle of a bunch of smaller towns."

He joined me at the map. "It doesn't have to be Fairfield, you know," he said quietly. "It was probably one of the outlying towns he had to reach. Try Hadley."

"Why Hadley? What would anyone want in Hadley at five o'clock in the morning?"

"The *Washington Flyer* stops there to take on water about that time," he said quietly.

"That's right too," I said. "I've heard that train many a night when I couldn't sleep. I'd hear it pulling in and then a minute or two later I'd hear the clock on the Methodist Chuch banging out five." I went back to my desk for a timetable. "The *Flyer* leaves Washington at 12:47 A.M. and gets into Boston at 8:00 A.M."

Nicky was still at the map measuring distances with a pencil.

"Exactly nine miles from Hadley is the Old Sumter Inn," he announced.

"Old Sumter Inn," I echoed. "But that upsets the whole theory. You can arrange for transportation there as easily as you can in a town."

He shook his head. "The cars are kept in an enclosure and you have to get an attendant to check you through the gate. The attendant would remember anyone taking out his car at a strange hour. It's a pretty conservative place. He could have waited in his room until he got a call from Washington about someone on the *Flyer*—maybe the number of the car and the berth. Then he could just slip out of the hotel and walk to Hadley."

I stared at him, hypnotized.

"It wouldn't be difficult to slip aboard while the train was taking on water, and then if he knew the car number and the berth—"

"Nicky," I said portentously, "as the Reform district attorney who campaigned on an economy program, I am going to waste the taxpayers' money and call Boston long distance. It's ridiculous, it's insane—but I'm going to do it!"

His little blue eyes glittered and he moistened his lips with the tip of his tongue.

"Go ahead," he said hoarsely.

I replaced the telephone in its cradle.

"Nicky," I said, "this is probably the most remarkable coincidence in the history of criminal investigation: *a man was found murdered in his berth on last night's 12:47 from Washington!* He'd been dead about three hours, which would make it exactly right for Hadley."

"I thought it was something like that," said Nicky. "But you're wrong about it being a coincidence. It can't be. Where did you get that sentence?"

"It was just a sentence. It simply popped into my head."

"It couldn't have! It's not the sort of sentence that pops into one's head. If you had taught composition as long as I have, you'd know that when you ask someone for a sentence of ten words or so, you get an ordinary statement such as 'I like milk'—with the other words made up by a modifying clause like, 'because it is good for my health.' The sentence you offered related to a *particular situation*."

"But I tell you I talked to no one this morning. And I was alone with you at the Blue Moon."

"You weren't with me all the time I paid my check," he said sharply. "Did you meet anyone while you were waiting on the sidewalk for me to come out of the Blue Moon?"

I shook my head. "I was outside for less than a minute before you joined me. You see, a couple of men came in while you were digging out your change and one of them bumped me, so I thought I'd wait—"

"Did you ever see them before?"

"Who?"

"The two men who came in," he said, the note of exasperation creeping into his voice again.

"Why, no—they weren't anyone I knew."

"Were they talking?"

"I guess so. Yes, they were. Quite absorbed in their conversation, as a matter of fact—otherwise, they would have noticed me and I would not have been bumped."

"Not many strangers come into the Blue Moon," he remarked.

"Do you think it was they?" I asked eagerly. "I think I'd know them again if I saw them."

Nicky's eyes narrowed. "It's possible. There had to be two—one to trail the victim in Washington and ascertain his berth number, the other to wait here and do the job. The Washington man would be likely to come down here afterward. If there were theft as well as murder, it would be to divide the spoils. If it was just murder, he would probably have to come down to pay off his confederate."

I reached for the telephone.

"We've been gone less than half an hour," Nicky went on. "They were just coming in and service is slow at the Blue Moon. The one who walked all the way to Hadley must certainly be hungry and the other probably drove all night from Washington."

"Call me immediately if you make an arrest," I said and hung up.

Neither of us spoke a word while we waited. We paced the floor, avoiding each other almost as though we had done something we were ashamed of. The telephone rang at last. I picked it up and listened. Then I said, "O.K." and turned to Nicky.

"One of them tried to escape through the kitchen but Winn had someone stationed at the back and they got him."

"That would seem to prove it," said Nicky with a frosty little smile.

I nodded agreement.

He glanced at his watch. "Gracious," he exclaimed, "I wanted to make an early start on my work this morning, and here I've already wasted all this time talking with you."

I let him get to the door. "Oh, Nicky," I called, "what was it you set out to prove?"

"That a chain of inferences could be logical and still not be true," he said.

"Oh."

"What are you laughing at?" he asked snappishly. And then he laughed too.

Stanley Ellin

The Speciality of the House

⁶⁶And this," said Laffler, "is Sbirro's." Costain saw a square brownstone façade identical with the others that extended from either side into the clammy darkness of the deserted street. From the barred windows of the basement at his feet, a glimmer of light showed behind heavy curtains.

"Lord," he observed, "it's a dismal hole, isn't it?"

"I beg you to understand," said Laffler stiffly, "that Sbirro's is the restaurant without pretensions. Beseiged by these ghastly, neurotic times, it has refused to compromise. It is perhaps the last important establishment in this city lit by gas jets. Here you will find the same honest furnishings, the same magnificent Sheffield service, and possibly, in a far corner, the very same spider webs that were remarked by the patrons of a half century ago!"

"A doubtful recommendation," said Costain, "and hardly sanitary."

"When you enter," Laffler continued, "you leave the insanity of this year, this day, and this hour, and you find yourself for a brief span restored in spirit, not by opulence but by dignity, which is the lost quality of our time."

Costain laughed uncomfortably. "You make it sound more like a cathedral than a restaurant," he said.

In the pale reflection of the street lamp overhead, Laffler peered at his companion's face. "I wonder," he said abruptly, "whether I have not made a mistake in extending this invitation to you."

Costain was hurt. Despite an impressive title and large salary, he was no more than clerk to this pompous little man, but he was impelled to make some display of his feelings. "If you wish," he said coldly, "I can make other plans for my evening with no trouble."

With his large, cowlike eyes turned up to Costain, the mist drifting into the ruddy full moon of his face, Laffler seemed strangely ill at ease. Then, "No, no," he said at last, "absolutely not. It's important that you dine at Sbirro's with me." He grasped Costain's arm firmly and led the way to the wrought-iron gate of the basement. "You see, you're the sole person in my office who seems to know anything at all about good food. And on my part, knowing about Sbirro's but not

235

having some appreciative friend to share it, is like having a unique piece of art locked in a room where no one else can enjoy it."

Costain was considerably mollified by this. "I understand there are a great many people who relish that situation."

"I'm not one of that kind!" Laffler said sharply. "And having the secret of Sbirro's locked in myself for years has finally become unendurable." He fumbled at the side of the gate and from within could be heard the small, discordant jangle of an ancient pull-bell. An interior door opened with a groan and Costain found himself peering into a dark face whose only discernible feature was a row of gleaming teeth.

"Sair?" said the face.

"Mr. Laffler and a guest."

"Sair," the face said again, this time in what was clearly an invitation. It moved aside and Costain stumbled down a single step behind his host. The door and gate creaked behind him and he stood blinking in a small foyer. It took him a moment to realize that the figure he now stared at was his own reflection in a gigantic pier glass that extended from floor to ceiling. "Atmosphere," he said under his breath and chuckled as he followed his guide to a seat.

He faced Laffler across a small table for two and peered curiously around the dining room. It was no size at all, but the half dozen guttering gas jets which provided the only illumination threw such a deceptive light that the walls flickered and faded into uncertain distance.

There were no more than eight or ten tables about, arranged to insure the maximum privacy. All were occupied, and the few waiters serving them moved with quiet efficiency. In the air was a soft clash and scrape of cutlery and a soothing murmur of talk. Costain nodded appreciatively.

Laffler breathed an audible sigh of gratification. "I knew you would share my enthusiasm," he said. "Have you noticed, by the way, that there are no women present?"

Costain raised inquiring eyebrows.

"Sbirro," said Laffler, "does not encourage members of the fair sex to enter the premises. And, I can tell you, his method is decidedly effective. I had the experience of seeing a woman get a taste of it not long ago. She sat at a table for not less than an hour waiting for service which was never forthcoming."

"Didn't she make a scene?"

"She did." Laffler smiled at the recollection. "She succeeded in annoying the customers, embarrassing her partner, and nothing more."

"And what about Mr. Sbirro?"

"He did not make an appearance. Whether he directed affairs from behind the scenes or was not even present during the episode, I don't know. Whichever it was, he won a complete victory. The woman never reappeared, nor, for that matter, did the witless gentleman who by bringing her was really the cause of the entire contretemps."

"A fair warning to all present," laughed Costain.

A waiter now appeared at the table. The chocolate-dark skin, the thin, beautifully molded nose and lips, the large liquid eyes, heavily lashed, and the silver-white hair so heavy and silken that it lay on the skull like a cap, all marked him definitely as an East Indian of some sort, Costain decided. The man arranged the stiff table linen, filled two tumblers from a huge cut-glass pitcher, and set them in their proper places.

"Tell me," Laffler said eagerly, "is the special being served this evening?"

The waiter smiled regretfully and showed teeth as spectacular as those of the majordomo. "I am so sorry, sair. There is no special this evening."

Laffler's face fell into lines of heavy disappointment. "After waiting so long. It's been a month already, and I hoped to show my friend here—"

"You understand the difficulties, sair."

"Of course, of course." Laffler looked at Costain sadly and shrugged. "You see, I had in mind to introduce you to the greatest treat that Sbirro's offers, but unfortunately it isn't on the menu this evening."

The waiter said: "Do you wish to be served now, sair?" and Laffler nodded. To Costain's surprise the waiter made his way off without waiting for any instructions.

"Have you ordered in advance?" he asked.

"Ah," said Laffler, "I really should have explained. Sbirro's offers no choice whatsoever. You will eat the same meal as everyone else in this room. Tomorrow evening you would eat an entirely different meal, but again without designating a single preference."

"Very unusual," said Costain, "and certainly unsatisfactory at times. What if one doesn't have a taste for the particular dish set before him?"

"On that score," said Laffler solemnly, "you need have no fears.

I give you my word that no matter how exacting your tastes, you will relish evey mouthful you eat in Sbirro's."

Costain looked doubtful, and Laffler smiled. "And consider the subtle advantages of the system," he said. "When you pick up the menu of a popular restaurant, you find youself confronted with innumerable choices. You are forced to weigh, to evaluate, to make uneasy decisions which you may instantly regret. The effect of all this is a tension which, however slight, must make for discomfort.

"And consider the mechanics of the process. Instead of a hurly-burly of sweating cooks rushing about a kitchen in a frenzy to prepare a hundred varying items, we have a chef who stands serenely alone, bringing all his talents to bear on one task, with all assurance of a complete triumph!"

"Then you have seen the kitchen?"

"Unfortunately, no," said Laffler sadly. "The picture I offer is hypothetical, made of conversational fragments I have pieced together over the years. I must admit, though, that my desire to see the functioning of the kitchen here comes very close to being my sole obsession nowadays."

"But have you mentioned this to Sbirro?"

"A dozen times. He shrugs the suggestion away."

"Isn't that a rather curious foible on his part?"

"No, no," Laffler said hastily, "a master artist is never under the compulsion of petty courtesies. Still," he sighed, "I have never given up hope."

The waiter now reappeared bearing two soup bowls which he set in place with mathematical exactitude, and a small tureen from which he slowly ladled a measure of clear, thin broth. Costain dipped his spoon into the broth and tasted it with some curiosity. It was delicately flavored, bland to the verge of tastelessness. Costain frowned, tentatively reached for the salt and pepper cellars, and discovered there were none on the table. He looked up, saw Laffler's eyes on him, and although unwilling to compromise with his own tastes, he hesitated to act as a damper on Laffler's enthusiasm. Therefore he smiled and indicated the broth.

"Excellent," he said.

Laffler returned his smile. "You do not find it excellent at all," he said coolly. "You find it flat and badly in need of condiments. I know this," he continued as Costain's eyebrows shot upward, "because it was my own reaction many years ago, and because like yourself I found myself reaching for salt and pepper after the first mouthful. I also learned with surprise that condiments are not available in Sbirro's."

Costain was shocked. "Not even salt!" he exclaimed.

"Not even salt. The very fact that you require it for your soup stands as evidence that your taste is unduly jaded. I am confident that you will now make the same discovery that I did: by the time you have nearly finished your soup, your desire for salt will be nonexistent."

Laffler was right; before Costain had reached the bottom of his plate, he was relishing the nuances of the broth with steadily increasing delight. Laffler thrust aside his own empty bowl and rested his elbows on the table. "Do you agree with me now?"

"To my surprise," said Costain, "I do."

As the waiter busied himself clearing the table, Laffler lowered his voice significantly. "You will find," he said, "that the absence of condiments is but one of several noteworthy characteristics which mark Sbirro's. I may as well prepare you for these. For example, no alcoholic beverages of any sort are served here, nor for that matter any beverage except clear, cold water, the first and only drink necessary for a human being."

"Outside of mother's milk," suggested Costain dryly.

"I can answer that in like vein by pointing out that the average patron of Sbirro's has passed that primal stage of his development."

Costain laughed. "Granted," he said.

"Very well. There is also a ban on the use of tobacco in any form."

"But, good heavens," said Costain, "doesn't that make Sbirro's more a teetotaler's retreat than a gourmet's sanctuary?"

"I fear," said Laffler solemnly, "that you confuse the words *gourmet* and *gourmand*. The gourmand, through glutting himself, requires a wider and wider latitude of experience to stir his surfeited senses, but the very nature of the gourmet is simplicity. The ancient Greek in his coarse chiton savoring the ripe olive; the Japanese in his bare room contemplating the curve of a single flower stem—these are the true gourmets."

"But an occasional drop of brandy or pipeful of tobacco," said Costain dubiously, "are hardly overindulgences."

"By alternating stimulant and narcotic," said Laffler, "you seesaw the delicate balance of your taste so violently that it loses its most precious quality: the appreciation of fine food. During my years as a patron of Sbirro's, I have proved this to my satisfaction."

"May I ask," said Costain, "why you regard the ban on these things as having such deep esthetic motives? What about such mundane reasons as the high cost of a liquor license, or the possibility that patrons would object to the smell of tobacco in such confined quarters?"

Laffler shook his head violently. "If and when you meet Sbirro," he said, "you will understand at once that he is not the man to make decisions on a mundane basis. As a matter of fact, it was Sbirro himself who first made me cognizant of what you call 'esthetic' motives."

"An amazing man," said Costain as the waiter prepared to serve the entrée.

Laffler's next words were not spoken until he had savored and swallowed a large portion of meat. "I hesitate to use superlatives," he said, "but to my way of thinking, Sbirro represents man at the apex of his civilization!"

Costain cocked an eyebrow and applied himself to his roast, which rested in a pool of stiff gravy ungarnished by green or vegetable. The thin steam rising from it carried to his nostrils a subtle, tantalizing odor which made his mouth water. He chewed a piece as slowly and thoughtfully as if he were analyzing the intricacies of a Mozart symphony. The range of taste he discovered was really extraordinary, from the pungent nip of the crisp outer edge to the peculiarly flat yet soul-satisfying ooze of blood which the pressure of his jaws forced from the half raw interior.

Upon swallowing he found himself ferociously hungry for another piece, and then another, and it was only with an effort that he prevented himself from wolfing down all his share of the meat and gravy without waiting to get the full voluptuous satisfaction from each mouthful. When he had scraped his platter clean, he realized that both he and Laffler had completed the entire course without exchanging a single word. He commented on this, and Laffler said: "Can you see any need for words in the presence of such food?"

Costain looked around at the shabby, dimly lit room, the quiet diners, with a new perception. "No," he said humbly, "I cannot. For any doubts I had I apologize unreservedly. In all your praise of Sbirro's there was not a single word of exaggeration."

"Ah," said Laffler delightedly. "And that is only part of the story. You heard me mention the special, which unfortunately was not on the menu tonight. What you have just eaten is as nothing when compared to the absolute delights of that special!"

"Good Lord!" cried Costain, "what is it? Nightingale's tongues? Filet of unicorn?"

"Neither," said Laffler. "It is lamb."

"Lamb?"

Laffler remained lost in thought for a minute. "If," he said at last, "I were to give you in my own unstinted words my opinion of this dish, you would judge me completely insane. That is how deeply the mere thought of it affects me. It is neither the fatty chop, nor the too solid leg; it is, instead, a select portion of the rarest sheep in existence and is named after the species—lamb Amirstan."

Costain knit his brows. "Amirstan?"

"A fragment of desolation almost lost on the border which separates Afghanistan and Russia. From chance remarks dropped by Sbirro, I gather it is no more than a plateau which grazes the pitiful remnants of a flock of superb sheep. Sbirro, through some means or other, obtained rights to the traffic in this flock and is, therefore, the sole restaurateur ever to have lamb Amirstan on his bill of fare. I can tell you that the appearance of this dish is a rare occurrence indeed, and luck is the only guide in determining for the clientele the exact date when it will be served."

"But surely," said Costain, "Sbirro could provide some advance knowledge of this event."

"The objection to that is simply stated," said Laffler. "There exists in this city a huge number of professional gluttons. Should advance information slip out, it is quite likely that they will, out of curiosity, become familiar with the dish and thenceforth supplant the regular patrons at these tables."

"But you don't mean to say," objected Costain, "that these few people present are the only ones in the entire city, or for that matter in the whole wide world, who know of the existence of Sbirro's!"

"Very nearly. There may be one or two regular patrons who, for some reason, are not present at the moment."

"That's incredible."

"It is done," said Laffler, the slightest shade of menace in his voice, "by every patron making it his solemn obligation to keep the secret. By accepting my invitation this evening, you automatically assume that obligation. I hope you can be trusted with it."

Costain flushed. "My position in your employ should vouch for me. I only question the wisdom of a policy which keeps such magnificent food away from so many who would enjoy it."

"Do you know the inevitable result of the policy *you* favor?" asked

Laffler bitterly. "An influx of idiots who would nightly complain that they are never served roast duck with chocolate sauce. Is that picture tolerable to you?"

"No," admitted Costain. "I am forced to agree with you."

Laffler leaned back in his chair wearily and passed his hand over his eyes in an uncertain gesture. "I am a solitary man," he said quietly, "and not by choice alone. It may sound strange to you, it may border on eccentricity, but I feel to my depths that this restaurant, this warm haven in a coldly insane world, is both family and friend to me."

And Costain, who to this moment had never viewed his companion as other than tyrannical employer or officious host, now felt an overwhelming pity twist inside his comfortably expanded stomach.

By the end of two weeks the invitations to join Laffler at Sbirro's had become something of a ritual. Every day, at a few minutes after five, Costain would step out into the office corridor and lock his cubicle behind him; he would drape his overcoat neatly over his left arm, and peer into the glass of the door to make sure his Homburg was set at the proper angle. At one time he would have followed this by lighting a cigarette, but under Laffler's prodding he had decided to give abstinence a fair trial. Then he would start down the corridor, and Laffler would fall in step at his elbow, clearing his throat. "Ah, Costain. No plans for this evening, I hope."

"No," Costain would say, "I'm footloose and fancy-free," or "At your service," or something equally inane. He wondered at times whether it would not be more tactful to vary the ritual with an occasional refusal, but the glow with which Laffler received his answer and the rough friendliness of Laffler's grip on his arm forestalled him.

Among the treacherous crags of the business world, reflected Costain, what better way to secure your footing than friendship with one's employer? Already, a secretary close to the workings of the inner office had commented publicly on Laffler's highly favorable opinion of Costain. That was all to the good.

And the food! The incomparable food at Sbirro's! For the first time in his life, Costain, ordinarily a lean and bony man, noted with gratification that he was certainly gaining weight; within two weeks his bones had disappeared under a layer of sleek, firm flesh, and here and there were even signs of incipient plumpness. It struck Costain one night, while surveying himself in his bath, that the rotund Laffler himself might have been a spare and bony man before discovering Sbirro's.

So there was obviously everything to be gained and nothing to be lost by accepting Laffler's invitations. Perhaps after testing the heralded wonders of lamb Amirstan and meeting Sbirro, who thus far had not made an appearance, a refusal or two might be in order. But certainly not until then.

That evening, two weeks to a day after his first visit to Sbirro's, Costain had both desires fulfilled; he dined on lamb Amirstan, and he met Sbirro. Both exceeded all his expectations.

When the waiter leaned over their table immediately after seating them and gravely announced: "Tonight is special, sair," Costain was shocked to find his heart pounding with expectation. On the table before him he saw Laffler's hands trembling violently.

But it isn't natural, he thought suddenly: two full-grown men, presumably intelligent and in the full possession of their senses, as jumpy as a pair of cats waiting to have their meat flung to them!

"This is it!" Laffler's voice startled him so that he almost leaped from his seat. "The culinary triumph of all times! And faced by it you are embarrassed by the very emotions it distills."

"How did you know that?" Costain asked faintly.

"How? Because a decade ago I underwent your embarrassment. Add to that your air of revulsion and it's easy to see how affronted you are by the knowledge that man has not yet forgotten how to slaver over his meat."

"And these others," whispered Costain, "do they all feel the same thing?"

"Judge for yourself."

Costain looked furtively around at the nearby tables. "You are right," he finally said. "At any rate, there's comfort in numbers."

Laffler inclined his head slightly to the side. "One of the numbers," he remarked, "appears to be in for a disappointment."

Costain followed the gesture. At the table indicated, a gray-haired man sat conspicuously alone, and Costain frowned at the empty chair opposite him.

"Why, yes," he recalled, "that very stout bald man, isn't it? I believe it's the first dinner he's missed here in two weeks."

"The entire decade more likely," said Laffler sympathetically. "Rain or shine, crisis or calamity, I don't think he's missed an evening at Sbirro's since the first time I dined here. Imagine his expression when he's told that on his very first defection, lamb Amirstan was the *plat du jour*."

Costain looked at the empty chair again with a dim discomfort. "His very first?" he murmured.

"Mr. Laffler! And friend! I am so pleased. So very, very pleased. No, do not stand; I will have a place made." Miraculously a seat appeared under the figure standing there at the table. "The lamb Amirstan will be an unqualified success, hurr? I myself have been stewing in the miserable kitchen all the day, prodding the foolish chef to do everything just so. The just so is the important part, hurr? But I see your friend does not know me. An introduction, perhaps?"

The words ran in a smooth, fluid eddy. They rippled, they purred, they hypnotized Costain so that he could do no more than stare. The mouth that uncoiled this sinuous monologue was alarmingly wide, with thin mobile lips that curled and twisted with every syllable. There was a flat nose with a straggling line of hair under it; wide-set eyes, almost oriental in appearance, that glittered in the unsteady flare of gaslight; and long sleek hair that swept back from high on the unwrinkled forehead—hair so pale that it might have been bleached of all color. An amazing face surely, and the sight of it tortured Costain with the conviction that it was somehow familiar. His brain twitched and prodded but could not stir up any solid recollection.

Laffler's voice jerked Costain out of his study. "Mr. Sbirro. Mr. Costain, a good friend and associate." Costain rose and shook the proffered hand. It was warm and dry, flint-hard against his palm.

"I am so very pleased, Mr. Costain. So very, very pleased," purred the voice. "You like my little establishment, hurr? You have a great treat in store, I assure you."

Laffler chuckled. "Oh, Costain's been dining here regularly for two weeks," he said. "He's by way of becoming a great admirer of yours, Sbirro."

The eyes were turned on Costain. "A very great compliment. You compliment me with your presence and I return same with my food, hurr? But the lamb Amirstan is far superior to anything of your past experience, I assure you. All the trouble of obtaining it, all the difficulty of preparation, is truly merited."

Costain strove to put aside the exasperating problem of that face. "I have wondered," he said, "why with all these difficulties you mention, you even bother to present lamb Amirstan to the public.

Surely your other dishes are excellent enough to uphold your reputation."

Sbirro smiled so broadly that his face became perfectly round.
"Perhaps it is a matter of the psychology, hurr? Someone discovers
a wonder and must share it with others. He must fill his cup to the
brim, perhaps, by observing the so evident pleasure of those who
explore it with him. Or," he shrugged, "perhaps it is just a matter
of good business."

"Then in the light of all this," Costain persisted, "and considering
all the conventions you have imposed on your customers, why do
you open the restaurant to the public instead of operating it as a
private club?"

The eyes abruptly glinted into Costain's, then turned away. "So
perspicacious, hurr? Then I will tell you. Becuase there is more
privacy in a public eating place than in the most exclusive club in
existence! Here no one inquires of your affairs; no one desires to
know the intimacies of your life. Here the business is eating. We
are not curious about names and addresses or the reasons for the
coming and going of our guests. We welcome you when you are here;
we have no regrets when you are here no longer. That is the answer,
hurr?"

Costain was startled by this vehemence. "I had no intention of
prying," he stammered.

Sbirro ran the tip of his tongue over his thin lips. "No, no," he
reassured, "you are not prying. Do not let me give you that impression. On the contrary, I invite your questions."

"Oh, come, Costain," said Laffler. "Don't let Sbirro intimidate you.
I've known him for years and I guarantee that his bark is worse
than his bite. Before you know it, he'll be showing you all the privileges of the house—outside of inviting you to visit his precious
kitchen, of course."

"Ah," smiled Sbirro, "for that, Mr. Costain may have to wait a
little while. For everything else I am at his beck and call."

Laffler slapped his hand jovially on the table. "What did I tell
you!" he said. "Now let's have the truth, Sbirro. Has anyone, outside
of your staff, ever stepped into the sanctum sanctorum?"

Sbirro looked up. "You see on the wall above you," he said earnestly, "the portrait of one to whom I did the honor. A very dear
friend and patron of most long standing, he is evidence that my
kitchen is not inviolate."

Costain studied the picture and started with recognition. "Why," he said excitedly, "that's the famous writer—you know the one, Laffler—he used to do such wonderful short stories and cynical bits and then suddenly took himself off and disappeared in Mexico!"

"Of course!" cried Laffler, "and to think I've been sitting under his portrait for years without even realizing it!" He turned to Sbirro. "A dear friend, you say? His disappearance must have been a blow to you."

Sbirro's face lengthened. "It was, it was, I assure you. But think of it this way, gentlemen: he was probably greater in his death than in his life, hurr? A most tragic man, he often told me that his only happy hours were spent here at this very table. Pathetic, is it not? And to think the only favor I could ever show him was to let him witness the mysteries of my kitchen, which is, when all is said and done, no more than a plain, ordinary kitchen."

"You seem very certain of his death," commented Costain. "After all, no evidence has ever turned up to substantiate it."

Sbirro contemplated the picture. "None at all," he said softly. "Remarkable, hurr?"

With the arrival of the entrée Sbirro leaped to his feet and set about serving them himself. With his eyes alight he lifted the casserole from the tray and sniffed at the fragrance from within with sensual relish. Then, taking great care not to lose a single drop of gravy, he filled two platters with chunks of dripping meat. As if exhausted by this task, he sat back in his chair, breathing heavily. "Gentlemen," he said, "to your good appetite."

Costain chewed his first mouthful with great deliberation and swallowed it. Then he looked at the empty tines of his fork with glazed eyes.

"Good God!" he breathed.

"It is good, hurr? Better than you imagined?"

Costain shook his head dazedly. "It is as impossible," he said slowly, "for the uninitiated to conceive the delights of lamb Amirstan as for mortal man to look into his own soul."

"Perhaps," Sbirro thrust his head so close that Costain could feel the warm, fetid breath tickle his nostrils, "perhaps you have just had a glimpse into your soul, hurr?"

Costain tried to draw back slightly without giving offense. "Perhaps," he laughed, "and a gratifying picture it made: all fang and claw. But without intending any disrespect, I should hardly like to build my church on *lamb en casserole*."

Sbirro rose and laid a hand gently on his shoulder. "So perspicacious," he said. "Sometimes when you have nothing to do, nothing, perhaps, but sit for a very little while in a dark room and think of this world—what it is and what it is going to be—then you must turn your thoughts a little to the significance of the Lamb in religion. It will be so interesting. And now," he bowed deeply to both men, "I have held you long enough from your dinner. I was most happy," he nodded to Costain, "and I am sure we will meet again." The teeth gleamed, the eyes glittered, and Sbirro was gone down the aisle of tables.

Costain twisted around to stare after the retreating figure. "Have I offended him in some way?" he asked.

Laffler looked up from his plate. "Offended him? He loves that kind of talk. Lamb Amirstan is a ritual with him; get him started and he'll be back at you a dozen times worse than a priest making a conversion."

Costain turned to his meal with the face still hovering before him. "Interesting man," he reflected. "Very."

It took him a month to discover the tantalizing familiarity of that face, and when he did he laughed aloud in his bed. Why, of course! Sbirro might have sat as the model for the Cheshire cat in *Alice!*

He passed this thought on to Laffler the very next evening as they pushed their way down the street to the restaurant against a chill, blustering wind. Laffler only looked blank.

"You may be right," he said, "but I'm not a fit judge. It's a far cry back to the days when I read the book. A far cry, indeed."

As if taking up his words, a piercing howl came ringing down the street and stopped both men short in their tracks. "Someone's in trouble there," said Laffler. "Look!"

Not far from the entrance to Sbirro's two figures could be seen struggling in the near darkness. They swayed back and forth and suddenly tumbled into a writhing heap on the sidewalk. The piteous howl went up again, and Laffler, despite his girth, ran toward it at a fair speed with Costain tagging cautiously behind.

Stretched out full-length on the pavement was a slender figure with the dusky complexion and white hair of one of Sbirro's servitors. His fingers were futilely plucking at the huge hands which encircled his throat, and his knees pushed weakly up at the gigantic bulk of a man who brutally bore down with his full weight.

Laffler came up panting. "Stop this!" he shouted. "What's going on here?"

The pleading eyes almost bulging from their sockets turned toward Laffler. "Help, sair. This man—drunk—"

"Drunk am I, ya dirty—" Costain saw now that the man was a sailor in a badly soiled uniform. The air around him reeked with the stench of liquor. "Pick me pocket and then call me drunk, will ya!" He dug his fingers in harder, and his victim groaned.

Laffler seized the sailor's shoulder. "Let go of him, do you hear! Let go of him at once!" he cried, and the next instant was sent careening into Costain, who staggered back under the force of the blow.

The attack on his own person sent Laffler into immediate and berserk action. Without a sound he leaped at the sailor, striking and kicking furiously at the unprotected face and flanks. Stunned at first, the man came to his feet with a rush and turned on Laffler. For a moment they stood locked together, and then, as Costain joined the attack, all three went sprawling to the ground. Slowly Laffler and Costain got to their feet and looked down at the body before them.

"He's either out cold from liquor," said Costain, "or he struck his head going down. In any case, it's a job for the police."

"No, no, sair!" The waiter crawled weakly to his feet, and stood swaying. "No police, sair. Mr. Sbirro do not want such. You understand, sair." He caught hold of Costain with a pleading hand, and Costain looked at Laffler.

"Of course not," said Laffler. "We won't have to bother with the police. They'll pick him up soon enough, the murderous sot. But what in the world started all this?"

"That man, sair. He make most erratic way while walking, and with no meaning I push against him. Then he attack me, accusing me to rob him."

"As I thought." Laffler pushed the waiter gently along. "Now go on in and get yourself attended to."

The man seemed ready to burst into tears. "To you, sair, I owe my life. If there is anything I can do—"

Laffler turned into the areaway that led to Sbirro's door. "No, no, it was nothing. You go along, and if Sbirro has any questions send him to me. I'll straighten it out."

"My life, sair," were the last words they heard as the inner door closed behind them.

"There you are, Costain," said Laffler, as a few minutes later he drew his chair under the table, "civilized man in all his glory. Reeking with alcohol, strangling to death some miserable innocent who came too close."

Costain made an effort to gloss over the nerve-shattering memory of the episode. "It's the neurotic cat that takes to alcohol," he said. "Surely there's a reason for that sailor's condition."

"Reason? Of course there is. Plain atavistic savagery!" Laffler swept his arm in an all-embracing gesture. "Why do we all sit here at our meat? Not only to appease physical demands, but because our atavistic selves cry for release. Think back, Costain. Do you remember that I once described Sbirro as the epitome of civilization? Can you now see why? A brilliant man, he fully understands the nature of human beings. But unlike lesser men he bends all his efforts to the satisfaction of our innate natures without resultant harm to some innocent bystander."

"When I think back on the wonders of lamb Amirstan," said Costain, "I quite understand what you're driving at. And, by the way, isn't it nearly due to appear on the bill of fare? It must have been over a month ago that it was last served."

The waiter, filling the tumblers, hesitated. "I am so sorry, sair. No special this evening."

"There's your answer," Laffler grunted, "and probably just my luck to miss out on it altogether the next time."

Costain stared at him. "Oh, come, that's impossible."

"No, blast it." Laffler drank off half his water at a gulp and the waiter immediately refilled the glass. "I'm off to South America for a surprise tour of inspection. One month, two months, Lord knows how long."

"Are things that bad down there?"

"They could be better." Laffler suddenly grinned. "Mustn't forget it takes very mundane dollars and cents to pay the tariff at Sbirro's."

"I haven't heard a word of this around the office."

"Wouldn't be a surprise tour if you had. Nobody knows about this except myself—and now you. I want to walk in on them completely unsuspected. Find out what flimflammery they're up to down there. As far as the office is concerned, I'm off on a jaunt somewhere. Maybe recuperating in some sanatorium from my hard work. Anyhow, the business will be in good hands. Yours, among them."

"Mine?" said Costain, surprised.

"When you go in tomorrow you'll find yourself in receipt of a promotion, even if I'm not there to hand it to you personally. Mind you, it has nothing to do with our friendship either; you've done fine work, and I'm immensely grateful for it."

Costain reddened under the praise. "You don't expect to be in tomorrow. Then you're leaving tonight?"

Laffler nodded. "I've been trying to wangle some reservations. If they come through, well, this will be in the nature of a farewell celebration."

"You know," said Costain slowly, "I devoutly hope that your reservations don't come through. I believe our dinners here have come to mean more to me than I ever dared imagine."

The waiter's voice broke in. "Do you wish to be served now, sair?" and they both started.

"Of course, of course," said Laffler sharply, "I didn't realize you were waiting."

"What bothers me," he told Costain as the waiter turned away, "is the thought of the lamb Amirstan I'm bound to miss. To tell you the truth, I've already put off my departure a week, hoping to hit a lucky night, and now I simply can't delay any more. I do hope that when you're sitting over your share of lamb Amirstan, you'll think of me with suitable regrets."

Costain laughed. "I will indeed," he said as he turned to his dinner.

Hardly had he cleared the plate when a waiter silently reached for it. It was not their usual waiter, he observed; it was none other than the victim of the assault.

"Well," Costain said, "how do you feel now? Still under the weather?"

The waiter paid no attention to him. Instead, with the air of a man under great strain, he turned to Laffler. "Sair," he whispered. "My life. I owe it to you. I can repay you!"

Laffler looked up in amazement, then shook his head firmly. "No," he said; "I want nothing from you, understand? You have repaid me sufficiently with your thanks. Now get on with your work and let's hear no more about it."

The waiter did not stir an inch, but his voice rose slightly. "By the body and blood of your God, sair, I will help you even if you do not want! *Do not go into the kitchen, sair.* I trade you my life for yours, sair, when I speak this. Tonight or any night of your life, do not go into the kitchen at Sbirro's!"

Laffler sat back, completely dumbfounded. "Not go into the kitchen? Why shouldn't I go into the kitchen if Mr. Sbirro ever took it into his head to invite me there? What's all this about?"

A hard hand was laid on Costain's back, and another gripped the waiter's arm. The waiter remained frozen to the spot, his lips compressed, his eyes downcast.

"What is all *what* about, gentlemen?" purred the voice. "So opportune an arrival. In time as ever, I see, to answer all the questions, hurr?"

Laffler breathed a sigh of relief. "Ah, Sbirro, thank heaven you're here. This man is saying something about my not going into your kitchen. Do you know what he means?"

The teeth showed in a broad grin. "But of course. This good man was giving you advice in all amiability. It so happens that my too emotional chef heard some rumor that I might have a guest into his precious kitchen, and he flew into a fearful rage. Such a rage, gentlemen! He even threatened to give notice on the spot, and you can understand what that would mean to Sbirro's, hurr? Fortunately, I succeeded in showing him what a signal honor it is to have an esteemed patron and true connoisseur observe him at his work first hand, and now he is quite amenable. Quite, hurr?"

He released the waiter's arm. "You're at the wrong table," he said softly. "See that it does not happen again."

The waiter slipped off without daring to raise his eyes and Sbirro drew a chair to the table. He seated himself and brushed his hand lightly over his hair. "Now I am afraid that the cat is out of the bag, hurr? This invitation to you, Mr. Laffler, was to be a surprise; but the surprise is gone, and all that is left is the invitation."

Laffler mopped beads of perspiration from his forehead. "Are you serious?" he said huskily. "Do you mean that we are really to witness the preparation of your food tonight?"

Sbirro drew a sharp fingernail along the tablecloth, leaving a thin straight line printed in the linen. "Ah," he said, "I am faced with a dilemma of great proportions." He studied the line soberly. "You, Mr. Laffler, have been my guest for ten long years. But our friend here—"

Costain raised his hand in protest. "I understand perfectly. This invitation is solely to Mr. Laffler, and naturally my presence is embarrassing. As it happens, I have an early engagement for this evening and must be on my way anyhow. So you see there's no dilemma at all, really."

"No," said Laffler, "absolutely not. That wouldn't be fair at all. We've been sharing this until now, Costain, and I won't enjoy this experience half as much if you're not along. Surely Sbirro can make his conditions flexible this one occasion."

They both looked at Sbirro who shrugged his shoulders regretfully.

Costain rose abruptly. "I'm not going to sit here, Laffler, and spoil your great adventure. And then too," he bantered, "think of that ferocious chef waiting to get his cleaver on you. I prefer not to be at the scene. I'll just say goodbye," he went on, to cover Laffler's guilty silence, "and leave you to Sbirro. I'm sure he'll take pains to give you a good show." He held out his hand and Laffler squeezed it painfully hard.

"You're being very decent, Costain," he said. "I hope you'll continue to dine here until we meet again. It shouldn't be too long."

Sbirro made way for Costain to pass. "I will expect you," he said. *"Au 'voir."*

Costain stopped briefly in the dim foyer to adjust his scarf and fix his Homburg at the proper angle. When he turned away from the mirror, satisfied at last, he saw with a final glance that Laffler and Sbirro were already at the kitchen door; Sbirro holding the door invitingly wide with one hand, while the other rested, almost tenderly, on Laffler's meaty shoulders.

Joyce Harrington

The Purple Shroud

Mrs. Moon threw the shuttle back and forth and pumped the treadles of the big four-harness loom as if her life depended on it. When they asked what she was weaving so furiously, she would laugh silently and say it was a shroud.

"No, really, what is it?"

"My house needs new draperies." Mrs. Moon would smile and the shuttle would fly and the beater would thump the newly woven threads tightly into place. The muffled, steady sounds of her craft could be heard from early morning until very late at night, until the sounds became an accepted and expected background noise and were only noticed in their absence.

Then they would say, "I wonder what Mrs. Moon is doing now."

That summer, as soon as they had arrived at the art colony and even before they had unpacked, Mrs. Moon requested that the largest loom in the weaving studio be installed in their cabin. Her request had been granted because she was a serious weaver, and because her husband, George, was one of the best painting instructors they'd ever had. He could coax the amateurs into stretching their imaginations and trying new ideas and techniques, and he would bully the scholarship students until, in a fury, they would sometimes produce works of surprising originality.

George Moon was, himself, only a competent painter. His work had never caught on, although he had a small loyal following in Detroit and occasionally sold a painting. His only concessions to the need for making a living and for buying paints and brushes was to teach some ten hours a week throughout the winter and to take this summer job at the art colony, which was also their vacation. Mrs. Moon taught craft therapy at a home for the aged.

After the loom had been set up in their cabin Mrs. Moon waited. Sometimes she went swimming in the lake, sometimes she drove into town and poked about in the antique shops, and sometimes she just sat in the wicker chair and looked at the loom.

They said, "What are you waiting for, Mrs. Moon? When are you going to begin?"

One day Mrs. Moon drove into town and came back with two boxes full of brightly colored yarns. Classes had been going on for about two weeks, and George was deeply engaged with his students. One of the things the students loved about George was the extra time he gave them. He was always ready to sit for hours on the porch of the big house, just outside the communal dining room, or under a tree, and talk about painting or about life as a painter or tell stories about painters he had known.

George looked like a painter. He was tall and thin, and with approaching middle age he was beginning to stoop a little. He had black snaky hair which he had always worn on the long side, and which was beginning to turn gray. His eyes were very dark, so dark you couldn't see the pupils, and they regarded everything and everyone with a probing intensity that evoked uneasiness in some and caused young girls to fall in love with him.

Every year George Moon selected one young lady disciple to be his summer consort.

Mrs. Moon knew all about these summer alliances. Every year, when they returned to Detroit, George would confess to her with great humility and swear never to repeat his transgression.

"Never again, Arlene," he would say. "I promise you, never again."

Mrs. Moon would smile her forgiveness.

Mrs. Moon hummed as she sorted through the skeins of purple and deep scarlet, goldenrod yellow and rich royal blue. She hummed as she wound the glowing hanks into fat balls, and she thought about George and the look that had passed between him and the girl from Minneapolis at dinner the night before. George had not returned to their cabin until almost two in the morning. The girl from Minneapolis was short and plump, with a round face and a halo of fuzzy red-gold hair. She reminded Mrs. Moon of a Teddy bear; she reminded Mrs. Moon of herself twenty years before.

When Mrs. Moon was ready to begin, she carried the purple yarn to the weaving studio.

"I have to make a very long warp," she said. "I'll need to use the warping reel."

She hummed as she measured out the seven feet and a little over, then sent the reel spinning.

"Is it wool?" asked the weaving instructor.

"No, it's orlon," said Mrs. Moon. "It won't shrink, you know."

Mrs. Moon loved the creak of the reel, and she loved feeling the warp threads grow fatter under her hands until at last each planned thread was in place and she could tie the bundle and braid up the end. When she held the plaited warp in her hands she imagined it to be the shorn tresses of some enormously powerful earth goddess whose potency was now transferred to her own person.

That evening after dinner, Mrs. Moon began to thread the loom. George had taken the rowboat and the girl from Minneapolis to the other end of the lake where there was a deserted cottage. Mrs. Moon knew he kept a sleeping bag there, and a cache of wine and peanuts. Mrs. Moon hummed as she carefully threaded the eye of each heddle with a single purple thread, and thought of black widow spiders and rattlesnakes coiled in the corners of the dark cottage.

She worked contentedly until midnight and then went to bed. She was asleep and smiling when George stumbled in two hours later and fell into bed with his clothes on.

Mrs. Moon wove steadily through the summer days. She did not attend the weekly critique sessions for she had nothing to show and was not interested in the problems others were having with their work. She ignored the Saturday night parties where George and the girl from Minneapolis and the others danced and drank beer and slipped off to the beach or the boathouse.

Sometimes, when she tired of the long hours at the loom, she would go for solitary walks in the woods and always brought back curious trophies of her rambling. The small cabin, already crowded with the loom and the iron double bedstead, began to fill up with giant toadstools, interesting bits of wood, arrangements of reeds and wild wheat.

One day she brought back two large black stones on which she painted faces. The eyes of the faces were closed and the mouths were faintly curved in archaic smiles. She placed one stone on each side of the fireplace.

George hated the stones. "Those damn stonefaces are watching me," he said. "Get them out of here."

"How can they be watching you? Their eyes are closed."

Mrs. Moon left the stones beside the fireplace and George soon forgot to hate them. She called them Apollo I and Apollo II.

The weaving grew and Mrs. Moon thought it the best thing she had ever done. Scattered about the purple ground were signs and symbols which she saw against the deep blackness of her closed eyelids when she thought of passion and revenge, of love and wasted years and the child she had never had. She thought the barbaric colors spoke of those matters, and she was pleased.

"I hope you'll finish it before the final critique," the weaving teacher said when she came to the cabin to see it. "It's very, very good."

Word spread through the camp and many of the students came to the cabin to see the marvelous weaving. Mrs. Moon was proud to show it to them and received their compliments with quiet grace.

"It's too fine to hang at a window," said one practical Sunday-painting matron. "The sun will fade the colors."

"I'd love to wear it," said the life model.

"You!" said a bearded student of lithography. "It's a robe for a pagan king!"

"Perhaps you're right," said Mrs. Moon, and smiled her happiness on all of them.

The season was drawing to a close when in the third week of August, Mrs. Moon threw the shuttle for the last time. She slumped on the backless bench and rested her limp hands on the breast beam of the loom. Tomorrow she would cut the warp.

That night, while George was showing color slides of his paintings in the main gallery, the girl from Minneapolis came alone to the Moons' cabin. Mrs. Moon was lying on the bed watching a spider spin a web in the rafters. A fire was blazing in the fireplace, between Apollo I and Apollo II, for the late-summer night was chill.

"You must let him go," said the golden-haired Teddy bear. "He loves me."

"Yes, dear," said Mrs. Moon.

"You don't seem to understand. I'm talking about George." The girl sat on the bed. "I think I'm pregnant."

"That's nice," said Mrs. Moon. "Children are a blessing. Watch the spider."

"We have a relationship going. I don't care about being married—that's too feudal. But you must free George to come and be a father image to the child."

"You'll get over it," said Mrs. Moon, smiling a trifle sadly at the girl.

"Oh, you don't even want to know what's happening!" cried the girl. "No wonder George is bored with you."

"Some spiders eat their mates after fertilization," Mrs. Moon remarked. "Female spiders."

The girl flounced angrily from the cabin, as far as one could be said to flounce in blue jeans and sweatshirt . . .

George performed his end-of-summer separation ritual simply and brutally the following afternoon. He disappeared after lunch. No one knew where he had gone. The girl from Minneapolis roamed the camp, trying not to let anyone know she was searching for him. Finally she rowed herself down to the other end of the lake, to find that George had dumped her transistor radio, her books of poetry, and her box of incense on the damp sand and had put a padlock on the door of the cottage.

She threw her belongings into the boat and rowed back to the camp, tears of rage streaming down her cheeks. She beached the boat, and with head lowered and shoulders hunched she stormed the Moons' cabin. She found Mrs. Moon tying off the severed warp threads.

"Tell George," she shouted, "tell George I'm going back to Minneapolis. He knows where to find me!"

"Here, dear," said Mrs. Moon, "hold the end and walk backwards while I unwind it."

The girl did as she was told, caught by the vibrant colors and Mrs. Moon's concentration. In a few minutes the full length of cloth rested in the girl's arms.

"Put it on the bed and spread it out," said Mrs. Moon. "Let's take a good look at it."

"I'm really leaving," whispered the girl. "Tell him I don't care if I never see him again."

"I'll tell him." The wide strip of purple flowed garishly down the middle of the bed between them. "Do you think he'll like it?" asked Mrs. Moon. "He's going to have it around for a long time."

"The colors are very beautiful, very savage." The girl looked closely at Mrs. Moon. "I wouldn't have thought you would choose such colors."

"I never did before."

"I'm leaving now."

"Goodbye," said Mrs. Moon.

George did not reappear until long after the girl had loaded up her battered bug of a car and driven off. Mrs. Moon knew he had been watching and waiting from the hill behind the camp. He came into the cabin whistling softly and began to take his clothes off.

"God, I'm tired," he said.

"It's almost dinnertime."

"Too tired to eat," he yawned. "What's that on the bed?"

"My weaving is finished. Do you like it?"

"It's good. Take it off the bed. I'll look at it tomorrow."

Mrs. Moon carefully folded the cloth and laid it on the weaving bench. She looked at George's thin naked body before he got into bed and smiled.

"I'm going to dinner now," she said.

"Okay. Don't wake me up when you get back. I could sleep for a week."

"I won't wake you up," said Mrs. Moon.

Mrs. Moon ate dinner at a table by herself. Most of the students had already left. A few people, the Moons among them, usually stayed on after the end of classes to rest and enjoy the isolation. Mrs. Moon spoke to no one.

After dinner she sat on the pier and watched the sunset. She watched the turtles in the shallow water and thought she saw a blue heron on the other side of the lake. When the sky was black and the stars were too many to count, Mrs. Moon went to the toolshed and got a wheelbarrow. She rolled this to the door of her cabin and went inside.

The cabin was dark and she could hear George's steady heavy breathing. She lit two candles and placed them on the mantelshelf. She spread her beautiful weaving on her side of the bed, gently so as not to disturb the sleeper. Then she quietly moved the weaving bench to George's side of the bed, near his head.

She sat on the bench for a time, memorizing the lines of his face by the wavering candlelight. She touched him softly on the forehead with the pads of her fingertips and gently caressed his eyes, his hard cheeks, his raspy chin. His breathing became uneven and she withdrew her hands, sitting motionless until his sleep rhythm was restored.

Then Mrs. Moon took off her shoes. She walked carefully to the fireplace, taking long quiet steps. She placed her shoes neatly side by side on the hearth and picked up the larger stone, Apollo I. The face of the kouros, the ancient god, smiled up at her and she returned that faint implacable smile. She carried the stone back to the bench beside the bed, and set it down.

Then she climbed onto the bench, and when she stood she found she could almost touch the spider's web in the rafters. The spider crouched in the heart of its web, and Mrs. Moon wondered if spiders ever slept.

Mrs. Moon picked up Apollo I, and with both arms raised took careful aim. Her shadow, cast by candlelight, had the appearance of a priestess offering sacrifice. The stone was heavy and her arms grew weak. Her hands let go. The stone dropped.

George's eyes flapped open and he saw Mrs. Moon smiling tenderly down on him. His lips drew back to scream, but his mouth could only form a soundless hole.

"Sleep, George," she whispered, and his eyelids clamped over his unbelieving eyes.

Mrs. Moon jumped off the bench. With gentle fingers she probed beneath his snaky locks until she found a satisfying softness. There was no blood and for this Mrs. Moon was grateful. It would have been a shame to spoil the beauty of her patterns with superfluous colors and untidy stains. Her mothlike fingers on his wrist warned her of a faint uneven fluttering.

She padded back to the fireplace and weighed in her hands the smaller, lighter Apollo II. This time she felt there was no need for added height. With three quick butter-churning motions she enlarged the softened area in George's skull and stilled the annoying flutter in his wrist.

Then she rolled him over as a hospital nurse will roll an immobile patient during bedmaking routine, until he rested on his back on one-half of the purple fabric. She placed his arms across his naked chest and straightened his spindly legs. She kissed his closed eyelids, gently stroked his shaggy brows, and said, "Rest now, dear George."

She folded the free half of the royal cloth over him, covering him from head to foot with a little left over at each end. From her sewing box she took a wide-eyed needle and threaded it with some difficulty in the flickering light. Then, kneeling beside the bed, Mrs. Moon began stitching across the top. She stitched small careful stitches that would hold for eternity.

Soon the top was closed and she began stitching down the long side. The job was wearisome, but Mrs. Moon was patient and she hummed a sweet, monotonous tune as stitch followed stitch past George's ear, his shoulder, his bent elbow. It was not until she reached his ankles that she allowed herself to stand and stretch her aching knees and flex her cramped fingers.

Retrieving the twin Apollos from where they lay abandoned on George's pillow, she tucked them reverently into the bottom of the cloth sarcophagus and knelt once more to her task. Her needle flew faster as the remaining gap between the two edges of cloth grew smaller, until the last stitch was securely knotted and George was sealed into his funerary garment. But the hardest part of her night's work was yet to come.

She knew she could not carry George even the short distance to the door of the cabin and the wheelbarrow outside. And the wheelbarrow was too wide to bring inside. She couldn't bear the thought of dragging him across the floor and soiling or tearing the fabric she had so lovingly woven. Finally she rolled him onto the weaving bench and despite the fact that it only supported him from armpits to groin, she managed to maneuver it to the door. From there it was possible to shift the burden to the waiting wheelbarrow.

Mrs. Moon was now breathing heavily from her exertions, and paused for a moment to survey the night and the prospect before her. There were no lights anywhere in the camp except for the feeble glow of her own guttering candles. As she went to blow them out she glanced at her watch and was mildly surprised to see that it was ten minutes past three. The hours had flown while she had been absorbed in her needlework.

She perceived now the furtive night noises of the forest creatures which had hitherto been blocked from her senses by the total concentration she had bestowed on her work. She thought of weasels and foxes prowling, of owls going about their predatory night activities, and considered herself in congenial company. Then, taking up the handles of the wheelbarrow, she trundled down the well defined path to the boathouse.

The wheelbarrow made more noise than she had anticipated and she hoped she was far enough from any occupied cabin for its rumbling to go unnoticed. The moonless night sheltered her from any wakeful watcher and a dozen summers of waiting had taught her the nature and substance of every square foot of the camp's area. She could walk it blindfolded.

When she reached the boathouse she found that some hurried careless soul had left a boat on the beach in defiance of the camp's rules. It was a simple matter of leverage to shift her burden from barrow to boat and in minutes Mrs. Moon was heaving inexpertly at the oars. At first the boat seemed inclined to travel only in wide arcs and head back to shore, but with patient determination Mrs. Moon established a rowing rhythm that would take her and her passenger to the deepest part of the lake.

She hummed a sea chanty which aided her rowing and pleased her sense of the appropriate. Then, pinpointing her position by the silhouette of the tall solitary pine that grew on the opposite shore, Mrs. Moon carefully raised the oars and rested them in the boat.

As Mrs. Moon crept forward in the boat, feeling her way in the darkness, the boat began to rock gently. It was a pleasant, soothing motion and Mrs. Moon thought of cradles and soft enveloping comforters. She continued creeping slowly forward, swaying with the motion of the boat, until she reached the side of her swaddled passenger. There she sat and stroked the cloth and wished that she could see the fine colors just one last time.

She felt the shape beneath the cloth, solid but thin and now rather pitiful. She took the head in her arms and held it against her breast, rocking and humming a long-forgotten lullaby.

The doubled weight at the forward end of the small boat caused the prow to dip. Water began to slosh into the boat—in small wavelets at first as the boat rocked from side to side, then in a steady trickle as the boat rode lower and lower in the water. Mrs. Moon rocked and hummed; the water rose over her bare feet and lapped against her ankles. The sky began to turn purple and she could just make out the distant shape of the boathouse and the hill behind the camp. She was very tired and very cold.

Gently she placed George's head in the water. The boat tilted crazily and she scrambled backward to equalize the weight. She picked up the other end of the long purple chrysalis, the end containing the stone Apollos, and heaved it overboard. George in his shroud, with head and feet trailing in the lake, now lay along the side of the boat weighting it down.

Water was now pouring in. Mrs. Moon held to the other side of the boat with placid hands and thought of the dense comfort of the muddy lake bottom and George beside her forever. She saw that her feet were frantically pushing against the burden of her life, running away from that companionable grave.

With a regretful sigh she let herself slide down the short incline of the seat and came to rest beside George. The boat lurched deeper into the lake. Water surrounded George and climbed into Mrs. Moon's lap. Mrs. Moon closed her eyes and hummed, "Nearer My God to Thee." She did not see George drift away from the side of the boat, carried off by the moving arms of water. She felt a wild bouncing, a shuddering and splashing, and was sure the boat had overturned. With relief she gave herself up to chaos and did not try to hold her breath.

Expecting a suffocating weight of water in her lungs, Mrs. Moon was disappointed to find she could open her eyes, that air still entered and left her gasping mouth. She lay in a pool of water in the bottom of the boat and saw a bird circle high above the lake, peering down at her. The boat was bobbing gently on the water, and when Mrs. Moon sat up she saw that a few yards away, through the fresh blue morning, George was bobbing gently too. The purple shroud had filled with air and floated on the water like a small submarine come up for air and a look at the new day.

As she watched, shivering and wet, the submarine shape drifted away and dwindled as the lake took slow possession. At last, with a grateful sigh, green water replacing the last bubble of air, it sank just as the bright arc of the sun rose over the hill in time to give Mrs. Moon a final glimpse of glorious purple and gold. She shook herself like a tired old gray dog and called out, "Goodbye, George." Her cry echoed back and forth across the morning and startled forth a chorus of bird shrieks. Pandemonium and farewell. She picked up the oars.

Back on the beach, the boat carefully restored to its place, Mrs. Moon dipped her blistered hands into the lake. She scented bacon in the early air and instantly felt the pangs of an enormous hunger. Mitch, the cook, would be having his early breakfast and perhaps would share it with her. She hurried to the cabin to change out of her wet clothes, and was amazed, as she stepped over the doorsill, at the stark emptiness which greeted her.

Shafts of daylight fell on the rumpled bed, but there was nothing for her there. She was not tired now, did not need to sleep. The fireplace contained cold ashes, and the hearth looked bare and unfriendly. The loom gaped at her like a toothless mouth, its usefulness at an end. In a heap on the floor lay George's clothes where he had dropped them the night before. Out of habit she picked them up, and as she hung them on a hook in the small closet she felt a rustle in the shirt pocket. It was a scrap of paper torn off a drawing pad; there was part of a pencil sketch on one side, on the other an address and telephone number.

Mrs. Moon hated to leave anything unfinished, despising untidiness in herself and others. She quickly changed into her town clothes and hung her discarded wet things in the tiny bathroom to dry. She found an apple and munched it as she made up her face and combed her still-damp hair. The apple took the edge off her hunger, and she decided not to take the time to beg breakfast from the cook.

She carefully made the bed and tidied the small room, sweeping a few scattered ashes back into the fireplace. She checked her summer straw pocketbook for driver's license, car keys, money, and finding everything satisfactory she paused for a moment in the center of the room. All was quiet, neat, and orderly. The spider still hung inert in the center of its web and one small fly was buzzing helplessly on its perimeter. Mrs. Moon smiled.

There was no time to weave now—indeed, there was no need. She could not really expect to find a conveniently deserted lake in a big city. No. She would have to think of something else.

Mrs. Moon stood in the doorway of the cabin in the early sunlight, a small frown wrinkling the placid surface of her round pink face. She scuffled slowly around to the back of the cabin and into the shadow of the sycamores beyond, her feet kicking up the spongy layers of years of fallen leaves, her eyes watching carefully for the right idea to show itself. Two grayish-white stones appeared side by side, half covered with leaf mold. Anonymous, faceless, about the size of cantaloupes, they would do unless something better presented itself.

Unceremoniously she dug them out of their bed, brushed away the loose dirt and leaf fragments, and carried them back to the car.

Mrs. Moon's watch had stopped sometime during the night, but as she got into the car she glanced at the now fully risen sun and guessed the time to be about six thirty or seven o'clock. She placed the two stones snugly on the passenger seat and covered them with her soft pale-blue cardigan. She started the engine, and then reached over and groped in the glove compartment. She never liked to drive anywhere without knowing beforehand the exact roads to take to get to her destination. The road map was there, neatly folded beneath the flashlight and the box of tissues.

Mrs. Moon unfolded the map and spread it out over the steering wheel. As the engine warmed up, Mrs. Moon hummed along with it. Her pudgy pink hand absently patted the tidy blue bundle beside her as she planned the most direct route to the girl in Minneapolis.

Jack Finney

The Widow's Walk

I'm so mad I could spit.

I walked into her room that morning as always; quietly, though not on tiptoe. The loose board creaked, but she didn't move, of course: she sleeps like a pig. At the side of her bed I stood looking down. She lay flat on her back, her skin, even her eyelids, yellow and wrinkled, her skull showing behind the sagging old flesh, and her mouth, without her teeth, puckered to a slit. How I hate it when I have to kiss her. It takes a day for the feeling to leave my lips.

Her pillow was on the floor. It always is, though I've often spoken about it. I wore gloves and my suede jacket and skirt. I picked up her pillow and held it tightly at each end, stretched between my hands. I edged closer to her bed, almost touching it. The rest I went through only in imagination, for I was rehearsing: I had to be certain, first, that I could really do it. But I saw it in my mind as though it were happening. I could even feel tentative little muscle movements.

Down with the pillow, flat across her face, a knee on the bed, shoulders hunched over my arms, the knuckles of each fist pressed deep in the mattress. A moment of utter silence, then her bony hands shoot out, clawing rapidly, senselessly, at my arms and hands, scratching at the leather. Then they tug purposefully at my wrists. A silent, almost motionless struggle—and now her old hands begin to relax.

Suddenly a new picture flashed through my mind, and up to that moment this possibility had never occurred to me. Suddenly, and I could hear it in my brain, her feet began to drum on the mattress. Fast! Fast as a two-year-old's in a tantrum, and loud!

I couldn't stand that. Not even in imagination. I could feel the blood drop from my face. Perhaps I made a sound, I don't know. And I don't like to think how my face must have looked. But when I turned it to hers—I'd been staring straight ahead—those mean blue eyes were boring into mine.

"What are you doing?" she said in her flat, cold voice. The panic remained for a moment. Then I could speak.

"Nothing, Mother," and my voice was easy. "I decided to shop

264

early." That explained my jacket and gloves. "And I thought I'd tidy up your room first."

"Can't do much tidying while I'm still here."

"No, I guess not. It was foolish of me. I'm sorry I disturbed you. Try to sleep some more."

"Can't sleep once I've been waked up; you know that." She was trying to prolong the conversation, alert for a clue.

"I'm sorry, Mother. I'll be back in a few minutes and get you some breakfast." Then I went out to the stores, though there was really no shopping to do. I bought a few staples.

It's infuriating, though. So perfect, so simple—and I just can't do it. She wouldn't be smothered, you see. Her creaky old heart would give out! Her doctor has warned us, and he'd be the doctor I'd call. Then I'd phone Al: "I tiptoed into her room to see if she wanted breakfast, and she looked sort of funny, and—oh, Al, she's dead!"

Almost true, and it would have been true, really, by the time they arrived. I'd have run it over and over in my mind, like a film, till I believed it myself, almost. I know how to lie. But I'm just not a murderer, that's all. I'm simply a housewife.

I'm thirty-two years old, five feet five inches tall, wavy hair, dark-blue eyes, reasonably pretty, and I'm in love with my husband. I'm a homemaker, much as I dislike that word, and I want my home the way it was before she came.

We didn't do much then, Al and I. Evenings mostly at home, reading in the living room. In the spring and summer, the garden till dark. Bridge with the Dykes fairly often: we hardly see them now. And occasionally a movie. Daytimes I cleaned, I shopped, I cooked. That's all. But I liked it. I made a home—for my husband and me. And I want it back.

But now it's like this. The other morning I was doing the dishes. She sat on the back porch, "taking the air"—unpleasant phrase. I couldn't see her, actually, but I could see her in my mind, staring out at the pile of new lumber in the yard, hands folded in her lap. And thinking of me. As I was thinking of her. For a long time she made no sound, and then she cleared her throat. That doesn't mean anything to you, does it? But it did to me. And she knew it. It was a nasty, deliberate, spiteful reminder that she was present and existing, sharing my house and my husband. Do you see now what I mean? I can feel her, actually *feel* her, in every room of the house at all times, day and night! Even in our bedroom, which she never enters.

Oh, I'm going to kill her, all right. Al will get over it. He *must* hate it as much as I do. We've had four years of it. And it started as soon as she came.

We'd had a date with the Crowleys, made just before she arrived—a weekend at their cottage on the lake. And we kept it. She insisted. "You children go ahead. I'll be glad to get rid of you!"

"Sure now, Mother?" Al asked. "You know, a weekend's not important, and if—"

"Of course I am! I won't hear another word—you're going!"

The doctor was there when we returned Sunday evening. An ambulance in front of the house, a nurse inside with an oxygen tent. A heart attack. I know she did it deliberately; not faked, exactly, but somehow self-induced. She'd phoned a neighbor in the late afternoon, hardly able to talk. Our neighbor hurried over, called the hospital—and that's what we came home to. She's never had another attack, and we've never had another weekend.

I mentioned it again a few days ago. "Yes, I'd have got over it," Al said. "You can't foresee and guard against everything. But you have to try. I have to see that she has as long and happy a life as she can." And then he startled me by adding this, "But I know it's hard on you sometimes, Annie."

I'd thought he didn't realize, wasn't aware. Of course he must have been—a little, at least. But he'll never know how I really feel, that I'm sure of.

My new plan is so perfect, you see. It's going to be a push, a sudden push from a high place. So simple, but it took me a long time to think of it. I was afraid I couldn't trust myself to go through with any of the plans I was able to think of. And then it came to me. There's nothing, really, to go through with in a push! It's over before you can think, over the moment it's started! And then—well, I heard her gasp, turned around, and there she was, disappearing over the edge! Her heart, I suppose.

But what high place? She never leaves the house. The stairs, from our second floor to the first, turn at a landing; not much of a fall. It wouldn't be certain. I wish I could plan ahead and think more logically. Al says I'd be out of house and home in a month if he weren't here to plan for me. Maybe he's right, but I've always found, it seems to me, that things work themselves out in the long run.

And sure enough. One night Al and I were reading in the living room; his mother had gone to bed. One of my magazines had come that day. I was leafing through it and I came to an article on widow's walks—photographs of the originals in New England, sketches of modern adaptations. So cute. Perfect little porches, the article said, for sunbathing and for sitting of an evening. Perfect: a widow's walk with a knee-high railing.

Al's set in his ways, though, and I could just hear what he'd say if I suggested a widow's walk on *our* house!

I did, though. "Look, dear," I said, and he glanced up from his book. "Aren't these darling?" I held up the article.

"Uh huh," he answered. I smiled expectantly and didn't move. "Yeah, they are," Al said. I continued to wait, still smiling, still holding my magazine up. I know the game: we've been married six years. He was hoping I'd consider his comment sufficient and let him get back to his book. Or that I'd be the one to get up. So I waited. Al is a polite man, and he started to rise. In an instant I was on my feet, carrying the magazine over to him. And because he'd kept his comfort, I'd earned my interruption. He laid his book in his lap and took my magazine.

"Aren't they darling?" I knelt on the floor beside Al's chair. "Widow's walks, they're called."

"Yeah, I've seen them," Al said. "The old whaling days. The women watched for the men at sea."

"So that's what they're for!"

"Sure. That's why the name. Half the time the husbands never came back."

"Well, no danger of your drowning at the office, dear. And I could watch for you to come home after work. How about building one on our roof?"

That half irritated, half pitying look men reserve for women's impracticality came over his face, but before he could turn to look at me I was smiling. He grinned then. "Oh, sure," he said, "I'll start tomorrow."

I waited three nights before I mentioned it again. We were walking home from the movies. And I waited till we were less than a block from home; just time enough to voice his objections, not time enough to get dead set against it. "I've been thinking, Al. It *would* be nice to have a widow's walk. It'd be easy to build," and now I was excited and enthusiastic. "You're so handy with tools and the plans are all in the magazine. It'd be *so* nice in the evening. I'll bet we could see the river, and—"

"Oh, Annie," Al said, "in the first place—" And I listened, and nodded, and agreed.

"It was just an idea," I said. We had reached our porch and he took out his keys. "But you're right, it wouldn't be practical." And as we entered the house, I added only this, "Your mother would like it, though." Then we had to be quiet: she was asleep.

It took less than two days. Spring came to stay on a Thursday. The sun was warmer, closer, the ground moist and crumbling, and the air was alive. Al, I knew, would be aching to build something, anything. He's a marvel with tools and loves to work with them. The lumber was delivered on Friday, dumped in the back yard, and I signed the receipt.

I grinned when Al came home. "What's the wood for?" I asked, and Al grinned back. His mother had to be told, then, and I let Al tell her. She mumbled and muttered about the lumber on the flower beds. Was there anything she liked, anything that met with her royal approval? But I didn't care, not this time.

Sunday, it happened again. That damned unexpected panic! Maybe I relaxed too much—it was that kind of day. Everything green and alive, the outdoor sounds so new and clear and soft; the sort of day you think of when someone says Spring. It should have been perfect.

Al was working on the roof in the sun—no shirt. His mother and I on the lawn in canvas chairs, she with the Sunday paper, while I shelled peas. Dinner was a comfortable two hours off, the meat was on and needed no attention. You could feel the air, soft and cool, moving across the back of your hands. And it carried sound as it never does otherwise. A dog barking, many houses away, the chitter of birds, and the soft, clean sound of the wood as Al worked on the little, half finished platform he'd built on the roof. A pause, then the sudden loose clatter of light new planking as it dropped on the heavier timbers already in place. A grunt from Al as he got down on his knees, then the skilled tap of his hammer, nudging a board to position. The tiny rattle of nails, the sharp ping, pong as he set one in the wood, then the heavy, measured, satisfactory bang, bang, bang, on a rising scale, as he drove it home.

"He's going to fall," she said nastily.

"Oh, no, Mother, Al's light as a cat on his feet." I spoke gently, kindly and I smiled. She didn't answer directly, didn't look at me.

"Don't see the use of it, anyway. Porch on a roof!"

"But, Mother," I said, "you'll love that porch!" That was a mistake. Her face set. Any urging from me is like pulling a mule with a rope. I said nothing more, but I was annoyed at myself and at her. If you only knew, I thought, and then, without warning, the panic broke. I hadn't expected it, hadn't allowed for it, but suddenly the sound of that hammer, bang, bang, bang, was the sound of a hammer building a scaffold. The next plank scraped and bumped hollowly over the others, then dropped into place. And I couldn't bear to hear the next nail, to hear the sound of her scaffold moving nearer and nearer to completion. I rose, turned, set the bowl carefully on my chair, and ran to the house.

Al called to me, "What's the matter?" Then he yelled. "Annie!"

"The meat!" I shrieked, and yanked the screen door open.

I leaned on the kitchen table, hands flat on the top, my eyes closed. "Take hold of yourself, take hold of yourself," I muttered senselessly, and then, in a moment or two, I was all right. The heavy, hollow hammer sound began again and I listened. Yes, I thought, a scaffold. For her. Make it good and strong.

What a ridiculous weakness, though, not to be able to count on yourself, to trust yourself! Oh, I *wish* she'd die of her own accord!

She won't though. She knows I want her to. Yes, she's that stubborn! Al finished the porch—it's really very cute—but she wouldn't use it. He painted it Sunday night, a light green, and we went up next morning before he went to work. His mother, too: trust her to be in on everything. But she wouldn't go back. I'd try to keep from urging her, but sometimes I couldn't help it. Then she'd smile, stay just where she was, and answer, "No, you go up, dear. I'm comfortable right where I am." Then I'd have to go up there and sit.

Things work themselves out, though. I stopped talking about the porch and spent a lot of time there. It *was* rather nice, and presently she began to suspect that I liked getting away from her. And maybe she was a little lonely. Then, one evening at dinner, Al mentioned the porch. I told him how much I liked it, how quiet and so sort of away from things it seemed. Maybe it was my speaking of the pleasant quiet that gave her the idea. She thought it would be so nice to have a radio up there—the one from the kitchen, perhaps. She knows I use it when I'm cooking. I wanted her to start using the porch so much that I nearly agreed with her. But I caught myself.

"I don't know that a radio would be so good up there, Mother. It's—"

"Don't see why not!" she answered instinctively. "Like to hear a few programs myself sometimes, and if we're going to sit up there all the time—"

I was elated. "We'll see," I said coldly, and later when she'd gone to bed I told Al, "Put the radio up there tonight—from the kitchen. I hardly ever use it."

"You're sweet," he said, and kissed me. He's a darling.

Now she likes the porch. Loves it! She puffs and mutters her way up to the attic, rests for a few moments on the old cedar chest, then pulls herself up the new flight of stairs to the roof. And there she sits, with her fan and her handkerchief, all morning long, till the sun gets at it from the west. Of course she has me on the jump all the time. Downstairs for the mail, for her glasses, for a drink of water, for anything and everything she can think of. "Do you mind, Annie? I'd go myself, but—"

Sometimes I'll say, "In a minute," and then let her wait. But usually I answer, "Of course not, Mother, I have to go down anyway." And I don't mind. Not in the least. Because it makes me madder and madder every time she does it. And that's what I want.

I know I can't trust myself, can't be sure I won't stop an instant before it happens, unable to go through with it—unless I see red. I really do see red. Some people think that's a figure of speech, but it isn't. When I get really furiously angry, it's as though a sheet of red cellophane were in front of my eyes. I actually see red, and then I can do anything.

I think it's going to happen soon, now—about the radio. Things work themselves out, you see. She had to use it, of course, once it was up there. And she's discovered a particularly unpleasant program. It comes on at ten; old-time songs played on an organ, and an obnoxious-voiced man reading bad poetry. Ten, she knows, is when I've always listened to "Woman of Destiny." I asked her the other day if she'd mind my occasionally hearing it just to keep up with the story. She guessed not. But when I get up there, after breakfast dishes and the beds, there she sits listening to *her* program. Never a move, never a suggestion to change it to mine. I haven't said any more. I just sit there, seething. She knows it, too, and likes it.

One other thing has been happening lately. I've forgotten several times to fold the canvas chairs when we leave the porch for the day. Then next morning the seats are damp from the dew and she has to sit on the rail till the chairs dry. She's complained about it.

Oh, things do work themselves out. One of these mornings the chairs will be damp again. I'll come up at ten and there she'll be,

sitting on the rail listening to that sanctimonious fool on the radio.
I'll sit down beside her. She'll complain in that nagging voice of hers
that I forgot the chairs again yesterday. I'll suggest that she might
think of it herself occasionally. Then that sullen silence. I'll glance
at the radio, then back at her, hinting that she *might* just suggest
hearing my program for a change.

She'll ignore that, as always. My blood will start to boil. And I'll
let it. I'll feed the flames, remembering everything she's ever done,
and that's plenty. I'll start back through the years and remember
them all. And suddenly—I'll see red. Really *red,* just for an instant.
Then, afterwards—panic? Well, let it come! Who wouldn't be panicky
when she'd seen her mother-in-law fall two and a half stories to a
cement driveway? Things, you see, do work themselves out. And it'll
serve her right. It will! It'll—serve—her—right! The old *bitch!*

I don't know, now, why I wrote what you've read. I started, I
remember, with some idea of getting all my plans on paper. It became
something else, of course, but I continued to write just the same. I
meant to burn it, but I never have. I've kept it and read it, many
times, over and over again.

Somehow I didn't think much about Al's using the porch. Naturally he did, on weekends especially. He went up one Saturday morning, shortly after his mother. I'd forgotten the chairs again, the night
before, and she was sitting on the railing. I suppose, this time, her
attack was a real one. Al sat on the opposite rail, the width of the
porch away, and she couldn't have been sure he'd be able to reach
her in time. He almost did, though. When she started to fall, he shot
across that porch faster than I'd ever seen him move before. I was
watching; I was coming up the stairs and my eyes were level with
the floor of the porch.

He got a hand on her skirt, a tight, strong hold, reaching way over
the railing a split-second after she was clear of the porch. And then,
as she plunged, her skirt went taut, yanked on his arm with the
force of a whip, and the precarious balance he held, leaning way
over the rail, was gone.

Things do work themselves out, I suppose. Long after their husbands were dead and gone, the old seafarers' wives must have continued pacing the floors of their widow's walks. The name says that.
Back and forth, back and forth they walked, day after day after
hopeless day. As I do.

Patricia Highsmith

The Gracious, Pleasant
Life of Mrs. Afton

"Dr. Bauer did not often find such pleasant people among his patients—but then Mrs. Afton had come to him last Monday in regard to her husband, not in regard to herself" . . .

Prober: DR. FELIX BAUER

For Dr. Felix Bauer, the psychoanalyst, staring out the window of his ground-floor office on Lexington Avenue, the afternoon was a sluggish stream which had lost its current, or which might have been flowing either backward or forward. Traffic had thickened, but in the molten sunlight the cars only inched along behind red lights, their chromium twinkling as if with white heat. Dr. Bauer's office was air-conditioned, actually pleasantly cool; but something—his logic or his blood—told him it was hot, and the heat depressed him.

He glanced at his wristwatch. Miss Vavrica, who was scheduled for 3:30, was once more funking her appointment. He could see her now, wide-eyed in a movie theater probably, hypnotizing herself so as not to think of what she should be doing. There were things he could be doing in the empty minutes before his 4:15 patient, but he kept staring out the window.

What was it about New York, the doctor wondered, for all its speed and ambition, that deprived him of his initiative? He worked hard—he always had—but in America it was with a consciousness of working hard. It was not like living in Vienna or Paris, where he had been able to relax with wife and friends in the evenings, and then found energy for more work, more reading, until the early hours of the morning.

Suddenly he saw in his mind the image of Mrs. Afton, small, rather stout, but still pretty with a rare, radiant prettiness of middle-age—scented, he remembered, with a gardenia cologne. The image superimposed itself on the memory of the old European evenings.

Mrs. Afton was a very pleasant woman from the American South. She bore out what he had often heard about the American South—that it preserved a tradition of living in which there was time for meals and visits and conversation and, simply, for doing nothing. He had detected it in a few of Mrs. Afton's phrases that might not have been necessary but were gratifying to hear, in her quiet good manners—and good manners usually annoyed him—which her anxiety had not caused her to forget. Mrs. Afton reflected a way of life which, like an alchemy, made the world into quite another and more beautiful one whenever he was in her presence. Dr. Bauer did not often find such pleasant people among his patients—but then Mrs. Afton had come to him last Monday in regard to her husband, not in regard to herself.

His 4:15 patient, earnest Mr. Schriever, who got full value for every penny he paid, came and went without making a bobble on the afternoon's surface.

Alone again, Dr. Bauer passed a strong, neat hand over his brows, impatiently smoothed them, and made a final note about Mr. Schriever. The young man had talked off the top of his head again, hesitating, then rushing, and no question had been able to steer him into more promising paths.

It was such people as Mr. Schriever that one had to believe one could finally help. The first barrier was always tension—not the almost objective tension of war or of poverty that Dr. Bauer had found in Europe, but the American kind of tension which was different in each individual and which each individual seemed to clasp all the closer to himself when he came to a psychoanalyst to have it dissected out.

Mrs. Afton, he now recalled, had none of that tension. It was regrettable that a woman born for happiness, reared for it, should be bound so tightly to a man who had renounced it. And it was regrettable that Dr. Bauer could do nothing for her. Today, he had decided, he must tell her he could not help her.

At precisely 5:00, Dr. Bauer's foot found the buzzer under the blue carpet and pressed it twice. He glanced at the door, then got up and opened it. Mrs. Afton came in immediately, her step quick and buoyant for all her plumpness, her carefully waved, light-brown head held high.

"Good afternoon, Dr. Bauer." She loosened the blue chiffon scarf that did not quite match, yet blended with his carpet, and settled herself in the leather armchair. "It's so divinely cool here! I shall dread leaving today."

"Yes," he smiled. "Air-conditioning spoils one." Bent over his desk, he read through the notes he had jotted down on Monday:

Thomas Bainbridge Afton, 55. Gen. health good. Irritable. Anxiety about physical strength and training. In recent months, severe diet and exercise program. Room of hotel suite fitted with gym. equip. Exercises strenuously. Schizoid, sadist-masochist indics. Refuses treatment.

Specifically, Mrs. Afton had come to ask him how her husband might be persuaded, if not to stop his regimen, at least to temper it.

Dr. Bauer smiled at her uneasily across his desk. He should, he supposed, explain once more that he could not possibly treat someone through someone else. Mrs. Afton had pleaded with him to let her come for a second interview. And she was obviously so much more hopeful now that he found it hard to begin.

"How are things today?" he asked, as he always did.

"Very well." She hesitated. "I think I've told you almost everything there is to tell. Unless you've something to ask me." Then, as if realizing her intensity, she leaned back in her chair, blinked her blue eyes and smiled, and the smile seemed to say what she had actually said on Monday, "I know it's funny—a husband who flexes his arms in front of a mirror like a twelve-year-old boy admiring his muscles; but you can understand that when he trembles from exhaustion afterwards, I fear for his life."

With the same kind of smile and a nod of understanding, he supposed, if he should begin, "Since your husband refuses to come personally for treatment . . ." she would let herself be dismissed and leave his office with her burden of anxiety still within her. Mrs. Afton did not spill all her troubles out at once as so many middle-aged women of her type did, and she was too proud to admit such embarrassing facts as, for instance, that her husband had ever struck her. Dr. Bauer felt sure that he had.

"I suspect, of course," he began, "that your husband is rebuilding a damaged ego through his physical culture regime. His unconscious reasoning is that having failed in other things—his business, socially perhaps, losing the property in Kentucky that you told me about, not being as good a provider as he would like to be—he can compensate by being strong physically."

Mrs. Afton looked off and her eyes widened. Dr. Bauer had seen them widen before when he challenged her, when she tried to recollect something; and he had seen them narrow suddenly when something amused her, with a flirtatiousness of youth still sparkling through the curved brown lashes. Now the tilt of her head emphasized the wide cheekbones, the narrower forehead, the softly pointed chin—a motherly face, though she had no children.

Finally, very dubiously, she replied, "I suppose that might be logical."

"But you don't agree?"

"Not entirely." She lifted her head again. "I don't think my husband considers himself quite a failure. We still live very comfortably, you know."

"Yes, of course."

She looked at the electric clock whose second hand ate away silently at the precious forty-five minutes. Her knees parted a little as she leaned forward, and her calves, like an ornamental base, curved symmetrically down to her slender ankles that she kept close together. "You can't suggest *anything* that would help me to moderate his—his routine, Dr. Bauer?"

"There's not the remotest chance he might be persuaded to come and see me?"

"I'm afraid not. I told you how he felt about doctors. He says they can tinker with him once he's dead, but he's through with them for the rest of his life. Oh, I don't think I told you that he sold his body to a medical school." She smiled again, but he saw a twitch of shame or of anger in the smile. "He did that about six months ago. I thought you might be interested."

"Yes."

She went on with the least increase of importunity. "I do think if you could simply see him for a few moments—I mean, if he didn't know who you were—I'm sure you'd be able to learn so much more than I could ever tell you."

Dr. Bauer sighed. "You see, whatever I could tell you even then would be only guesswork. From you, or even from seeing your husband for a few moments, I cannot learn the facts that in the first place caused his obsession with athletics. I might advise you to help him build back what he has lost—his social contacts, his hobbies and so on. But I'm sure you have tried already."

Mrs. Afton conveyed with an uncertain nod that she had tried.

"And still, psychologically, that would be only correcting the surface," Dr. Bauer said, almost apologetically.

She said nothing. Her lips tightened at the corners, and she looked off at the four bright yellow echelons the venetian blinds made in a corner of the room. But despite the eagerness of her posture there was an air of hopelessness about her that made Dr. Bauer drop his eyes to the capped fountain pen that he kept rolling under one finger on his desk.

"Still, I'd be so grateful if you'd just *try* to see him, even if it's only across the lobby of our hotel. Then I'd feel that whatever you said about him was more—more definite."

Whatever I say *is* definite, he thought; then he abandoned his objection, his mind going on to what he must say next—that there was nothing left for her to do but go to a domestic relations court. The court would probably advise that her husband be taken away for treatment, and Mrs. Afton, he knew, would suffer a thousand times more than when he had suggested that her husband had been a failure. She still loved her husband, and divorce was not in her mind, she had said, or even a short separation. Not only did she still love him, she was proud of him, Dr. Bauer realized.

Then suddenly it occurred to him that seeing her husband, glimpsing him, might be the final gesture of courtesy he had been groping for. After he had seen him, he would feel that he had made the maximum effort it was possible for him to make.

"I can try," he said at last.

"Oh, thank you! I'm sure it will help—I know it will." She smiled and sat up taller. She shook her head at the cigarette that Dr. Bauer extended. "I'll tell you something else that happened," she said, and he felt her gratitude radiating toward him. "I was to see you at two thirty on Monday, you know; so to get away alone, I told Thomas I was to meet Mrs. Hatfield—my oldest friend at the hotel—at two thirty in Lord and Taylor's. Well, I was having lunch in the hotel dining room by myself at two o'clock, when Thomas came in unexpectedly. We never lunch together, because he goes to a salad bar on Madison Avenue. And there I was having lobster Newburgh, which Thomas thinks is the nearest thing to suicide, anyway. Lobster Newburgh is a specialty of the hotel on Mondays, and I always order it for lunch. Well, I'd just told Thomas I was to meet Mrs. Hatfield at two thirty, when Mrs. Hatfield herself came into the dining room. She's near-sighted and didn't see us, but my husband saw her as clearly as I did. She sat down at a table and ordered her lunch and obviously she was going to stay there an hour or more. Thomas just sat opposite me without a word, knowing I'd lied. He's like that sometimes. Then it all comes out at some other time when I'm least expecting it." She stopped, breathing quickly.

"And it came out—when?" Dr. Bauer prompted.

"Yesterday afternoon. He knew positively then that I'd gone to lunch with Mrs. Hatfield, because she came upstairs to fetch me. We had lunch at the Algonquin with a couple of our friends. When I came home at about three, Thomas was in a temper and accused me of having gone to see a picture both afternoons, though clearly there hadn't been time to go to a picture after lunch yesterday afternoon."

"He doesn't like you to go to films?"

She shook her head, laughing, a tolerant laugh that was almost gay. "The bad air, you know. He thinks all theaters should be torn down. Oh, dear, he is funny sometimes! And he thinks the pictures I like are the lowest form of entertainment. I like a good musical comedy now and then, I must say, and I go when I please."

Dr. Bauer was sure she did not. "And what else did he say?"

"Well, he didn't say much more, but he threw his gold watch down. It was such a petulant gesture for him, I could hardly believe my eyes."

She looked at him as if expecting some reaction, then opened her handbag, brought out a gold watch, and wrapped its chain once around her forefinger as if to display it to best advantage. As the watch turned, Dr. Bauer saw a monogram of interlocked initials on its back.

"It's the watch I gave him the first year we were married. I'm old-fashioned, I suppose, but I like a man to carry a big pocket watch. By a miracle, it's still running. I'm just taking it now to have a new crystal put in. I simply picked up the watch without saying anything to him, and he put on his coat and went out for his usual afternoon walk. He walks from three till five thirty every day, rain or shine, then comes home and showers—a cold shower—before we go out to dinner together, unless it's one of his evenings with Major Stearns. I told you Major Stearns was Thomas' best friend. They play pinochle or chess together several evenings a week. —Could you possibly see my husband this week, Dr. Bauer?"

"I think I can arrange it for Friday at noon, Mrs. Afton," he said. He worked at a clinic on Friday afternoons, and he could stop by the hotel just before. "Shall I call you Friday morning? We'll make our plans then. They're always better made as late as possible."

She got up when he did, smiling, erect. "All right. I'll expect your call then. Good day, Dr. Bauer. I feel *ever* so much better. But I'm afraid I've overstayed my time by two minutes."

He waved his hand protestingly, and held the door open for her. In a moment she was gone—all but the scent of her cologne that lingered faintly as he stood by his closed door, facing the dusk that had come at the window . . .

When Dr. Bauer arrived at his office the next morning at 9:00, Mrs. Afton had already called twice. She wanted him to call her immediately, his secretary told him, and he meant to as soon as he had hung up his hat; but his telephone buzzed first.

"Can you come this morning?" Mrs. Afton asked.

The tremor of fear in her voice alerted him. "I'm sure I can, Mrs. Afton. What has happened?"

"He knows I've been seeing you about him. Seeing *someone*, I mean. He accused me of it outright this morning, just after he came back from his morning walk—as if he'd discovered it out of thin air. He accused me of being disloyal to him and he packed his suitcases and said he was leaving. He's out now—not with the suitcases, they're still here, so I know he's just walking. He'll probably be back by ten or so. Could you possibly come now?"

"Is he in violent temper? Has he struck you?"

"Oh, no! Nothing like that. But I know it's the end. I know it can't go on after this."

Dr. Bauer calculated how many appointments he would have to cancel. His 10:15 appointment, and possibly his 11:00. "Can you be in the lobby at ten fifteen?"

"Oh, certainly, Dr. Bauer!"

He found it hard to concentrate during his 9:15 consultation, and remembering Mrs. Afton's voice, he wished he had started off immediately for her hotel. Whatever the circumstances, Mrs. Afton had engaged his services, and he was therefore responsible for her.

In a taxi at 10:03, he lighted a cigarette and sat motionless, unable to look at the newspaper he had brought with him. Mid-morning of a day in mid-June, he thought, and while he was borne passively in a taxi that continually turned corners and met red lights, Mrs. Thomas Bainbridge Afton was at the crisis of more than twenty-five years of marriage.

And of what use would he be to her? To call for help in case of violence, and to utter the usual phrases of comfort, of advice, if her husband had come back and then gone away with his suitcases? It was the end of the gracious, pleasant life of Mrs. Afton, who without her husband would never be quite so happy again with her friends.

He could hear the remarks she had already made to them: "Thomas has his peculiarities . . . he has his little fads." And finally, after embarrassments, compromises, to herself: "He is impossible." Yet through pride or breeding or duty, she had maintained, along with her sense of humor, the look of being happily married. "Thomas is an ideal husband—*was* . . ."

A swerve of the taxi interrupted his thoughts. They had stopped in the middle of a block between Fifth and Sixth Avenues in the Forties, at a hotel smaller and shabbier than he had anticipated—a narrow, tucked-away building that he supposed was filled with middle-aged people like the Aftons, residents of decades or more.

Mrs. Afton walked quickly toward him across the black and white tile floor, and her tense face broke into a smile of welcome. She wiped a handkerchief across her palm and extended her hand. "How good of you, Dr. Bauer! He's come back and he's upstairs now. I thought I might introduce you as a friend of a friend of mine—of Mrs. Lanuxe of Charleston. I could say you've just stopped by for a moment before you have to catch a train."

"As you like." He followed her toward the elevator, relieved to find her in such good command of herself.

They entered a tiny, rattling elevator manned by an old man, and were silent as the elevator climbed slowly. Close to her now, Dr. Bauer could see the traces of gray in her light-brown hair, and could hear her too fast breathing. The handkerchief was tightly clenched in one hand.

"It's this way."

They went along a darkish corridor, down a couple of steps to a different level, and stopped at a tall door.

"I'm sure he's in his own room, but I always knock," she whispered. Then she opened the door. "This is the living room."

Dr. Bauer had unconsciously stuffed his newspaper into his jacket pocket so that his hands would be free. Now he found himself in an empty, rather depressing room containing hotel furniture, a few books, a brass chandelier that was a spray of former gas pipes, and an undersized black fireplace.

"He's in here," she said, going toward another door. "Thomas?" She opened the door cautiously.

There was no answer.

"He isn't in?" Dr. Bauer asked.

Mrs. Afton seemed embarrassed for a moment. "He must have stepped out again. But you can come in meanwhile and see what I've been talking to you about. This is his gymnasium, as he calls it."

Dr. Bauer entered a room about half the size of the living room, and much dimmer, since it had only one fire-escape window. It took him a moment to make out the odd shapes lying on the floor and hanging from the ceiling. There was a punching bag, a large cylindrical sandbag for tackling, an exercise horse with handgrips, and two basketballs on the floor. He picked up a boxing glove from the floor and the other came with it, fastened by its laces.

"And he has a machine for rowing. It's in the closet there," Mrs. Afton said.

"Can we have more light?"

"Oh, of course." She pulled a cord and a bare lightbulb came on at the ceiling. "Any other day, he'd be right here now. I'm so sorry. I'm sure he'll be back any minute."

The laces of the boxing gloves, Dr. Bauer saw, were crisp and white, threading all the eyelets, as if they had never been undone. Under the light now he saw that all the equipment looked brand-new. The exercise horse was a little dusty, but its leather bore no sign of wear. He frowned at the tan-colored sandbag only a few inches from his eyes. On the side nearest to him a diamond-shaped paper label was still pasted. Certainly none of the equipment had been used. It was such a surprise to him that at first he did not realize what it meant.

"And there's the mirror." She pointed to a tall mirror resting on the floor but quite upright against a wall. She chuckled. "He's eternally in front of that."

Dr. Bauer nodded. Despite her smile, he saw more anxiety in her face than on the afternoon of their first interview—an anxiety that made ugly, tortured ridges of her thin eyebrows. Her hands shook as she picked up a measuring tape and began to roll it neatly around two fingers, waiting trustfully for some comment from him.

"Perhaps I should wait in the lobby," Dr. Bauer murmured.

"All right. I'll call down and have you paged when he comes in

He always uses the stairs. I suppose that's how we missed him when he went out."

The stairway was directly in front of Dr. Bauer when he went out into the hall. He took it somewhat dazedly. A slight blond man came up the stairs, seemed to eye him a moment before he passed, but Dr. Bauer was sure it could not be Mr. Afton.

He felt stunned, without knowing exactly what had stunned him. In the lobby he looked one way, then the other, and finally went to the desk that was half hidden under a different set of stairs.

"You have a Mrs. Afton registered here," he said, stating it more than asking.

The young man at the switchboard looked up from his newspaper. "Afton? No, sir."

"Mrs. Afton in Room Thirty-two."

"No, sir. No Afton here at all."

"Then who is it in Room Thirty-two?" At least he was sure of the room number.

The young man checked quickly with his list over the switchboard. "That's Miss Gorham's suite." And slowly, as he looked at Dr. Bauer, his face took on an amused smile.

"Miss Gorham? She's not married?" Dr. Bauer moistened his lips. "She lives by herself?"

"Yes, sir."

"Do you know the person I mean? A woman about fifty, somewhat plump, light-brown hair?"

He knew, he *knew*—but he had to make sure, doubly sure.

"Miss Gorham, yes—Miss Frances Gorham."

Dr. Bauer looked into the smiling eyes of the young man who knew Miss Gorham, and wondered what the clerk knew that he didn't. Many a time Mrs. Afton must have smiled at this young man, too, ingratiated herself as she had with him in his office.

"Thank you," he said. Then absently, "Nothing more."

He faced in the other direction, staring at nothing, setting his teeth until the sensation of reality's crumbling stopped and the world righted itself again and became hard, a little shabby like the hotel lobby . . . until there was definitely no more Mrs. Afton.

He was walking toward the door when a compulsion to return to routine made him look at his wristwatch, made him realize he could be back for his 11:00 appointment after all, because it was not quite 10:40. He veered toward the coffin-like form of a telephone booth that was nearly hidden behind a large jar of palms. A shelf with telephone directories was at the side under a light, and some stubborn, some senseless curiosity prompted him to turn to the A's in the Manhattan directory.

There was only one Afton, and that was the trade name of some kind of shop.

He entered the booth and dialed his office number.

"Would you try to reach Mr. Schriever again," he told his secretary, "and ask him if he can still come at eleven. With my apologies for the changes. And when is Mrs. Afton's next appointment?"

"Just a moment. We have her tentatively scheduled for two thirty Monday."

"Would you change that please to an appointment for Miss Gorham?" he said distinctly. "Miss Frances Gorham for the same time?"

"Gorham? That's G-o-r-h-a-m?"

"Yes. I suppose so."

"That's a new patient, Dr. Bauer?"

"Yes," he said.

Julian Symons

Credit to Shakespeare

This first-night performance of "Hamlet" was notable for various reasons: one was the scandalous background of some of the cast; another was such stuff as Shakespeare never dreamed on . . .

Detective: FRANCIS QUARLES

66 **I**t won't do," said acidulous dramatic critic, Edgar Burin, to private detective, Francis Quarles. "The fact is that this young producer's too clever by half. You can't play about with a masterpiece like *Hamlet*."

Burin wrinkled his thin nose in distaste as the curtain rose on Act Five.

This *Hamlet* first night was notable because the production was by a young man still in his twenties named Jack Golding, who had already obtained a reputation for eccentric but ingenious work. It was also notable because of the casting. Golding had chosen for his Hamlet a star of light comedy named Giles Shoreham. His Laertes, John Farrimond, had been given his part on the strength of Golding's intuition, since Farrimond had played only one walk-on part in the West End.

Olivia Marston as the Queen and Roger Peters as the King were acknowledged Shakespearean actors, but their choice was remarkable in another sense. For the name of Olivia Marston, an impressive personality on the stage and a notorious one off it, had been linked by well-informed gossip with those of Peters, Farrimond, and even with Jack Golding himself.

Those were the rumors. What was certain was that Olivia, a tall handsome woman in her forties, had been married a few weeks ago to Giles Shoreham who was fifteen years her junior.

This agreeably scandalous background was known to most of the first-night audience, who watched eagerly for signs of tension among the leading players. So far, however, they had been disappointed of anything more exciting than a tendency on the part of Giles Shore-ham to fluff his lines.

By Act Five the audience had settled to the view that this was, after all, only another performance of *Hamlet*, marked by abrupt changes of mood from scene to scene, and by the producer's insistence on stressing the relationship between Hamlet and the Queen.

So the curtain rose on Act Five. Golding had taken unusual liberties with the text, and Burin sucked in his breath with disapproval at the omission of the Second Gravedigger at the beginning of this scene. Giles Shoreham, slight and elegant, was playing now with eloquence and increased confidence.

.Then came the funeral procession for Ophelia and Hamlet's struggle with Laertes in Ophelia's grave. Here one or two members of the audience sat forward, thinking they discovered an unusual air of reality as Shoreham and Farrimond struggled together, while Roger Peters, as the King, restrained them and Olivia Marston looked on.

Shoreham, Quarles thought, had gained impressiveness as the play went on. With Osric he was now splendidly ironical, and in the opening of the duel scene he seemed to dominate the stage for all his slightness of stature compared with Farrimond's height and breadth of shoulder.

This scene was played faster than usual, and Quarles vaguely noted cuts in the speeches before the duel began. There was Laertes choosing his poisoned foil; there was the poisoned cup brought in and placed on a side table. Then foils were flashing, Hamlet achieved a hit, took the cup to drink and put it down without doing so, with the speech, "I'll play this bout first; set it by a while."

Then another hit, and the Queen came over to wipe Hamlet's brow, picked up the cup, and drank. Laertes wounded Hamlet with his poisoned foil, and Hamlet snatched it from him and wounded Laertes. The Queen, with a cry, sank down as she was returning to the throne, and at once there was a bustle around her.

Osric and two attendants ran to her. The King moved upstage in her direction.

"How does the Queen?" Hamlet asked, and the King made the appropriate reply. "She swoons to see them bleed."

There was a pause.

Should not the Queen reply?

Quarles searched his memory while Burin grunted impatiently by his side.

Hamlet repeated, "How does the Queen?" and knelt down by her side.

The pause this time was longer.

Then Hamlet looked up, and on his face was an unforgettable expression of mingled anguish and irresolution. His lips moved, but he seemed unable to speak. When the words came they seemed almost ludicrous after the Shakespearean speech they had heard.

"A doctor," he cried. "Is there a doctor in the house?"

The other players looked at him in consternation. The curtain came down with a rush. Five minutes later, Roger Peters appeared before it and told the anxious audience that Miss Marston had met with a serious accident.

When Burin and Quarles came onto the stage, the players were standing together in small, silent groups. Only Giles Shoreham sat apart in his red court suit, head in hands.

A man bending over Olivia Marston straightened up and greeted Quarles, who recognized him as the well-known pathologist, Sir Charles Palquist.

"She's dead," Palquist said, and his face was grave. "She took cyanide, and there's no doubt she drank it from that cup. Somebody knocked the cup over and it's empty now, but the smell is still plain enough."

"Now I wonder who did that?" Quarles said. But his meditation on that point was checked by the arrival of his old friend, brisk, grizzled Inspector Leeds.

The Inspector had a wonderful capacity for marshaling facts. Like a dog snapping at the heels of so many sheep, he now extracted a story from each of the actors on the stage, while Quarles stood by and listened.

When the Inspector had finished, this was the result. The cup from which Olivia Marston had taken her fatal drink was filled with red wine and water. The cup had been standing ready in the wings for some time, and it would have been quite easy for anybody on the stage—or, indeed, anybody in the whole company—to drop poison into it unobserved.

As for what had happened on the stage, the duel scene had been played absolutely to the script up to the point where Peters, as the King, said, "She swoons to see them bleed." The Queen should then have replied to him, and her failure to do so was the reason for the very obvious pause that had occurred.

Shoreham, as Hamlet, then improvised by repeating his question, "How does the Queen?" and went on his knees to look at her, thinking that she felt unwell. But when he saw her face, half turned to the floor, suffused and contorted, he knew that something was seriously wrong. Shoreham was then faced with a terrible problem.

Clasping his hands nervously, white-faced, Shoreham said to the Inspector, "I could have got up and gone on as though nothing had happened—after all, in the play the Queen was dead—and within ten minutes the play would have been over. That way we should have completed the performance." Shoreham's large eyes looked pleadingly round at the other members of the cast. "But I couldn't do it. I couldn't leave her lying there—I just couldn't."

"Since the poor lady was dead, it didn't make any difference," said the Inspector in his nutmeg-grater voice. "Now, this lady became Mrs. Shoreham a few weeks ago, I believe? And she was, I imagine, a pretty wealthy woman?"

Giles Shoreham's head jerked up. "Do you mean to insinuate—?"

"I'm not insinuating, sir—I'm merely stating a fact."

Quarles coughed. "I think, Inspector, that there may be other motives at work here."

He took the Inspector aside and told him of the rumors that linked the names of Farrimond, Peters, and Golding with Olivia Marston. The Inspector's face lengthened as he listened.

"But that means any of the four might have had reason to kill her."

"If they felt passionately enough about her—yes. Which would you pick?"

The Inspector's glance passed from Farrimond, big and sulky, to the assured, dignified, gray-haired Peters and on to the young producer Jack Golding, who looked odd in his lounge suit and thick horn-rimmed spectacles among this collection of Elizabethans. "I'm hanged if I know."

"May I ask a few questions?" The Inspector assented. Quarles stepped forward. "A small point perhaps, gentlemen, but one I should like to clear up. The cup was found on its side with the liquid spilled out of it. Who knocked it over?"

There was silence.

With something threatening behind his urbanity Quarles said, "Very well. Let us have individual denials. Mr. Shoreham?"

Shoreham shook his head.

"Mr. Farrimond?"

"Didn't touch a thing."

"Mr. Peters?"

"No."

"Any of you other gentlemen who were on the stage? Or did anyone see it done?" There were murmurs of denial. "Most interesting. Miss Marston replaced the cup on the table and then some unknown agency knocked it on its side."

The Inspector was becoming impatient. "Can't see what you're getting at, Quarles. Do you mean she didn't drink out of it?"

Quarles shook his head. "Oh, no, she drank from it, poor woman. Mr. Shoreham, did you know that you had some rivals for your wife's affections? And did she ever hint that any one of them was particularly angry when she decided to marry you?"

A wintry suggestion of a smile crossed Shoreham's pale face. "She once said she'd treated everybody badly except me and that one of these days she'd get into trouble. I thought she was joking."

"Mr. Golding." The producer started. "I'm not a Shakespearean scholar, but I seem to have noticed more cuts in this *Hamlet* than are usually made."

"No," said Golding. The thickness of his spectacles effectively masked his expression. "*Hamlet* is very rarely played in full. I haven't made more cuts than usual, I've simply made different ones."

"In this particular scene, for instance," Quarles went on, "you've cut the passage early—where the King drinks and sends somebody across to Hamlet with the cup."

"That's right. It seems to me an unnecessary complication."

"What about the rest of the scene? Any cuts in that?"

"None at all. After what you saw we adhere to the standard printed version."

Quarles bent his whole great body forward and said emphatically, "Doesn't that suggest something to you, Mr. Golding? Remember that the cup was knocked over and emptied. Do you understand?"

On Golding's face there was suddenly amazed comprehension.

The Inspector had been listening with increasing irritation. "What's all this got to do with the murder? Why the devil was that cup emptied?"

"*Because the murderer thought he would have to drink from it.* Remember what happens after the Queen dies, crying that her drink was poisoned. Laertes tells Hamlet that he has been the victim of treachery. Hamlet stabs the King. And what happens *then*, Mr. Peters?"

Roger Peters, truly kingly in his robes, was smiling. "Hamlet puts the poisoned cup to the King's mouth and forces him to drink."

"Correct. In fact, Shoreham stopped the play before that point was reached. But the murderer couldn't be sure that Shoreham's instinct as an actor wouldn't impel him to go on and say nothing. And then what would have happened? The King would also have had to drink from the poisoned cup. You couldn't risk that, could you, Mr. Peters?"

Peters' hand was at his mouth. "No. You are a clever man, Mr. Quarles."

"So there was only one person who would have had any motive for knocking over that cup."

"Only one person. But you are a little late, Mr. Quarles. I had two capsules. I swallowed the second a few seconds ago. I don't think, anyway, that I would have wanted to live without Olivia."

Peters' body seemed to crumple suddenly. Farrimond caught him as he fell.

"Well," said Burin, the dramatic critic, afterward, "you had no evidence, Quarles, but that was a pretty piece of deduction."

"I was merely the interpreter," Quarles said mock-modestly. "The credit for spinning the plot and then unraveling it goes to someone much more famous."

"Who's that?"

"William Shakespeare."

Christianna Brand

Blood Brothers

Inspector Cockrill said, "Well, well, so you're the famous Birds-
well twins! . . . An almost mystic bond, I hear? . . . In fact, you
might properly be called—blood brothers?" . . .

Detective: INSPECTOR COCKRILL

A nd devoted, I hear? . . . David and Jonathan?" he said. "In
fact, you might properly be called," he said, with that glitter
in his eye, "blood brothers?"

Well, he can sneer, but it's true we was pally enough, Fred and
me, till Lydia came along. Shared the same digs in the
village—Birdswell's our village, if you know it?—Birdswell, in Kent.

Everyone in Birdswell knows us—even if they can't easily tell the
difference between us—and used to say how wonderful it was, us
two so alike, with our strong legs and big shoulders and curly red
hair, like a kid's; and what a beautiful understanding we always
had, what a bond of union. Well, people talk a lot of nonsense about
identical twins.

Lydia couldn't tell the difference between us either—seemingly.
Was that my fault? Fair enough, she was Fred's girl first—unless
you counted her husband, and to some extent you did have to count
him: six foot five, he is, and it isn't only because he's the blacksmith
that they call him Black Will.

But she switched to me of her own accord, didn't she?—even if I
wasn't too quick to disillusion her, the first time she started with
her carryings-on, mistaking me for Fred. "*I* can't help it if she fancies
me more than you, now," I said to Fred.

"You'll regret this, you two-timing, double-crossing skunk," said
Fred. He always did have a filthy temper, Fred did.

Well, I did regret it, and not so very long after. Fred and me shares
a car between us—a heavy, old, bashed-up, fourth-hand "family
model," but at least it goes. And one evening, when he'd slouched

off, ugly and moody as he was those days, to poach the river down by the Vicarage woods, I picked up Lydia and took her out in it, joyriding.

Not that there was much joy in it. We hadn't been out twenty minutes when, smooching around with Lydia, I suppose, and not paying enough attention to the road—well, I didn't see the kid until I'd hit him. Jogging along the grass verge the kid was, with his little can of blackberries, haring home as fast as his legs would go, a bit scared, I daresay, because the dark was catching up on him.

Well, the dark caught him up all right, poor little kid. I scrambled out and knelt down and turned him over; and got back again, quick. "He's gone," I said to Lydia, "and we'd best be gone too."

She made a lot of fuss, womanlike, but what was the point of it? If he wasn't dead now, he would be mighty soon, there wasn't any doubt of it, lying there with the can still clutched in his fat little hand and the blackberries spilt, and scattered all around him. I couldn't do nothing; if I could have, I daresay I'd have waited, but I couldn't. So what was the use of bringing trouble on myself, when the chances were that I could get clear away with it?

And I did get clear away with it. The road was hard and dry, the cars that followed and stopped must have obscured my tire marks, if there were any. They found half a footprint in the dried mud, where I'd bent over him; but it was just a cheap, common make of shoe, pretty new so that it had no particular marks to it; and a largish size, of course, but nothing out of the ordinary.

So no one knew I'd been on that road—everything Lydia did with us two was done in deep secret, because of Black Will. Will was doing time at the moment, for beating up a keeper who came on him, poaching (we all spent most of our evenings poaching). But he'd be back some day, Black Will would.

And Fred promised me an alibi when I told him about it, clutching at his arm, shaking a bit by this time, losing confidence because Lydia was threatening to turn nasty. "I'll say you was in the woods with me," he said.

And he did, too. They came to our door—"regulation police inquiries." But Lydia didn't dare tell, not really—I could see that in the light of day—and they had no other sort of reason to suspect me, especially. And nobody did—it could have been any stranger, speeding along the empty country roads.

Fred pretended to be reluctant to alibi me, cagey about saying where we was—because of the poaching. He managed it fine, sort of threw their interest halfway in a different direction. I thought it was decent of Fred, considering about me and Lydia. But brotherly love is a wonderful thing, isn't it?

Or is it? Because it hadn't been all for nothing. No sooner was I clear of that lot than he said to me, "Well, has she told you?"

"Told me what?" I said. "Who? Lydia?"

"Lydia," he said. "She's having a baby."

"Well, don't look at me," I said, and quick. "I've only been going with the girl a couple of weeks."

"And her husband hasn't been going with her at all," said Fred. "On account of he's been in prison for the past five months."

"For half killing a man," I said thoughtfully; and I looked Fred up and down. Fred and me are no weeds, like I said, but Black Will, he's halfway to a giant.

"And due out at the end of October," said Fred.

"Well, good luck to the two of you," I said. "It's nothing to do with me. I went with her for a couple of weeks, and now even that's over. She reckons I ought to have stopped and seen to the kid; she's given me the air."

"She'll give you more than the air," he said, "and me too, when Will comes home. When he knows about the baby he'll beat the rest out of her; and then God help you and me too."

"The baby could be Jimmy Green's," I said. "Or Bill Bray's. She's been out with them, too."

"That's her tales," he said, "to make you jealous. They're a sight too scared of Will to let Lydia make up to them. And so ought you and I have been too, if we'd had any sense." Only where Lydia was concerned, there never seemed to be time to have sense; and six months ago, Fred said, Black Will's return had seemed like a century away.

"So what are you going to do?" I said.

"What are *you* going to do?" he said. "A hit-and-run driver—you can get a long stretch for that."

Good old brotherly love!—Fred worrying about me, when after all I *had* pinched his girl. And him in such trouble himself.

We went out in the car where no one could hear us—our old landlady's pretty deaf and takes no interest at all in our comings and goings, but Fred wasn't taking no chances.

Because it was all Fred's idea; that I will say, and stick to it—it was all Fred's idea. Dead men tell no tales, said Fred; nor dead girls, neither. "If they find she's in the family way—it's like you said, she'd been going with half the men in the village. So once she was past talking, Will couldn't pin it on us two—not to be certain, he couldn't."

"Speak for yourself," I said.

"She'd be past talking about the hit-and-run, too," he said. "You say she's sore about that. She won't tell now, because it means admitting she was joy-riding with you; but once Black Will gets it out of her that she was—and he will, you can bet on it—then she'll tell about the accident too; it'll make her feel easier."

"So what do you suggest?" I said. "*I'm* not killing the girl, I can tell you that, flat."

"No," he said, "I'll do that. You've done one killing—that'll do for you. All I want from you now is an alibi."

"What, me alibi you?" I said. "No one'd believe it for a minute. One twin speaking up for another—the whole village would testify how 'close' we are."

But Fred had thought of all that too. If a straight alibi failed, he said, there were other ways of playing it. He had it all worked out—suspiciously well worked out, I should have thought; but he gave me no time for thinking. "It won't come to any alibi, our names probably won't even come into it—as you say, the baby could have been fathered by half the male population of Birdswell. But if it does—well, you alibi for me and I alibi for you. They'll know it was one of us, but they'll never know which one; and if they don't know which of us, they'll have to let both of us go."

"And Black Will?" I said. "When we've not only seduced his wife, but murdered her—which one of us will *he* let go?"

"Oh, well," he said, "we'd have to clear out if it got as far as that, start again somewhere else. But the chances are a hundred to one it'll never come to that. After all, no one suspected you of the hit-and-run affair, did they?"

He kept coming back to that, sort of nastily. I didn't forget that I'd done him wrong, pinching his girl. But that was his lever, really—while he kept reminding me, he could pretty well force me to go in with him. He was in trouble—but I was in trouble even deeper.

So we worked it out—we worked out everything to the last detail. This was Tuesday, and we'd do it Thursday night. I'd see nothing more of the girl; but he'd get her to go driving with him on the pretense of talking over the baby business. And he'd lead round to the accident, advising her to confess to the police it was me, and then drive past where it happened. And get her out of the car and show him just where the boy was lying. And then—well, then there'd be a second hit-and-run killing on that lonely spot. "*You* got away with it once," he kept saying. "Why not another?"

There was a kind of—well, justice, in it, I thought. After all, it was because she was threatening to tell about the hit-and-run that I was letting her be murdered.

"But what about clues?" I said. "Even I left a footprint."

He had worked that out too. He and I are the same size, of course, and most of our clothes are the same as one another's. Not for any silly reason like dressing identical, but simply because when he'd go along shopping, I'd go along too, and mostly we liked the same things; or he'd buy something and it'd be a success, so I'd buy the same, later.

We'd dress the same Thursday night, he said, because of the alibi; and we checked our stuff over—shoes, gray slacks, shirts, without jackets—this all happened in September.

Our blue poplins were in the wash—we'd worn them clean Sunday, and second-day Monday; so it would have to be the striped wool-and-nylon—a bit warm for this weather, if anyone remarked it, but we'd have to risk that, I said, we daren't ask the old woman to wash out our blue ones special. The last thing we wanted was to do anything out of the ordinary. That was what the police looked for—a break in routine. That was asking for it.

Our shoes were the same—same size, same make, bought together, with a rubber sole that had bars across it; but, like I said, new enough not to be worn down, or have any peculiarities. And everything else we'd wear would be identical—not only for the alibi, but in case of bits caught in the girl's fingernails or whatnot—you've only got to read the papers to know what they look for.

Not that he meant to get near enough for that. But she might not—well, she might not kick in at once, if you see what I mean; he might have to get out of the car and do something about it. And in case of scratches, he said, I'd better be prepared to get some scratches on my own hands too—we could say we'd been blackberrying or something.

"Blackberrying," I said. "That'd be bloody likely! We both detest blackberries—everybody knows it; or anyway, the old woman knows it, we never touch her blackberry pie."

I knew he'd only said it to remind me of the kid—him and his little can of blackberries, spilt all around him.

"Oh, well," he said, "say we got scratched pushing through the brambles down by the river. Do your poaching down by the bramble patch."

But she didn't scratch him. It was all a bit grim, I think; he couldn't be sure she was properly done in and he had to get out of the car and have a look and—well, go back and take a second run at her. But she didn't have the strength left to scratch him.

All the same, he looked pretty ghastly when finally we met in the moonlight, in the Vicarage woods. He didn't say anything, just stood there, staring at me with a sort of sick, white heaviness.

I couldn't exactly say anything either; it was worse than, talking it over, I'd thought it ever would be. I sort of—well, looked a question at him; and he gave me a weary kind of nod and glanced away towards the river. It was easier to talk about my angle, so I said, at last, "Well, I saw the Vicar."

"But did he see you?" he said. We'd agreed on the Reverend because he always walked across to the church of a Thursday evening; you'd be sure of passing him if you went at a certain time.

"Yes," I said. "He saw me. I gave a sort of grunt for 'good evening,' and he said, 'Going poaching?' and gave me a bit of a grin. You'd better remember that." He nodded again but he said nothing more; and more to ease the silence than anything else, I said, "Is the car all right? Not marked?"

"What does it matter if it is?" he said. "It's marked all over, no one could say what's old or what's new—you know that, from bashing the boy." As for bits of her clothing and—well, blood and all that, he'd had the idea of spreading a bit of plastic over the front of the car before he—well, did it. He produced the plastic folded in brown paper, and we wrapped the whole lot round a stone and sank it, then and there, in the river. There was blood on the plastic, all right. It gave me the shudders.

But next thing he said that I really had something to shudder at. "Anyway, *your* number's up, mate. She's shopped you."

"Shopped me?" I said. I stood and stared at him.

"Shopped you," he said. "She'd already sent off an anonymous note to the police. About the hit-and-run."

"How do you know?" I said. I couldn't believe it.

"She told me so," he said. "It was on her conscience, what you'd done."

Her conscience! Lydia's conscience! I started to laugh, a bit hysterical, I suppose, with the strain of it. He put his hand on my wrist and gave me a little shake.

"Steady lad," he said. "Don't lose your head. I'm looking after you." It wasn't like him to be so demonstrative, but there you are—it's like the poem says, when times are bad, there's no friend like a brother. "It's just a matter of slanting the alibi," he said.

Well, we'd worked that out, too. There'd always be a risk that they wouldn't accept a brother's alibi, that the two of us was together. The other time, about the accident, they'd had no special reason to suspect me, so they'd accepted that all right; but this time it might at any moment turn into a murder inquiry—and a murder inquiry into *us*, now that they knew about the hit-and-run.

But as Fred said—we had the alternative all ready.

I hadn't counted on its being Inspector Cockrill. When I realized it was him—come all the way over from Heronsford—I knew they meant business. And to be honest, it struck a bit of chill into the heart of me.

A little man he is, for a policeman, and near retiring age he must be—looks like a grandfather; but his eyes are as bright as a bird's and they seem to look right into you. He came into the old woman's best parlor and he had us brought in there, and he looked us up and down.

"Well, well," he said, "so you're the famous Birdswell twins! You certainly are identicals, aren't you?" And he gave us a look of a sort of fiendish glee, or so it seemed to me, and said, "And devoted, I hear? An almost mystic bond, I hear? David and Jonathan, Damon and Pythias, and all the rest of it? In fact," he said, "you might properly be called—blood brothers?"

We stood in front of him, silent. He said at last, "Well, which is which?—and no nonsense."

We told him—*and* no nonsense.

"So you're the one that killed the child?" he said to me. "And drove on, regardless."

"I never was near the child," I said. "I was in the woods that evening—poaching."

"Yours is the name stated in the anonymous letter."

"I don't know who wrote the letter," I said. "But no one can tell us apart, me and my brother."

"Even your fancy girl?" he said. "It appears it was she who wrote the letter."

"I don't know what you mean," I said, "by my fancy girl."

"Well, everyone else does," he said. "All the village knows she was playing you off, one against the other. And all the village has been grinning behind their hands, waiting for her husband's homecoming."

"But I tell you none of them can tell us apart," I said. "I was out poaching."

"That's a damn lie," said Fred, playing it the way we'd agreed upon. "That was me, poaching."

"One of you was poaching?" said Inspector Cockrill, very smooth, "And one of you was with the lady? And even the lady couldn't have said which was which?"

He said it sort of, well, suggestive. "I daresay she might," I said, "later on in the proceedings. But there couldn't have been any proceedings that night—there wouldn't have been time because the accident happened."

"Why should she say so positively it was you, then?"

"I daresay she thought it was me," I said. "I daresay he told her so. She'd finished with him—it would be the only way he could get back at her."

"I see," said Inspector Cockrill. "How very ingenious!" I didn't know whether he meant how ingenious of Fred to have thought of it then, or of me to think of it now.

"Don't you listen to him, sir," said Fred. "He's a bloody liar. I wasn't with the girl that night. I tell you I was poaching."

"All right, you were poaching," said Inspector Cockrill. "Any witnesses?"

"Of course not. You don't go poaching with witnesses. I used to go with him," said Fred bitterly, gesturing with his head towards me, "but not since he pinched my girl, the bloody so-and-so."

"And last night?" said the Inspector softly. "When the girl was murdered?"

"Last night too," said Fred. "I was in the woods, poaching."

"You call me a liar!" I said. "It was me in the woods. The Vicar saw me going there."

"It was me the Vicar saw," said Fred. "I told him, Good evening, and he laughed and said, 'Going poaching?' "

"There!" said Inspector Cockrill to me, like a teacher patiently getting the truth from a difficult child. "How could he know that? Because the Vicar will surely confirm it."

"He knows it because I told him," I said. "I told him I'd been poaching and I hoped the Vicar hadn't realized where I was going."

"Very ingenious," said Inspector Cockrill again. "Very ingenious."

It seemed like he couldn't get over it all, sitting there, shaking his head at the wonder of it. But I knew he was playing for time. I knew that we'd foxed him.

And Fred knew too. He suggested, reasonably, "Why should you be so sure, sir, that the girl was murdered? Why not just a second hit-and-run?"

"A bit of a coincidence?" said Inspector Cockrill mildly. "Same thing in the same place and so soon after? And when on top of it, we find that the girl was threatening a certain person with exposure, about the first hit-and-run . . . " He left it in the air. He said to his sergeant, "Have you collected their clobber?"

"Yes, sir," said the sergeant. "Two pairs of shoes—" and he gave the Inspector a sort of nod, as if to say, Yes, they look as if they'll match very nicely—"and all the week's laundry."

"Including Monday's?" said Cockrill.

"Including Monday evening's, sir. The old woman washes of a Monday morning. Anything they've worn after that—which includes two shirts to each, sir—is in two laundry baskets, one in each bedroom."

"Two baskets?" he says, looking more bright-eyed than ever. "That's a bit of luck. Their laundry's kept separate, is it?"

"Yes, it is," said Fred, though I don't know what call he had to butt in. "His in his room, mine in mine."

"And no chance of its getting mixed up?" said Inspector Cockrill. He fixed Fred with that beady eye of his.

Fred, of course, was maintaining the mutual-accusation arrangement we'd agreed upon. "Not a chance, sir," he said a bit too eagerly.

I wasn't going to be left out. I said, "Not the slightest."

"That's right, sir," says the sergeant. "The old lady confirms it."

"Good," said Cockrill. He gave a few orders and the sergeant went away. People were still buzzing about, up in our bedrooms. "I'm coming," the Inspector called up to someone at the head of the stairs. He turned back to us. "All right, Cain and Abel," he said. "I'll leave you to stew in it. But in a day or two, as the song says, 'I'll be seeing you.' And when I do, it'll be at short notice. So stick around if you know what's good for you."

"And if we don't?" I said. "You've got nothing against us. You can't charge us, so you've got no call to be giving us orders."

"Who's giving orders?" he said. "Just a little friendly advice. But before you ignore the advice take a good, hard, long look at yourselves. You won't need any mirrors. And ask yourselves," he said, giving us a good, hard, long look on his own account, from the soles of our feet to the tops of our flaming red heads, "just how far you'd get."

So that was that; and for the next two days, we "stewed in it." David and Jonathan, Cain and Abel—like he'd said, blood brothers.

On the third day he sent for us, to Heronsford Police Station. They shoved Fred into one little room and me in another. He talked to Fred first, and I waited. All very chummy, cigs and cups of tea and offers of bread and butter; but it was the waiting . . .

Long after I knew I couldn't stand one more minute of it, the Inspector came in. I suppose they muttered some formalities, but I don't remember. Fred and I might hate one another, and by this time we did, well and truly, there's no denying it—but it was worse, a thousand times worse, without him there. My head felt as though it were filled with gray cottonwool, little, stuffy, warm clouds of it.

Inspector Cockrill sat down in front of me. He said, "Well, have you come to your senses? Of course you killed her."

"If anyone killed her," I said, clinging to our patter, "it must have been him."

"Your brother?" he said. "But why should your brother have killed her?"

"Well," I said, "if the girl was having a baby—"

"A baby?" he said surprised, and his eyes got that bright, glittering look in them. "But she wasn't."

"She wasn't?" I said. "She *wasn't*? But she'd told him—"

Or had she told him? Something like an icicle of light—ice-cold, piercing, brilliant—thrust itself into the dark places of my cotton-wool mind. I said, "The bloody, two-timing, double-crossing. . . !"

"*He* didn't seem," said the Inspector softly, "to expect her to have been found pregnant."

So that was it! So *that* was it! So as to get me to agree to the killing, to get me to help him with it . . . I ought to have been more fly—why should Fred, of all people, be so much afraid of Black Will as to go in for murder? Will's a dangerous man, but Fred's not exactly a softie.

The icicle turned in my mind and twisted, probing with its light rays into the cotton wooliness. Revenge! Cold, sullen, implacable revenge on the two of us—because Lydia had come over to me, because I had taken her away from him. Death for her—and I to be the accomplice in her undoing, and in my own undoing.

I knew now who had sent the anonymous note about the hit-and-run accident—so easily to be "traced" (after she was dead) to Lydia.

But yet, he was still as deep in it as I was—even deeper had he but known it. I said, fighting my way up out of the darkness, "Even if she *had* been pregnant, it wouldn't have been my fault. I'd only been going with her a couple of weeks."

"That's what you say," Cockrill said.

"But all the village—"

"All the village knew there were goings-on, but nobody knew just where they went on, or how long. You must, all three, have been remarkably careful."

I tried another tack. "But if she wasn't pregnant, why should I have killed her?"

"You've just told me yourself that you thought she was," he said.

"Because he told me—my brother told me. Now, look, Inspector," I said, trying to think it out as I went along, trying to ram it home to him, "you say she wasn't having a baby? So why should I have thought she was? *She* wouldn't have told me, if she hadn't been. So it was he who told me—my own brother. But you say yourself, he knew it wasn't true. So why should he have told me?"

He looked at me, cold as ice, and he said, "That's easy. He wanted *you* to kill *her* for *him*."

He wanted *me* to kill her! I could have laughed. The thing was getting fantastic, getting out of hand; and yet at the same time I had a feeling that the fantasy was a hard, gripping, grim fantasy, that once it had its hold on me it would never shake loose. I stammered out, "Why should he have wanted her killed?"

"Because," he said, "she was threatening to tell that it was he who ran the child down, and left it to die." And the Inspector said, cold and bitter, "I have no wish to trap you. We know that it was your brother who killed the child—we have proof of it. And we know it was you who killed the girl—we have proof of that too. There's her blood on your cuff."

On my cuff. Where Fred had put his hand that night—taking my wrist in his grasp, giving me a brotherly little shake "to steady me." I remembered how I'd thought, even then, that it wasn't like him to be so demonstrative.

Putting his hand on my wrist—fresh from the blood-smeared plastic he'd put on the front of the car. Making such a point, later on, about there being no chance of our soiled shirts getting confused, one with the other's.

So there it is. I wonder if we'll be doing our time in the same prison, sharing the same cell, maybe?—we two being blood brothers.

Because he'll be doing time all right, as well as me. While I'm doing my time for *his* killing the girl, he'll be doing his time for *my* killing the child.

Well, that's all right with me. He'll be first out, I daresay. Is it murder to leave a kid to die? I suppose not; the actual knocking down would be accidental, after all, not planned. So Fred'll be out first, and Black Will will be there to meet him. By the time I get out, I daresay Will will be back "in" for what he done to Fred—so it looks like being a very long time away, my ever meeting Black Will, I mean.

But can you beat it?—Fred working it out so far ahead, leading up to it so patiently, so softly, so craftily? Planting the blood on my cuff—and then leading up to it so softly, so craftily. And all for revenge—revenge on his own twin brother! And him planning and expecting me to pay for it all, and him planning to go scot-free.

After all, what *I* did, was done in self-preservation—there was no venom in it against Fred. That night after the car accident, I mean, when, clutching his arm and begging him to help me, when just to be on the safe side I rubbed his sleeve with the juice of a blackberry.

Isaac Asimov

The Man Who Never Told a Lie

At this session of the Black Widowers the guest, brought by artist
Mario Gonzalo, gives the club a problem in pure logic. Mr. John
Sand seemed to be the only possible culprit; yet he denied guilt,
and as everyone knew (and the reader can take this as gospel),
Mr. Sand always told the truth, the whole truth, and nothing but
the truth . . .

Detectives: THE BLACK WIDOWERS

When Roger Halsted made his appearance at the head of the
stairs on the day of the monthly meeting of the Black Widowers, the only others yet present were Avalon, the patent-attorney,
and Rubin, the writer. They greeted him with jubilation.

Emmanuel Rubin said, "Well, you've finally managed to stir yourself up to the point of meeting your old friends, have you?" He trotted
over and held out both his hands, his straggly beard stretching to
match his grin. "Where've you been the last two meetings?"

"Hello, Roger," said Geoffrey Avalon, smiling from his stiff height.

Halsted shucked his coat. "Damned cold outside. Henry, bring—"

Henry, the only waiter the Black Widowers ever had or ever would
have, already had the drink waiting. "I'm glad to see you again,
sir."

Halsted took it with a nod of thanks. "Twice running something
came up—Say, you know what I've decided to do?"

"Give up mathematics and make an honest living?" asked Rubin.

Halsted sighed. "Teaching math at a junior high school is as honest
a living as one can find. That's why it pays so little."

"In that case," said Avalon, swirling his drink gently, "why is
free-lance writing so dishonest a racket?"

"Free-lance writing is *not* dishonest," said free-lance Rubin, rising
to the bait at once.

"What have you decided to do, Roger?" asked Avalon.

"It's this project I've dreamed up," said Halsted. His forehead rose white and high, showing no signs of the hairline that had been there perhaps ten years ago, though the hair was still copious enough around the sides and in the back. "I'm going to rewrite the *Iliad* and the *Odyssey* in limericks, one for each of the forty-eight books they contain."

Avalon nodded. "Any of it written?"

"I've got the first book of the *Iliad* taken care of. It goes like this:

"Agamemnon, the top-ranking Greek,

To Achilles in anger did speak.

They argued a lot,

Then Achilles grew hot,

And went stamping away in a pique."

"Not bad," said Avalon. "In fact, quite good. It gets across the essence of the first book in full. Of course, the proper name of the hero of the *Iliad* is Achilleus, with the 'ch' sound as in—"

"That would throw off the meter," said Halsted.

"Besides," said Rubin, "everyone would think the 'u' was a typographical error and that's all they'd see in the limerick."

Mario Gonzalo, the artist, came racing up the stairs. He was host for this session and he said, "Anyone else here?"

"Nobody here but us old folks," said Avalon.

"My guest is on his way up. Real interesting guy. Henry will like him because he never tells a lie."

Henry lifted an eyebrow as he produced Mario's drink.

"Don't tell me you're bringing the ghost of George Washington!" said Halsted.

"Roger! A pleasure to see you again. —By the way, Jim Drake won't be here with us today. He sent back the card saying there was some family shindig he had to attend. The guest I'm bringing is a fellow named Sand—John Sand. I've known him on and off for years. Real crazy guy. Horse race buff who never tells a lie. I've heard him *not* telling lies. It's about the only virtue he has." And Gonzalo winked.

Avalon nodded. "Good for those who can. As one grows older, however—"

"And I think it will be an interesting session," added Gonzalo hurriedly, visibly avoiding one of Avalon's long-winded confidences. "I was telling him about the Black Widowers Club and how the last two times we had mysteries on our hands—"

"Mysteries?" said Halsted, with sudden interest.

Gonzalo said, "You're a member of the club in good standing, so we can tell you. But get Henry to do it. He was a principal both times."

"Henry?" Halsted looked over his shoulder in mild surprise. "Are they getting you involved in their idiocies?"

"I assure you, Mr. Halsted, I tried not to be," said Henry.

"Tried not to be!" exclaimed Rubin. "Listen, Henry was the Sherlock of the session last time. He—"

"The point is," said Avalon, "that you may have talked too much, Mario. What did you tell your friend about us?"

"What do you mean, talked too much? I'm not Manny Rubin, you know. I carefully told Sand that we were priests at the confessional, one and all, as far as anything in this room is concerned, and he said he wished he were a member because he has a difficulty that's been driving him wild, and I said he could come the next time because it was my turn to be host and he could be my guest and—here he is!"

A slim man, his neck swathed in a thick scarf, was mounting the stairs. The slimness was emphasized when he took off his coat. Under the scarf his tie gleamed blood-red and seemed to lend color to a thin and pallid face. He was thirtyish.

"John Sand," said Mario, introducing him all round in a pageant that was interrupted by Thomas Trumbull's heavy tread on the steps and the code expert's loud cry of "Henry, a Scotch and soda for a dying man!"

Rubin said, "Tom, you could be here early if only you'd relax and stop trying so hard to be late."

"The later I come," said Trumbull, "the less I have to hear of your stupid remarks. Ever think of that?" Then he was introduced too, and they all sat down.

Since the menu for that meeting had been so incautiously planned as to begin with artichokes, Rubin launched into a dissertation on the preparation of the only proper sauce. Then, when Trumbull said disgustedly that the only proper preparation for artichokes involved a large garbage can, Rubin said, "Sure, *if* you don't have exactly the right sauce."

Sand ate uneasily and left at least one-third of his excellent steak untouched. Halsted, who had a tendency to plumpness, eyed the remains enviously. His own plate was the first one to be cleaned. Only a scraped bone and some fat were left.

Sand seemed to grow aware of Halsted's eyes and said, "Frankly, I'm too worried to have much appetite. Would you care for the rest of my steak?"

"Me? No, thank you," said Halsted glumly.

Sand smiled. "May I be frank?"

"Of course. If you've been listening to the conversation around the table, you'll realize frankness is the order of the day."

"Good, because I would be anyway. It's my—fetish. You're lying, Mr. Halsted. Of course you want the rest of my steak, and you'd eat it, too, if you thought no one would notice. That's perfectly obvious, but social convention requires you to lie. You don't want to seem greedy and you don't want to seem to ignore the elements of hygiene by eating something possibly contaminated by the saliva of a stranger."

Halsted frowned. "And what if the situation were reversed?"

"And I was hungry for more steak?"

"Yes."

"Well, I might not want to eat yours for hygienic reasons, but I would admit I wanted it. Almost all lying is the result of a desire for self-protection or out of respect for social conventions. To me, however, a lie is rarely a useful defense and I am not at all interested in social conventions."

Rubin said, "Actually, a lie *is* a useful defense if it is a thoroughgoing one. The trouble with most lies is that they don't go far enough."

"Been reading *Mein Kampf* lately?" said Gonzalo.

Rubin's eyebrows went up. "You think *Hitler* was the first to use the technique of the big lie? You can go back to Napoleon III; you can go back to Julius Caesar. Have you read his *Commentaries?*"

Henry was bringing the baba au rhum and pouring the coffee delicately when Avalon said, "Let's get to our honored guest."

Gonzalo said, "As host and chairman of this session I'm going to cancel the grilling. Our guest has a problem and I direct him to favor us with its details." He was drawing a quick caricature of Sand on the back of the menu card, with a thin sad face accentuated into the face of a distorted bloodhound.

Sand cleared his throat. "I understand everything said in this room is in the strictest confidence. But—"

Trumbull followed Sand's glance, then growled. "Don't worry about Henry. He is the best of us all. If you want to doubt someone's discretion, doubt someone else."

"Thank you, sir," murmured Henry, setting up the brandy glasses on the sideboard.

Sand said, "The trouble, gentlemen, is that I am suspected of a crime."

"What kind of crime?" demanded Trumbull. It was his duty, ordinarily, to grill the guests, and the look in his eye was that of a person who had no intention of missing his opportunity.

"Theft," said Sand. "There is a sum of money and a wad of negotiable bonds missing from a safe in my company. I'm one of those who knows the combination, and I've had a chance to open the safe unobserved. I also have a motive—I've had bad luck at the races and needed cash urgently. So it doesn't look good for me."

Gonzalo said eagerly, "But he didn't do it. That's the point. He didn't do it."

Avalon twirled the half drink he was not going to finish and said, "I think in the interest of coherence we ought to allow Mr. Sand to tell his story."

"Yes," said Trumbull, "how do *you* know he didn't do it, Mario?"

"That's the whole point, damn it. He *says* he didn't do it," replied Gonzalo, "and if he says so, that's good enough for me. Maybe not for a court, but it's good enough for anyone who knows him. I've heard him admit enough rotten things that other people wouldn't—"

"Suppose I ask him myself, okay?" said Trumbull. "*Did* you take the stuff, Mr. Sand?"

Sand paused. His blue eyes flicked from face to face, then he said, "Gentlemen, I am telling the absolute truth. I did not take the cash or the bonds."

Halsted passed his hand upward over his forehead, as though trying to clear away doubts.

"Mr. Sand," he said, "you seem to have a position of some trust. You can get into a safe with negotiable assets in it. Yet you play the horses."

"Lots of people do."

"And lose."

"I didn't quite plan it that way."

"But don't you risk losing your job?"

"My advantage, sir, is that I am employed by my uncle, who is aware of my weakness, but who also knows I don't lie. He knew I had the means and the opportunity to steal, and he knew I had debts. He also knew I had recently paid off my gambling debts. I told him so. Yet the circumstantial evidence against me looked bad.

But then he asked me directly if I was responsible for the loss and I told him exactly what I told you: I did not take the cash or the bonds. Since he knows me well, he believes me."

"How were you able to pay off your gambling debts?" said Avalon.

"Because a long shot came through. That happens, too, sometimes. It happened shortly before the theft was discovered and I paid off the bookies."

"But then you didn't have a motive," said Gonzalo.

"I can't say that. The theft might have been committed as long as two weeks before its discovery. No one looked in that particular drawer in the safe for that period of time—except the thief, of course. It could be argued that after I took the cash and bonds, the horse came through and made the theft unnecessary—too late."

"It might also be argued," said Halsted, "that you took the money in order to place a large bet on the horse."

"The bet wasn't that large, and I had other sources. But, yes, it could also be argued that way."

Trumbull broke in, "But if you still have your job, as I suppose you do, and if your uncle isn't prosecuting you, as I assume he isn't— Has he notified the police at all?"

"No, he can absorb the loss and he feels the police will only try to pin it on me. He knows that what I have told him is true."

"Then what's the problem, for God's sake?"

"There's simply no one else who could have done it. My uncle can't think of any other way of accounting for the theft. Nor, for that matter, can I. And as long as he can't see any alternative, there will always be a residuum of uneasiness, of suspicion, in his mind. He will always keep his eye on me. He will always be reluctant to trust me. I'll keep my job, but I'll never be promoted; and I may be made uncomfortable enough to be forced to resign. If I do, I can't count on a wholehearted recommendation, and from an uncle, a half-hearted one would be ruinous."

Rubin was frowning. "So you came here, Mr. Sand, because Gonzalo said we solve mysteries. You want us to tell you who really took the stuff."

Sand shrugged. "Maybe not. I don't even know if I can give you enough information. It's not as though you're detectives who can go to the scene of the crime and make inquiries. If you could just tell me how it *might* have been done—even if it's far-fetched, that would help. If I could go to my uncle and say, 'Uncle, it might have been done this way, mightn't it?' Even if he couldn't be sure, even if he couldn't ever get the money and bonds back, it would at least spread the suspicion. He wouldn't have the eternal nagging thought that I was the *only possible* thief."

"Well," said Avalon, "we can try to be logical, I suppose. How about the other people who work with you and your uncle? Would any of them need money badly?"

Sand shook his head. "Enough to risk the possible consequences of being caught? I don't know. One of them might be in debt, or one might be paying blackmail, or one might be greedy, or just had the opportunity and acted on impulse. If I were a detective I could go about asking questions, or I could track down documents, or whatever it is they do. As it is—"

"Of course," said Avalon, "we can't do that either. —Now you say you had both means and opportunity. Did anyone else have them?"

"At least three people could have got into the safe more easily than I and got away with it more easily, but not one of them knew the combination, and the safe wasn't broken into; that's certain. There are two people besides my uncle and myself who know the combination, but one has been hospitalized over the entire period in question and the other is such an old and reliable member of the firm that to suspect him seems unthinkable."

"Aha," said Mario Gonzalo, "there's our man right there."

"You've been reading too many Agatha Christies," said Rubin. "The fact of the matter is that in almost every crime on record, the most suspicious person turns out to be the criminal."

"That's beside the point," said Halsted, "and too dull besides. What we have here is a pure exercise in logic. Let's have Mr. Sand tell us everything he knows about every member of the firm, and we can all try to see if there's any way in which we can work out motive, means, and opportunity for some other person."

"Oh, hell," said Trumbull, "who says it has to be *one* person? So someone's in a hospital. Big deal. The telephone exists. He phones the combination to a confederate."

"All right, all right," said Halsted hastily, "we're bound to think up all sorts of possibilities and some may be more plausible than others. After we've thrashed them out, Mr. Sand can choose the most plausible and tell it to his uncle."

"May I speak, sir?" Henry spoke so quickly, and at a sound level so much higher than his usual murmur, that everyone turned to face him.

Henry said, this time softly, "Although I'm not a Black Widower—"

"Not so," said Rubin. "You *know* you're a Black Widower. In fact, you're the only one who's never missed a single meeting."

"Then may I point out, gentlemen, that if Mr. Sand carries your conclusion, whatever it may be, to his uncle, he will be carrying the proceedings of this meeting beyond the walls of this room."

There was an uncomfortable silence. Halsted said, "In the interest of saving an innocent person's reputation, surely—"

Henry shook his head gently. "But it would be at the cost of spreading suspicion to one or more other people, who might also be innocent."

Avalon said, "Henry's got something there. We seem to be stymied."

"Unless," said Henry, "we can come to a definite conclusion that will satisfy the club and will not involve the outside world."

"What do you have in mind, Henry?" asked Trumbull.

"If I may explain—I was, as Mr. Gonzalo said before dinner, interested to meet someone who never tells a lie."

"Now come, Henry," said Rubin, "you're pathologically honest yourself. You know you are. That's been established more than once."

"That may be so," said Henry, "but I *do* tell lies."

"Do you doubt Sand? Do you think he's lying?" said Rubin.

"I assure you—" began Sand, almost in anguish.

"No," said Henry, "I believe that every word Mr. Sand has said is true. He didn't take the money or the bonds. He is the logical one at whom suspicion points. His career may be ruined. His career, on the other hand, may not be ruined if some reasonable alternative explanation can be found, even if that does not actually lead to a solution. And, since he can think of no reasonable alternative himself, he wants us to help find one for him. I am convinced, gentlemen, that all this is true."

Sand nodded. "Well, thank you."

"And yet," said Henry, "what is truth? For instance, Mr. Trumbull, I think that your habit of perpetually arriving late with a cry of 'Scotch and soda for a dying man' is rude, unnecessary, and, worse yet, has grown boring. I suspect others here feel the same."

Trumbull flushed, but Henry went on firmly, "Yet if, under ordinary circumstances, I were asked whether I disapproved of it, I would say I did not. Strictly speaking, that would be a lie, but I like you for other reasons, Mr. Trumbull, that far outweigh this verbal trick of yours; so telling the strict truth, which would imply a dislike for you, would end up being a greater lie. Therefore I lie to express a truth—my liking for you."

Trumbull muttered, "I'm not sure I like your way of liking, Henry."

Henry said, "Or consider Mr. Halsted's limerick on the first book of the *Iliad*. Mr. Avalon quite rightly said that Achilleus is the correct name of the hero, or even Akhilleus with a 'k,' I suppose, to suggest the correct sound. But then Mr. Rubin pointed out that the truth would seem like a typographical error and spoil the effect of the limerick. Again, literal truth creates a problem.

"Mr. Sand said that all lies arise out of a desire for self-protection or out of respect for social conventions. But we cannot always ignore self-protection and social conventions. If we cannot lie, we must make the truth lie for us."

Gonzalo said, "You're not making sense, Henry."

"I think I am, Mr. Gonzalo. Few people listen to exact words, and many a literal truth tells a lie by implication. Who should know that better than a person who always tells the literal truth?"

Sand's pale cheeks were less pale, or his red tie was reflecting more color upward. He said, "What the hell are you implying?"

"I would like to ask you just one question, Mr. Sand? If the members of the club are willing, of course."

"I don't care if they are or not," said Sand, glowering at Henry. "If you take that tone I might not choose to answer."

"You may not have to," said Henry. "The point is that each time you deny having committed the crime, you deny it in precisely the same words. I couldn't help but notice since I made up my mind to listen to your exact words as soon as I heard that you never lied. Each time, you said, 'I did not take the cash or the bonds.' "

"And that is perfectly true," said Sand loudly.

"I'm sure it is, or you wouldn't have said so," said Henry. "Now this is the question I would like to ask you. Did you, by any chance, take the cash *and* the bonds?"

There was a short silence. Then Sand rose and said, "I'll get my coat now. Goodbye. I remind you all that nothing said here can be repeated outside."

When Sand was gone, Trumbull said, "Well, I'll be damned."

To which Henry replied, "Perhaps not, Mr. Trumbull. Don't despair."

Joyce Porter

Dover Does Some Spadework

S. S. Van Dine's Philo Vance was once described as the fictional detective one loved to hate. It might be said that Joyce Porter's Chief Inspector Wilfred Dover is the fictional detective one hates to love. The snarling, scowling, glaring, growling, grumbling, grunting, groaning, sneering, scoffing man from Scotland Yard may be a sloppy sleuth (clothingwise) and an invidious investigator (personalitywise), but as a detective he's, no question about it, one of a kind and no one else would dare create another! . .

Detective: CHIEF INSPECTOR DOVER

"You're supposed to be a detective, aren't you?"

Chief Inspector Dover—unwashed, unshaved, still in his dressing gown and more than half asleep—stared sullenly across the kitchen table at his wife. The great man was not feeling at his best. "I'm on leave," he pointed out resentfully as he spooned a half pound of sugar into his tea. "Supposed to be having a rest."

"All right for some," muttered Mrs. Dover crossly. She slapped down a plate of bacon, eggs, tomatoes, mushrooms, sausages, and fried bread in front of her husband.

Dover had been sitting with his knife and fork at the ready but now he poked disconsolately among the goodies. "No kidney?"

"You want it with jam on, you do!"

Dover responded to this disappointment with a grunt. "Besides," he said a few minutes later when he was wiping the egg yolk off his chin with the back of his hand, "I'm Murder Squad. You can't expect me to go messing around with piddling things like somebody nicking your garden tools. Ring up the local coppers if something's gone missing."

"And a fine fool I'd look, wouldn't I?" Mrs. Dover sat down and

310

poured out her own cup of tea. "My husband a Chief Inspector at Scotland Yard and me phoning the local police station for help! And I told you, Wilf—nobody stole anything. They just broke in."

Dover considerately remembered his wife's oft-reiterated injunctions and licked the knife clean of marmalade before sticking it in the butter. Well, it didn't do to push the old girl too far. "It's like asking Picasso to decorate the back bedroom for you, you see," he explained amid a spray of toast crumbs. "And if there's nothing actually missing. . ."

"Two can play at that game, you know." Mrs. Dover sounded ominously like a woman who had got all four aces up her sleeve.

A frown of sudden anxiety creased Dover's hitherto untroubled brow. "Whadderyemean?" he asked nervously.

Mrs. Dover ignored the question. "Have another piece of toast," she invited with grim humor. "Help yourself. Enjoy your breakfast. Make the most of it while it's here!"

"Oh, 'strewth!" groaned Dover, knowing only too well what was coming.

Mrs. Dover patted her hair into place. "If you can't do a bit of something for me, Wilf," she said with feigned reasonableness, "you may wake up one of these fine days and find that I can't do something for you. Like standing over a hot stove all the live-long day!"

"But that's your job," protested Dover. "Wives are supposed to look after their husbands' comfort. It's the law!"

But Mrs. Dover wasn't listening. "I wasn't brought up just to be your head cook and bottle washer," she claimed dreamily. "My parents had better things in mind for me than finishing up as your unpaid skivvy. Why"—she soared off misty-eyed into the realms of pure fantasy—"I might have been a concert pianist or a lady judge or a TV personality, if I hadn't met you."

"And pigs might fly," sniggered Dover, being careful to restrict his comment to the range of his own ears. "Well," he said aloud and making the promise, perhaps a mite too glibly, "I'll have a look at the shed for you. Later on. When the sun's had a chance to take the chill off things a bit."

Mrs. Dover was too battle-scarred a veteran of matrimony to be caught like that.

"Suit yourself, Wilf," she said equably. "Your lunch will be ready and waiting for you . . . just as soon as you come up with the answer." She began to gather up the dirty crockery. "And not before," she added thoughtfully . . .

"So that," snarled Dover, "is what I'm doing here! Since you were so gracious as to ask!"

Detective Sergeant MacGregor could only stand and stare. Almost any comment, he felt, was going to be open to misinterpretation.

But even a tactful silence gave no guarantee of immunity from Dover's quivering indignation.

"Cat got your tongue now, laddie?"

MacGregor suppressed a sigh. He didn't usually come calling when his boss was on leave, having more than enough of the old fool when they were at work in the normal way; but he needed a countersignature for his Expenses Claim Form and, since most of the money had been dispensed on Dover's behalf, it was only fitting that his uncouth signature should grace the document.

So when, at eleven o'clock, the sergeant had called at the Dovers' semidetached suburban residence, he had been quite prepared to find that His Nibs was still, on a cold and foggy December morning, abed. What he had not expected was Mrs. Dover's tightlipped announcement that her better half was to be found in the tool shed at the bottom of the garden. It had seemed a highly improbable state of affairs but, as MacGregor was now seeing for himself, it was true.

Dover, arrayed as for a funeral in his shabby black overcoat and his even shabbier bowler hat, was sunk dejectedly in a deck chair. He glared up at his sergeant. "Well, don't just stand there like a stick of Blackpool rock, you moron! Come inside and shut that damn door!"

Even with the door closed the tool shed was hardly a cosy spot, and MacGregor was gratified to notice that Dover's nose was already turning quite a pronounced blue. "Er—what exactly is the trouble, sir? Mrs. Dover wasn't actually very clear about why you were out here."

Dover cut the cackle with the ruthlessness of desperation. "She's got this idea in her stupid head that somebody bust their way into this shed during the past week and borrowed a spade. Silly cow!"

"I see," said MacGregor politely.

"I doubt it," sniffed Dover. "Seeing as how you're not married."

"A stolen spade, eh, sir?" For the first time MacGregor turned his attention to his surroundings and discovered to his amazement that he was standing in the middle of a vast collection of implements which, if hygiene and perfect order were anything to go by, wouldn't have looked out of place in a hospital operating theater. As MacGregor's gaze ran along the serried ranks of apparently brand-new tools he wondered what on earth they were used for. Surely not for the care and maintenance of that miserable strip of barren, cat-infested clay which lay outside between the shed and the house? Good heavens, they must have bought the things wholesale!

The walls were covered with hoes and rakes and forks and spades and trowels, all hung on special hooks and racks. A couple of shelves groaned under a load of secateurs, garden shears, seed trays, and a set of flower pots arranged in descending order of size, while the floor was almost totally occupied by wheelbarrows, watering cans, and a well-oiled cylinder lawn mower. MacGregor only tore his mind away from his inventory of sacks of peat and fertilizer when he realized that the oracle had said something. "I beg your pardon, sir?"

"I said it wasn't stolen," snapped Dover. "It was only borrowed." The lack of comprehension on MacGregor's face appeared to infuriate the Chief Inspector. "That one, you idiot!"

MacGregor followed the direction of Dover's thumb which was indicating the larger of two stainless-steel spades. He leaned forward to examine the mirror-like blade more closely. "Er—how does Mrs. Dover know it was—er—borrowed, sir?"

Dover blew wearily down his nose. "Why don't you use your bloomin' eyes?" he asked. "Look at it all!" He flapped a cold-looking hand at the tools on the wall. "They're all hanging on their own hooks, aren't they? Right! Well, every bloody Tuesday morning with-out fail Mrs. Dover comes down here and turns 'em all round. Get it? Regular as ruddy clockwork. One week all these spades and trowels and things have got their backs facing the wall and then, the next week, they've got the backs of their blades facing out to the middle of the shed. Follow me?"

"I understand perfectly, thank you, sir," said MacGregor stiffly.

Dover scowled. "Then you're lucky," he growled, "because it's more than I do. She reckons it evens out the wear, you know. Silly cow! Anyhow!"—he heaved himself up in his deck chair again and jerked his thumb at the spade—"that thing is hanging the wrong way round. Savvy? So that means somebody moved it and that means, since this shed is kept locked up tighter than the Bank of England, that somebody must have broken in to do it."

He sank back and the deck chair groaned and creaked in under-standable protest. "Mrs. Dover's developed into a very nervous sort of woman over the years."

MacGregor's agile mind had already solved the problem. "But, if

you'll forgive me saying so, sir, the spade *isn't* the wrong way round."
He moved across to the appropriate wall so as to be able to demonstrate his thesis in a way that even a muttonhead like Dover could
understand. "All the tools are currently hanging with their backs
turned towards the shed wall, aren't they? With the prongs and
the—er—sharp edges pointing outward towards us. Right? Well, the
spade in question is hanging on the wall in just the same way as all
the other tools, isn't it? So, it's *not* hanging the wrong way round,
unless of course"—he ventured on a rather patronizing little chuckle—"Mrs. Dover has got a special routine for that particular spade."

Dover didn't bother opening his eyes. It would be a bad day, he
reflected, when he couldn't outsmart young MacGregor with both
hands tied behind his back. "She killed a spider with it last week,"
he explained sleepily. "When she was in doing a security check. God
knows what a spider was doing in this place, apart from starving
to death, but there it was. On the floor. Mrs. Dover's allergic to
spiders, so she grabbed that spade and flattened the brute."

"I see, sir," said MacGregor who had not, hitherto, suspected that
Mrs. Dover was a woman of violence.

"Then," said Dover, pulling his overcoat collar up closer round his
ears, "the spade had to be washed, didn't it? And disinfected, too,
I shouldn't wonder." He tried to rub some warmth back into his
frozen fingers. "Well, nobody in their right senses, it seems, would
dream of hanging a newly washed spade with its back up against
a shed wall. In case of rust. So Mrs. Dover broke the habit of a
lifetime and replaced the spade the wrong way round so that the air
could circulate freely about it."

"I see," said MacGregor for the second time in as many minutes.
"Our mysterious borrower, when he returned the spade, then un-
derstandably hung it back on its hook in the same way that all the
other implements were hung—with their backs to the wall. Yes"—he
nodded his head—"a perfectly natural mistake to make."

" 'Strewth, don't you start!"

"Sir?"

Dover wriggled impatiently in his deck chair. "Talking as though
this joker really exists. He damn well doesn't!"

"Then how do you explain the fact that the spade is hanging the
wrong way round, sir?"

"I don't!" howled Dover. "I wouldn't be sitting here freezing to
death if I could, would I, dumbbell?"

There was a moment's pause after this outburst. By rights

MacGregor should have emulated Mrs. Dover's way of dealing with pests by seizing hold of the nearest sufficiently heavy instrument and laying Dover's skull open with it; but the Metropolitan Police do too good a job on their young recruits. MacGregor swallowed all his finer impulses and concentrated hard on trying to be a detective. "Are there any signs of breaking in, sir?"

There was a surly grunt from the deck chair. "Search me!"

MacGregor crossed the shed and opened the door to examine the large padlock which had been left hooked carelessly in the staple. It looked as though it had recently been ravaged by some sharp-toothed carnivore.

Dover had got up to stretch his legs. He squinted over MacGregor's shoulder. "I had a job getting the damn thing open."

Oh, well, it wasn't the first time that Dover had ridden roughshod over what might have been a vital clue, and it wouldn't be the last. Just for the hell of it, MacGregor gave Dame Fortune's wheel a half-hearted whirl. "I suppose you didn't happen to notice when you unlocked the padlock, sir, if—"

Dover was not the man to waste time nurturing slender hopes. "No," he said, "I didn't."

MacGregor closed the door. "Well, presumably our chappie knows how to pick a lock. That's some sort of lead."

"Garn," scoffed Dover, "they learn that with their mother's milk these days." He began to waddle back to his deck chair. "Got any smokes on you, laddie?" he asked. "I'm dying for a puff."

MacGregor often used to bewail the fact that he couldn't include all the cigarettes he provided for Dover on his swindle sheet but, as usual, he handed his packet over with a fairly good grace. He waited patiently until Dover's clumsy fingers had extracted a crumpled coffin nail and then gave him a light.

"Fetch us one of those plant pots," ordered Dover. "A little one."

A look of horror flashed across MacGregor's face. A plant pot? Surely Dover wasn't actually going to—

"For an ashtray, you bloody fool!" snarled Dover. "Mrs. Dover'll do her nut if she finds we've made a mess all over her floor."

MacGregor felt quite weak with the relief. "I've been thinking, sir," he said.

"The age of miracles is not yet past," snickered Dover.

MacGregor turned the other cheek with a practised hand. "We can deduce quite a bit about our Mr. Borrower."

"Such as what?" Dover leered up suspiciously at his sergeant.

MacGregor ticked the points off on well-manicured fingers. "The spade must have been purloined for some illicit purpose." He saw from the vacant look on Dover's face that he'd better watch his language. "If the fellow just wanted a spade for digging potatoes or what-have-you, sir, he'd have just asked for it, wouldn't he? Taking a spade without permission and picking a padlock to get at it must add up to some criminal activity being concerned, don't you agree, sir?"

Dover nodded cautiously, unwilling to commit himself too far at this stage. "You reckon he nicked the spade to dig something up?" he asked, eyes bulging greedily. "Like buried treasure?"

"I was thinking more along the lines of him wanting to hide something, actually, sir. By concealing it in the ground. He returned the spade to the shed, you see. Surely, if he was merely digging up buried treasure, he wouldn't have gone to the trouble of putting the spade back carefully in its place?"

"*Burying* buried treasure?" Dover, dribbling ash down the front of his overcoat, tried this idea on for size.

"Or a dead body, sir," said MacGregor. "That strikes me as a more likely explanation."

Dover's heavy jowls settled sullenly over where his shirt collar would have been if he'd been wearing one. For a member (however unwanted) of Scotland Yard's Murder Squad, dead bodies were in his mind inextricably connected with work, and work always tended to bring Dover out in a cold sweat. He tried to concentrate on an occupation more to his taste: nit-picking. "How do you know it's a 'he'?" he demanded truculently. "It could just as well be a woman."

MacGregor was so anxious to display his superior powers of reasoning and deduction that he, perhaps, showed insufficient regard for Dover's slower wits. "Oh, I doubt that, sir! I don't know whether you've noticed, but Mrs. Dover had two spades hanging on the wall. The one that was 'borrowed' and a smaller one which is called, I believe, a border spade. You see? Now, surely if our intruder were a woman, she would have taken the lighter, more manageable border spade?"

Dover's initial scowl of fury was gradually replaced by a rather constipated expression, a sure indication that his thought processes were beginning to swing into action.

MacGregor waited anxiously.

"A *young* man!" said Dover at last.

"Sir?"

"You'd hardly find an old-age pensioner nipping over garden fences and picking locks and digging bloomin' great holes big enough to take a dead body, would you? 'Strewth, what you know about the real world, laddie, wouldn't cover a pinhead. We've had a frost out here for weeks! The ground's as hard as iron."

MacGregor's unabashed astonishment at this feat of unsolicited reasoning was not exactly flattering, but Dover, the bit now firmly between his National Health teeth, didn't appear to notice.

"And I'll tell you something else, laddie," he went on, "if our joker borrowed my missus's spade to bury a dead body with, I'll lay you a pound to a penny that it's his wife!"

MacGregor perched himself gingerly on the edge of a wheelbarrow, having first inspected and then passed it for cleanliness. Mrs. Dover certainly ran a tight garden shed. There was another deck chair stacked tidily in a corner but, since it was still in its plastic wrapper, MacGregor didn't feel he could really make use of it.

Having settled himself as comfortably as he could, MacGregor gave his full attention to putting the damper on Dover's enthusiasm. "Oh, steady on, sir," he advised.

"Steady on—nothing!" Dover had his fixations and he wasn't going to have any pipsqueak of a sergeant talking him out of them. In Dover's book, wives were always killed by their husbands. This was a simple rule of thumb which had more than a little basis in fact and saved a great deal of trouble all round—except for the odd innocent husband, of course, but no system is perfect. "A strapping young man with a dead body to get rid of, nicking a neighbor's spade. Use your brains, laddie, who else could it be except his wife?"

MacGregor retaliated by taking a leaf out of Dover's book and, instead of dealing with the main issue, quibbled over a minor detail. "A *neighbor's* spade, sir? I don't think we can go quite as far as—"

Dover went over his sergeant's objection like a steamroller over a cream puff. "Well, he didn't bloomin' well come over by Tube from Balham, did he, you nitwit? Twice? Once to get the bloody spade and once to put it back? Of course he comes from somewhere round here. He wouldn't have known about our tool shed otherwise, would he?"

Without really thinking about it, MacGregor had pulled his notebook out. He looked up from an invitingly blank page that was just aching to be written on. "Actually, sir, I have been wondering why anybody would pick on this particular tool shed to break into in the first place."

Dover had no doubts. "Spite!" he said.

"There must be dozens of garden sheds round here, sir. Why choose this one?"

Dover belched with touching lack of inhibition. His exile was playing havoc with his insides. "Could be pure ruddy chance," he grunted.

"He had to prize open a good-quality padlock to get in here, sir. There must be plenty of sheds that aren't even locked."

Dover turned a lacklustre eye on his sergeant. "All right, Mr. Clever Boots, so what's the answer?"

"It's because Mrs. Dover's tools are all kept so spotlessly clean, sir, and in such immaculate order. I'm sure our unwelcome visitor thought he'd be able to take the spade and return it without it ever being noticed that it had so much as been touched. You see, if the shed were dirty and dusty and untidy and covered, say, with cobwebs, it would be virtually impossible to borrow a tool and put it back without disturbing something. Do you follow me, sir? He'd be bound to leave a trail of clues behind him. But here"—MacGregor swept an admiring hand round the shed—"our chap had every reason to believe that, as long as he cleaned the spade and replaced it neatly on the wall with all the others, no suspicions would ever be aroused."

"He was reckoning without my old woman," said Dover with a kind of gloomy pride. "Like a bloodhound. More so, if anything." He shook off his reminiscent mood. "Anyhow, what you're saying just goes to show for sure that this joker is living somewhere round here. That's how he knows this is the cleanest garden shed in the country."

He broke off to stare disgustedly around him. "She got all this lot with trading stamps, you know. It's taken her years and years. Never asks me if there's anything *I* want, mind you," he mused resentfully, "though they've definitely got long woolly underpants because I've seen 'em in the damn catalogue."

"I agree our chap probably does live near here, sir," said MacGregor, who'd only been debating the point just to keep his end up. "It's hard to see how he could have known about the tool shed or the tools otherwise. On the other hand, he must be something of a newcomer."

Dover snapped his fat fingers for another cigarette and used the time it took to furnish him with one in trying to puzzle out what MacGregor was getting at. He was forced to concede defeat. "Regular little Sherlock Holmes, aren't you?" he sneered.

Privately, MacGregor thought he was a jolly sight smarter than this supposed paragon, but he wasn't fool enough to confide such an opinion to Dover. "Our Mr. Borrower would hardly have come breaking into this particular tool shed, sir, if he'd known that you were a policeman. A Chief Inspector from New Scotland Yard, in fact."

Dover, almost invisible in a cloud of tobacco smoke, mulled this over. He was rather taken with the idea that all the barons of the underworld might be going in fear and trepidation of him. "He might be potty," he observed generously. "Otherwise he'd know he couldn't hope to pull the wool over the eyes of a highly trained observer like me."

Another thought struck him and he flopped back in his deck chair, suffering from shock. " 'Strewth," he gasped, "it's only a couple of hours since I first heard about this crime, and look at me now! I've solved it, near as damn it! All we've got to do is find a young, newly married villain who's recently moved into the district. And I'll lay odds he's living in that new block of flats they've built just across the way. They've got the dregs of society in that place.

"So, all we've got to do now is get onto the local cop shop and tell 'em to send a posse of coppers round to make a few inquiries. Soon as they find somebody who fits the bill, all they've got to do is ask him to produce his wife. If he can't—well, Bob's your uncle, eh? And that," added Dover, seeing that MacGregor was dying to interrupt and being determined to thwart him, "is why he had to borrow a spade in the first place! Because people who live in flats don't have gardens, and if they don't have gardens they don't have gardening tools, either!"

MacGregor put his notebook away and stood up. "Oh, I don't think our man is living in a flat, do you, sir?"

Dover's eye immediately became glassy with suspicion, resentment, and chronic dyspepsia. "Why not?"

"He'd have nowhere to bury the body, sir."

Dover's scowl grew muddier. "He could have shoved it in somebody else's garden, couldn't he?" he asked, reasonably enough.

MacGregor shook his head. "Far too risky, sir. Digging a hole big enough to inter a body would take an hour or more, I should think. Now, it would be bad enough undertaking a job like that in one's own garden, but in somebody else's—" MacGregor pursed his lips in a silent whistle and shook his head again. "No, I doubt it, sir, I really do. I think we must take it, as a working hypothesis, that—"

"He could have planted her in the garden of an empty house," said

Dover doggedly and, as a gesture of defiance against society, dropped his cigarette end into the empty watering can.

"Well, I suppose it's a possibility, sir," said MacGregor with a sigh, "and I agree that we ought to bear it in mind. The thing is, though, that you're hardly in the depths of the country out here, are you? I mean—well, everywhere round here does tend to be a bit visible, doesn't it?"

There are plenty of suburban mortgage holders who would have taken deep umbrage at such a damaging assessment of their property, but Dover was not cursed with that kind of pride. He simply reacted by nodding his head in sincere agreement. "Too right, laddie!" he rumbled.

"There's another point that's been puzzling me, sir," MacGregor said. "Why did our chap go to all this trouble to *borrow* a spade? The way he broke into this shed may carry all the hallmarks of a professional job, but he was still running a terrible risk. Anybody might have seen him and blown the whistle on him."

"He'd do it after dark," said Dover, "and, besides, you don't go in for murder if you aren't prepared to chance your arm a bit. And what choice did he have? With a dead body on his hands and no spade? He could hardly start digging his hole with a knife and fork."

"He could have bought a spade, sir."

"Eh?"

"He could have bought a spade," repeated MacGregor, quite prepared for the look of horror that flashed across Dover's pasty face. The Chief Inspector regarded the actual purchasing of anything as a desperate step, only to be contemplated when all the avenues of begging, borrowing, and stealing had been exhaustively explored. "It wouldn't have cost all that much, sir, and it would have been a much less hazardous operation."

Dover wrinkled up his nose. "The shops were shut?" he suggested. "Or he didn't have any money?"

"A professional villain, sir? That doesn't sound very likely, does it? And if he's going to nick something, why not nick the money? A handful of cash wouldn't be as compromising, if something went wrong, as Mrs. Dover's stainless-steel spade would be."

Dover shivered and shoved his hands as deep as they would go in his overcoat pockets. The shed wasn't built for sitting in and there was a howling gale blowing under the door. The sooner he got out of this dump and back into the warmth and comfort of his own home, the better. "That's why he didn't buy a spade!"

"Sir?"

"Put yourself in the murderer's shoes, laddie. You've just knocked your missus off and you're proposing to get rid of the body by burying it in a hole. Sooner or later people are going to come around asking questions. Well, I'd have said the last thing you wanted was a bloomin' spade standing there and shouting the odds. No, borrowing the spade and putting it back again shows our chap has a bit of class about him. He's somebody who can see further than the end of his nose. An opponent," added Dover with a smirk, "worthy of my steel. Well"—he raised a pair of motheaten eyebrows at his sergeant—"what are you waiting for? Christmas?"

Dover sighed heavily and dramatically. "It's no wonder you've never made Inspector," he sneered. "You're as thick as two planks. Look, laddie, what's a detective got to do if he wants to be everybody's little white-haired boy, eh?"

MacGregor wondered what on earth they were supposed to be talking about now. "Well, I don't quite know, sir," he said uncertainly. "Er—solve his cases?"

" 'Strewth!" snarled Dover, giving vent to his opinion with unwonted energy. "Look, you know what they're like, all Commissioners and Commanders and what-have-you. They're forever yakking about a good detective being the one who goes out and finds his own cases, aren't they?"

"Oh, I see what you mean, sir."

"Well, look at me!"

"Sir?"

"I'm on leave, aren't I?" asked Dover, warming gleefully to the task of blowing his own trumpet. "But I don't go around sitting with my ruddy feet up! On the contrary, from the very faintest of hints—the sort any other jack would have brushed aside as not worth his attention—I've uncovered a dastardly murder that nobody else even knows has been committed."

Too late MacGregor saw the danger signals. "But, sir—"

"But, nothing!" snapped Dover. "With the information I'm giving 'em, the local police'll have our laddie under lock and key before you can say Sir Robert Peel!"

"But we can't go to the local police, sir," said MacGregor, breaking out in a sweat at the mere idea. "After all, we've only been theorizing."

Dover's face split into an evil grin. "Of course *we* are not going to the local police, laddie," he promised soothingly. "Just you!" There was a brief interval while the old fool laughed himself nearly sick. "Ask for Detective Superintendent Andy Andrews and mention my name—clearly! Tell him what we've come up with so far—that we're after a young, agile newlywed villain who's just moved into a house in this area. A specialist in picking locks."

"Oh, sir!" wailed MacGregor.

"There can't be all that many jokers knocking around who'd fit that bill," Dover went on. "And, if there are, Andrews will soon spot our chap because he'll be the one with a newly turned patch of soil in his garden and no wife."

"You're not serious, sir?"

"Never been more serious in my life," growled Dover. "And I've just thought of something else. If they're newcomers to the district, that's why nobody's reported the wife missing. She won't have had time to establish a routine yet or have made any close friends. Her husband will be able to give any rubbishy explanation for her absence." He realized that MacGregor was still standing there. "What's got into you, laddie? You're usually so damn keen they could use you for mustard!"

"It's just that I don't feel we're quite ready, sir."

But Dover wasn't having any argument about it. He cut ruthlessly through his sergeant's feeble protests. "And stick to old Andrews like a limpet, see? Don't move from his side till you've got the handcuffs on our chummie—I don't want Andrews stealing my thunder. I've solved this case and I'm going to get the glory for it. Well"—he glared up at a very shrinking violet—"what are you waiting for now? A Number Nine bus?"

MacGregor answered out of a bone-dry throat. "No, sir."

"Leave us your cigarettes," said Dover, not the man to get his priorities mixed. "You'll not be having time to smoke."

Reluctantly MacGregor handed over his pack of cigarettes and even found a spare packet of matches. When, however, he'd got his hand on the door handle he paused. "Er—you're staying here, sir?"

In all the excitement Dover had not overlooked his own personal predicament. "Call in at the house on your way out and tell Mrs. Dover that I've solved the problem of her bloody spade and that you're off to arrest the bloke for murder. I'll give you five minutes' start, so she's got time to digest the good news, and then I'll follow you. And I don't mind telling you, laddie"—he surveyed the scene of his exile with a marked lack of enthusiasm—"I'll be glad to get back to my own armchair by the fire." He waggled his head in mild bewilderment. "Do you know, she's never let me come in here on my own before. Funny, isn't it?"

Long before the allotted five minutes was up, however, Dover was infuriated to discover that Sergeant MacGregor was coming back down the garden path at the double. Extricating himself from his deck chair, he dragged the door open and voiced his feelings in a penetrating bellow. "That damn woman! Is she never satisfied?"

MacGregor glanced around nervously, although the silent, unseen watchers weren't his neighbors and he really didn't care what they thought about the Dovers. "It's not that, actually, sir."

"Then what is it, *actually?*" roared Dover, mimicking his sergeant's minor public-school accent.

"It's a message from Mrs. Dover, sir."

Dover knew when he was being softened up for the breaking of bad news. "Spit it out, laddie," he said bleakly.

MacGregor grinned foolishly out of sheer embarrassment. "It's just that she's remembered she turned the spade round herself, sir. Mrs. Dover, I mean. It had quite slipped her mind, she says, but she popped down to the shed before she went to church on Sunday morning to count how many tie-on labels she'd got and the spade being hung the wrong way round got on her nerves, she says. And since she reckoned it must have dried off after being washed, she—"

"You can spare me the details," said Dover as all his dreams of fame and glory crumbled to dust and ashes in his mouth.

"Mrs. Dover was going to come down and tell you herself, sir, when she'd finished washing the leaves of the aspidistras."

Dover seemed indifferent to such graciousness. "You didn't get in touch with Superintendent Andrews, did you?"

MacGregor shook his head. "There didn't seem much point, sir. As it was Mrs. Dover who changed the spade back to its proper position, well"—he shrugged—"that did rather seem to be that. Nobody broke into the shed to borrow the spade and, if nobody borrowed the spade, that means there was no dead body to be buried. And if there's no dead body to be buried, that means that we haven't got a wife murderer and—"

But Dover had switched off. He had many faults, but crying over spilt milk wasn't one of them. He was already lumbering out through the shed door, his thoughts turning to the future. He tossed a final question back over his shoulder.

"Did she say what she was giving me for my dinner?"

Ellery Queen

The Adventure of the
Three R's

Ellery Queen's CALENDAR OF CRIME, *published in 1952, is a series of twelve stories, each story dealing with an important aspect of a different month of the year. For example, January offers a New Year's mystery, February a tale of George Washington's Birthday, and so on through December, which is a Christmas detective story. Here is the return-to-school month, the September story, about Mr. Chipp, a member of the faculty of Barlowe College, Barlowe, Missouri, and the strange events that preceded his summer vacation . . .*

Detective: ELLERY QUEEN

Hail Missouri! which is North and also South, upland and riverbottom, mountain, plain, factory, and farm. Hail Missouri! for MacArthur's corncob and Pershing's noble mule. Hail! for Hannibal and Mark Twain, for Excelsior Springs and James, for Barlowe and . . . Barlowe? Barlowe is the site of Barlowe College.

Barlowe College is the last place in Missouri you would go to (Missouri, which yields to no State in the historic redness of its soil) if you yearned for a lesson in the fine art of murder. In fact, the subject being introduced, it is the rare Show Me Stater who will not say, with an informative wink, that Barlowe is the last place in Missouri, and leave all the rest unsaid. But this is a smokeroom witticism, whose origin is as murky as the waters of the Big Muddy. It may well first have been uttered by the alumnus of some Missouri university whose attitude toward learning is steeped in the traditional embalming fluid—whereas, at little Barlowe, learning leaps: Jove and jive thunder in duet, profound sociological lessons are drawn from *Li'l Abner* and *Terry and the Pirates*, and in the seminars of the Philosophy Department you are almost certain to find Faith, as a matter of pedagogic policy, paired with Hope.

Scratch a great work and find a great workman.

Dr. Isaiah St. Joseph A. Barlowe, pressed for vital statistics, once remarked that while he was old enough to have been a Founder, still he was not so old as to have calcified over a mound of English ivy. But the good dean jested; he is as perennial as a sundial. And the truth is, in the garden where he labors, there is no death and a great deal of healthy laughter.

One might string his academic honors after him, like dutiful beads; one might recount the extraordinary tale of how, in the manner of Uther Pendragon, Dr. Barlowe bewitched some dumfounded Missourians and took a whole series of substantial buildings out of their pockets; one might produce a volume on the subject of his acolytes alone, who have sped his humanistic gospel into the far corners of the land. Alas, this far more rewarding reportage must await the service of one who has, at the very least, a thousand pages at his disposal. Here there is space merely to record that the liveliness of Barlowe's alarming approach to scholarship is totally the inspiration of Dr. Isaiah St. Joseph A. Barlowe.

Those who would instruct at Barlowe must pass a rather unusual entrance examination. The examination is conducted *in camera*, and its nature is as sacredly undisclosable as the Thirty-Third Rite; nevertheless, leaks have occurred, and it may be significant that in its course Dr. Barlowe employs a 16-millimeter motion-picture projector, a radio, a portable phonograph, one copy each of The Bible, *The Old Farmer's Almanac*, and *The Complete Sherlock Holmes*; and the latest issue of *The Congressional Record*—among others. During examinations the voices of Donald Duck and Young Widder Brown have been reported; and so on. It is all very puzzling, but perhaps not unconnected with the fact that visitors often cannot distinguish who are Barlowe students and who are Barlowe professors. Certainly a beard at Barlowe is no index of dignity; even the elderly among the faculty exude a zest more commonly associated with the fuzzy-chinned undergraduate.

So laughter and not harumphery is rampant upon the Gold and the Puce; and, if corpses dance macabre, it is only upon the dissection tables of Bio III, where the attitude toward extinction is roguishly empirical.

Then imagine—if you can—the impact upon Barlowe, not of epic murder as sung by the master troubadours of Classics I; not of romantic murder (Abbot, Anthony to Zangwill, Israel) beckoning from the rental shelves of The Campus Book Shop; but of murder loud and harsh.

Murder, as young Professor Bacon of the Biochemistry Department might say, with a stink.

The letter from Dr. Barlowe struck Ellery as remarkably woeful.

"One of my faculty has disappeared," wrote the President of Barlowe College, "and I cannot express to you, Mr. Queen, the extent of my apprehension. In short, I fear the worst.

"I am aware of your busy itinerary, but if you are at all informed regarding the institution to which I have devoted my life, you will grasp the full horror of our dilemma. We feel we have erected something here too precious to be befouled by the nastiness of the age; on the other hand, there are humane—not to mention legal—considerations. If, as I suspect, Professor Chipp has met with foul play, it occurred to me that we might investigate *sub rosa* and at least present the not altogether friendly world with *un mystère accompli*. In this way, much anguish may be spared us all.

"Can I prevail upon you to come to Barlowe quietly, and at once? I feel confident I speak for our Trustees when I say we shall have no difficulty about the coarser aspects of the association."

The letter was handwritten, in a hasty and nervous script which seemed to suggest guilty glances over the presidential shoulder.

It was all so at variance with what Ellery had heard about Dr. Isaiah St. Joseph A. Barlowe and his learned vaudeville show that he scribbled a note to Inspector Queen and ran. Nikki, clutching her invaluable notebook, ran with him.

Barlowe, Missouri lay torpid in the warm September sunshine. And the distant Ozarks seemed to be peering at Barlowe inquisitively.

"Do you suppose it's got out, Ellery?" asked Nikki *sotto voce* as a sluggish hack trundled them through the slumbering town. "It's all so still. Not like a college town at all."

"The fall term doesn't begin for another ten days," Ellery remarked.

They were whisked into Dr. Barlowe's sanctum.

"You'll forgive my not meeting you at the station," muttered the dean as he quickly shut the door. He was a lean and gray-thatched man with an Italianate face and lively black eyes whose present preoccupation did not altogether extinguish the lurking twinkle. Missouri's Petrarch, thought Ellery with a chuckle. As for Nikki, it was love at first sight. "Softly, softly—that must be our watchword."

"Just who is Professor Chipp, Dr. Barlowe?"

"American Lit. You haven't heard of Chipp's seminar on Poe? He's an authority—it's one of our more popular items."

"Poe," exclaimed Nikki. "Ellery, that should give you a personal interest in the case."

"Leverett Chisholm Chipp," nodded Ellery, remembering. "Monographs in *The Review* on the Poe prose. Enthusiasm and scholarship. That Chipp."

"He's been a Barlowe appendage for thirty years," said the dean. "We really couldn't go on without him."

"When was Professor Chipp last seen?"

Dr. Barlowe snatched his telephone. "Millie, send Ma Blinker in now. Ma runs the boarding house on the campus where old Chipp's had rooms ever since he came to Barlowe to teach, Mr. Queen. Ah, Ma! Come in. And shut the door."

Ma Blinker was a brawny old Missourian who looked as if she had been summoned to the council chamber from her Friday's batch of apple pies. But it was a landlady's eye she turned on the visitors from New York—an eye which did not surrender until Dr. Barlowe uttered a cryptic reassurance, whereupon it softened and became moist.

"He's an old love, the Professor is," she said brokenly. "Regular? Ye could set your watch by that man."

"I take it," murmured Ellery, "Chipp's regularity is relevant?"

Dr. Barlowe nodded. "Now, Ma, you're carrying on. And you with the blood of pioneers! Tell Mr. Queen all about it."

"The Professor," gulped Ma Blinker, "he owns a log cabin up in the Ozarks, 'cross the Arkansas line. Every year he leaves Barlowe first of July to spend his summer vacation in the cabin. First of July, like clockwork."

"Alone, Mrs. Blinker?"

"Yes, sir. Does all his writin' up there, he does."

"Literary textbooks," explained the dean. "Although summer before last, to my astonishment, Chipp informed me he was beginning a novel."

"First of July he leaves for the cabin, and one day after Labor Day he's back in Barlowe gettin' ready for the fall term."

"One day after Labor Day, Mr. Queen. Year in, year out. Unfailingly."

"And here 'tis the thirteenth of September and he ain't showed up in town!"

"Day after Labor Day. Ten days overdue."

"All this fuss," asked Nikki, "over a measly ten days?"

"Miss Porter, Chipp's being ten days late is as unlikely as—as my being Mrs. Hudson in disguise! Unlikelier. I was so concerned, Mr. Queen, I telephoned the Slater, Arkansas, authorities to send someone up to Chipp's cabin."

"Then he didn't simply linger there past his usual date?"

"I can't impress upon you too strongly the inflexibility of Chipp's habit-pattern. He did not. The Slater man found no sign of Chipp but his trunk."

"But I gathered from your letter, Doctor, that you had a more specific reason for suspecting—"

"And don't we!" Ma Blinker broke out frankly now in bosomy sobs. "I'd never have gone into the Professor's rooms—it was another of his rules—but Dr. Barlowe said I ought to when the Professor didn't show up, so I did, and—and—"

"Yes, Mrs. Blinker?"

"There on the rug, in front of his fireplace," whispered the landlady, "was a great . . . big . . . stain."

"A stain!" gasped Nikki. "A *stain?*"

"A bloodstain."

Ellery raised his brows.

"I examined it myself, Mr. Queen," said Dr. Barlowe nervously "It's—it's blood, I feel certain. And it's been on the rug for some time. We locked Chipp's rooms up again, and I wrote to you."

And although the September sun filled each cranny of the dean's office, it was a cold sun suddenly.

"Have you heard from Professor Chipp at all since July the first, Doctor?" asked Ellery with a frown.

Dr. Barlowe looked startled. "It's been his habit to send a few of us cards at least once during the summer recess . . ." He began to rummage excitedly through a pile of mail on his desk. "I've been away since early June myself. This has so upset me I . . . Why didn't I think of that? Ah, the trained mind . . . Mr. Queen, here it is!"

It was a picture postcard illustrating a mountain cascade of improbable blue surrounded by verdure of impossible green. The message and address were in a cramped and spidery script.

July 31.

Am rewriting my novel. It will be a huge surprise to you all.
Regards—

Chipp

"His 'novel' again," muttered Ellery. "Bears the postmark Slater,
Arkansas, July thirty-first of this year. Dr. Barlowe, was this card
written by Professor Chipp?"

"Unmistakably."

"Doesn't the writing seem awfully awkward to you, Ellery?" asked
Nikki, in the tradition of the detectival secretary.

"Yes. As if something were wrong with his hand."

"There is," sniffled Ma Blinker. "Middle and forefinger missin' to
the second joint—poor, poor old man!"

"Some accident in his youth, I believe."

Ellery rose. "May I see that stain on Chipp's rug, please?"

A man may leave more than his blood on his hearth; he may leave
his soul.

The blood was there, faded brown and hard, but so was Professor
Chipp, though *in absentia*.

The two small rooms overlooking the campus were as tidy as a
barrack. Chairs were rigidly placed. The bed was a sculpture. The
mantelpiece was a shopwindow display; each pipe in the rack had
been reamed and polished and laid away with a mathematical hand.
The papers in the pigeon holes of the old pine desk were ranged
according to size. Even the missing professor's books were disciplined: no volume on these shelves leaned carelessly, or lolled dream-
ing on its back. They stood in battalions, company after company,
at attention. And they were ranked by author, and arranged in
alphabetical order.

"Terrifying," he said; and he turned to examine a small ledger-
like volume lying in the exact center of the desk's dropleaf.

"I suppose this invasion is unavoidable," muttered the dean, "but
I must say I feel as if I were the tailor of Coventry! What's in that
ledger, Mr. Queen?"

"Chipp's personal accounts. His daily outlays of cash . . . Ah. This
year's entries stop at the thirtieth day of June."

"The day before he left for his cabin."

"He's even noted down what one postage stamp cost him—"

"That's the old Professor," sobbed Ma Blinker. Then she raised her fat arms and shrieked, "Heavens to Bessie, Dr. Barlowe! It's Professor Bacon back!"

"Hi, Ma!"

Professor Bacon's return was in the manner of a charge from third base. Having flung himself at the dean as at home plate and pumped the dean's hand violently, with large stained fingers, the young man immediately cried, "Just got back to the shop and found your note, Doctor. What's this nonsense about old Chipp's not showing up for the fall brawl?"

"It's only too true, Bacon," said Dr. Barlowe sadly, and he introduced the young man as a full professor of chemistry and biology, another of Ma Blinker's boarders, and Chipp's closest faculty friend.

"You agree with Dr. Barlowe as to the gravity of the situation?" Ellery asked him.

"Mr. Queen, if the old idiot's not back, something's happened to him." And for a precarious moment Professor Bacon fought tears. "If I'd only known," he mumbled. "But I've been away since the middle of June—biochemical research at Johns Hopkins. Damn it!" he roared. "This is more staggering than nuclear fission!"

"Have you heard from Chipp this summer, Professor?"

"His usual postcard. I may still have it on me . . . Yes!"

"Just a greeting," said Ellery, examining it. "Dated July thirty-first and postmarked Slater, Arkansas—exactly like the card he sent Dr. Barlowe. May I keep this, Bacon?"

"By all means. Chipp not back . . ." And then the young man spied the brown crust on the hearthrug. He collapsed on the missing man's bed, gaping at it.

"Ellery!"

Nikki was standing on tiptoe before Chipp's bookshelves. Under Q stood a familiar phalanx.

"A complete set of *your* books!"

"Really?" But Ellery did not seem as pleased as an author making such a flattering discovery should. Rather, he eyed one of the volumes as if it were a traitor. And indeed there was a sinister air about it, for it was the only book on all the shelves—he now noted for the first time—which did not exercise the general discipline. It stood on the shelf upside-down.

"Queer . . ." He took it down and righted it. In doing so, he opened the back cover; and his lips tightened.

"Oh, yes," said the dean gloomily "Old Chipp's quite unreasonable about your books, Mr. Queen."

"Only detective stories he'd buy," muttered Professor Bacon. "Rented the others."

"A mystery bug, eh?" murmured Ellery. "Well, here's one Queen title he didn't buy." He tapped the book in his hand.

"*The Murderer Was a Fox*," read Nikki, craning. "Rental library!"

"The Campus Book Shop. And it gives us our first confirmation of that bloodstain."

"What do you mean," asked Bacon quickly, jumping off the bed.

"The last library stamp indicates that Professor Chipp rented this book from The Campus Book Shop on June twenty-eighth. A man as orderly as these rooms indicate, who moreover scrupulously records his purchase of a postage stamp, would scarcely trot off on a summer vacation and leave a book behind to accumulate eleven weeks' rental-library charges."

"Chipp? Impossible!"

"Contrary to his whole character."

"Since the last entry in that ledger bears the date June thirtieth, and since the bloodstain is on this hearthrug," said Ellery gravely, "I'm afraid, gentlemen, that your colleague was murdered in this room on the eve of his scheduled departure for the Ozarks. He never left this room alive."

No one said anything for a long time.

But finally Ellery patted Ma Blinker's frozen shoulder and said, "Did you actually see Professor Chipp leave your boardinghouse on July first, Mrs. Blinker?"

"No, sir," said the landlady. "The expressman came for his trunk that mornin', but the Professor wasn't here. I . . . thought he'd already left."

"Tell me this, Mrs. Blinker: did Chipp have a visitor on the preceding night—the night of June thirtieth?"

A slow change came over the woman's blotchy features.

"He surely did," she said. "He surely did. That Weems."

"Weems?" Dr. Barlowe said quickly. "Oh, no! I mean . . ."

"Weems," said Nikki. "Ellery, didn't you notice that name on The Campus Book Shop as we drove by?"

Ellery said nothing.

Young Bacon muttered: "Revolting idea. But then . . . Weems and old Chipp were always at each other's throats."

"Weems is the only other one I've discussed Chipp's nonappearance with," said the dean. "He seemed so concerned!"

"A common interest in Poe," said Professor Bacon fiercely.

"Indeed," smiled Ellery. "We begin to see a certain unity of plot elements, don't we? If you'll excuse us for a little while, gentlemen, Miss Porter and I will have a chat with Mr. Weems."

But Mr. Weems turned out to be a bustly, bald little Missouri countryman, with shrewdly humored eyes and the prevailing jocular manner, the most unmurderous-looking character imaginable. And he presided over a shop so satisfyingly full of books, so aromatic with the odors of printery and bindery, and he did so with such a naked bibliophilic tenderness, that Nikki—for one—instantly dismissed him as a suspect.

Yep, Mr. Queen'd been given to understand correctly that he, Claude Weems, had visited old Chipp's rooms at Ma Blinker's on the night of June thirty last; and, yep, he'd left the old chucklehead in the best of health; and, no, he hadn't laid eyes on him since that evenin'.

He'd shut up shop for the summer and left Barlowe on July fifteenth for his annual walking tour cross-country; didn't get back till a couple of days ago to open up for fall.

"Doc Barlowe's fussin' too much about old Chipp's not turnin' up," said little Mr. Weems, beaming. "Now I grant you he's never done it before, and all that, but he's gettin' old, Chipp is. Never can tell what a man'll do when he passes a certain age."

Nikki looked relieved, but Ellery did not.

"May I ask what you dropped in to see Chipp about on the evening of June thirtieth, Mr. Weems?"

"To say goodbye. And then I'd heard tell the old varmint'd just made a great book find—"

"Book find! Chipp had 'found' a book?"

Mr. Weems looked around and lowered his voice. "I heard he'd picked up a first edition of Poe's *Tamerlane* for a few dollars from some fool who didn't know its worth. You a collector, Mr. Queen?"

"A *Tamerlane* first!" exclaimed Ellery.

"Is that good, Ellery?" asked Nikki with the candor of ignorance.

"Good! A *Tamerlane* first, Nikki, is worth a fortune!"

Weems chuckled. "Know the market, I see. Yes, sir, bein' the biggest booster old Edgar Allan ever had west of the Missip', I wanted to see that copy bad, awful bad. Chipp showed it to me, crowin' like a cock in a roostful. Lucky dog," he said without audible rancor. " 'Twas the real article, all right."

Nikki could see Ellery tucking this fact into one of the innumerable cubbyholes of his mind—the one marked *For Future Consideration*. So she was not surprised when he changed the subject abruptly.

"Did Professor Chipp ever mention to you, Weems, that he was engaged in writing a novel?"

"Sure did. I told ye he was gettin' old."

"I suppose he also told you the *kind* of novel it was?"

"Dunno as he did."

"Seems likely, seems likely," mumbled Ellery, staring at the rental-library section where murder frolicked.

"*What* seems likely, Ellery?" demanded Nikki.

"Considering that Chipp was a mystery fan, and the fact that he wrote Dr. Barlowe his novel would be a 'huge surprise,' it's my conclusion, Nikki, the old fellow was writing a whodunit."

"Say," exclaimed Mr. Weems. "I think you're right."

"Oh?"

"Prof Chipp asked me—in April, it was—to find out if a certain title's ever been used on a detective story!"

"Ah. And what was the title he mentioned, Weems?"

"*The Mystery of the Three R's.*"

"Three R's . . . Three R's?" cried Ellery. "But that's incredible! Nikki—back to the Administration Building!"

"Suppose he was," said Professor Bacon. "Readin', 'Rithmetic! Abracadabra and Rubadubdub. What of it?"

"Perhaps nothing, Bacon," scowled Ellery, hugging his pipe. "And yet . . . see here. We found a clue pointing to the strong probability that Chipp never left his rooms at Ma Blinker's alive last June thirtieth. What was that clue? The fact that Chipp failed to return his rented copy of my novel to Weems' lending library. Novel . . . book . . . *reading*, gentlemen. The first of the traditional Three R's."

"Rot!" bellowed the professor, and he began to bite his fingernails.

"I don't blame you," shrugged Ellery. "But has it occurred to you that there is also a *writing clue?*"

At this Nikki went over to the enemy.

"Ellery, are you sure the sun . . .?"

"Those postcards Chipp wrote, Nikki."

Three glances crossed stealthily.

"But I fail to see the connection, Mr. Queen," said Dr. Barlowe soothingly. "How are those ordinary postcards a clue?"

"And besides," snorted Bacon, "how could Chipp have been bumped off on June thirtieth and have mailed the cards a full month later, on July thirty-first?"

"If you'll examine the date Chipp wrote on the cards," said Ellery evenly, "you'll find that the *3* of *July 31* is crowded between the *y* of *July* and the *1* of *31*. If that isn't a clue, I never saw one."

And Ellery, who was as thin-skinned as the next artist, went on rather tartly to reconstruct the events of the fateful evening of June the thirtieth.

"Chipp wrote those cards in his rooms that night, dating them a day ahead—July first—probably intending to mail them from Slater, Arkansas, the next day on his way to the log cabin—"

"It's true Chipp loathed correspondence," muttered the dean.

"Got his duty cards out of the way before his vacation even began—the old sinner!" mumbled young Bacon.

"Someone then murdered him in his rooms, appropriated the cards, stuffed the body into Chipp's trunk—"

"Which was picked up by the expressman next morning and shipped to the cabin?" cried Nikki.

And again the little chill wind cut through the dean's office.

"But the postmarks, Mr. Queen," said the dean stiffly. "The postmarks also say July *thirty*-first."

"The murderer merely waited a month before mailing them at the Slater, Arkansas, post office."

"But *why?*" growled Bacon. "You weave beautiful rugs, man—but what do they mean?"

"Obviously it was all done, Professor Bacon," said Ellery, "to leave the impression that on July thirty-first Professor Chipp was *still alive* . . . to keep the world from learning that he was really murdered on the night of June thirtieth. And that, of course, is significant." He sprang to his feet. "We must examine the Professor's cabin—most particularly, his trunk."

It was a little trunk—but then, as Dr. Barlowe pointed out in a very queer voice, Professor Chipp had been a little man.

Outdoors, the Ozarks were shutting up shop for the summer, stripping the fainter-hearted trees and busily daubing hillsides; but in the cabin there was no beauty—only dust, and an odor of dampness—and something else.

The little steamer trunk stood just inside the cabin doorway.

They stared at it.

"Well, well," said Bacon finally. "Miss Porter's outside—what are we waiting for?"

And so they knocked off the rusted lock and raised the lid—and found the trunk quite empty.

Perhaps not quite empty; the interior held a pale, dead-looking mass of crumbly stuff.

Ellery glanced up at Professor Bacon.

"Quicklime," muttered the chemistry teacher.

"Quicklime!" choked the dean. "But the body. Where's the body?"

Nikki's scream, augmented a dozen times by the encircling hills, answered Dr. Barlowe's question most unpleasantly.

She had been wandering about the clearing, dreading to catch the first cry of discovery from the cabin, when she came upon a little cairn of stones. And she had sat down on it.

But the loose rocks gave way, and Miss Porter found herself sitting on Professor Chipp—or, rather, on what was left of Professor Chipp. For Professor Chipp had gone the way of all flesh—which is to say, he was merely bones, and very dry bones, at that.

But that it was the skeleton of Leverett Chisholm Chipp could not be questioned: the medius and index finger of the right skeletal hand were missing to the second joint. And that Leverett Chisholm Chipp had been most foully used was also evident: the top of the skull revealed a deep and ragged chasm, the result of what could only have been a tremendous blow.

Whereupon the old pedagogue and the young took flight, joining Miss Porter, who was quietly being ill on the other side of the cabin; and Mr. Queen found himself alone with Professor Chipp.

Later Ellery went over the log cabin with a disagreeable sense of anticipation. There was no sensible reason for believing that the cabin held further secrets; but sense is not all, and the already chilling air held a whiff of fatality.

He found it in a cupboard, in a green steel box, beside a rusty can of moldering tobacco.

It was a stapled pile of neat papers, curled by damp, but otherwise intact.

The top sheet, in a cramped, spidery hand, read:

The Mystery of the Three R's
by

L. C. Chipp

The discovery of Professor Chipp's detective story may be said to mark the climax of the case. That the old man had been battered to death in his rooms on the night of June thirtieth; that his corpse had been shipped from Barlowe, Missouri, to the Arkansas cabin in his own trunk, packed in quicklime to avert detection en route; that the murderer had then at his leisure made his way to the cabin, removed the body from the trunk, and buried it under a heap of stones—these were mere facts, dry as the professor's bones. They did not possess the aroma of the grotesque—the *bouffe*—which rose like a delicious mist from the pages of that incredible manuscript.

Not that Professor Chipp's venture into detective fiction revealed a new master, to tower above the busy little figures of his fellow toilers in this curious vineyard and vie for cloud space only with Poe and Doyle and Chesterton. To the contrary. *The Mystery of the Three R's*, by L. C. Chipp, was a labored exercise in familiar elements, distinguished chiefly for its enthusiasm.

No, it was not the murdered professor's manuscript which was remarkable; the remarkable thing was the manner in which life had imitated it.

It was a shaken group that gathered in Chipp's rooms the morning after the return from the Arkansas cabin. Ellery had called the meeting, and he had invited Mr. Weems of The Campus Book Shop to participate—who, on hearing the ghastly news, stopped beaming, clamped his Missouri jaws shut, and began to gaze furtively at the door.

Ellery's own jaws were unshaven, and his eyes were red.

"I've passed the better part of the night," he began abruptly, "reading through Chipp's manuscript. And I must report an amazing—an almost unbelievable—thing.

"The crime in Chipp's detective story takes place in and about a small Missouri college called . . . Barleigh College."

"Barleigh," muttered the dean of Barlowe.

"Moreover, the victim in Chipp's yarn is a methodical old professor of American Literature."

Nikki looked puzzled. "You mean that Professor Chipp—?"

"Took off on himself, Nikki—exactly."

"What's so incredible about that?" demanded young Bacon. "Art imitating life—"

"Considering the fact that Chipp plotted his story long before the events of this summer, Professor Bacon, it's rather a case of life imitating art. Suppose I tell you that the methodical old professor of American Literature in Chipp's story owns a cabin in the Ozarks where his body is found?"

"Even *that?*" squeaked Mr. Weems.

"And more, Weems. The suspects in the story are the President of Barleigh College, whose name is given as Dr. Isaac St. Anthony E. Barleigh; a local bookshop owner named Claudius Deems; a young professor of chemistry known as Macon; and, most extraordinary of all, the three main clues in Chipp's detective story revolve about—are called—Readin', 'Ritin', and 'Rithmetic!"

And the icy little wind blew once more.

"You mean," exclaimed Dr. Barlowe, "the crime we're investigating—Chipp's own death—is *an exact counterpart of the fictional crime Chipp invented in his manuscript?*"

"Down to the last character, Doctor."

"But Ellery," said Nikki, "how can that possibly be?"

"Obviously, Chipp's killer managed to get hold of the old fellow's manuscript, read it, and with hellish humor proceeded to copy in real life—actually to duplicate—the crime Chipp had created in fiction." Ellery began to lunge about the little room, his usually neat hair disordered and a rather wild look on his face. "Everything's the same: the book that wasn't returned to the lending library—the readin' clue; the picture postcards bearing forged dates—the 'ritin' clue—"

"And the 'rithmetic clue, Mr. Queen?" asked the dean in a quavering voice.

"In the story, Doctor, the victim has found a first edition of Poe's *Tamerlane*, worth many thousands of dollars."

Little Weems cried, "That's 'rithmetic, all right!" and then bit his lip.

"And how," asked Professor Bacon thickly, "how is the book integrated into Chipp's yarn, Mr. Queen?"

"It furnishes the motive for the crime. The killer steals the victim's authentic *Tamerlane*, substituting for it a facsimile copy which is worth only a few dollars."

"But if everything else is duplicated—" began Dr. Barlowe in a mutter.

"Then that must be the motive for Professor Chipp's own murder!" cried Nikki.

"It would seem so, wouldn't it?" Ellery glanced sharply at the proprietor of The Campus Book Shop. "Weems, where is the first edition of *Tamerlane* you told me Chipp showed you on the night of June thirtieth?"

"Why—why—why, reckon it's on his shelves here somewheres, Mr. Queen. Under *P*, for Poe."

And there it was. Under *P*, for Poe.

And when Ellery took it down and turned its pages, he smiled. For the first time since they had found the skeleton under the cairn, he smiled.

"Well, Weems," he said affably, "you're a Poe expert. Is this an authentic *Tamerlane* first?"

"Why—why—why, must be. 'Twas when old Chipp showed it to me that night—"

"Really? Suppose you re-examine it—now."

But they all knew the answer before Weems spoke.

"It ain't," he said feebly. "It's a facsim'le copy."

"The *Tamerlane*—stolen," whispered Dr. Barlowe.

"So once again," murmured Ellery, "we find duplication. I think that's all. Or should I say, it's too much?"

And he lit his pipe and seated himself in one of Professor Chipp's chairs, puffing contentedly.

"All!" exclaimed Dr. Barlowe. "I confess, Mr. Queen, you've—you've baffled me no end in this investigation. All? It's barely begun! *Who* has done all this?"

"Wait," said Bacon slowly. "It may be, Doctor, we don't need Queen's eminent services at that. If the rest has followed Chipp's plot so faithfully, why not the most important plot element of all?"

"That's true, Ellery," said Nikki with shining eyes. *"Who is the murderer in Professor Chipp's detective story?"*

Ellery glanced at the cowering little figure of Claude Weems.

"The character," he replied cheerfully, "whom Chipp had named Claudius Deems."

The muscular young professor snarled, and he sprang.

"In your enthusiasm, Bacon," murmured Ellery, without stirring from his chair, "don't throttle him. After all, he's such a little fellow, and you're so large."

"Kill old Chipp, would you!" growled Professor Bacon; but his grip relaxed a little.

"Mr. Weems," said Nikki, looking displeased. "Of course! The murderer forged the dates on the postcards so we wouldn't know the crime had been committed on June thirtieth. And who'd have reason to falsify the true date of the crime? The one man who'd visited Professor Chipp that night!"

"The damned beast could easily have got quicklime," said Bacon, shaking Weems like a rabbit, "by stealing it from the Chemistry Department after everyone'd left the college for the summer."

"Yes!" said Nikki. "Remember Weems himself told us he didn't leave Barlowe until July fifteenth?"

"I do, indeed. And Weems's motive, Nikki?"

"Why, to steal Chipp's *Tamerlane.*"

"I'm afraid that's so," groaned the dean. "Weems as a bookseller could easily have got hold of a cheap facsimile to substitute for the authentic first edition."

"And he said he'd gone on a walking tour, didn't he?" Nikki added, warming to her own logic. "Well, I'll bet he 'walked' into that Arkansas post office, Ellery, on July thirty-first, to mail those postcards!"

Weems found his voice.

"Why, now, listen here, little lady, I didn't kill old Chipp—" he began in the most unconvincing tones imaginable.

They all eyed him with scorn—all, that is, but Ellery.

"Very true, Weems," said Ellery, nodding. "You most certainly did not."

"He didn't—" began Dr. Barlowe, blinking.

"I . . didn't?" gasped Weems, which seemed to Nikki a remarkable thing for him to have said.

"No, although I'm afraid I've been led very cleverly to *believe* that you did, Weems."

"See here, Mr. Queen," said the dean of Barlowe in a terrible voice. "Precisely what *do* you mean?"

"And how do you know he didn't?" shouted Bacon. "I told you, Doctor—this fellow's grossly overrated. The next thing you'll tell us is that Chipp hasn't been murdered at all!"

"Exactly," said Ellery. "Therefore Weems couldn't have murdered him."

"Ellery—" moaned Nikki.

"Your syllogism seems a bit perverted, Mr. Queen," said Dr. Barlowe severely.

"Yes!" snarled Bacon. "What about the evidence—?"

"Very well," said Ellery briskly, "let's consider the evidence. Let's consider the evidence of the skeleton we found near Chipp's cabin."

"Those dry bones? What about 'em?"

"Just that, Professor—they're so very dry. Bacon, you're a biologist as well as a chemist. Under normal conditions, how long does it take for the soft parts of a body to decompose completely?"

"How long . . .?" The young man moistened his lips. "Muscles, stomach, liver—from three to four years. But—"

"And for decomposition of the fibrous tissues, the ligaments?"

"Oh, five years or so more. But—"

"And yet," sighed Ellery, "that desiccated skeleton was supposed to be the remains of a man who'd been alive *a mere eleven weeks before*. And not only that—I now appeal to your chemical knowledge, Professor. Just what is the effect of quicklime on human flesh and bones?"

"Why, it's pulverulent. Would dry out a body—"

"Would quicklime destroy the tissues?"

"Er, no."

"*It would tend to preserve them?*"

"Er, yes."

"Therefore the skeleton we found couldn't possibly have been the mortal remains of Professor Chipp."

"But the right hand, Ellery," cried Nikki. "The missing fingers—just like Professor Chipp's—"

"I shouldn't think," said Ellery dryly, "snapping a couple of dry bones off a man dead eight or ten years would present much of a problem."

"Eight or ten years—"

"Surely, Nikki, it suggests the tenant of some outraged grave . . . or, considering the facts at our disposal, the far likelier theory that it came from a laboratory closet in the Biology Department of Barlowe College." And Professor Bacon cringed before Ellery's accusing glance, which softened suddenly in laughter. "Now, really, gentlemen. Hasn't this hoax gone far enough?"

"Hoax, Mr. Queen?" choked the dean of Barlowe with feeble indignation.

"Come, come, Doctor," chuckled Ellery, "the game's up. Let me review the fantastic facts. What is this case? A detective story come to life. Bizarre—fascinating—to be sure. But really, Doctor, so utterly unconvincing!

"How conveniently all the clues in Chipp's manuscript found reflections in reality! The lending-library book, so long overdue—in the story, in the crime. The postcards written in advance—in the story, in the crime. The *Tamerlane* facsimile right here on Chipp's shelf—exactly as the manuscript has it. It would seem as if Chipp collaborated in his own murder."

"Collab—I can't make hide nor hair of this, Mr. Queen," said little Mr. Weems.

"Now, now, Weems, as the bookseller-Poe-crony you were the key figure in the plot! Although I must confess, Dr. Barlowe, *you* played your role magnificently, too—and, Professor Bacon, you missed a career in the theater; you really did. The only innocent, I daresay, is Ma Blinker—and to you, gentlemen, I gladly leave the trial of facing that doughty lady when she finds out how her honest grief has been exploited in the interest of commerce."

"Commerce?" whimpered Nikki, who by now was holding her pretty head to keep it from flying off.

"Of course, Nikki. I was invited to Barlowe to follow an elaborate trail of carefully placed 'clues' in order to reach the conclusion that Claude Weems had 'murdered' Professor Chipp. When I announced Weems's 'guilt,' the hoax was supposed to blow up in my face. *Old Chipp would pop out of his hiding place grinning from ear to ear.*"

"Pop out . . . You mean," gasped Nikki, "you mean Professor Chipp is *alive?*"

"Only conclusion that makes sense, Nikki. And then," Ellery went on, glaring at the three men, "imagine the headlines. 'Famous Sleuth Tricked by Hoax—Pins Whodunit on Harmless Prof.' Commerce? I'll say! Chipp's *Mystery of the Three R's*, launched by such splendid publicity, would be swallowed by a publisher as the whale swallowed Jonah—and there we'd have—presumably—a sensational best-seller.

"The whole thing, Nikki, was a conspiracy hatched by the dean of Barlowe College, his two favorite professors, and their good friend the campus bookseller—a conspiracy to put old Chipp's first detective story over with a bang!"

And now the little wind blew warm, bringing the blood of embarrassment to six male cheeks.

"Mr. Queen—" began the dean hoarsely.

"Mr. Queen—" began the bio-chemistry professor hoarsely.

"Mr. Queen—" began the bookseller hoarsely.

"Come, come, gentlemen!" cried Ellery. "All is not lost! We'll go through with the plot! I make only one condition. Where the devil is Chipp? I want to shake the old scoundrel's hand."

Barlowe is an unusual college.

Ernest Bramah

The Tragedy at Brookbend Cottage

To refresh your memory: the first blind detective in modern fiction made his appearance in 1914—"wise, witty, gentle" Max Carrados, born Max Wynn. In compensation for his blindness, Max Carrados can run his fingertips along the surface of a newspaper, find the infinitesimal height of printers' ink, and "read" any type larger than long primer. There was one amazing moment in his career when a stranger sauntered past Max Carrados and in that fleeting moment the blind detective deduced with impeccable logic that the stranger was wearing a false mustache . . .

Detective: MAX CARRADOS

"Max," said Mr. Carlyle, when Parkinson had closed the door behind him, "this is Lieutenant Hollyer, whom you consented to see."

"To hear," corrected Carrados, smiling straight into the healthy and rather embarrassed face of the stranger before him. "Mr. Hollyer knows of my disability?"

"Mr. Carlyle told me," said the young man, "but, as a matter of fact, I had heard of you before, Mr. Carrados, in connection with the foundering of the *Ivan Saratov*."

Carrados wagged his head in good-humored resignation.

"And the owners were sworn to inviolable secrecy!" he exclaimed. "Well, it is inevitable, I suppose. Not another scuttling case, Mr. Hollyer?"

"No, mine is quite a private matter," replied the lieutenant. "My sister, Mrs. Creake—but Mr. Carlyle would tell you better than I can."

"No, no; Carlyle is a professional. Let me have it in the rough, Mr. Hollyer. My ears are my eyes."

"Very well, sir. I can tell you what there is to tell, right enough, but I feel that when all's said and done it must sound very little to another, although it seems important to me."

"We have occasionally found trifles of significance ourselves," said Carrados encouragingly.

Lieutenant Hollyer began: "I have a sister, Millicent, who is married to a man called Creake. She is about twenty-eight now and he is at least fifteen years older. Neither my mother (who has since died) nor I cared very much about Creake. We had nothing particular against him, except, perhaps, the disparity of age, but none of us appeared to have anything in common. He was a dark, taciturn man, and his moody silence froze up conversation. As a result, of course, we didn't see much of each other."

"This, you must understand, was four or five years ago, Max," interposed Mr. Carlyle officiously.

Lieutenant Hollyer continued: "Millicent married Creake after a very short engagement. It was a frightfully subdued wedding—more like a funeral to me. The man professed to have no relations and apparently he had scarcely any friends or business acquaintances. He was an agent for something or other and had an office off Holborn. I suppose he made a living out of it then, although we knew practically nothing of his private affairs, but I gather that it has been going down since, and I suspect that for the past few years they have been getting along almost entirely on Millicent's little income. You would like the particulars?"

"Please," assented Carrados.

"When our father died about seven years ago, he left six thousand pounds. It was invested in Canadian stock and brought in a little over two hundred a year. By his will my mother was to have the income of that for life and on her death it was to pass to Millicent, subject to the payment of a lump sum of five hundred pounds to me. But my father privately suggested to me that if I should have no particular use for the money at the time, he would propose my letting Millicent have the income of it until I did want it, as she would not be particularly well off. You see, Mr. Carrados, a great deal more had been spent on my education and advancement than on her; I had my pay, and, of course, I could look out for myself better than a girl could."

"Quite so," agreed Carrados.

"Therefore I did nothing about that," continued the lieutenant. "Three years ago I was over again but I did not see much of them.

They were living in lodgings. That was the only time since the marriage that I have seen them until last week. In the meanwhile our mother had died and Millicent had been receiving her income. She wrote me several letters at the time. Otherwise we did not correspond much, but about a year ago she sent me their new address—Brookbend Cottage, Mulling Common—a house that they had taken. When I got two months' leave I invited myself there as a matter of course, fully expecting to stay most of my time with them, but I made an excuse to get away after a week. The place was dismal and unendurable, the whole life and atmosphere indescribably depressing." He looked round with an instinct of caution, leaned forward earnestly, and dropped his voice. "Mr. Carrados, it is my absolute conviction that Creake is only waiting for a favorable opportunity to murder Millicent."

"Go on," said Carrados quietly. "A week of the depressing surroundings of Brookbend Cottage would not alone convince you of that, Mr. Hollyer."

"I am not so sure," declared Hollyer doubtfully. "There was a feeling of suspicion and—before me—polite hatred that would have gone a good way towards it. All the same there *was* something more definite. Millicent told me this the day after I went there. There is no doubt that a few months ago Creake deliberately planned to poison her with some weed-killer. She told me the circumstances in a rather distressed moment, but afterwards she refused to speak of it again—even weakly denied it—and, as a matter of fact, it was with the greatest difficulty that I could get her at any time to talk about her husband or his affairs. The gist of it was that she had the strongest suspicion that Creake doctored a bottle of stout which he expected she would drink for her supper when she was alone. The weed-killer, properly labeled, but also in a beer bottle, was kept with other miscellaneous liquids in the same cupboard as the beer, but on a high shelf. When he found that it had miscarried he poured away the mixture, washed out the bottle, and put in the dregs from another. There is no doubt in my mind that if he had come back and found Millicent dead or dying he would have contrived it to appear that she had made a mistake in the dark."

"Yes," assented Carrados. "The open way, the safe way."

"You must understand that they live in a very small style, Mr. Carrados, and Millicent is almost entirely in the man's power. The only servant they have is a woman who comes in for a few hours every day. The house is lonely and secluded. Creake is sometimes away for days and nights at a time, and Millicent, either through pride or indifference, seems to have dropped off all her old friends and to have made no others. He might poison her, bury the body in the garden, and be a thousand miles away before anyone began even to inquire about her. What am I to do?"

"He is less likely to try poison than some other means now," pondered Carrados. "That having failed, his wife will always be on her guard. He may know, or at least suspect, that others know. No. . . . The common-sense precaution would be for your sister to leave the man, Mr. Hollyer. She will not?"

"No," admitted Hollyer, "she will not. I at once urged that." The young man struggled with some hesitation for a moment and then blurted out: "The fact is, Mr. Carrados, I don't understand Millicent. She is not the girl she was. She hates Creake and treats him with a silent contempt that eats into their lives like acid, and yet she is so jealous of him that she will let nothing short of death part them. It is a horrible life they lead. I stood it for a week and I must say, much as I dislike my brother-in-law, that he has something to put up with. If only he got into a passion like a man and killed her it wouldn't be altogether incomprehensible."

"That does not concern us," said Carrados. "In a game of this kind one has to take sides and we have taken ours. It remains for us to see that our side wins. You mentioned jealousy, Mr. Hollyer. Have you any idea whether Mrs. Creake has real ground for it?"

"I should have told you that," replied Lieutenant Hollyer. "I happened to strike up with a newspaperman whose office is in the same block as Creake's. When I mentioned the name he grinned. 'Creake,' he said, 'oh, he's the man with the romantic typist, isn't he?' 'Well, he's my brother-in-law,' I replied. 'What about the typist?' Then the chap shut up like a knife. 'No, no,' he said, 'I didn't know he was married. I don't want to get mixed up in anything of that sort.' "

Carrados turned to his friend.

"I suppose you know all about the typist by now, Louis?"

"We have had her under efficient observation, Max."

"Is she unmarried?"

"Yes; so far as ordinary repute goes."

"That is all that is essential for the moment. Mr. Hollyer opens up three excellent reasons why this man might wish to dispose of his wife. Well, we will go forward on that. Have you got a photograph of Mr. Creake?"

The lieutenant took out his pocketbook.

"Mr. Carlyle asked me for one. Here is the best I could get."

Carrados rang the bell.

"This, Parkinson," he said, when the man appeared, "is a photograph of a Mr.—What first name, by the way?"

"Austin," said Hollyer.

"—of a Mr. Austin Creake. I may require you to recognize him."

Parkinson glanced at the print and returned it to his master's hand.

"May I inquire if it is a recent photograph of the gentleman, sir?" he asked.

"About six years ago," said the lieutenant. "But he is very little changed."

"Thank you, sir. I will endeavor to remember Mr. Creake, sir."

Lieutenant Hollyer stood up as Parkinson left the room. The interview seemed to be at an end.

"Oh, there's one other matter," he remarked. "I am afraid that I did rather an unfortunate thing while I was at Brookbend. It seemed to me that as all Millicent's money would probably pass into Creake's hands sooner or later I might as well have my five hundred pounds, if only to help her with afterwards. So I broached the subject and said that I should like to have it now as I had an opportunity for investing."

"And you think?"

"It may possibly influence Creake to act sooner than he otherwise might have done. He may even have got possession of the principal and find it very awkward to replace it."

"So much the better. If your sister is going to be murdered it may as well be done next week or two. Excuse my brutality, Mr. Hollyer, but this is simply a case to me and I regard it strategically. Now Mr. Carlyle's organization can look after Mrs. Creake for a few weeks, but it cannot look after her forever. By increasing the immediate risk we diminish the permanent risk."

"I see," agreed Hollyer. "I'm awfully uneasy but I'm entirely in your hands."

"Then we will give Mr. Creake every inducement and every opportunity to get to work. Where are you staying now?"

"Just now at St. Albans."

"That is too far." The inscrutable eyes retained their tranquil depth but a new quality of quickening interest in the voice made Mr. Carlyle sit up. "Give me a few minutes, please. The cigarettes are behind you, Mr. Hollyer." The blind man walked to the window and seemed to look out over the cypress-shaded lawn. The lieutenant lit a cigarette and Mr. Carlyle picked up *Punch*. Then Carrados turned round again.

"You are prepared to put your own arrangements aside?" he demanded of his visitor.

"Certainly."

"Very well. I want you to go down now—straight from here—to Brookbend Cottage. Tell your sister that your leave is unexpectedly cut short and that you sail tomorrow."

"The *Martian?*"

"No, no; the *Martian* doesn't sail. Look up the movements on your way there and pick out a boat that does. Say you are transferred. Add that you expect to be away only two or three months and that you really want the five hundred pounds by the time of your return. Don't stay in the house long, please."

"I understand, sir."

"St. Albans is too far. Make your excuse and get away from there today. Put up somewhere in town, where you will be in reach of the telephone. Let Mr. Carlyle and myself know where you are. Keep out of Creake's way. I don't want actually to tie you down to the house, but we may require your services. We will let you know at the first sign of anything doing. . . ."

"Is there nothing more that I can do now?"

"Nothing. In going to Mr. Carlyle you have done the best thing possible; you have put your sister into the care of the shrewdest man in London."

"Well, Max?" remarked Mr. Carlyle tentatively when they were alone.

"Well, Louis?"

"Of course, it wasn't worth while rubbing it in before young Hollyer, but, as a matter of fact, every single man carries the life of any other man—only one, mind you—in his hands, do what you will."

"Provided he doesn't bungle," acquiesced Carrados.

"Quite so."

"And also that he is absolutely reckless of the consequences."

"Of course."

"Two rather large provisos. Creake is obviously susceptible to both. Have you seen him?"

"No. As I told you, I put a man on to report his habits in town. Then, two days ago, as the case seemed to promise some interest—for he certainly is deeply involved with the typist, Max, and the thing might take a sensational turn at any time—I went down to Mulling Common myself. Although the house is lonely it is on the electric tram route—you know the sort of market-garden rurality about a dozen miles out of London—alternate bricks and cabbages. It was easy enough to get to know about Creake locally. He mixes with no one there, goes into town at irregular times but generally every day, and is reputed to be devilish hard to get money out of. Finally, I made the acquaintance of an old fellow who used to do a day's gardening at Brookbend occasionally. He has a cottage and a garden of his own with a greenhouse, and the business cost me the price of a pound of tomatoes."

"Was it a profitable investment?"

"As tomatoes, yes; as information, no. The old fellow had the fatal disadvantage from our point of view of laboring under a grievance. A few weeks ago Creake told him that he would not require him again as he was going to do his own gardening."

"That is something, Louis."

"However, the chatty old soul had a simple explanation for everything that Creake did. Creake was mad. He had even seen him flying a kite in his garden where it was bound to get wrecked among the trees. A lad of ten would have known better, he declared."

"A good many men have been flying kites of various kinds lately," said Carrados. "Is he interested in aviation?"

"I daresay. He appears to have some knowledge of scientific subjects. Now what do you want me to do, Max?"

"Will you do it?"

"Implicitly."

"Keep your man on Creake in town and let me have his reports after you have seen them. Lunch with me here now. Phone your office that you are detained on unpleasant business and then give the deserving Parkinson an afternoon off by looking after me while we take a motor run round Mulling Common. If we have time we might go on to Brighton, feed at the 'Ship,' and come back in the cool."

"Amiable and thrice lucky mortal," sighed Mr. Carlyle.

But, as it happened, Brighton did not figure in that day's itinerary It had been Carrados' intention merely to pass Brookbend Cottage on this occasion, relying on his highly developed faculties, aided by Mr. Carlyle's description, to inform him of the surroundings. A hundred yards before they reached the house he had given an order to his chauffeur to drop into the lowest speed and they were leisurely drawing past when a discovery by Mr. Carlyle modified their plans.

"By Jupiter!" that gentleman suddenly exclaimed, "there's a board up, Max. The place is to be let."

Carrados picked up the tube again. A couple of sentences passed and the car stopped by the roadside, a score of paces past the limit of the garden. Mr. Carlyle took out his notebook and wrote down the address of a firm of house agents.

"You might raise the hood and have a look at the engine, Harris," said Carrados. "We want to be occupied here for a few minutes."

"This is sudden; Hollyer knew nothing of their leaving," remarked Mr. Carlyle.

"All the same, Louis, we will go on to the agents and get a card to view whether we use it today or not."

A thick hedge, in its summer dress effectively screening the house beyond from public view, lay between the garden and the road. Above the hedge showed an occasional shrub; at the corner nearest to the car a chestnut flourished. The wooden gate, once white, which they had passed, was grimed and rickety. The road itself was still the unpretentious country lane that the advent of the electric tram had found it. When Carrados had taken in these details there seemed little else to notice. He was on the point of giving Harris the order to go on when his ear caught a trivial sound.

"Someone is coming out of the house, Louis," he warned his friend. "It may be Hollyer."

"I don't hear anyone," replied the other, but as he spoke a door banged noisily and Mr. Carlyle slipped into another seat and ensconced himself behind a copy of *The Globe*.

"Creake himself," he whispered across the car, as a man appeared at the gate. "Hollyer was right; he is hardly changed. Waiting for the tram, I suppose."

But the tram very soon swung past them from the direction in which Mr. Creake was looking and it did not interest him. For a minute or two longer he continued to look expectantly along the road. Then he walked slowly up the drive to the house.

"We will give him five or ten minutes," decided Carrados. "Harris is behaving very naturally."

Before even the shorter period had run out they were repaid. A telegraph boy cycled leisurely along the road, and, leaving his machine at the gate, went up to the cottage. Evidently there was no reply, for in less than a minute he was trundling past them back again. Round the bend an approaching tram clanged its bell noisily, and quickened by the warning sound, Mr. Creake again appeared, this time with a small portmanteau in his hand. With a backward glance he hurried on towards the next stopping-place, and boarded the car as it slackened down.

"Very convenient of Mr. Creake," remarked Carrados, with quiet satisfaction. "We will now get the order and go over the house in his absence. It might be useful to have a look at the telegram as well."

"It might, Max," acquiesced Mr. Carlyle. "But if it is, as it probably is, in Creake's pocket, how do you propose to get it?"

"By going to the telegraph office."

"Quite so. Have you ever tried to see a copy of a telegram addressed to someone else?"

"I don't think I have had occasion yet," admitted Carrados. "Have you?"

"In one or two cases I have perhaps been an accessory to the act. It is generally a matter either of extreme delicacy or considerable expenditure."

"Then for Hollyer's sake we will hope for the former."

A little later, having left the car at the beginning of the straggling High Street, the two men called at the village telegraph office. They had already visited the house agent and obtained an order to view Brookbend Cottage, declining with some difficulty the clerk's persistent offer to accompany them. The reason was soon forthcoming. "As a matter of fact," explained the young man, "the present tenant is under *our* notice to leave."

"Unsatisfactory, eh?" said Carrados, encouragingly.

"He's a corker," admitted the clerk, responding to the friendly tone. "Fifteen months and not a bit of rent have we had. That's why I should have liked—"

"We will make every allowance," replied Carrados.

The telegraph office occupied one side of a stationer's shop. It was not without some inward trepidation that Mr. Carlyle found himself committed to the adventure. Carrados, on the other hand, was the personification of bland unconcern.

"You have just sent a telegram to Brookbend Cottage," he said to the young lady behind the brass-work lattice. "We think it may have come inaccurately and should like a repeat." He took out his purse. "What is the fee?"

The request was evidently not a common one. "Oh," said the girl uncertainly, "wait a minute, please." She turned to a pile of telegram duplicates behind the desk and ran a doubtful finger along the upper sheets. "I think this is all right. You want it repeated?"

"Please."

"It will be fourpence. If there is an error the amount will be refunded."

Carrados put down his coins.

"Will it take long?" he inquired.

"You will most likely get it within a quarter of an hour," she replied.

"Now you've done it," commented Mr. Carlyle, as they walked back to their car. "How do you propose to get that telegram, Max?"

"Ask for it."

And stripping the artifice of any elaboration, he simply asked for it and got it. The car, posted at a convenient bend in the road, gave him a warning note as the telegraph-boy approached. Then Carrados took up a convincing attitude with his hand on the gate while Mr. Carlyle lent himself to the semblance of a departing friend. That was the inevitable impression when the boy rode up.

"Creake, Brookbend Cottage?" inquired Carrados, holding out his hand, and without a second thought the boy gave him the envelope.

"Some day, my friend," remarked Mr. Carlyle, looking nervously towards the unseen house, "your ingenuity will get you into a tight corner."

"Then my ingenuity must get me out again," was the retort. "Let us have our 'view' now. The telegram can wait."

An untidy workwoman took their order and left them standing at the door. Presently a lady whom they both knew to be Mrs. Creake appeared.

"You wish to see the house?" she said, in a voice that was utterly devoid of any interest. Then, without waiting for a reply, she turned to the nearest door and threw it open.

"This is the drawing-room."

They walked into a sparsely furnished, damp-smelling room and made a pretense of looking round.

"The dining-room," she continued, crossing the narrow hall.

Mr. Carlyle ventured a genial commonplace in the hope of inducing conversation. The result was not encouraging. Doubtless they would have gone through the house under the same frigid guidance had not Carrados been at fault in a way that Mr. Carlyle had never known him fail before. In crossing the hall he stumbled over a mat and almost fell.

"Pardon my clumsiness," he said to the lady. "I am, unfortunately, quite blind."

"Blind!" she exclaimed. "Oh, I beg your pardon. Why did you not tell me? You might have fallen."

"I generally manage fairly well," he replied. "But, of course, in a strange house—"

She put her hand on his arm very lightly.

"You must let me guide you," she said.

The house, without being large, was full of passages and inconvenient turnings. Carrados asked an occasional question and found Mrs. Creake quite amiable without effusion. Mr. Carlyle followed them from room to room in the hope, though scarcely the expectation, of learning something that might be useful.

"This is the last one. It is the largest bedroom," said their guide. Only two of the upper rooms were fully furnished and Mr. Carlyle at once saw, as Carrados knew without seeing, that this was the one which the Creakes occupied.

"A very pleasant outlook," declared Mr. Carlyle.

"Oh, I suppose so," admitted the lady vaguely. The room, in fact, looked over the leafy garden and the road beyond. It had a French door opening onto a small balcony, and to this, under the strange influence that always attracted him to light, Carrados walked.

"I expect that there is a certain amount of repair needed?" he said, after standing there a moment.

"I am afraid there would be," she confessed.

"I ask because there is a sheet of metal on the floor here," he continued. "Now that, in an old house, spells dry-rot to the wary observer."

"My husband said that the rain, which comes in a little under the window, was rotting the boards there," she replied. "He put that down recently. I had not noticed anything myself."

It was the first time she had mentioned her husband; Mr. Carlyle pricked up his ears.

"Ah, that is a less serious matter," said Carrados. "May I step out onto the balcony?"

"Oh, yes, if you like to." Then, as he appeared to be fumbling at the catch, "Let me open it for you."

But the window was already open, and Carrados, facing the various points of the compass, took in the bearings.

"A sunny, sheltered corner," he remarked. "An ideal spot for a deckchair and a book."

"I daresay," she replied, "but I never use it."

"Sometimes, surely," he persisted mildly. "It would be my favorite retreat. But then—"

"I was going to say that I had never even been out on it, but that would not be quite true. It has only two uses for me: occasionally I shake a duster from it, and when my husband returns late without his latchkey he wakes me up and I come out here and drop him mine."

Further revelation of Mr. Creake's nocturnal habits was cut off, greatly to Mr. Carlyle's annoyance, by a cough of unmistakable significance from the foot of the stairs. They had heard a trade cart drive up to the gate, a knock at the door, and the heavyfooted woman tramp along the hall.

"Excuse me a minute, please," said Mrs. Creake.

"Louis," said Carrados, in a sharp whisper, the moment they were alone, "stand against the door."

With extreme plausibility Mr. Carlyle began to admire a picture so situated that while he was there it was impossible to open the door more than a few inches. From that position he observed his confederate go through the curious procedure of kneeling down on the bedroom floor and for a full minute pressing his ear to the sheet of metal that had already engaged his attention. Then he rose to his feet, nodded, dusted his trousers, and Mr. Carlyle moved to a less equivocal position.

"What a beautiful rose-tree grows up your balcony," remarked Carrados, stepping into the room as Mrs. Creake returned. "I suppose you are very fond of gardening?"

"I detest it," she replied.

"But this *Gloire,* so carefully trained—?"

"Is it?" she replied. "I think my husband was nailing it up recently." By some strange fatality Carrados' most aimless remarks seemed to involve the absent Mr. Creake. "Do you care to see the garden?"

The garden proved to be extensive and neglected. Behind the house was chiefly orchard. In front, some semblance of order had been kept up; here it was lawn and shrubbery, and the drive they had walked along. Two things interested Carrados: the soil at the foot of the balcony, which he declared on examination to be particularly suitable for roses, and the fine chestnut-tree in the corner by the road.

As they walked back to the car Mr. Carlyle lamented that they had learned so little of Creake's movements.

"Perhaps the telegram will tell us something," suggested Carrados.

Mr. Carlyle cut open the envelope, glanced at the enclosure, and in spite of his disappointment could not restrain a chuckle.

"My poor Max," he explained, "you have put yourself to an amount of ingenious trouble for nothing. Creake is evidently taking a few days' holiday and prudently availed himself of the Meteorological Office forecast before going. Listen: *Immediate prospect for London warm and settled. Further outlook cooler but fine.* Well, well; I did get a pound of tomatoes for *my* fourpence."

"You certainly scored there, Louis," admitted Carrados. "I wonder," he added speculatively, "whether it is Creake's peculiar taste usually to spend his week-end holiday in London."

"Eh?" exclaimed Mr. Carlyle, looking at the words again. "By gad, that's rum, Max. They usually go to Weston-super-Mare. Why on earth should he want to know about London?"

"I can make a guess, but before we are satisfied I must come here again. Take another look at that kite, Louis. Are there a few yards of string hanging loose from it?"

"Yes, there are."

"Rather thick string—unusually thick for the purpose?"

"Yes; but how do you know?"

As they drove home again Carrados explained, and Mr. Carlyle sat aghast, saying incredulously: "Good God, Max, is it possible?"

An hour later he was satisfied that it was possible. In reply to his inquiry someone in his office telephoned him the information that "they" had left Paddington by the four thirty for Weston.

It was more than a week after his introduction to Carrados that Lieutenant Hollyer had a summons to present himself at the Carrados home again. He found Mr. Carlyle already there and the two friends awaiting his arrival.

"I hope everything is all right?" he said, shaking hands.

"Excellent," replied Carrados. "You'd better eat something before we start. We have a long and perhaps an exciting night before us."

"And certainly a wet one," assented the lieutenant. "It was thundering over Mulling way as I came along."

"That is why you are here," said his host. "We are waiting for a certain message before we start, and in the meantime you may as well understand what we expect to happen. As you saw, there is a thunderstorm coming on. The Meteorological Office forecast predicted it for the whole of London if the conditions remained. Within an hour it is now inevitable that we shall experience a deluge. Here and there damage will be done to trees and buildings; here and there a person will probably be struck and killed."

"Yes."

"It is Mr. Creake's intention that his wife should be among the victims."

"I don't exactly follow," said Hollyer, looking from one man to the other. "I quite admit that Creake would be immensely relieved if such a thing did happen, but the chance is surely an absurdly remote one."

"Yet unless we intervene it is precisely what a coroner's jury will decide has happened. Do you know whether your brother-in-law has any practical knowledge of electricity, Mr. Hollyer?"

"I cannot say. He was so reserved, and we really knew so little of him—"

"Yet in 1896 an Austin Creake contributed an article on 'Alternating Currents' to the American *Scientific World.*"

"But do you mean that he is going to direct a flash of lightning?"

"Only into the minds of the doctor who conducts the post-mortem, and the coroner. This storm, the opportunity for which he has been waiting for weeks, is merely the cloak to his act. The weapon which he has planned to use—scarcely less powerful than lightning but much more tractable—is the high-voltage current of electricity that flows along the tram wire at his gate."

"Oh!" exclaimed Lieutenant Hollyer.

"Some time between eleven o'clock tonight—about the hour when your sister goes to bed—and one thirty in the morning—the time up to which he can rely on the current—Creake will throw a stone up at the balcony window. Most of his preparation has long been made; it only remains for him to connect up a short length to the window handle and a longer one at the other end to tap the live wire. That done, he will wake his wife in the way I have said. The moment she moves the catch of the window—and he has carefully filed its parts to ensure perfect contact—she will be electrocuted as effectually as if she sat in the executioner's chair in Sing Sing prison."

"But what are we doing here!" exclaimed Hollyer, starting to his feet, pale and horrified. "It is past ten now and anything may happen."

"Quite natural, Mr. Hollyer," said Carrados, reassuringly, "but you need have no anxiety. Creake is being watched, the house is being watched, and your sister is as safe as if she slept tonight in Windsor Castle. Be assured that whatever happens he will not be allowed to complete his scheme; but it is desirable to let him implicate himself to the fullest limit. Your brother-in-law, Mr. Hollyer, is a man with a peculiar capacity for taking pains."

"He is a damned cold-blooded scoundrel!" exclaimed the young officer fiercely. "When I think of Millicent five years ago—"

"Well, for that matter, an enlightened nation has decided that electrocution is the most humane way of removing its superfluous citizens," suggested Carrados, mildly. "He is certainly an ingenious-minded gentleman. It is his misfortune that in Mr. Carlyle he was fated to be opposed by an even subtler brain—"

"No, no! Really, Max!" protested the embarrassed gentleman.

"Mr. Hollyer will be able to judge for himself when I tell him that it was Mr. Carlyle who first drew attention to the significance of the abandoned kite," insisted Carrados, firmly. "Then, of course, its object became plain to me—as indeed to anyone. For ten minutes, perhaps, a wire must be carried from the overhead line to the chestnut-tree. Creake has everything in his favor, but it is just within possibility that the driver of an inopportune tram might notice the appendage. What of that? Why, for more than a week he has seen a derelict kite with its yards of trailing string hanging in the tree. A very calculating mind, Mr. Hollyer. It would be interesting to know what line of action Mr. Creake has mapped out for himself afterwards. I expect he has half a dozen artistic little touches up his sleeve. Possibly he would merely singe his wife's hair, burn her feet with a red-hot poker, shiver the glass of the French door, and be content with that to let well alone. You see, lightning is so varied in its effects that whatever he did or did not do would be right. He is in the impregnable position of the body showing all the symptoms of death by lightning shock and nothing else but lightning to account for it—a dilated eye, heart contracted in systole, bloodless lungs shrunk to a third the normal weight, and all the rest of it. When he has removed a few outward traces of his work Creake might quite safely 'discover' his dead wife and rush off for the nearest doctor. Or he may have decided to arrange a convincing alibi, and creep away, leaving the discovery to another. We shall never know; he will make no confession."

"I wish it was over," admitted Hollyer.

"Three more hours at the worst, Lieutenant," said Carrados, cheerfully. "Ah-ha, something is coming through now."

He went to the telephone and received a message from one quarter; then made another connection and talked a few minutes.

"Everything working smoothly," he remarked between times over his shoulder. "Your sister has gone to bed, Mr. Hollyer."

Then he turned to the house telephone and distributed his orders. "So we," he concluded, "must get going."

By the time they were ready a large closed motor-car was waiting. The lieutenant thought he recognized Parkinson in the well-swathed form beside the driver, but there was no temptation to linger on the steps. Already the stinging rain had lashed the drive into the semblance of a frothy estuary; all around the lightning jagged its course through the incessant tremulous glow of more distant lightning, while the thunder only ceased its muttering to turn at close quarters and crackle viciously.

"One of the few things I regret missing," remarked Carrados, tranquilly; "but I hear a good deal of color in it."

"We are not going direct?" suddenly inquired Hollyer, after they had traveled perhaps half a dozen miles.

"No; through Hunscott Green and then by a field path to the orchard at the back," replied Carrados. "Keep a sharp lookout for the man with the lantern about here, Harris," he called through the tube.

"Something flashing just ahead, sir," came the reply, and the car slowed down and stopped.

Carrados dropped the near window as a man in glistening waterproof stepped from the shelter of a lich-gate and approached.

"Inspector Beedel, sir," said the stranger, looking into the car.

"Quite right, Inspector," said Carrados. "Get in."

"I have a man with me, sir."

"We can find room for him."

"We are very wet."

"So shall we all be soon."

The lieutenant changed his seat and the two burly forms took places side by side. In less than five minutes the car stopped again, this time in a grassy country lane.

"Now we have to face it," announced Carrados. "The inspector will show us the way."

The car slid round and disappeared into the night, while Beedel led the party to a stile in the hedge. A couple of fields brought them to the Brookbend boundary. There a figure stood out of the black foliage, exchanged a few words with their guide and piloted them along the shadows of the orchard to the back door.

"You will find a broken pane near the catch of the scullery window," said the blind man.

"Right, sir," replied the inspector. "I have it. Now, who goes through?"

"Mr. Hollyer will open the door for us. I'm afraid you must take off your boots and all wet things, Lieutenant. We cannot risk a single spot inside."

They waited until the back door opened, then each one divested himself in a similar manner and passed into the kitchen, where the remains of a fire still burned. The man from the orchard gathered together the discarded garments and disappeared.

Carrados turned to the lieutenant.

"A rather delicate job for you now, Mr. Hollyer. I want you to go up to your sister, wake her, and get her into another room with as little fuss as possible. Tell her as much as you think fit and let her understand that her very life depends on absolute stillness when she is alone. Don't be unduly hurried, but not a glimmer of a light."

Ten minutes passed by the measure of the battered old alarm on the dresser shelf before he returned.

"I've had rather a time of it," he reported, with a nervous laugh, "but I think it will be all right now. She is in the spare room."

"Then we will take our places. You and Parkinson come with me to the bedroom. Inspector, you have your own arrangements. Mr. Carlyle will be with you."

They dispersed silently about the house. Hollyer glanced apprehensively at the door of the spare room as they passed it, but within was as quiet as the grave. Their room lay at the other end of the passage.

"You may as well take your place in the bed now, Hollyer," directed Carrados when they were inside and the door closed. "Keep well down among the clothes. Creake has to get up on the balcony, you know, and he will probably peep through the window, but he dare come no farther. Then when he begins to throw up stones slip on this dressing-gown of your sister's. I'll tell you what to do."

The next sixty minutes drew out into the longest hour that the lieutenant had ever known. Occasionally he heard a whisper pass between the two men who stood behind the window curtains, but he could see nothing. Then Carrados threw a guarded remark in his direction.

"He is in the garden now."

Something scraped slightly against the outer wall. But the night was full of wilder sounds, and in the house the boards creaked and sprang between the yowling of the wind among the chimneys, the rattle of the thunder and the pelting of the rain. It was a time to quicken the steadiest pulse, and when the crucial moment came, when a pebble suddenly rang against the pane with a sound that the tense waiting magnified into a shivering crash, Hollyer leaped from the bed on the instant.

"Easy, easy," warned Carrados; feelingly. "We will wait for another knock." He passed something across. "Here is a rubber glove. I have cut the wire but you had better put it on. Stand just for a moment at the window, move the catch so that it can blow open a little, and drop immediately. *Now.*"

Another stone had rattled against the glass. For Hollyer to go through his part was the work merely of seconds. But an unforeseen and in the circumstances rather horrible interval followed, for Creake, in accordance with some detail of his never-revealed plan, continued to shower missile after missile against the panes until even the unimpressionable Parkinson shivered.

"The last act," whispered Carrados, a moment after the throwing had ceased. "He has gone round to the back. Keep as you are. We take cover now."

From half a dozen places of concealment ears were straining to catch the first guiding sound. Creake moved very stealthily, burdened, perhaps, by some strange scruple in the presence of the tragedy that he had not feared to contrive, paused for a moment at the bedroom door, then opened it very quietly, and in the fickle light read the consummation of his hopes.

"At last!" they heard the sharp whisper drawn from his relief. "At last!"

He took another step and two shadows seemed to fall upon him from behind, one on either side. With primitive instinct a cry of terror and surprise escaped him as he made a desperate movement to wrench himself free, and for a short second he almost succeeded in dragging one hand into a pocket. Then his wrists slowly came together and the handcuffs closed.

"I am Inspector Beedel," said the man on his right side. "You are charged with the attempted murder of your wife, Millicent Creake."

"You are mad," retorted Creake, falling into a desperate calmness. "She has been struck by lightning."

"No, you blackguard, she hasn't," wrathfully exclaimed his brother-in-law, jumping up. "Would you like to see her?"

"I also have to warn you," continued the inspector impassively, "that anything you say may be used as evidence against you."

A startled cry from the farther end of the passage arrested their attention.

"Mr. Carrados," called Hollyer, "oh, come at once."

At the open door of the other bedroom stood the lieutenant, his eyes still turned towards something in the room beyond, a little bottle in his hand.

"Dead!" he exclaimed tragically, with a sob, "with this beside her. Dead just when she would have been free of the brute."

The blind man passed into the room, sniffed the air, and laid a gentle hand on the pulseless heart.

"Yes," he replied. "That, Hollyer, does not always appeal to the woman, strange to say."

Roy Vickers

Blind Man's Buff

Roy Vickers was our most gifted practitioner of the "inverted" storytelling method invented by R. Austin Freeman. Vickers raised this detective-story method to new heights. His Department of Dead Ends stories relate the full case histories of unusual murders—"a minute and detailed description of the crime, setting forth the antecedents, motives, and all attendant circumstances." Readers "see the crime committed, know all about the criminal."

In the novelet, "Blind Man's Buff," Robert Swilbey is compelled by circumstances to change from a promising young lawyer to a successful playwright. In the process Swilbey teaches himself how to create a new personality—rather how to split his personality—to meet each new condition in his life . . .

Detectives: DEPARTMENT OF DEAD ENDS

Until he committed murder, Robert Swilbey was a model citizen. Everyone admired him for one or another of his qualities, including the go-getters who admired only his business abilities. The example of his courage under a devastating affliction helped other sufferers. Many who knew him well would speak of him almost reverently.

Yet he was, in vulgar parlance, a tough guy, with a toughness that would have frightened any gangster who had brain enough to understand it—a toughness with which even Scotland Yard was impressed.

"That man," said Chief Inspector Karslake, "practises all the virtues as if they were vices." All that, from Karslake, after a single murder!

His father was a country solicitor who, perceiving Robert to be something exceptional, scraped and saved and sent him to the Bar. He died when Robert was twenty-three, leaving him about a thousand pounds. Having no influence, Robert at first secured only dock briefs in defense of impecunious criminals. Through these he soon attracted favorable attention. But as his income remained perilously low, he occupied his spare time in writing sketches for West End revues—cheeky little seven-minute playlets—with enough success to enable him to carry on at the Bar without dipping into his small reserve.

His knowledge of law was but little above the average, but his advocacy was of a high order, and he had the adroitness of an old hand in humoring his Judges. His early success was helped, in some measure, by his magnificent physique, his full-toned voice, and his handsome face. Win or lose, he always made the most of his case. As generally happens to young defenders who show consistent ability, the Crown gave him a chance to function as prosecutor.

In his fourth year at the Bar, when he was twenty-six, he earned nearly a thousand pounds—six hundred in practice—the balance deriving from a minute share in the royalties of a revue to which he had contributed three playlets. He was already crawling along the road to success—a road along which he intended to gallop.

He had surprised himself by falling in love with Mildred Keltson, the daughter of a doctor who had attended him for a trifling ailment. Women tended to favor him: he had had his share of adventures and believed himself free from the danger of a serious entanglement. But Mildred did not appear to him as an entanglement. Tall and exquisitely shaped, with grey-green eyes and chestnut hair, intelligent and perceptive but temperamentally docile, she attracted him as he had not been attracted before. Considered impartially, he told himself, she was an ideal wife for a man such as himself. He proposed and was accepted in February: they were to be married in the Easter vacation.

In this phase he is seen only as a successful young man obviously destined for a brilliant career. He was bumptious, but no more so than any other rising barrister, and certainly no tougher. The toughness was, as it were, flashed into being, a few days before the Easter vacation by a wretched woman called May Dinton, the associate of a burglar whom Swilbey was prosecuting.

It required no great ingenuity on Swilbey's part to destroy the alibi the girl was trying to create for her man. But he carried on for another hour and with some subtlety, extracted from her additional facts which aggravated the prisoner's guilt.

At dusk, when Swilbey was returning to his lodgings, May Dinton appeared from behind a pillar box.

"You got my boy seven years when the cops said the judge 'ud only give 'im three," she accused.

"My dear girl, what the cops say means nothing to me. I am sorry if you have been made unhappy, but you know that sort of thing is my job."

"You did more than you had to do for your pay. Twistin' my words round like that! You've made Ted think I ratted on him. But he won't think it any more—*now!*"

He had seen her draw a broad-stoppered bottle from under her coat: he supposed indifferently that she was about to swallow poison. He put up no guard—with the result that some three fluid ounces of vitriol splashed into his face.

On regaining consciousness after the operation, he asked when he would be likely to recover the use of his eyes. The doctor stalled, but broke down under Swilbey's expert questioning.

"Very well! Perhaps you'd better take the full shock while you are under our care. I am very sorry, Mr. Swilbey—there is no hope at all. Moreover—well, bluntly, old man, for appearance's sake, you'll have to wear two glass eyes."

"Thank you," said Swilbey. In the time it took to utter those two words he re-planned his career.

Inspector Karslake himself had come to the hospital. They were personally acquainted, and respected each other's work.

"D'you feel strong enough now, Mr. Swilbey, to tell us what happened?"

"I haven't the least idea."

It was not the smallest of Swilbey's achievements that he was able to think clearly while his body was racked with pain.

"We know it was May Dinton," prompted Karslake.

"But you can't prove it or we shouldn't be talking about it—you'd charge her. Sorry, Karslake! I can't afford vengeance. Got to be very economical. Got to avoid law courts. Got to forget I was once a lawyer."

The bumptious young barrister had been drowned in three ounces of vitriol, and Swilbey's unquenchable vitality was already creating a new personality, which had to be coddled during its infancy. He must forget May Dinton as well as the Law. The new personality must have no grievance against life, or it would not make the grade.

Through a nurse, he wrote to Mildred: *Please don't come to see me until the pain has passed. Pain in your presence would confuse me.*

These words show he was aware that, no matter how much his personality might change, he would still have a normal nervous system, would still be sensitive to the charm of women, with all its disturbances. Mildred, of course, would be in charge of that side of his life. So there need be no disturbances.

Mildred's father visited him every day. Swilbey found the visits tedious, except when they were talking about Mildred.

"You'll very soon feel well enough to let her come, won't you?"

"Practically ready now. Say the day after tomorrow."

"I'll tell her." Dr. Keltson cleared his throat. "There's one thing I want to mention before then. I can safely say that Mildred will keep her promise to marry you, if she sees that you wish to—er—hold her to it."

"There's no means by which a man can 'hold' a woman to such a promise."

"Oh, yes, there is, my friend!" The father was fighting for his daughter's happiness and dared not soften his words. "When Mildred accepted you, you were on the threshold of a brilliant career. She must have looked forward—quite properly—to sharing fame and prosperity with you. By a tragic accident you can now offer her only poverty and a treadmill of small services to yourself. Show that you expect her to stick to you, and she will. As would any woman of character."

Dr. Keltson had done his painful duty. The answer brought him but cold comfort.

"You want me to humbug her with a wistful little speech about my not having the right to blight her life. Wistfulness is not in my program. You needn't worry. I shall not blight her life. I shall give her a square deal."

He meant what he said. Indeed, Swilbey never lied to himself nor anyone else—except, eventually, to the police. But he failed to see that in the matter of Mildred he had appointed himself judge to his own cause—to his own ultimate ruin.

When she came to the hospital, he was still bandaged—was in a chair on a terrace overlooking the river. A motor launch was passing and he did not hear her approach.

"I'm here, Robert," she said and thrust her hand in his. The significance of having to announce herself to him upset her self-control. A tear dropped on his wrist.

"Darling, you've got the wrong slant on this!" he exclaimed eagerly. "To us it won't make any essential difference. I've adapted my thoughts to it and know I can manage it. Listen! Believe I'm telling the truth and not just trying to cheer you up. These last few seconds—while I've been holding your hand—I've taken a great leap forward. You've touched some nerve or other. I can *visualize!*"

"I'm glad, dear, but I don't understand. Go on talking about it—it'll make it easier."

"Darkness!" he exclaimed. "At first you're always waiting, waiting for the light. Having breakfast in total darkness! It muddles your other senses, produces a sort of animal fear. I found difficulty in thinking of things by their shape and color. But now—holding your hand—I can see the sun shining on your hair, making the wavy bit in front look like copper wire. I can get the angle of the sun, too. It doesn't matter a damn if the sun isn't actually shining at the moment. The important thing is that I can visualize the effect of light under the stimulus of an emotional urge—meaning you. That guarantees I shall be able to visualize stage lighting."

Fascinated by the mechanism of his own brain, he pursued his thoughts in silence, which she broke.

"While you're here, could I come every day to teach you Braille?"

"I'm not going to learn Braille—nor anything else the blind learn. I'm not going to be a blind man. I'm an ordinary man, who can't see."

That which she believed to be his pathetic courage, his gallant faith in the wreck of himself, destroyed her judgment—though it is easy to see, even at this stage, that there was no pathos in his courage, and that he had not been wrecked by his blindness.

"This is the program. I've got one toe in the theatre with those sketches. I intend to plant both feet. Now, when I've paid up here I shall have about fourteen hundred pounds, all told. I shall want five hundred for my working expenses, which will include the purchase of a dictaphone."

He proceeded to detail a practical plan of domestic finance. "Allow a hundred and fifty for our honeymoon and unforeseen expenses after we move in, and we shall have a reserve of eighteen months at the rate of five hundred a year. I shall be well in the swim within six months. Have you made notes of all this?"

"Yes, Robert." Prudence was awakening. Suppose he were not "well in the swim"—ever?

"If you'll see my bank manager we'll fix a power of attorney so

that you can deal with the checks and the contracts. Remember, I
can't sign my name. By the way, you'll have to do a lot of reading
for me at first. Shall you mind?"

She answered that she would not mind. Her tone made him ask:

"I say, darling! The program as a whole? Including me? I've been
rushing on, building a new life on your shoulders. Feel like it—or
not?"

She was, in the words of her father, a woman of character. To
leave him in the lurch would be utterly impossible. She bent and
kissed him.

"It will be wonderful—building together," she said, which was
exactly what he had expected her to say. He visualized the expression on her face as she said it. But the visualized expression was
quite different from her actual expression of honest doubt of herself
and him.

"I shall have these bandages off in a fortnight," he told her—and
altogether failed to visualize the shudder that followed his words.

For the next few years we see Robert Swilbey as the embodiment
of the virtues extolled in the literature of success. In him character
really did triumph against enormous odds. He did laugh at his set-
backs. He did believe that failure was impossible. Also, of course,
"luck came to him who earned it." His stage plays happened to be
adaptable to a certain comedian in whom Hollywood had sunk a
good deal of capital, and Swilbey's rates rose with each success.

In the first year he climbed on Mildred's shoulders more than he
realized. Indeed, Mildred herself did not know that it was she who
put him so quickly into the West End. His first full-length farcical
comedy was tried out in the provinces, seven months after their
wedding. It was undercapitalized and badly mounted and was in
some danger of collapse, when Turley Wain saw it in Liverpool.

Wain was a company promoter, mainly in the cotton market, with
no expert knowledge of the theatre, who had the amateur's belief
that he could spot a winner. He was impressed by Swilbey's dynamic
drive, but he was more impressed, in a different way, by Mildred's
courage and devoted care. He could see that he was in a position to
dictate terms, but in Mildred's presence he held his hand and let
Swilbey drive him. True that he eventually made money out of the
play. But Swilbey made so much that he was able to finance his
next play himself. Before the run had ended, Wain came to live in

London and thereafter saw much of Midred, without suspecting danger.

At the end of six years, living in affluence and with strong financial reserves, Swilbey believed that his marriage was as successful as his career. He was unaware that after the first eighteen months of struggle Mildred had been extremely unhappy. Even on their honeymoon, he had refused to perceive that her feeling for him had become exclusively maternal and protective. This feeling had been steadily thwarted by his progressive efficiency.

While they were still comparatively poor she had the arduous task of keeping him abreast of events and ideas by reading to him for long stretches every day. Then she had to take him for walks and in the intervals run the home with inadequate assistance. But the comradeship of it sustained her, gave her a sense of fulfillment.

Yet even in this first phase of their marriage, she had what one may call the first premonition of the ultimate disaster. She took her fear to her father.

"He drives himself so hard, Daddy. And although in a way it's all so splendid, I'm a little worried as to whether it's quite—healthy. I know you'll think I'm a fool—I think so myself—but this happens. When we're discussing plans for the week, he speaks as if he and I were making arrangements about someone else. He even says: '*he* must go to that rehearsal, and if we can get *him* back in good time we'll let *him* try a re-write of that last scene before *he* goes to bed.' The frightening part is that it's not meant to be funny. He only speaks like that when he is very concentrated."

"There's nothing in that," said Dr. Keltson. "I suspect you've been reading some stuff about split personality without, my dear, quite understanding what you read. I'm no psychiatrist, but I can tell you that, though it does attack exceptionally clever people sometimes, there's no fear at all with a balanced, mentally disciplined man like Robert. I've never met any man I admire more—for mental discipline, I mean."

Six years later she again approached her father on the same subject.

"He's begun to 'split' me now," she told him. "Yesterday, I read a contract to him. He said: "Ah! *There's* something for him to tell his wife!" And he did tell me, last night. He always does tell me how wonderful he is. This time he spoke as if I knew nothing about the contract."

Dr. Keltson was still unimpressed. He asked: "Anything else? Has he any morbid habits?"

"Not that I know of. But I see so little of him except for business, or when others are there. He won't go for walks any more. He 'goes for a row' in that rowing contraption in the gym that makes a noise like a real boat on real water. And a bicycle-thing that can make him feel he's going up and down hills. And he has a journalist to read to him. If anything gets in his way he invents an expensive gadget so that he need not ask me to help him. He has so built things round him—things and persons—that I don't believe he any longer wishes he could see. Perhaps that's morbid."

"You aren't happy with him, Mildred, are you?"

"No!" She added: "What makes it uncanny is that he *is* happy with me. I suppose I'm beastly to him pretty often. It never hurts his feelings. He never retaliates—just cleverly makes me feel ashamed of myself. And then"—she shuddered—"we make up!"

"Well, at least he is loyal to you. At the back of my mind—"

"Loyal?" It was as if she asked herself a question. "Women run after him. He's so big and strong—and handsome, if you can ignore his poor, staring eyes. But I think he's afraid they might put him out of his stride. He's positively Victorian with them. When he's going to rehearse a new actress he sends for me. He says to the girl: 'It's essential that I should be able to visualize you. May I touch you?' And then I have to chip in and say something pleasant."

"At the back of my mind—"

" '*May I touch you!*' " she repeated bitterly. "With me standing by to make it impersonal and uncompromising. That's what I'm for. I'm not his wife. I'm just—*women!*"

"At the back of my mind, my dear girl, there has been for some time the feeling that I ought to warn you that there are whispers about your friendship with Mr. Wain. I know there can be nothing in it—but there it is!"

About the same time the whisper reached Swilbey.

Every Tuesday night Swilbey gave a party in his house in St. John's Wood, a couple of miles from theatreland. For the rest of the week he was strictly not-at-home to anybody to whom he had not given a definite appointment.

In the lofty L-shaped drawing-room that was also his working room he would hold an inner court round his gadget-laden armchair.

Now and again he would rise and walk among his guests, who

were required merely to avoid impeding his progress. His system enabled him always to know where he was standing in his house or in the theatre. On first nights he could walk unaided to the proper spot from which to take his author's call—for which purpose he wore spectacles and a careful makeup; for he did not wish his public to know that he "could not see."

It was by the bend of the "L" that he overheard the whisper; and for the first time since he lost his sight he found himself shirking a reality.

For some days he vacillated. Mildred's behavior to himself was the same as it had been for years. He worked out ways of asking her for details—a frank approach. But in his heart he was afraid of receiving a frank answer that would break the smooth routine of his career. On the fourth day he wrote to Wain, under a thin pretense of being able to offer him another flutter in the theatre.

He received him, as he received everybody, alone in the drawing-room.

"I say, old man! Some infernal scandalmongers have been coupling your name and Mildred's. I thought you and I had better get together about it. Cards on the table and all that!"

He was alarmed by the length of the pause before Wain answered.

"Before I say anything else, Swilbey, I have nothing to confess to you. I've never so much as touched her hand. I can't imagine what is being said. We have always taken care not to give the talkers a chance."

That killed the last hope that there might be nothing in it. Wain seemed to think that Mildred had already discussed it.

"I'd better go on." Wain's voice sounded unctuous and sentimental. "I've been in love with her for years, and shall be all my life. But I doubt whether she knows it's any more than friendship. Anyhow, if circumstances were normal I would speak to her—then ask you for a divorce. I've told you all there is to tell, Swilbey."

"I appreciate that." The fellow, thought Swilbey, was a mere sentimentalist, who would run from a challenge. "But I don't follow that bit about 'normal circumstances.' Why not speak to her? I have never regarded women as property. I stake no prior claim. How do we know she wouldn't be happier with you?"

Sentimentalist or not, Wain shook the edifice of six years with his answer.

"Swilbey, you asked for cards on the table. So you'll let me say that we both know she would be happier with me—if I could retain my self-respect. But how could I? Knowing I had taken his wife from a blind man?"

In the recesses of Swilbey's brain, a voice was speaking about Swilbey: *That'll upset him—calling him a blind man! Mind he doesn't do anything rash.*

Through darkness the other voice, that of Wain, penetrated.

"To Mildred, your well-being is a sacred mission, Swilbey. Her power of attorney has more than legal significance. She stands between you and the outside world with which you could not cope, even with all your assistants and servants. You would be the first to acknowledge that you owe your career not only to your own qualities but also to hers."

Again came the illusion of an inner voice speaking: *Look out! That'll make him worse. Wain is telling him that he's a blind man living on the charity of his wife's eyes.*

"I quite agree." Swilbey's voice was calm as ever. "By the way, years ago—when I was starting—did you finance my play because of Mildred?"

"N-no. At least, I don't think so. Not altogether. Does it matter, now?"

The personality had been thumped into numbness. Only the mannerisms remained active—and some resolution he did not yet understand. Swilbey rose from his chair.

"I'm glad we've had this talk. One way and another, Wain, you've been a factor in my life. I would like to be able to visualize you. May I touch you?"

"Of course! I'm a shrimp compared with you."

"Yes, you're shorter. And you've kept slim." The hands crept lightly to the head, crept over the features, outlining the heavy, prominent chin with a dimple in it, crept below the chin to the throat—

Don't let him do anything rash!

But how would it be possible to keep "him" quiet? For the first time for six years consciousness of the perpetual darkness returned, and with it the animal fear.

At six o'clock, Menceman, the journalist, came as usual with a digest of the day's papers. Swilbey barely heard a word throughout the hour's reading. At seven-thirty, when he was going upstairs to prepare for dinner, he crashed into the balustrade.

The parlormaid, who had been with him for years, gasped with astonishment. Never before had she seen him miss his direction.

"Have you hurt yourself, sir?"

"No, thanks. My foot slipped," he lied.

That evening, alone with Mildred in her little sitting-room up-stairs, he got up to go to bed, faltered, and then: "Will you take me to my room, please?"

Sheer astonishment made her ask: "Why, Robert?"

"Because I'm blind!" he cried, and broke down like a child.

The next day Mildred beat down his protests and took him for a holiday up the river where he could scull for hours while she steered. The first nervous crisis passed. She made no mention of Wain.

He evolved, during that holiday, an interim personality—an understudy to sustain the role of Robert Swilbey. All the mannerisms were faithfully copied, but the inspiration was lacking. The interim personality could not write dialogue that sparkled with clever nonsense. He was working then on *Playgirl Wanted*, but had to abandon it before he had completed the first act.

"Menceman, I'm going to try my hand at straight drama. I shall have a background of police work, treated realistically. You might begin by going through the verbatim reports of trials, picking out the small points overlooked by intelligent murderers."

Now and again, the inner voice would register a half-hearted warning. *He's planning to kill Wain. Better humor him.*

"David Durham advised me to have a model theatre on the table beside me, as he does," he told Mildred. "Of course, my sense of touch isn't developed enough for that sort of thing. But I could rig up a model stage at the other end of the drawing-room." He meant at the short end of the "L." "Scale about one to four I should think. I could use it, too, for rehearsing special scenes."

He spent sixteen hundred pounds on what became not a model but a miniature stage, with many of the fitments of a full-sized stage. Unable to concentrate enough for original work, he rehearsed revivals on the miniature stage.

At rehearsals he necessarily worked through a subordinate stage manager.

"I want to be able to handle the rigging myself—get the feel of the controls," said Swilbey, because he now knew that he intended to hang Wain, thereby giving the murder the outward semblance of an execution.

There is no doubt that Swilbey planned the murder of Wain in minute detail. But there is considerable doubt whether he meant to carry it out. Remember that daydreams and fancies and castles-in-the-air possess a special kind of reality to a playwright—they become as real to him as a parcel of speculative shares is to a business man.

In a sense, Swilbey soothed his wounded ego by murdering Wain every night. The taunt of being a blind man, who could only hold his woman by invoking her pity, was nightly avenged by the fatal blow that was not actually struck. Nightly, too, the heads of Scotland Yard were made to confess themselves beaten by the dazzling brilliance of Robert Swilbey—a man who, as it happened, could not see.

Certain it is that for two years he made no attempt to use the "engine of death," as counsel called it—more simply, the essential parts of a gallows, disguised as rigging for shifting scenes and the heavier stage properties. Nor did he take any step to lure Wain to the house. Ironically, Wain was, as it were, put on the spot by Mildred herself.

"I want to ask something of you, Robert," she began. "About Turley Wain. It's two years now since he gave you an explanation. He told me at the time that you had been very kind to him."

"He was very kind to me. I told him I'd fix a divorce, if you wanted it."

He hoped she would say she had never, and would never, want a divorce. But she did not. The darkness came down on him again.

"We exchanged parting gifts. I have only seen him once since then. Today. He is very changed. I drew from him that things have gone very badly with him, and he expects to be made bankrupt. Will you help him?"

"Of course, I will! Apart from your friendship with him, he did me a good turn when he financed *Brenda Gets Married*."

He felt her approaching. The darkness vanished as he visualized her physical beauty against the background of a sun-lit flower garden. She thanked him warmly—because he had said he would help Turley Wain.

"When shall I tell him to come and see you about it?"

In the nightly murder Wain always arrived at five-thirty on a winter afternoon. And Mildred was always out of the house. He reminded himself now that, on Fridays, Mildred always visited her parents, who were in retirement in Canterbury.

"Next Friday at five-thirty," he answered, and added: "February fifteenth—my birthday—good omen for Wain!"

It was about five-thirty when he came, Inspector. I was in the rehearsal theatre. I showed him the tackle for shifting the heavier pieces.

That was part of the scene in which the police, every night, were "hopelessly baffled."

On Friday Mildred left for Canterbury after lunch; she would stay for dinner, returning on the last train.

At five-thirty precisely, the parlormaid announced Wain. Speaking from the miniature stage, Swilbey greeted him with the opening lines composed two years ago.

"Hullo, Wain! I've just finished here. You haven't seen this little rigout before, have you?" Swilbey could hear the parlormaid drawing the curtains. He spoke loudly enough for her to hear. "It's the engineering I'm proud of. Have to haul everything up to the flies when we want a change. With the double reduction on these pulleys, a child could manage it—designed the whole thing myself. How's that for a blind man, eh! Have a cigarette?"

He felt for his cigarette case in one pocket and another. Like many a sighted man, he was never sure of his pockets.

"You dropped it on that bench, sir." The parlormaid left the curtains, hurried to the stage, recovered the cigarette case, and handed it to Swilbey.

Wain, who did not know that the very word "blind" was a danger signal, made polite murmurs. When Swilbey heard the parlormaid draw the last curtain, he said:

"Let's go and sit down. I won't bother to put the tackle away."

Back together down the short arm of the "L," a left turn into the long arm, to his armchair and the group of chairs round it. Swilbey felt the hands of his watch. Five thirty-four. Not a minute to waste.

"Mildred told me you might go bankrupt. How much do you want?"

"Bankruptcy is one thing. There's another!" Judging by his voice, Wain had gone to pieces—he was almost cringing. "To leave out technicalities, I got caught in a landslide, Swilbey. I swear to you I didn't try to save myself at the expense of others. I threw in all my own resources, including even my furniture, when I need not have done so. It wasn't nearly enough. In trying to save the investments of others I committed a technical breach of the criminal law. At this moment I am actually wanted by the police."

"Better give me the figures!" Thirty-eight minutes past five. The babble must not last more than another four minutes. And he mustn't forget Wain's cigarette. It might set the house on fire—which would disarrange the plan.

Wain seemed to shrink from coming to the point.

"Last week a detective came to see me. Very decent fellow. Karslake. He knew you when you were at the Bar. I drew wool over his eyes because I didn't want to be arrested there and then. And now I'm keeping out of his way."

"Wain, old man, how much do you want?"

"The technical breach—well, five thousand pounds would cover that. But look here, Swilbey, I've no excuse for asking you."

"Yes, you have. You and Mildred together made it possible for a blind man to make a living. My career pivots on you two. She hinted that you might want a wad of ready cash. Come with me."

Swilbey felt some squeamishness in promising money that would never be given. But there is no gentlemanly method of committing murder.

"D'you mind putting your cigarette out, old man? Have to be careful of fire where we're going."

On the way back round the turn of the "L," to the rehearsal theatre, he asked:

"And what about the bankruptcy?"

"Astronomical! Fifty thousand pounds, if a penny!"

"Hm! We'll have to talk about that later. We're going over the stage. That door at the back is still in use. All right! I can manage. In their own place, the blind can manage as if they were not blind. Mind that pulley!"

Wain, as he had himself said, was a shrimp beside Swilbey. Moreover, he did not know how to use what little weight and strength he had. So the "compensatory fantasy" was translated into reality without muscular strain.

When Wain was dead, Swilbey turned on the main switch which flooded the stage with light. The room lights of the short arm of the "L" had been turned on by the parlormaid.

The parlormaid! Halfway to the corner he stopped. He had had a sudden mental picture of the parlormaid handing him his cigarette case after he had dropped it on the bench.

"If I've dropped anything this time—"

He went back to the stage and groped on the bench: he was leaving when his foot touched something on the floor which ought not to have been there. He bent down.

"That damned case again!" Like frightened snakes, his fingers slid over the tessellated pattern of the slim gold case. "Phew! I had a sort of intuition. Subconscious memory. Good! It means '*he*' won't make any mistakes!"

He thrust the case into his breast pocket and hurried away.

At four mintues to six Swilbey, back in his gadget-laden armchair, switched on the radio. Luck again came to him who had earned it. A drama critic was talking.

At six punctually, just as the radio critic was finishing, Menceman, the journalist, came in.

Swilbey turned off the radio and spoke as if Wain were sitting near him.

"Wain," he said, "let me introduce Mr. Menceman who—"

"There's no one in the room but ourselves, Mr. Swilbey."

"Oh, then Wain must have slipped out—I had to listen to that critique! My fairy godfather. Backed my first play. Badly hit in the Slump. Let's have the Slump news first."

There was no fear of Menceman strolling about the room, turning the bend of the "L" and seeing the corpse.

Swilbey gave his full attention. The plan was fulfilling itself. Menceman would leave at seven. By domestic routine a housemaid would discover the body of Turley Wain at seven-thirty, by which time he would be in his room dressing for dinner.

But at nine minutes to seven the sequence of the plan was broken by the house telephone.

"An officer from Scotland Yard, sir. Chief Inspector Karslake. He wants to speak to Mr. Wain."

For a second only Swilbey hesitated.

"Mr. Wain left a long time ago. But tell Mr. Karslake I would like to see him if he can spare the time."

With a nod he dismissed Menceman and concentrated on the problem of the detective.

Swilbey held out his hand and waited, as the blind do, for Karslake to grip it.

"It's good to see you after all these years, Mr. Swilbey. I always take the wife to one of your plays when I get the chance."

"And it's good to hear your voice!" echoed Swilbey. "We must have a chat sometime. At present you've got something on your mind, and Wain has told me what it is. You may take it that will be settled at once—in full."

"Well, I'm glad to hear it, since he's a friend of yours. All the same, I can't stop the machinery at this stage, as you know. Can I see him, please?"

"He's not here," said Swilbey. "Left about six."

There was a short, strained silence.

"Mr. Swilbey, his coat and hat are in your vestibule."

"Surely not! Wait a minute." On the house telephone he spoke to the parlormaid.

"What time did Mr. Wain leave?"

"He hasn't left, sir. I thought he was in the drawing room with you."

Swilbey repeated the girl's words.

"Then d'you mean to say he sneaked out of the room without saying goodbye or anything?" asked Karslake.

"Apparently, he did. I'd told him what I could do for him, and we'd really finished. I asked him to excuse me for a few minutes as I wanted to hear the end of a dramatic critique on the radio. At six, when Menceman came in—you saw him just now—I began to introduce them, when Menceman told me Wain wasn't here."

Karslake noted a half-smoked cigarette on the ashtray by his side: nothing in the tray within Swilbey's reach. That tallied with what Swilbey was saying.

"He left the room, then, but not the house," said Karslake.

"He wouldn't wander about my house without permission," asserted Swilbey. "It's much more likely that he heard Menceman arrive and thought it was you coming to collect him. He was in a very nervy state."

"If he left the house—without his hat and coat—which way did he go?" pressed Karslake.

Swilbey had seen that question coming—had seen, too, that he was in no danger, provided he did not shirk the logic of his position.

"He could have got into the garden by going through the door at the back of my rehearsal stage, and along the corridor. That door was locked on this side. If he slipped out that way, it must be unlocked now."

"Can I have a look at that door?"

Swilbey stood up.

"Come with me," he invited. "The stage is in this room—round the corner."

Karslake followed Swilbey round the corner of the "L." A corpse, as such, could not shake Karslake's nerve. But his nerve was shaken this time, partly because he thought, for a second or two, that the corpse was a stage property.

Looking some thirty feet down the short arm of the "L," he saw a well-lit stage-set of a saloon bar. Left back, at an angle, was the bar, with shining pump handles; left, a pin-table; right, a bench in green plush; and centre, a human form suspended by its neck in what appeared to be a noose attached to the hook of a pulley block.

Two paces nearer he recognized the features of Turley Wain.

"What?" Swilbey stopped in his stride. "Did you speak?"

"No. It's all right." Karslake was thinking quickly. "Carry on, please, Mr. Swilbey."

Swilbey, a couple of feet ahead, walked on. With the steadiness of a sighted man, he stepped on to the stage. He passed within a dozen inches of the man who was obviously dead. So to the back of the miniature stage.

"Nothing doing!" exclaimed Swilbey. "The door is still locked on this side."

Fascinated, Karslake watched Swilbey return, wondering whether, this time, he would collide with the dangling corpse. Again there were a dozen inches to spare. Perhaps, he reflected, the blind always walked in the same track in familiar surroundings.

"Surely it isn't worth investigating, Karslake! The charge against him is pretty certain to be dropped, after restitution. Forget it for a few minutes and have a drink."

"That sounds like a good idea," said Karslake, who had meantime satisfied himself that there was no hope of saving life.

Back, with the blind man, round the corner of the "L" to his chair. Swilbey sat down. Sitting gave him the range of all the gadgets. He leaned forward and opened the door of a cabinet.

"Whiskey, gin or—"

"Whiskey, please." Karslake glanced uneasily at a row of decanters. "Allow me!"

"It's all right, thanks. You sit down." Swilbey's voice had a slight edge to it. He passed his guest the whiskey decanter, a tumbler and a siphon, then held out his hand for the return of the decanter.

"Can I pour yours for you, Mr. Swilbey?"

"No, thanks!" Swilbey's tone barely escaped rudeness.

Karslake watched Swilbey pour his own drink with a deftness that made his hands seem like independent agents, able to think and act for themselves. Meantime, he was groping for a line of action. That corpse, actually in the same room with them, presented a tricky problem in presence of mind.

"Cigarette, Karslake?"

"Oh—er—thanks!"

Swilbey thrust his hand into his breast pocket for his cigarette case—kept it there for seconds as if his arm were paralyzed. Then he tried his side pockets.

Karslake saw a thin, tessellated gold cigarette case on the ledge, flush with the dictaphone. But he had observed that Swilbey was very touchy about being helped. So Karslake said nothing.

"Dammit, I thought I had my case on me!"

Karslake was glad of the respite. His mind on the corpse, he watched Swilbey's hand creeping, spiderlike, along the ledge by the dictaphone.

"Ah, here it is!"

For an instant the hand hovered, quivering over the case as if it were puzzled. Karslake dismissed this eerie fancy, took the offered cigarette, and made his decision.

"To come back to Wain for a moment," said Karslake, "you might tell me exactly what happened while he was here."

This was the cue for the scene in which the police were "hopelessly baffled."

He had but to repeat the oft-repeated words.

"It was about five-thirty when he came. I was in the rehearsal theatre. I showed him the tackle for shifting the heavier pieces. Then we came back here and talked. He told me he had committed a technical breach of the criminal law and that he was playing tag with you. Mentioned you by name and said you remembered me. I said I'd let him have the five thousand in the morning. Then he explained that he would be in for a civil bankruptcy to the tune of fifty thousand pounds. I said bluntly I couldn't manage that much—after which things became mildly unpleasant."

"What sort of unpleasantness?"

"After I'd turned down the fifty thousand idea, he said something about the five thousand being wasted—that it would be cheaper for all if he jumped off Waterloo Bridge on a dark night—the usual suicide threat that is never implemented. Between ourselves, Karslake, I don't like that man. He financed my first play. I admit he was thundering useful to me at the time, and I'm glad to let him have the five thousand. Fifty thousand is another pair o' shoes. So I made the excuse that I had to listen to the radio critique. And I suppose he buzzed off in a huff as well as a panic.

"He's coming here tomorrow morning for the five thousand, and he's sure to surrender to you as soon as he's got it, so you don't have to worry. Have another drink?"

"No thanks. May I use your telephone?"

Karslake dialed the Yard, asked for an internal number, then gave Swilbey's address.

"Homicide!" said Karslake. "I'll be here when the team arrives." He hung up. "Wain is on that stage of yours, Mr. Swilbey—with his neck in that scene-shifting tackle."

"My God! Doing it in my house!" exclaimed Swilbey. "That's a dirty, malicious trick, Karslake! The publicity will do me no good—no darned good at all."

It was near the truth to say that Robert Swilbey was disappointed when it appeared that the police were not "baffled"—that they hadn't the wit to see that there was anything to be baffled about. On the other hand, he received, in the Coroner's court, a severe shock which put him momentarily in fear of his life. For the Coroner described exactly how Wain had been murdered—which Swilbey had thought no one could ever guess.

"Accident," said the Coroner to his jury, when all the evidence had been heard, "may be ruled out. If you are to return a positive verdict, therefore, you must decide between murder and suicide. Let us consider what evidence, if any, supports the theory of murder."

He dwelt on the virtual impossibility of anyone entering the drawing-room without the servants or Swilbey being aware of it—he elaborated obvious absurdities.

"Apart from such absurdities, you have to postulate—to sustain the hypothesis of murder—a very powerful man who suddenly attacked the deceased, constricting his victim's throat so that he could not cry out—or the servants, to say nothing of Mr. Swilbey, would have heard him. For this purpose he used a curtain cord, an item in the fittings of the stage set. This hypothetical murderer then proceeded, in the clumsiest possible manner, to attach his victim to the hook on the pulley block.

"As you have been told, the device of a noose, or slip-knot, was not employed. A curtain cord, itself a stage property securing a curtain on the stage set, was wound round the throat of the deceased in such a manner as to make four complete coils. This cord was tied at the back of deceased's neck with three knots—the kind of simple knot which one uses for one's shoe laces, the difference being that this simple knot was tied three times instead of once. Through three of the coils, the hook beneath the pulley block was inserted, greatly increasing the pressure of the coils round the neck. The hands were unbound. Medical evidence as to the condition of the hands—and microscopic examination of the ropes above the pulley block—make it clear that the unhappy man attempted to free himself by reaching above his head and pulling on the ropes.

"Why did our hypothetical murderer permit this attempt to frustrate his purpose? Add that this eccentric murderer must have swung the dead, or unconscious, body in such a way that the shoes could be pressed into the upholstery of the bench—and you may come to the conclusion that no such person as the murderer existed."

The Coroner had reconstructed the murder in order to ridicule the theory of murder. As a dramatist, Swilbey knew the danger of playing tricks like that on an audience, who would sometimes pick up an unexpected angle. But the fact of his blindness—above all, Karslake's evidence of his behavior in the presence of the corpse—headed off suspicion.

Swilbey's dread was dispelled when the Coroner went on to say what Swilbey had intended him to say.

"On the hypothesis of suicide the deceased slipped silently away when Mr. Swilbey turned on the radio. After adjusting the pulley to the height he required, he wound the curtain cord round his throat, as one might wind a narrow scarf, and tied it, as described, at the back. He stood on the bench, worked the hook under the coils, then swung himself off the bench. Police measurements, on the chart before you, show that the ropes would then swing, pendulum-wise, to the centre of the stage, bringing the feet of the deceased within three and a half inches of the floor.

"Like many a suicide and would-be suicide before him, he repented of his act before it had been completed, and tried to interrupt it. Had he secured himself with a noose, he would in all probability have succeeded. To free the hook from the coils of curtain cord was a great deal more difficult than loosening a slip-knot—doubly so, through the fact that his jaw was large and prominent."

The jury, ever ready to believe that a simple explanation must be the true one, accepted the Coroner's interpretation. Only Chief Inspector Karslake was heard to mumble that the suicide had been clear-headed enough to measure the pendulum swing, correct to three and a half inches. After a verdict of suicide while of unsound mind, public interest in the case evaporated.

On the evening following the inquest, Robert Swilbey resumed work on the first act of *Playgirl Wanted*, abandoned two years previously. The play was put on the following autumn. It ran all through the following year.

Eighteen months later he was at work on another play—when the end came.

A junior detective from another department flung open the door of the Department of Dead Ends and ushered in a seedy individual with patched trousers but a very decent sports coat.

"This is Mr. Joe Byker, sir," said the detective facetiously. "Hensons', the pawnbrokers, 'phoned us. Mr. Byker was trying to pawn this." He laid on the table a slim gold cigarette case with a tessellated design. "Mr. Byker says the case is his and he bought it with his own money."

Among the burglaries, petty thefts and whatnot in Detective-Inspector Rason's file were eleven missing gold cigarette cases, five with tessellated design. He opened the case in the hope of finding some identifying mark.

For Remembrance he read. No name. No initials.

"You bought it, eh, Byker! From a man in a pub whose name you don't know?"

"No, sir. I bought it right enough, a matter o' six weeks ago, off a respectable dealer name o' Clawson's, Theobalds Road."

"They're second-hand clothes dealers, Byker."

"That's right, sir. Matter o' six weeks ago I bought this 'ere sports coat as I'm wearin' this very minute, sir, and I didn't know till this morning when I was havin' me breakfast that I'd bought that cigarette-case with it. In here it was, sir." He took the coat off. "In between these two bits o' stiffening—that's where I had to cut the lining to get it out. And me walking about with it for a matter of six weeks."

Clawson, the dealer, was able to supply the name and address of the man from whom he had bought the sports coat. Interviewed by Rason, the vendor of the coat was inclined to be indignant.

"Yes, I sold it to Clawson's—and what's the matter with that? The missis gave it to me to do what I liked with."

"And who is the missis?"

"Mrs. Swilbey—wife of the gentleman who writes all them plays. I'm his gardener."

Swilbey, a writer of plays! In a few minutes Rason remembered the freak suicide of eighteen months ago. Byker would drop in for "stealing by finding" if Mrs. Swilbey would consent to prosecute, he reflected on his way to the house in St. John's Wood.

"Perhaps you could tell me, Mrs. Swilbey whether this is your husband's cigarette case?"

"It looks like it. I wonder where he dropped it!"

Mildred took the case, opened it, and caught her breath.

"No," she said. "It is not my husband's."

"But you do know whose it is, Mrs. Swilbey!" It was a statement, not a question.

"It belonged to a friend of ours who—is dead. A Mr. Wain. I gave it to him myself. It is exactly like the one I gave to my husband—bought at the same place. That's why I thought at first it was his."

"Mr. Wain," repeated Rason. "I remember. Very sad. You're sure this is the case you gave Mr. Wain?"

"Quite!" She added the name of the jeweler where she had bought both cases. "How did it come into your hands, Mr. Rason?"

"It has been stolen," answered Rason, and bowed himself out.

He checked up at the jeweler's, then decided reluctantly that he must bring Chief Inspector Karslake into it.

"He was a lawyer once," warned Karslake, as it was Rason's case. "You won't get him to admit anything. But I'll stooge you all I can."

At five-thirty that afternoon they were being shown into the "L" shaped drawing-room. Karslake introduced Rason with a somewhat elaborate heartiness.

"I've got to worry you about the estate in bankruptcy of the late Turley Wain, Mr. Swilbey," said Rason.

"Before we start, Mr. Swilbey," cut in Karslake, "d'you mind if we smoke?"

"Do! Here, have a cigarette!" Swilbey felt in one pocket and then another, then found his cigarette case on the ledge that was flush with the dictaphone. "I don't know anything about Wain's affairs."

Rason observed the cigarette case. It looked exactly like Wain's—the same tessellated design. It would feel the same to a blind man—and that was all Rason wanted to know.

"What an extraordinary thing!" exclaimed Rason. "That case is exactly like Turley Wain's." He added carefully. "You may remember—it dropped out of Wain's pocket—onto the floor of your stage—during the poor chap's struggles."

There was a tiny perceptible stiffening of the large frame. But it was the long pause that made Rason sure of his ground.

"I don't remember, because I was never told," said Swilbey.

"You didn't need telling! You picked the cigarette case up after you had killed him. You thought it was yours, put it in your pocket.

It was in your pocket when you were sitting in here, offering Mr. Karslake a cigarette."

"Any ass can make wild assertions!" snapped Swilbey. "Are you in this foolery, Karslake?"

"Well, Mr. Swilbey, I must say I do remember your offering me a cigarette out of a gold case."

"Then I wonder, my dear Karslake—" Swilbey had pounced as, years ago, he would pounce on a witness "—I wonder whether you also remember that the case was *not* in my pocket, as I thought it was, but on this ledge here?"

"Y-yes, I do remember, now you mention it, Mr. Swilbey." Karslake spoke as one making a reluctant admission. "Rason, I think you'll have to apologize."

"Wait a minute!" said Rason. "*Suppose* the case on the ledge there, out of which he offered you a cigarette, was his own case? And *suppose* Wain's case, which Swilbey had put in his pocket, had slipped down the lining. And *suppose*—"

"Suppose my grandmother's foot!" Swilbey emitted a roar of laughter. "Karslake, haven't you taught this man any evidence?" Swilbey leaned forward in the direction of Rason. "My good man! If you could prove that I put Wain's cigarette case in my pocket—eighteen months ago, mark you!—we would not be talking about it. Mr. Karslake would charge me with murder—wouldn't you, Karslake?"

"Yes," said Chief Inspector Karslake. In sudden silence, the distant rumble of traffic seemed to fill the vast drawing-room. Presently Karslake added: "Perhaps you'd like to ring the bell, Swilbey, and tell them to pack you a suitcase?"